FAMILIAR
MAGIC

The Land of Enchantment #1

KATHLENA L. CONTRERAS

Flying Tiger Press
flyingtigerpress.com

To Patricia Askren, who made me believe
it was possible

ACKNOWLEDGEMENTS

I have so many people to thank. Always at the top of the list, my husband, Bob, and my dad, the best boosters I could ever ask for. Laura Carlson and LaVonne Jordan, critiquers extraordinaire, for their patience and for going above and beyond. Suzann Ledbetter for her expertise and great suggestions. Daniel Contreras, for his description of a high-rise building jobsite, and Jesse Contreras, for filling in the blanks on the car stuff I didn't know. Trish Mazzolini, for her knowledge of EMT protocol. The groups Toto and Genesis for the great imagery. And thanks to my old Opel Kadett and the adventures I had keeping it running.

Prelude

*H*e waited by the curbside, blind and deaf to the city life around. People sensed rather than saw the strangeness in him. Two chatting mothers with babies in strollers moved closer together and watched him from the corners of their eyes. A jogger puffed by, stared and ran on. Bicyclists glanced at him and away.

A skater glided down the hill, her ponytail swinging. One outflung hand brushed him, a fleeting touch across a sleeper's face.

Awareness flooded him, welling up from depths of oblivion.

He explored the edges of himself. Age had touched him, but that he could repair. He yet remained strong, implacable steel. Or when he wished, slippery shadow. He focused his attention outward.

He flinched and almost withdrew again. Magic seethed, corrosive as a toxic sea, chewing at the edges of reality. It was worse, much worse than before, chaos ready to engulf the world.

Yet there was the grit of pavement beneath him, the sharp, high-altitude sun on his body, the city that unrolled, foothills to mesas to winding river then back up again to a line of low volcanoes on the horizon. He scanned his surroundings—street, whooshing traffic, the squat blocks of apartment buildings, all ordinary, solid, sure. Then his attention fastened on her, the skater. He forgot everything else.

Latte macchiato skin. Dark hair bound at the nape of her neck. A swimmer's build, slim enough to appear taller than she was. Her head turned, showing a face not pretty, but pleasant to look upon.

And the very fragrance of soul he had been waiting for.

Exultation surged in him. He moved to catch her—

Then stopped himself. It was hard, hard. He yearned to savor the taste, revel in the brilliance of that soul. To make her his own. After so long…

After so long, he could wait a bit longer. But only a bit.

She reached the corner, swung onto the path that followed the boulevard. Budding desert willow and grey-green chamisa screened her.

He waited a moment more then stirred himself, fire and thunder, then the cough of his breath, the crackle of small stones beneath him. He moved to follow the skater. Close, but not too close behind her.

Chapter 1

The rumble of a big-bore engine echoed up the street. A sound like that didn't belong in a quiet Albuquerque neighborhood, among the little pueblo-style houses with their flat roofs and small, high windows and stucco walls. It didn't belong with new spring leaves, the Juicy Fruit scent of Spanish broom, the perfume of lilac, the mutter of grackles.

At the moment, Amethyst Rey was more interested in what was in the mail. Her skates leaned against the post and she stood in her socks by the mailbox cluster, sorting through envelopes.

Bill. Bill. She didn't even want to look at those. Credit card offer? No thanks. Sorry. Ah—finally! The check from Mrs. Blakely for the job she'd just finished—a series of dining room clerestory windows depicting mesas and clouds in stained glass. Amethyst tore open the envelope.

The engine fell silent and she looked up.

There it was again! That car! Past the Wesley's tidy sweep of gravel dotted with juniper and the stiff, prickly arms of cholla cactus, past the Griego's defiant green lawn and two enormous elms, it crouched black as a curse at the curbside in front of her house.

She waited for the car's door to open, the driver to climb out. No one did. She leaned down to pick up her skates.

An odd, silvery prickle scuttled across her skin, as if someone watched her. She jerked upright, looking for…whoever it was. The sidewalks were empty, the front doors closed. No face peered through a window, no one stood within the shadow of a garage door. So who—?

The car still sat there two houses down, silent, waiting as she waited.

Waiting, *hell*. She stuffed the mail in the back pocket of her jeans and strode toward the car. Time to let this person know that people in this neighborhood kept an eye on things.

The car was some kind of classic, probably older than Amethyst—Mustang, she decided. One in perfect condition, the sort of thing a middle-aged man would spend hours waxing, reminiscing about days of big, throaty engines and admiring girls. Not a vehicle that would blend in, if someone were up to no good.

Sunlight slid along the car's gleaming black body. The dark-tinted windows seemed to regard her, like a man's appraising stare behind blackout sunglasses. An arc of dash showed through the windshield, the curve of a seatback.

No driver? She'd looked around the moment the engine had shut off. So was he hiding in the back seat, or what?

A shudder stroked down her back, but she set her jaw and kept walking. No front plates in New Mexico, so she had to go a little past her driveway to see the car's tail end. The plate was the old, bright red-on-yellow one with the yucca in the corner. It read *TALYS*.

A lot of good it did her. It wasn't like she could call the cops and complain that someone had been parking in front of her house for the last week. She didn't own the street. Still…

She strode up her cracked driveway to the walk, past pansies struggling against the still-chill high-desert nights. She stopped short on the front porch and dropped her skates.

A pomegranate rested on the doormat. It hadn't been there when she'd unlocked the door two minutes ago.

She took a step back. No, no, no. There was no way this could be here—this…this gift. *Another* gift, these strange little offerings she'd been finding on her front porch. The big, shiny acorn with the cap still on. The keychain—no keys—with a wand-shaped fob of clear plastic filled with floating, multicolored stars. An issue of *Car and Driver* magazine, a few months old and a little battered around the edges.

She swallowed the little flutter that started in her throat. Another gift, but who had left it? And how? And *why?*

Although she had a pretty good idea what the gift-giver drove.

She clenched her fists. It was broad daylight. This was *her* house. Damned if she'd let someone keep playing these games with her. The pomegranate was going right back where it came from: to whoever was driving that car.

She scooped it up and headed back down the walk.

"Amethyst, *hola!*"

She jumped, but it was only Oscar Griego from next door.

He met her on the section of sidewalk between their driveways. "Hey, you okay? Did I scare you?"

She forced a laugh. "I'm fine, Oscar. I just…" Against her will, her eyes slid to the car.

"Yeah, I was gonna ask you about that," he said, following her gaze. "Sixty-nine Mach One. Woo! New boyfriend?"

"No! It's…uh… No."

Boyfriends were painful and complicated. Work and friends filled the days much more comfortably.

He grinned, showing a silver-capped front tooth. "*Bueno.* Gary'll be happy. Mama told him he don't stand a chance against the guy who drives something like that."

'Mama' was an accurate term for Oscar's wife. She even tried to mother Amethyst: What was a nice Spanish girl doing living all by herself? And with a young man like her son Gary right next door! Amethyst didn't even have to go visit her own mother in San Cristobal to get quizzed on her love life. Or more accurately, the lack thereof.

She cupped the pomegranate as unobtrusively as possible. "So…have you seen who drives it?"

Oscar shook his head. "No. Mama hasn't, either." He gave an apologetic shrug. "And she's been looking." He spun his car keys around a finger and frowned. "Why? Trouble?"

Was there? What was going on here, anyway? Was she being *stalked?*

Sure, like anyone would want to stalk a skinny, not-much-to-look-at computer geek turned stained glass artist.

The pomegranate prickled in her hand, round and mottled red and about as innocuous as the one the Lord of the

Underworld had presented his kidnapped Persephone. *Just a taste, my dear. No strings attached, upon my word...*

"No trouble as far as I know," she said. "I just wonder why someone keeps parking in front of my house."

Oscar grunted thoughtfully. "Mama's been saying your new boyfriend must be a *brujo*." He used the Spanish word for sorcerer. "Since she never sees him. So now she'll be happy too. No *brujos* hanging around next door." He opened his pickup's door. "Time to go fight with the VA. When you see this guy," he tipped his chin at the Mustang, "make sure you send him over. I'd sure like a chance behind the wheel." He climbed into his pickup and with a wave, drove off.

Amethyst waved back. A *brujo*. Thanks, Oscar. The supernatural as an alternative to a stalker.

The skittery, nervous feeling returned, as if something ominous prowled just beyond the light of her everyday life, and all she could perceive of it was the pad of a soft footfall, the gleam of a reflective eye.

She gave the pomegranate a disgusted look. It was all stupid. Gifts. Unseen watchers. And sorcerers only existed in stories. She would *not* stand here shivering like a kid after a scary movie.

She set her teeth and took the few steps to the curb. Quickly, she reached across the car's hood to place the pomegranate just behind the scoop. Her thigh pressed against the fender.

Images swarmed into her mind: streets filled with old cars that weren't old at all, a man with a black terrier trotting by his side. A woman in a long, old-fashioned dress reading a book by firelight, stroking the black tomcat draped over her knee. The cat's eyes glinted silver through half-closed lids. A girl feeding a bit of apple to a mynah bird on its perch. Its bill, instead of yellow, was silvery-white, and it said in its croaking voice, "Amethyst—"

She jerked back and dropped the pomegranate. *Thump!* It struck the hood and rolled off.

Amethyst shook her head hard and backed away, rubbing her thigh. Her heart tried to crowd up her throat.

The car sat quietly. The door didn't jerk open, no angry voice demanded to know what the hell she thought she was doing. It was obviously—impossibly—empty.

Impossible. Just like the pomegranate. Like that sense of being watched…

When there was no one to watch her.

Amethyst took a step backward, then fled into the house.

Amethyst tucked the old plastic bowl on one hip, reached for the back gate latch, then hesitated. Through the gate's splintery boards only a slice of tumbleweeds and the concrete block wall on the opposite side of the alley were visible.

This is ridiculous, she told herself. She hadn't seen any sign of the black car since yesterday. There was no reason to get all twitchy.

She dropped her hand from the gate latch. "Caramela," she called.

Nothing. Then a rustle on the other side of the block wall, coming along the alley. She tensed, listening. At last, a whine outside the gate.

Amethyst took a breath and pulled the gate open.

A caramel-colored pit bull looked up at her. She wagged so hard everything behind her shoulders wiggled, and her wide, pink mouth stretched in a grin.

Amethyst rubbed the dog's ear and peeked up and down the alley. No car here, at least. So far.

She let out the breath and crouched to give the dog a good petting. "I think it's time you come live with me, Caramela. What do you think?"

Caramela wagged and panted, more intent on the affection than on the food in the bowl beside Amethyst. The dog's hip bones no longer showed, the xylophone of her ribs was less pronounced. Her big, blocky pit bull head looked like it fit her body better. She was still greasy and dirty, though, and smelled. The pink patch just above her nose was sunburned.

Amethyst picked up the bowl again and stood. "Well, come on in."

Caramela's head drooped. She still wagged, but it was an apologetic, regretful sort of wag now.

"Not yet, huh?" Amethyst sighed and set the bowl just outside the gate. Caramela dived on it. Amethyst waited the twenty seconds it took for the food to vanish then rubbed the dog's ear again. "I have to go now."

Caramela looked up at her. When no more caresses were forthcoming, she turned and trotted back up the alley, past other back gates, piles of grass clippings, tree trimmings and cardboard boxes. Finally, she pushed through a gate hanging askew a few houses distant.

The rumble of an engine echoed between the walls. Amethyst jumped and wrenched around. The alley remained empty, but traffic winked past the end, two blocks down. Must've just been a delivery truck on Eubank. She shut the gate and headed back to the house.

"You shouldn't be feeding that dog," an old voice said. "It's gonna kill somebody's pet. Or even a kid."

Mr. Meadows scowled at her over the block wall that divided their backyards. The top buttons of his shirt were misbuttoned, and his thin hair stood up in back. La-Z-Boy hair, Amethyst privately called it. The sound of spattering water rose from the other side of the wall. Mr. Meadows watered his yard a lot, especially when a neighbor was outside.

Amethyst sighed again. She really should raise that wall, but… Well, Mr., Meadows would say something about unneighborliness and how folks had visited over this wall for the last fifty years and what was wrong with people now that they felt they had to shut their neighbors out and what were they up to they had to hide, anyway?

Maybe stuff like feeding neglected dogs.

"She's a nice dog, Mr. Meadows. And nobody else is feeding her."

"Then call the pound. That animal shouldn't be wandering around, anyhow. It's a public menace."

"No, she's not. And calling the pound isn't a good idea."

"When I—" Mr. Meadows began, but Amethyst cut him off.

"I'm late, gotta go, sorry. Have a good day, Mr. Meadows."

"Don't even have a proper job," he muttered behind her. "How can you be late?"

◈ ◈ ◈

"You're late," Melodie Jarret said. Her arms were crossed over a University of New Mexico Lobos sweatshirt with the arms torn out, her light brown hair piled on top of her head in a silly-looking fountain of a ponytail. "I've been standing here baking in this parking lot when all those nice, cool trees are just over there."

She tossed her head in the direction of the Rio Grande River and its bordering cottonwoods, their leaves flashing white undersides in the rowdy spring wind.

Amethyst opened the rear door of her little Isuzu SUV. "I had to feed Caramela. Sorry."

Melodie came and leaned a hip on the faded rear fender of the Isuzu. "If you're that worried, why don't you just keep the dog?"

Amethyst threw up her hands. "Same reason I don't call Animal Control! The owners are the kind of people who'd rob you and trash your house to show you how unhappy they are that you took a dog they can't bother to care for."

Melodie studied her. "Hmm. Twenty minutes late when it takes maybe five, tops, to feed the dog. And grumpy, not like you. What *really* happened, Wiz?"

Wiz. The nickname coiled like a bad meal in her gut today.

Amethyst snagged her skates from the forward end of the cargo area, where they never failed to slide. "Nothing."

She wasn't about to say, *There was this pomegranate, and this car, and the car was parked outside all yesterday afternoon, and all night, too...* She slipped off a sneaker, worked her foot into the skate.

"Just... I don't know. Too much glass, I guess. Too much time home alone, working."

Melodie's eyes went round. "Did you say, 'Too much glass'? Is that what I heard you say?"

Amethyst sighed silently and fastened the skate straps. Melodie's needling was usually fun. Not today.

"You've had your days when you don't feel like convincing some Luddite the new software won't eliminate her job. Well, I get tired of work sometimes, too."

"Not you. Never." Melodie shook her head, and the silly fountain of hair bobbed. "It's all artistic rhapsodies, about how turning pieces of broken glass and strips of foil into something beautiful is like magic."

"I never said—"

"Yes, you did. 'Magic.' That's just the word you used." She sniffed. "And this from the woman who left everyone in UNM's IT department in the dust, from the precocious junior hackers to the pocket-protector graduate geeks. Miss Wiz."

A little one-sided smile tugged at Amethyst's lips. "Is that jealousy I hear? You should be happy I switched to Fine Arts, then, so you could shine. You never had a chance, otherwise."

Melodie propped fists on hips. "You don't think so?"

"Not a bit."

"Well, lock your truck, honey, because there's a reason when we take to the trail together, *you* wear skates while *I* depend on my own two feet."

More cars were trickling in. A pregnant mom waited while another woman unfolded a stroller and settled her child into it. Across the lot, a curly-haired man in jeans and boots and a shirt that said *Just Rope It* backed two horses out of a trailer. The horses thumped along the trailer floor, then clopped on the asphalt, looking around, ears perked and interested. The guy was cute. If she had the nerve, the horses would be a good excuse to go over and try to strike up a conversation. Melodie would even play along.

Amethyst turned away and slammed the rear door.

A flash of reflected sunlight caught her gaze. Glossy black paint. The glitter of chrome.

She snatched the key out of the lock. "Let's go."

Melodie's grin went out like a popped light bulb. "Wiz, what—"

Amethyst didn't take the time to put the keys away in her fanny pack. Fisting them, she skated toward the rustic-looking posts that marked the trail entrance.

She sped across the bridge spanning the riverside drain. Metal girders and brown water flashed past. The cottonwoods lining the river rose ahead, furrow-barked, spring-green leaves quivering against a vibrant blue sky. She swung onto the paved path on the ditchbank above the tangled vegetation of the bosque.

The car couldn't follow her here.

But the driver could. And she didn't know what he looked like.

Melodie sprinted along not far behind. "Wiz, wait!"

Amethyst did a neat turn and stop. "God, Mel, I'm sorry."

"What happened?" Melodie panted.

Amethyst flicked a glance back, along the path, across the bridge. "Nothing. I just thought—" She unzipped her fanny pack, dropped in the car keys. "Nothing."

Still panting, Melodie caught her arm, pulled her along the path. "You don't—light out—for nothing."

"Mel—"

Her friend dropped onto to a bench. "Sit down. Tell me. Something's really spooked you. And you don't usually spook."

Clumping awkwardly on the skates, Amethyst sat too. She pulled a water bottle from her fanny pack, but just gripped it with both hands.

The riverside drain—the irrigation canal that paralleled the river—ran between the trail and houses' backyards. The full socioeconomic spectrum was on display there: equestrian stables, ponds and gazebos separated by fences and screens of elms or poplars from dirt yards, tumbleweeds and junked cars. The Sandia Mountains loomed beyond the house- and treetops, five thousand feet of sheer granite rearing above the mile-high heights of Albuquerque.

Amethyst's mouth was dry. She took a sip of water, swallowed, but the dryness came right back. "I might be— I'm not sure, but it seems—"

Melodie tugged the bottle away, drank and wiped her mouth. "Just tell me."

It was going to sound so stupid. "I think I'm being stalked."

"*Stalked?*" Melodie looked back along the path, then at Amethyst. "By who?"

Not, *are you sure*, but, *by who?* Melodie's faith in her judgment made something in her middle untwist.

She hitched one shoulder. "I don't know. I've never seen him."

"But then how—"

"Somebody's been leaving…things…on my front porch. Nothing much, just junk, but…" She threw up her hands, frustrated. "The wind couldn't have blown them there, and—"

No, she'd better not say anything about how the car, even unoccupied, seemed to watch her. About the visions that had come when she touched it.

"And? What?" Melodie said. "Calls? Letters?"

"Nothing like that." She hesitated. "But I think I've seen someone following me."

Melodie studied her. "And you saw that someone pull into the parking lot?"

Always perceptive, was Melodie.

Amethyst clenched her hands together. "I thought so."

"But you were sure enough to take off like a cat with a stepped-on tail. What's he driving?"

"Something black. Old."

"Old *and* black. Now there's a description to go on."

Amethyst sat back and folded her arms. "It isn't like I can call the cops or anything. What am I going to say? 'Officer, someone has been leaving threatening pomegranates on my doorstep. You've got to stop him before he leaves a watermelon.'"

"*Pomegranates?*"

Amethyst bit her tongue. "Never mind."

Melodie put a hand on her arm. "Pomegranates."

"I told you it was just stuff. But when was the last time you saw a pomegranate in the grocery store?"

For that matter, where did that big, fat acorn come from, when the only acorns you'd find around this part of New Mexico were those little bitty ones from the scrub oaks up in the mountains?

"Maybe they ship them up from Chile."

"Sure." And the acorns, too.

"No unstable boyfriends I wouldn't know about?"

"Oh, right. I've left such a trail of broken hearts behind me."

Melodie pressed her lips together in impatience. "Okay, okay, let's not go into the old whine about how little use men have for smart women."

"You can't talk. You got lucky with Marl. Lawyers like someone who can challenge them."

Melodie had been dating Marl Odham for something like three years now.

"You're the one who won't let me hook you up with one of his associates," Melodie said.

"I'm trying to save Marl the embarrassment of hearing how the date went."

Melodie rolled her eyes. "Since you're smart, I'm sure you've considered that someone's playing a joke on you."

Suddenly, the conversation was no longer fun. "If they are, the joke is almost as scary as a stalker. Way, way too elaborate." Amethyst smoothed a finger along the hem of her shorts. "I don't know, Mel. Something about the whole situation is really strange."

"Stranger than a stalker?"

Amethyst took a drink to avoid answering.

Melodie wasn't one to tactfully drop a subject. "So what're you going to do?"

Sighing, Amethyst pushed to her feet. "Right now? Go for a skate. Finish that atrium window for the DeBacas. Start going in and out exclusively through the garage door. Or maybe through the back gate into the alley."

"You don't sound as worried as you should be," Melodie said.

Amethyst shrugged. "It's crazy, that somebody could be stalking me. Look at me."

She spread her arms. About the only thing she had going for her was the dark, rich fall of her hair, and her eyes: violet in sunlight, dark indoors. Her dad had named her for those unusual eyes long before it became obvious she'd grow into anything but a jewel.

"I mean," she said, "who'd bother?"

Melodie didn't dignify that last comment with a reply. "So what's the alternative? You're imagining things?"

"Thanks, Mel. You're such a comfort."

Melodie flicked away the sarcasm with toss of her head. "Maybe you were right the first time, and you're just tired, or stressed. Maybe you need a change of routine."

This sounded an awful lot like the beginning of another get-back-into-the-computer-field-you're-wasting-your-talent lecture. But she loved the glass, loved her independence.

Melodie scowled. "Don't look like that. It's not what you think. I was going to say that Bree is singing in the youth opera tomorrow." Bree was Marl's oldest daughter. "You don't even have to dress up. We can stop and have dessert afterwards. It'll be fun."

A chance to think about something other than this crazy car business couldn't hurt. And Bree was a nice kid.

"Mmm," Amethyst said. "You and Marl won't shout and whistle from the stands this time, will you?"

"Please. Are you going to come, or just stand there and be snide?"

Amethyst gave a little curtsey, though her skates didn't entirely cooperate. "I thank you for your gracious invitation. I shall be delighted to join you and your gentleman friend at the opera Friday night."

Melodie tilted her chin up. "We are honored by your condescension." She stood and tightened her ponytail. "Now come on. If somebody's really stalking you, let's make him work for his twisted pleasure." She jogged off along the path.

Amethyst wouldn't look. She wouldn't.

Her head turned. Two bicyclists in wraparound sunglasses and helmets like weird-colored alien skulls hunched over their handlebars. They didn't look particularly threatening.

If she really were being stalked, did it make sense to get too far from her friend?

Amethyst pushed off, fast enough even the cyclists didn't catch her.

On the return trip, she eyed the nearing bridge for signs of suspicious-looking loiterers.

Melodie puffed obliviously beside her. A few strands escaped from the ponytail stuck to her cheeks and neck, and her sweatshirt was damp down the back and under the arms.

The parking lot held nothing more frightening than a large, noisy group of grade-school kids on a field trip. If they'd come hoping to see the bald eagles or cranes, she suspected they'd be disappointed. Anything mobile would remove itself before the kids came within a half a mile.

Amethyst unlocked the Isuzu's doors and opened them to let out the heat. She sat on the cargo bed to pull off her skates.

Melodie sat beside her. "Listen, Wiz. You may not be able to call the cops, but you can call me if you need to. Or Marl. You have his number, don't you?"

"I don't think Marl would appreciate—"

"Call us. Either one. Or both. You're not the sort to have the vapors."

Amethyst let go a breath. "Thanks, Mel. That's really—that means a lot."

"I'm serious. Should I ask Marl to pull some strings somewhere? See what can be done?"

Amethyst hesitated. Maybe. But what if the whole thing turned out to be harmless?

"That's okay. I'll call. If it's necessary."

Melodie nodded. "Good. See you Friday." She ambled off across the parking lot.

Amethyst took off the other skate and peeled off her socks. Melodie was the best. If anything really was wrong…

She closed the rear doors and tiptoed barefoot across the hot pavement. The car couldn't possibly be anything as outrageous as a stalker. And the silly little gifts were likely a kid's prank.

She slid into the driver's seat. She probably only thought she'd seen the same car pulling into the parking lot earlier this morning. After all, she hadn't stuck around to get a really good look at it. For all she knew, it might've been one of the new retro-styled Mustangs, and not the one from in front of her house at all.

She checked the rearview mirrors for pedestrians or oncoming cars, fumbling at the ignition with her key. A glint of color snared her eye.

On the dash, resting in the angle of the windshield was a large marble. It looked as if it were made of crystal. Purple crystal. Amethyst.

Light leapt from flaw to flaw in the crystal. Cold stalked across her scalp and down her back.

The doors had been locked. She remembered the click of the lock when she'd turned the key. There was no way this could've gotten in here. No way—

Unless someone had the skill—or a master key—to unlock her truck, carefully place the marble where she would see it, then just as carefully lock the door behind him.

Chapter 2

"**S**o what's this we're going to see?" Amethyst said.

She sat with Melodie in the semidarkness of the theater thumbing through a program, trying to pretend everything was normal. Well, actually, everything was normal—right now. No car. No gifts. Yet.

"It's called *Mayhem and Malarkey*," Melodie said. "It's for kids, a conglomeration of fairy tales. A comedy. You should see Bree, though." She laughed fondly. "You'd think she's performing at the Santa Fe Opera."

Amethyst summoned an answering smile. Even with an extended family about as large and close as any old Spanish clan in northern New Mexico, kids were a foreign tribe as far as she was concerned. Teenagers were a little more comprehensible than most. At least you could carry on a conversation about computer gaming with them.

Most of the couples around her looked in their thirties and forties—Marl's age, old enough to have teenaged kids. Lots of kids in the audience, too, probably siblings and classmates of the performers. She didn't see anyone who looked like a stalker—whatever a stalker would look like.

Sighing—well, more like breathing again, after having held it too long—she sat back in her seat again. The obligatory red curtains hid the stage.

"Where's Marl? And Jenna?" Jenna was Marl's younger daughter.

Melodie gestured behind them. "Jenna's back there, with a couple friends. Thankfully." Jenna was at the goofy, giggly age. "Marl is backstage with Bree. She's singing a lead part."

Thinking of Bree's long, coppery hair, Amethyst said, "They wouldn't type-cast her as Red Riding Hood, would they?"

Melodie only gave her a withering look.

People shuffled in their seats to let Marl pass. Melodie

smiled at him. He gave her a quick kiss and sat down. His thick, reddish-brown hair was forever falling in his eyes, and he swept it back now with a practiced gesture. "I think I have her convinced that she won't squeak on the high notes."

Melodie squeezed his hand where it rested on her knee. "She's her father's daughter. She'll be perfect."

Marl was a nice guy, gentle and steady and good for Melodie. They really ought to get married, but maybe Melodie was worried about his two daughters, about becoming a stepmom. Or maybe Marl wasn't ready yet—he'd lost his wife a few years ago when a bullet from a gang shooting went astray. Or maybe—

Maybe she should just mind her own business and let them work it out for themselves.

Amethyst busied herself with the program in her lap.

A Wizard's Journey

it said amid a framework of ornate scrolls. She pushed out her lower lip. Didn't sound like the right program. Marl and Melodie still had their heads close together in conversation. She opened the program and looked for a date, but couldn't find one.

The Players

said the first page, and she scanned down the list, searching for Bree's name.

Talys – The Familiar
Koro – The Old Wizard; Harreken – The Young Wizard
Chauncy, Meredydd – The Lost—

Certainly the wrong program, from some play far more Tolkienesque than what Melodie had described. But it was something to look at until the curtain came up. She settled back into her seat.

Welcome!

the text began in a large and fancy font.

Prepare yourself for a journey beyond your imaginings, a

journey into wonder and adventure! Discover within yourself power and potential of which you never dreamed. Dive beneath the dull surface of the commonplace to immerse yourself in the vivid depths and vital currents of magic.

Amethyst turned the page.

You fear the unfamiliar, but that is to be expected. Trust that the unfamiliar shall become the familiar, your Familiar, your other half, the expression, direction and refinement of your power. I am Talys, and I have waited long and long for you.

Talys. Where had she seen that name? And why did it give her such a bad feeling?

A scattering of notes came from the orchestra pit as the musicians warmed up. She turned another page.

Magic is grown disused and forgotten, to the impoverishment of the world. And to its peril. For the magic grows wild, volatile, dangerous. But in a world that scorns sorcery as superstition and mocks magic as madness, whose power will calm the coming storm? Who will find and face the hunger that drives it?

The license plate. The one on the Mustang. That was where she'd seen that name. How could it possibly be printed here, too? Her fingers, suddenly damp, dimpled the paper. She turned it over.

You will, Amethyst Rey. Do not fear. Come to me.

Amethyst slapped the program shut and jammed it between her seat and Melodie's. Startled, Melodie turned to her. Over her shoulder, Marl's mouth was open, his lips still shaping a word.

Melodie touched her arm. "What's wrong, Wiz?"

Amethyst pointed down. A corner of the program poked up from between the seats, taunting her.

Melodie followed her pointing finger and drew out the bent and crumpled booklet. "What happened to this?"

Amethyst's voice wouldn't come for a moment, then it did. "Read it."

Melodie looked as if she were unsure whether to be worried or amused. "'Mayhem and Malarkey.'" She opened the cover. "'The Players.'"

"Turn to the fourth page," Amethyst said. "What does it say at the bottom?"

A worried line appeared between Melodie's brows. "'We would like to thank the following people for their generous contributions—'"

"No," Amethyst interrupted. She grabbed the program. "Look right here. It says—"

It said just what Melodie had read. Other people's names. Not Amethyst's. The world tilted and the booklet fluttered to the floor.

She struggled to her feet. "Where's the ladies room?" She had to get herself together. The program drew her eye, sentient and jeering.

"Why?" Melodie said. "Amethyst, are you okay? Are you sick?"

Marl rose. "Come on, I'll show you."

He stood there tall and grave and gallant in his sport jacket and narrow tie. God. She must look like a hysterical idiot.

"That's okay, I'm fine. I just need to splash a little water on my face." At his doubtful look, she gave a shaky laugh. "Really, I'll be fine." *Just as soon as driverless cars stop chasing me and opera programs stop addressing me personally.* She kept her mouth closed.

Marl held out his hand. She took it, a warm clasp of reality. Why couldn't she find someone like this? Well…probably because she couldn't bear the process of looking. The discomfort, embarrassment and outright terror.

"I'll be right back," he said to Melodie, then led Amethyst past the shuffling, muttering people to the aisle.

"Stay and watch the play. I'll be fine," Amethyst said again. "Just point the way."

He hesitated, then said, "Through the doors, to the left, just before the lobby."

Amethyst squeezed his arm and continued alone. The aisle

stretched ahead, patterned carpet lined with tiny floor lights. She wobbled a little on unaccustomed heels. The teenaged usher eyed her as she pushed through the doors, maybe suspecting her of desertion. She went through into a hall lit by frosted sconces that spilled semicircles of soft light on fawn-colored walls. Two women came toward her, chatting and making small adjustments to their clothes. They didn't seem real. When opera programs started talking to you, what was real, and what wasn't?

In the lobby ahead, people stood in well-dressed, murmuring groups. The darkness outside the glass entrance doors reflected distorted images. Shuddering, she turned away, looking for the restroom.

Then she was in the parking lot, under tall sodium lights gleaming on rows of parked cars.

Amethyst stumbled to a stop. The theater lay a long walk back, lights gleaming like a distant haven. Mary, Jesus and all the saints in heaven, how had she gotten here?

Suddenly shaking, she started walking toward the safety of lights and people. Her heels made small tappings on the asphalt, carrying her forward into the alternation of darkness and pooled orange light.

Night wind slithered cold along her calves. What had she done, sleepwalked? Gone into a trance? She couldn't possibly be so stressed—so distressed—as to aim for the bathroom only to end up in the middle of the parking lot. She raked one hand through her hair. God. Was she going crazy?

"Hey, babe."

Her heart tripped, then stumbled all over itself.

Him. The stalker.

She spun, dry-mouthed, blood roaring in her ears.

Three punks, saggy-pantsed, hoodie-shirted, stood grinning like caricatures in the faint light. A grey glitteryness shivered at the edges of her vision.

"Hey, I'm talkin' to ya. Where ya goin'?"

Damn, damn, damn! She forced herself to breathe, to speak. "Back," she said with a curt nod and started walking again, toward the beckoning theater. Don't hurry. Head up, walk, listen behind. Look strong, not like prey.

Footsteps followed, heavy and unhurried. Crude words were bandied amid unpleasant laughter.

Fine. This was the game: Let's Terrify a Lone Woman. Instinct told her to run. Reason told that was the worst thing to do. The long, full folds of her broomstick skirt tangled around her legs, but she kept walking, ignoring the hoots and rude calls behind her.

Light flared, splayed her shadow across the asphalt ahead of her. Stark eyes of headlights silhouetted the punks behind her, rimmed them with a white glare. A big-bore engine coughed to life, then gave a dragstrip howl. Tires squealed and the lights lunged forward.

The headlights grew, and the engine snarled louder. Her muscles locked, shorted out, disconnected from drive. The punks yelled and scattered, cursing, shouting threats. *Move*, she told herself. *Stupid,* move. But she didn't. Couldn't. Her mouth tasted of rusty metal.

In a skunky haze of burned rubber, the car screeched to a stop. The long, black hood gleamed like Death's river, scoop gaping in the middle. Amethyst could have touched it if she raised her hand. The grille was a dark maw. The windshield watched her, a depthless eye of night.

She knotted her hands in her skirt and shook. Concern, reassurance…came from somewhere. She tottered backward, on the edge of breaking into a run, then caught herself.

The punks—

Nothing nearby but asphalt and cars, but they couldn't have gone far. The Mustang rumbled at her knee.

Her head abruptly went around like she'd topple over where she stood. She flung out a hand, and her fingers touched something solid. She leaned against it, resting her face on her forearm until the world stopped rocking. She raised her head, found herself braced against the car's roof and snatched her arm away.

The car waited, muttering. Maybe the punks did, too. She took a few trembling steps.

The car crackled over the asphalt, keeping pace with her. She tensed, ready for the driver's door to swing open. But it remained closed. Even the driver's window stayed rolled up. Why didn't he get out, at least roll down the window and ask if she was okay?

"What the hell do you want?" Her voice shook, not the sneering challenge she'd meant. "Why don't you just—" *leave me alone*, she almost said. Except being alone hadn't been—still wasn't—a good idea.

She could cut through the ranks of parked cars and ditch the nutcase driving the Mustang. But she stayed to the middle of the aisle. In the light, easy to see if anyone was looking.

Like an oversized Rottweiler, the Mustang grumbled along at her side all the way to the theatre entrance. She glanced back once through the lobby doors, but it didn't drive away.

She still shook, and was now sick to her stomach, too. She took some deep breaths, finally made it to the restroom to wipe her face and neck with a damp paper towel and wobbled her way back to the dim theatre.

"Where have you been?" Melodie whispered as Amethyst lowered herself into her seat. "You've missed almost all of the first act!"

On stage, a tall young man in thigh-high boots sang, one hand on chest, the other dramatically upraised. Amethyst took a long breath. She leaned close and whispered, "I went outside and walked around for a while. Just to get some air."

Melodie eyed her. "You don't look good. Do you need to go home?"

Home. Was she any safer there? Was anywhere safe? "No, thanks, I'm fine, really."

Melodie didn't look convinced.

"Just—a little tired, I think," Amethyst said. "I really do want to hear Bree sing. I hope I haven't missed her."

Melodie shook her head. "No, but promise to tell me if you change your mind."

Amethyst squeezed her friend's hand. "I will." She was glad it was too dim to see the open programs the people beside her held.

When the house lights came back up, she was also glad she wasn't required to recite the storyline. Or, in fact, do anything more challenging than agree that, oh, yes, Bree had a wonderful voice, and yes, she looked quite the diva in that costume.

Everything still seemed strange, off-balance. Every thought, every action had to be carefully pre-planned. She ached to tell Melodie about what had just happened.

Had the stalker parked his car and followed her into the theatre? Was he here, now? He might be the tall, heavyset kid with the Bluetooth clipped over his ear, or the man in the navy blue suit and combover intent on the screen of his iPhone. He could be anyone. She forced herself to stop staring suspiciously into faces. After all, she was with other people, one of them male, and the stalker was probably smart enough to keep a low profile.

She couldn't keep herself from peering through the doors as they crossed the lobby, but the only vehicles pulled up at the curb outside were an enormous SUV and a minivan.

Marl held the door. A cluster of girls in long dresses preened and fluttered for three good-looking young men who stood on the sidewalk. A little distance along the theatre's front, angry voices echoed.

The punks from the parking lot crowded like sheep around two police officers. Pointing and waving their tattooed arms like overwrought actors, they now seemed no more than blustering kids.

"I'm tellin' ya, the sonofabitch tried to run us over! We was just hangin, y'know what I mean, man? And he tried to run us over!"

One of the officers made quieting gestures and spoke in a low tone.

One of the punks said, "It was somethin' old. And black. A Camaro or somethin' like that. Real old, but in good shape. Shiny, y'know?" The numbers "505," central New Mexico's area code, were shaved onto his scalp, pale in the dark fuzz of his hair.

Amethyst stopped herself from grabbing Melodie and saying, *Listen! They saw it too!* No. Definitely not. But if she joined the group and added her version of the story to the mix, along with a proper description of the car... That might take care of both kids and car.

Melodie took her arm and tugged. "Come on, Wiz. Coffee. A great big slice of pie, remember? The fun here is over with."

One could only hope.

The parking lot stretched ahead, rows of innocuous cars and vans and mile-high pickups washed to monochromes by the orange glow of sodium lights. Amethyst pulled her sweater tight. Parents and youngsters plunged heedlessly into the chilly spring night. Safety in numbers, right?

"Where'd you park?" Melodie asked.

Amethyst pointed. "Right over there, by that light standard."

The night chill insinuated itself through the inadequate knit of her sweater.

Cars idled past, headlights drawing their shadows long and then short on the pavement. Behind them, Bree and Jenna teased and giggled.

They came to where she'd parked her Isuzu. Amethyst stopped with a click of heels on pavement.

Red plastic taillight fragments littered the asphalt. The bumper was pushed up under the shattered rear window, into the cargo area. Both rear wheels tilted at painful angles, and one tire was flat.

Swallowing shouts and curse words, she walked the length of the vehicle. Doors sprung. Hood buckled. Oil and radiator fluid pooling on the pavement like blood. Front bumper wrapped around the light standard.

Bree's eyes were huge, her hands pressed over her mouth. Jenna clutched her dad's arm.

"Oh, Amethyst," Melodie finally breathed and hugged her.

The shout and curse words deserted her. "I quit carrying full coverage insurance on it last year. It's too old. It wasn't worth it."

Thin lipped, Marl said, "At least the police are already here. I'll go get in line." He stalked off, back toward the theater.

Melodie slid her free arm around Jenna and jiggled Amethyst's shoulders. "We'll take you home when you're done with the police. Get a good night's sleep and call me in the morning when you get up. I'll run you around wherever you need to go."

Amethyst stared down at the florescent green fluid by the toe of her shoe and nodded. It was all she was good for at the moment.

Chapter 3

"Wizzzzzz," a voice whispered.

Amethyst shot upright in bed, fingers clenched in the covers. Her bedroom curtains billowed, and the pages of the paperback on her nightstand fluttered. Her heart fluttering much the same, she gusted a breath.

The wind, risen as it sometimes did at night, hissed through the gap in the casement. Tomorrow would also be windy, probably—no surprise for spring in the Southwest.

She flipped back the covers and got up, rubbing her arms. The wind plastered her pajamas to her body as she cranked the casement closed. The backyard was sketched in the ghastly orange glow of streetlights. An overgrown lilac bush loomed dark against the pale concrete block wall enclosing the yard. A gust of wind flicked a scrap of paper like a small, fleeing ghost.

Something crashed in the alley beyond the back wall. A dog began barking, wild, snarling barks.

Amethyst stopped mid-crank. Caramela? The barking came closer, staccato bursts connected by long rips of snarls, right on the other side of her back wall. Then a dog's screaming wail of pain.

She yanked out a robe and grabbed the baseball bat she kept in a corner of the closet. She ran down the hall for the dining room and the back door, belting on the robe with sharp little tugs.

The wind nearly slammed the door into her face. She hefted the baseball bat and surged out into the backyard. Her hair whipped around her head, and the robe ballooned threateningly. The bat slipped in her sweaty grip. Taking a firmer hold, she hauled open the back gate.

The alley was a wind tunnel. Scraps of paper, even small boxes scuttled like rats, vague in the glow of a distant streetlight.

A tree hung a blot of darkness over the pavement a few houses down.

"Caramela?"

Amethyst caught her hair, dragged it back out of her face. She'd heard a dog. Not in someone's backyard. Here, right behind her own. And she knew that bark was Caramela's—she'd heard her barking and howling often enough in her own yard, hungry, lonely and neglected.

Amethyst stepped a little farther into the alley, shading her eyes against the streetlight's gleam. Twigs and grains of sand peppered her. A gust whipped her hair stingingly into her eyes. The gate banged closed behind her.

She whirled and pressed a hand to her chest. With a breathy little laugh, she pulled the string that unlatched the gate from the outside.

It snapped, dropping the latch into place again. A frayed length of string hung useless in her hand.

Cursing would do absolutely no good. She'd still have to scramble back over the wall, or else hike around the block. In the middle of the night. In a windstorm. In her robe and slippers. She felt like sneaking over to Caramela's gate, just to peek in and make sure she was all right, that she hadn't fled in pain to the only home she knew. But not like this.

The alley was lower than her back yard, so the wall here rose well over her head. Amethyst leaned the bat against the wall and backed up to get a running start.

A full-throated growl sounded, as if from something large and predatory. Her heart kicked her breastbone. Taillights in triplicate flared in that overhanging tree's shadow. Walls and weed-invaded pavement suddenly glowed a lurid red. Then tires squealed and the lights lunged toward her.

Amethyst leapt for the wall. One hand hit the cold, rough surface of concrete block, the other, the top of the gate. Splinters drove into her fingers and she fell back again. The taillights, red and glaring, were almost on her. She snatched at the bat, but it clattered to the ground and rolled away. She ran.

The rumble grew louder. The stink of exhaust choked her, breathed hot on her legs. A fender eased alongside, barely brushing her hip. She dodged against the wall. In that awful, endless moment came the distinctive clack of a car door opening, then the door jostled her, swept her up.

Her head and back knocked something hard. She gave a strangled scream, landed wedged upside down. A door thumped, and the rush of the wind ceased.

She struck out. Her fists met air, a seat, her feet a padded door panel. No one spoke. No one grabbed her. Somehow, she righted herself, scrambled up.

The driver's seat was empty.

Instrument lights glowed green on the inside of the cabin. The steering wheel nudged itself left and right. The engine quaked with a cement-mixer growl. She gasped, unable to get enough air, wrenched at the door handle. It lifted, but the door didn't budge. She threw herself across the center console into the driver's seat, yanked at the driver's door handle. Nothing. Nothing. Locked in—*pull the damn door lock, Amethyst*—but it wouldn't pull up, the doors wouldn't open, the window cranks were frozen.

She clenched her hands in the nubby fabric of her robe and collapsed back into the seat. The shift lever moved of its own accord from reverse to first, then to second. Beyond the windshield, the alley scrolled by. Piles of yard trimmings squatted, broken glass sparkled in the headlights.

Reality shuddered and collapsed. No human stalker lurked to kidnap and rape her, just a car, *only* a car, alone, undriven, lying in wait to lure her out and snatch her up into some impossible craziness. She hugged herself, trying to steady her breathing, forcing herself to think.

It was just—had to be—remote control, servos, cameras, some techie's idea of a twisted joke. If she had the money and equipment, she could rig up something like it herself.

A laugh escaped her, one that teetered on the edge of hysteria. A sicko techie stalker was better?

She pulled the sleeves of her robe over her fists and hammered at the dark-tinted window.

A sense of presence stole over her, smoothing the edges of her terror, murmuring calm in a subliminal whisper. Just like in the theatre parking lot—

Amethyst spun to look in the backseat. Empty. A street now slid slowly by outside, quiet houses and parked cars as remote as a scene in a movie. She turned forward again, gripped the wheel and planted both feet on the brake. The wheel moved under her hands, but to its own impulsion. The brake pedal might have been welded to the floorboard.

"Let me out," she said, and her voice came out high and thin. "Or do I have to reach under the dash and start ripping out wires? Or maybe—" She caught a breath. "Maybe a few fuses will do it."

She twisted around under the wheel. The sense of soothing warred with her fear. No one—*no one*—else was in this car. No one to be aware of her. No one to soothe her. She wouldn't look again, because if she did, she'd only see—

The pitch of the engine changed. The brake and clutch pedals depressed. She fumbled under the dash. For an instant, she felt as if someone took her hand, gently.

She snatched her hand away and thrust herself upright. Her knees knocked hard on the steering wheel. "Let me go!"

The car eased to a stop. With a click, the driver's door swung open.

Amethyst tumbled out, staggered to catch her balance on a driveway. The wind still blew, tangling her hair in her face. She wanted to be home, safe in her own bed, where all of this would turn out to be just a dream. She stumbled backward. A line of low bushes snatched at her robe, raked her legs. A house, dark and blind, faced her. She reeled.

She stood at the edge of her own driveway.

The car's deep-voiced engine abruptly fell silent. The wind rushed, whistled through wires, jangled the low chain link fence around Mr. Meadows' front yard. She backed into the garage door with a thump. It rattled as she edged along it.

Heat radiated from the car's grille, warm against her cold flesh. Lit by the Halloween glow of the streetlights, the Mustang gleamed like black water, quiescent now as a car should be. But from somewhere, she caught a sense of rueful amusement.

Amethyst bolted. The gate by the garage burst open, spilling her into the side yard. The back door was unlocked—she'd only shut it behind her.

She groped at the back doorknob, flung open the door and slammed it shut again. Fingers shaking so hard she could scarcely control them, she locked it behind her.

It had to be a dream. Just a dream. Cars didn't drive themselves, and they certainly didn't lure people outside in the middle of the night and abduct them.

Early morning sunlight slanted along the alley behind her yard, showing every undeniable detail. Those wide, black streaks on the pavement were definitely tire tracks, fresh enough to have cleared the gravel off the decaying asphalt. And what about the wide, red scrape on her right leg, and the bluish, lumpy bruises on her shins? The splinters in her hand? Not to mention that it was pretty hard to dream anything while wedged into a corner of the couch, wide awake and keeping an eye on both the front and back doors.

She followed the marks of rubber until they hooked and disappeared. Caramela's crazy-hanging gate was just ahead. Amethyst stopped just short and bit her lip. She didn't remember hearing Caramela bark while she was running down the damned alley last night. She didn't need more trouble, but if that dog crying had been Caramela—

She pressed against the wall and peeked through the gate, into the backyard. Wrinkled and torn aluminum foil plastered the inside of the house's back windows. The backyard was overrun with tree-of-heaven suckers. Playing hide and seek among them were a gutted washing machine, a rusted-out water heater lying on its side, broken toilet, engines in various stages of disassembly and car seats leaking stuffing. A transmission with its torque converter vomited fluid on the oil-blackened dirt.

A growl rumbled on the other side of the gate and a head pushed through.

"Caramela!" Amethyst whispered. "You're okay?"

The dog wiggled through the gate, already wagging. Then her tail stopped and quivered, and Caramela intently sniffed Amethyst up and down. Her short fur bristled, making a darker line along her back.

Amethyst wished she could ask the dog what she smelled. A freak with enough money, time and obsession to rig up a full-sized remote-controlled car?

Or the almost-speaking *presence* Amethyst had sensed last night?

Reality started to slide scarily askew again. Maybe there wasn't a stalker. Maybe there was only the car.

She rapped her knuckles on her head. "No, no, no." There was someone behind all this. And cars had VINs, and registrations.

She had a computer she knew how to use.

"Come on, Caramela," she said. "Let's take a walk."

She retraced the route she'd taken—unwillingly—last night, a couple of blocks along the alley to Eubank. She couldn't remember which way the car had turned then. Left, probably, away from Flint, her street. It had seemed like too long for a trip not quite around the block. But then, she'd been terrified, too. Five seconds would've seemed like forever.

Morning commute traffic stretched and compressed between lights like pulled taffy. Amethyst kept an eye on it, but nothing low, black and classic glided by. Caramela trotted ahead, sniffing the corner house's zero-scaping—a yard whose contribution to water conservation was an expanse of gravel interspersed with patches of puncture vine.

Flint was just ahead. Her house was two blocks uphill, out of sight from here. So was the street in front of her house.

Amethyst's heart beat too fast. She *wanted* to find the car there this time, she reminded herself.

She forced herself to keep walking, past yards, past innocuous, half-familiar parked cars. The traffic noise on Eubank dwindled, leaving the rush of the wind, someone's clamoring windchime, the gurgle of a mourning dove. A dog barked. Caramela lifted her head but kept on trotting. Just a little farther, then Amethyst would be able to see.

Her stomach twisted into slow knots. Whoever (or *whatever*, a little voice whispered) motivated the damned car wouldn't try anything in broad daylight. She'd be able to see the VIN through the windshield, standing safely in front of the car door to see it.

Amethyst drifted to the edge of the sidewalk and stretched her neck.

The car wasn't there. Not in the street, not in her driveway. She should have felt relieved. She didn't.

The doorbell rang. Amethyst looked up from her computer screen—*Car Rentals*—pushed up from the dining room table and walked to the front door, phone still pressed to her ear. Melodie, looking unaccountably happy, stood outside.

"Uh-huh. Do you have anything cheaper?" Amethyst said to the clerk on the other end of the line. Giving Melodie a wan smile, she motioned her in and returned to her scribbled pad of notes.

"Okay. Well, thanks for your help." She thumbed off the phone and dropped her head in her hands.

The dining room chair beside her scraped over the floor.

"You don't look too good, Wiz. Are you still upset about last night?"

"Of course I am!" Amethyst blurted.

"Well, I know it was a shock," Melodie said a little defensively. "But you've got the problem covered now, don't you?"

"You have to be—" Wait. Last night… The wreck of her

Isuzu had been only the prelude. Melodie hadn't been around for the big event. Amethyst pressed fingertips to eyes and started over. "I don't see how."

"I don't see how *not*."

Amethyst sighed and tilted her chair onto its back legs. How many times had Dad told her not to do that? And here she was, all grown up and still doing it. But Dad wasn't here to tell her, "Thistle, you're gonna ruin the legs of that chair, and you know what? It won't be you they'll break under, it'll be me, and I won't be a bit happy when they do, let me tell you."

Everyone seemed to have a different nickname for her. Dad called her "Thistle," Mama called her "Violita." Purple names. Except for Melodie's "Wiz."

"Mel," she said, "I can hardly meet clients and deliver windows on the bus. And you're a wonderful friend, but I don't expect you chauffer me indefinitely."

Melodie's brows crooked. "But…what about the car in your driveway?"

Amethyst's stomach fell. "What car?"

Melodie stared at her as if trying to decide if she were joking or not, then rolled her eyes. "You know," she said with exaggerated care. "The one that looks like something straight out of the Muscle Car Nationals?" She cocked a suggestive eyebrow. "Or do you have a visitor I didn't see?"

Amethyst gripped the edge of the table. The tips of her fingers turned white. No. No, no, no…

She shoved to her feet.

"Wiz?"

She didn't answer, only stomped through the kitchen and living room, out the door and down the walk. Melodie followed, growing, from the tone of her questions, ever more concerned.

Amethyst swung around at the end of the walk and faced the car. Low. Black. Muscular. She sensed a smile of triumph—from somewhere.

From the Mustang.

No.

Yes.

Sweat prickled along her hairline, and she swallowed a whimper.

Melodie glanced at the car and back at Amethyst. "It isn't yours? I saw it in your driveway and thought—"

"It is *not* mine," Amethyst said. Her voice quavered a little.

"Then whose is it?"

"I'd love to know."

Melodie studied her. "It— Wait. Is it—? This isn't the one—"

"Yes."

Melodie's eyes narrowed. "It doesn't belong in your driveway, then." She took a determined step toward the passenger door. "Let's find out who's about to wish they hadn't started playing games with you."

Amethyst caught her arm. "Mel, don't—"

"The hell." Melodie was giving out mad vibes that would run a generator. "I'll break the damn window if I have to."

But the door swung open most cooperatively under her hand. Amethyst peered over Melodie's shoulder. The car was—what else?—empty.

Melodie plopped into the passenger seat and snapped opened the glove box. The compartment within was immaculate: no petrified sticks of gum, no old matchbooks, no dried-up ballpoint pens, dead flashlights or tattered maps. Just a single slip of white paper. Melodie plucked it up, studied it, then raised her eyes to Amethyst's.

Amethyst's voice wasn't cooperating. She cleared her throat. "Registration?" she finally managed.

Melodie held it out, but Amethyst couldn't bring herself to touch it, much less take it.

"Yours." Melodie shook it at her. If you're Amethyst M. Rey at 10638 Flint Avenue, Northeast, Albuquerque, New Mexico."

"But it's not—it can't be—" Another gift? A really big one,

this time, a step or two hundred up from pomegranates and acorns.

Melodie flicked the edge of the paper with a fingernail, then slid it back into the glove compartment. "Awfully convenient, isn't it? Someone nukes your truck last night, and this shows up in your driveway this morning."

Amethyst wrapped her arms around herself and squeezed. "*Why?* Why are you doing this to me?"

Melodie climbed out of the car and took Amethyst's arm. "There's nobody here."

Amethyst shifted her jaw sideways. "No, but he damn sure can—" *hear me*, she almost said, but bit back the words.

Somewhere, the bastard was watching. There had to be cameras and mikes to go with the remote control. The better to enjoy the victim's fear.

Then she thought, appalled, *Cameras? Microphones?* This was turning into real paranoia, complete with delusions of grandeur.

"The VIN," she said suddenly.

A sort of vindictive triumph leapt up in her. She circled the car and peered through the driver's side windshield. "I don't see it…" She yanked open the door and searched the inside edges, then the jamb. "Where the hell is it? These old cars had VIN's, didn't they?" She slammed the door and stalked around to the passenger side again. "Let me see that registration slip again." She opened the glove compartment and scrabbled out the registration.

Melodie caught her arm. "Wiz. Come on. Let's go inside a minute." Amethyst balked, but Melodie tugged her up the driveway. "Come on."

Amethyst let herself be led into the dining room. She plunked down at the table and dropped her head into her hands.

Melodie slid into the chair beside her. She laced and re-laced her fingers. "Wiz, are you sure there's a stalker? This is just…so weird. I mean, could someone register a car in your name without you knowing anything about it?"

"I don't know," Amethyst said into her hand, then raised

her head. "What about when someone buys a car as a gift?" No, she didn't want to think about gifts right now.

Melodie shrugged.

She was right. The whole thing was crazy, and getting crazier. But whatever was going on, Amethyst knew *she* wasn't crazy. Or at least, she couldn't be *that* crazy. She wouldn't forget buying a car. And she flat out didn't have the funds to buy a fully restored classic.

She slid the registration slip across the table and stared into the kitchen. A stained glass window-hanging, one of her early projects, spangled the worn Formica of the breakfast bar with green and scarlet and gold shapes. Grocery store dishes and glasses peeking through geometric-patterned stained glass inserts in the kitchen cabinets became mysterious and exotic. She'd always liked the mysterious and exotic. But now that it had decided to take over—

"I didn't buy that car, Mel. Why would I? Do I look like I have any desire to tinker with an antiquated, gas-guzzling, lead-burning monstrosity I can't even take off a paved road? Do you suppose I want to frequent *swap meets* for parts and spend my weekends waxing it?" She massaged her temples. A headache was coming on. "And how the hell am I supposed to deliver windows in something like that?"

Melodie reached out a conciliatory hand. "Okay, okay." She straightened. "Hey, you have evidence now! You can call the police."

Amethyst sucked in a swift, hopeful breath, then slumped. "It's the same problem as with the rest of the gifts. What law's been broken?"

Melodie's mouth dropped open. "Last night—!"

"You heard what the cops said. Without witnesses, who's to prove who did it? And that thing," she jerked her chin in the direction of the front door, "doesn't have a dent on it. No way could it have crunched up my truck like that."

"But—" Frowning, Melodie drummed fingers on the table. "Okay. Forget about the car's provenance for a minute."

Amethyst made a skeptical face, but Melodie went on.

"The registration is in your name, all nice and legal. I'd drive the damn thing, if only to flush your secret admirer out of the shrubbery."

"That's what I'm afraid of," Amethyst muttered, then narrowed her eyes. She pulled the registration toward her. "This'll have the damned VIN."

Printed in the Vehicle Identification Number box was Y0UN33DN'7B0TH3R. The printer must've skipped on the figure just before the "7". Then her brain made the jump from an unreadable string of letters and numbers to a phrase: *you needn't bother.*

Amethyst cursed.

Melodie grabbed the slip. "So you can't read the VIN. Don't worry about it. The question is, what're you going to do? You can't just ignore the car."

"Watch me."

Melodie stood. "C'mon."

Amethyst braced her hands against the table. "Where?"

"Outside, to make your feelings clear." She walked out of the room.

"What are you going to do?" Amethyst scrambled after her.

"*I* will watch while *you* move the damned car out of your driveway." Melodie marched out the front door, down the walk to the car. She made to open the driver's door.

"Are you crazy?" Amethyst said, grabbing her hand. "Don't you know—" What? That whoever operates the car by remote control is liable to take over at any moment? Gee, might as well just go ahead and tell her all about the presence she sensed. The one that tried to soothe her during her short-term kidnapping. The one she'd sensed just a few minutes ago.

Melodie waited, attentive. "Don't I know what?"

"*Him.* The stalker. He's got to be around. Somewhere."

"Do you see him?" Melodie made a show of peering around. "Nope, I don't see him." She made an elaborate gesture of invitation.

Damn! She *couldn't* tell her, not when Melodie was already beginning to doubt the ordinary stalker theory.

The chrome door handle winked in the sunlight. Amethyst wiped a damp palm down the leg of her jeans, then pushed the button of the old-fashioned door latch. On a breath of cool, new-car-scented air, the door clicked and swung open in well-greased silence.

Cool air. A black car sitting in the sun, and it was cool inside. Was there a new-car-smell foo-foo hanging from the rear-view mirror, too? No.

Melodie leaned over Amethyst's shoulder. "Keys in the ignition. Ever thoughtful, this fellow."

"Sure. *Thanks*, Mr. Stalker."

She hesitated by the open door. After all, the car had been completely capable of driving off with her before.

"Mel…"

"What?"

"I—" *I have to look for the receiver for the remote control.* And where would that be? "I don't think this is a good idea."

"Got a better one?" Melodie said.

"Yeah. Call a tow truck and have this baby hauled to the junkyard. Let the damned stalker buy it back, if he wants it."

This—this—bastard was doing everything in his power to force his attentions on her, scare her, make her vulnerable. If she didn't do something, this latest gift would represent her surrender to him.

She leaned in and snatched the keys out of the ignition. The keychain was the wand-shaped fob with the little floating stars she'd found on her doorstep a week ago. The one she'd thrown in the trash. How the hell had he gotten it? How the hell had he known where to look for it?

Shuddering, she flung it into the street. The keys gave a sort of jingling wail when they hit the asphalt.

"Wiz!" Melodie said.

"Forget it. I don't want anything to do with it. As far as I'm concerned, the damned car can sit here and rust."

Melodie folded her arms. "So what are you going to do?"

"I'll figure something out." Amethyst headed for Melodie's chile-pepper-red Honda Insight. "Come on. I'm sick of thinking about it. I want to do something normal, like get breakfast."

Melodie got into her car. Amethyst buckled into the passenger seat.

"I know you don't want to hear this right now," Melodie said, "but for all intents and purposes, it's your car. You can do whatever you want with it. Sell it, for example."

Amethyst brightened, then slumped against the door. "No title."

"Hmmm. There is that. I guess your stalker isn't as thoughtful as we'd like."

Still, Motor Vehicles should be able to print one. The thought made her a little happier. "Maybe I can trade it in for a Subaru Outback."

"Get a Toyota Highlander. A hybrid."

"Does that mean we're going car shopping?"

"After breakfast. One must be properly fortified for that kind of work."

Amethyst grinned. "So where're we going?"

"Double Lightning," Melodie said. "I feel like a big, fat, crispy Belgian waffle with whipped cream and strawberries piled this high on top."

"You're going to *look* like a big, fat Belgian plow horse if you start eating like that."

"Sure, Wiz. Rub it in that you can eat anything and not worry about your figure."

Amethyst stuck her tongue out sideways. "Rub it in that you *have* a figure."

This was better, pretending that everything was just the way it always was. Here in the new-forged light of morning, she could think of getting rid of the car.

Double Lightning wasn't a bad drive in the lighter traffic of a Saturday morning, although they somehow managed to hit every red light on Eubank. Strip malls, churches and apartment buildings seemed to crawl by until they finally turned into Double Lightning's parking lot, which was, of course, full.

Inside the restaurant, the smells of baked goods and bacon curled invitingly. The waitress, a substantial presence in her purple-and yellow uniform, led them to a window booth. Amethyst slid into the booth opposite her friend.

Melodie waved off the menu. "I already know what I want. An espresso and one of your wonderful strawberry Belgian waffles."

"Hot chocolate, please," Amethyst said, taking the menu. Double Lightning made a great breakfast casserole, with green chile sausage and potatoes, black beans and red peppers. They also made a whole lot of other yummy things. Sometimes it was hard to decide.

The waitress scribbled on her pad and left the menu. The clink of cutlery and drone of conversation created a comforting background.

"Espresso. Ecch," Amethyst said and opened her menu. "Might as well drink used motor oil."

Right under *Breakfast Delights*, the menu said, *Don't try to sell me, Amethyst.*

She dropped it.

Melodie looked up, startled. "Didn't see anything you wanted?"

So much for pretending that everything was just fine. "It says—"

Me, it said. Don't try to sell *me*. As if—

As if the car itself were talking to her.

Amethyst wrenched around. Outside the window, the usual assortment of vehicles winked and flashed in the morning sunlight. There was no telltale glimpse of chrome and sleek black fender.

That didn't mean the car wasn't out there. Waiting. Like at the opera.

"What?" Melodie said.

Slowly, Amethyst pulled the menu toward her. "Sorry. I

guess I'm still jumpy. After…everything." She took a long breath.

Under *Eggs and More*, the menu said,

I seriously advise you...........................*$8.95*

to desist in a scheme.............................*$8.95*

which will prove....................................*$9.65*

sadly deleterious...................................*$9.95*

to your comfort, ease...........................*$10.50*

and peace of mind...............................*$11.95*

Of course. She should have realized it before. However she tried to get rid of the damned car, it would just show up in her driveway again. If she sold it, she'd probably find the angry buyer on her doorstep, too. If the stalker didn't get there first. Maybe being crazy beat the alternative.

She pushed the menu across the table. "I think I'll stick with the hot chocolate. I'm not too hungry right now."

Chapter 4

Amethyst had to be dreaming, because certain things were wrong. For one thing, she couldn't find the light switch on the wall beside her, no matter how many times she swept her hand over the place it should be. For another, the, unlighted space around her was cold and echoey, not the close, soft dimness of her bedroom. And strangest of all, someone was there with her.

Maybe, under the circumstances, the fact that it wasn't her bedroom was a good thing.

"Why are you doing this?" she said, still fumbling across the wall. Where was the damned switch?

A sigh gusted from somewhere nearby. "I fear I can't help it," a male voice replied, deep and tinged with some sort of unplaceable accent. "You're a wizard, you see. I'm a familiar, and the awkward fact of the matter is, I need you. I'd be highly ill-advised to leave you, for an assortment of reasons."

Which of the several parts of that statement was the most alarming? She forgot about the light switch for the moment. "A wizard. You mean like with a long white beard and tall pointy hat and purple robe sewn all over with moons and stars and horoscope symbols?"

Out of the darkness came a laugh as rich and warm as cocoa. "Rather like that."

She should've been able to hear the rustle of clothes, small shiftings of weight. Nothing. Nothing but the sounds she herself made. "You're crazy," she said.

"Not in the least," the voice replied.

"Then *I* must be," she muttered.

"Why," the voice said, sounding annoyed, "would you prefer to think yourself insane than to accept the evidence of your own senses?"

"Um…maybe because there's no such thing as magic?"

"Are you quite sure of that?"

She made a disgusted noise. "Of course I'm sure! I haven't noticed anybody throwing lightning or making things appear out of thin air."

"Not even a lowly pomegranate? And the opera program and menu were rather peculiar, wouldn't you say?"

She went cold. "How the hell do you know about that?"

"Oh, I think you know."

"Okay. For the sake of argument, let's say that was m-magic." She suddenly had trouble saying the word. "But that doesn't mean I am. Magic, that is. My god, I'm twenty-eight years old. If I had any unusual abilities, you'd think they'd've cropped up by now."

"There is an excellent reason for that," the voice said.

"Like what?" Why was she even asking? It wasn't like any of this was real.

"Since you insist on disbelieving, it hardly seems profitable to explain."

"I never said—" She hadn't said it, but that's exactly what she'd thought just now. She scrambled to her feet. "Dammit, you—"

"Talys."

"What?"

"Talys. My name. If you must curse me, it should be helpful to know it."

"Stay out of my head!"

A sigh. "Forgive me. It's part and parcel of being your familiar. After all, you are able to sense me quite keenly."

"I don't want to sense you. I want to wake up in my bed, find my Isuzu in the garage and realize all this has been nothing but a dream brought on by a bit of bad beef, a blot of mustard."

"Or a fragment of underdone potato? Dickens, wasn't it? I do assimilate my hosts' knowledge."

"*Hosts?*" she said, horrified. "As in parasites?"

"I am *not* a parasite." The voice sounded irritated and a little outraged. "Parasites subsist to the detriment of the host. If you must use a biological analogy, I'm a symbiont. While the magic you possess offers me certain advantages, I provide benefits in the form of amplification and refinement of your powers, as well as access to my immeasurable experience and knowledge."

Certainly no one could accuse him, whatever he was, of being humble. She knotted her hands in her hair and pulled. "Wake up, Amethyst."

"Why, with each passing century," the voice was exasperated now, "have humans grown more skeptical of anything they cannot touch and feel, manipulate and dissect? Never mind. I know perfectly well the answer to that question."

Passing centuries. And humans, as if speaking of another sort of being. Amethyst took her hands out of her hair, wadded the hem of her nightshirt instead and swallowed a moan. "If you'd just *tell* me, rather then dropping cryptic hints, it might help."

"Perhaps it will. Very well. Because wizards are become so very rare."

Are become? This—guy, for lack of a better term—had read way too many nineteenth century novels. She laughed—or rather, a laugh popped out. "No kidding. More like wizards don't exist."

He tutted. "My, you're obstinate. No, the few wizards who remain are extremely circumspect."

"Yeah?" she said. "Why?"

"Do you plan on displaying your abilities for one and all to see?"

She pushed a breath through pursed lips. "Leaving aside that my abilities have yet to be proven, this argument is becoming suspiciously circular. Which leads me to believe you're avoiding an answer."

"Perceptive, yes." He sounded annoyed. "If you insist. The number of wizards had been declining for some few centuries. Then it seemed suddenly scarcely any were left at all."

"Thin gene pool, huh?"

"Power is not necessarily inherited. As the present example should demonstrate."

She wouldn't keep arguing the latter point. "You know, if you're not going to answer my questions, I don't see why we should continue this conversation." She felt behind her for the doorknob.

"I am merely a familiar. My knowledge is extensive, but I am hardly omniscient."

"Which *still* isn't an answer."

"Nevertheless, I refuse to alarm you with baseless speculation."

"Why stop now?" She gave up on the doorknob, which she couldn't find any more than the light switch.

"Because my task is presently difficult enough! Not only have I the burden of this absurdly material culture to struggle against, but also an intransigent woman!"

"Oh, well, gee. Sorry. But just think, all's not lost. You can still find a real wizard to familiarize with. Then we'll both be happy."

"Ah," he said. "But it was your magic awakened me. Your bright, young power might deliver me from my long exile."

Long exile. Another hint. Put with the others, it laid a breadcrumb trail to something he didn't want her to know. If she kept him talking long enough, she might finally manage to piece it together. "So, it was only random mischance that delivered you to my doorstep."

"Tsk," he chided. "The first thing I must teach you is that nothing in wizardry is random. Every life, every thought, every event is interconnected, a part of the universal pattern."

"A familiar that spouts quantum mechanics," Amethyst muttered.

"Some truths go beyond the arrogance of science."

She waved a dismissive hand. "Now we're getting into philosophy. Okay, so you affirmed me into being, or…what?"

"*You* attracted *me*—your power, your soul, your potentialities."

"Potential for what?"

"Ah-ah," he said. "We're getting a bit ahead of ourselves, aren't we? First there is the little matter of your believing me."

"And what if I do believe in all this bull—these assertions of yours?"

Warmth, as of a smile, came through the cold darkness. "Well, love, that's when the fun begins."

Amethyst clawed herself awake. Her head banged back on something hard. It was dark in the room, too dark. Where was the wan orange glow of the streetlight? And the wall behind her was still cold …

Concrete cold under her bare feet, the smell of oil and old grease. She started shivering. No *way*.

Echoing her dream, she swept the wall beside her for the light switch. This time, she found it. She hesitated.

What was she afraid of? Okay, fine. She was in the garage instead of her bedroom, where she belonged. Maybe she'd sleepwalked. When the light came on, she'd see the usual clutter: the lawn mower, the scarred old workbench with its pegboard back, the rusty cans of paint on plank shelves, the oil spots on the floor, the empty space her old Isuzu had occupied. Nothing else.

Amethyst sucked in a breath and flipped the switch.

The florescent bulbs flickered on with stuttering clicks, settled into a faint hum. Before her, filling her single-car garage, stretched the gleaming black length of the car, silent, aware and smug.

◊ ◊ ◊

It had just been a dream.

Yet in defiance of all things dreamlike, the Mustang filled the dim, narrow space, like a bodybuilder in a too-small jacket.

Amethyst stood on the step between the garage and the utility room, morning light slanting through the utility room window behind her. "I did not drive you in here. I threw the keys into the street, remember?"

She bit her lip, waiting, but the car didn't answer.

Answer, right. *Hello*, Amethyst. Cars don't talk!

Taking a shaky breath, she stepped down. The car door didn't open, so she took another step, then dashed to the side garage door and flung it open, in case she needed an escape. The car sat quietly.

She edged up to the car door. If the windows weren't so darkly tinted, she'd be able to see inside. She'd have to open the door. Well, she'd opened it yesterday. Nothing had happened then. Melodie had been with her, though. Sweat prickled her palms.

"Stop being stupid," she told herself. Something weird was going on, but bottom line, it was just a car. If she didn't prove that to herself right now, she was lost for sure.

She took a deep breath and opened the door.

Still empty. She slid into the driver's seat.

The door closed with an ear-popping *whump*. She jerked around. She hadn't pulled it closed behind her. Had she? Before her, the dash spread in woodgrain, glossy black vinyl and chrome; great, big, round speedometer and tach dominated the instrument array. The key was in the ignition. The wand-fob dangled from it.

"I did not pick up those keys, either." But that didn't have anything to do with magic, or a talking car. It could be explained. Somehow.

The Mustang remained silent, still, as blank and innocent as any car. She touched the shift knob, ran her fingers over the wheel.

She abruptly stomped on the clutch, twisted the key in the ignition. The engine woke like a beast. She turned it off just as quickly. It stayed off.

She was breathing too fast. "Okay," she said. This was going to be the hardest part.

Amethyst climbed out and opened the garage door. Morning light spilled in, the inevitable spring wind, the faint smell of dust blown off the West Mesa. The car's paint was glossy and immaculate, without a trace of dust. She tried to convince herself this was interesting, not eerie. Outside, everything was normal.

She got back in the car and started it.

Funny, how the whole idea of a stalker seemed less scary than what had happened—what she'd *dreamed*—last night. That the Mustang held *something's* consciousness, and that something wanted to convince her she was a wizard and attach itself—himself?—to her. Or that she was going crazy.

The gearshift and pedals moved gently, easily under her hand and feet as if trying to win her approval.

She shook her head. Maybe that would shake the craziness out of it. Nothing was here to want her approval.

"No hand brake," she grumbled, groping automatically for the nonexistent lever between the seats. "I hate American cars. Whose stupid idea was it to put in an emergency brake that you can't control?" She finally found the brake release below the dash, popped it and backed out.

To shut the garage door, she had to turn her back on the car. She hauled on the bit of knotted rope, and the door went rattling down. The skin along her spine tickled with the feather-touch of someone's gaze. She spun. Of course, no one lurked behind but the Mustang.

"It's just a car," she said through clenched teeth. Her feet refused to move closer, though. "Get in, Amethyst. *Drive* it."

The Mustang only crouched over its wheels, muttering.

The car felt strange: heavy, powerful. She wished for her nice, clattery, unthreatening Isuzu. She drove down the street, made a right onto Eubank. Two kids sat at a bus stop, one perched on the back of the bench, the other slouched on it. They straightened and their heads swiveled as she drove by.

She made another right. Just a little cruise through the neighborhood, nice and slow, driving the Mustang like she would any other car. Houses passed by, rentals with cars parked in dirt front yards. Some houses had funny, pointed Swiss-chalet roofs and upturned eaves, as out-of-place in the Southwest as a yodeler in a mariachi band. Amethyst had always wondered what the developer was thinking. Then she was back on Flint, driving up the hill. A guy was outside in the dirt front yard of Caramela's house, leaning shirtless over the engine compartment of a rust-speckled, primer-grey coupe. He straightened and watched her pass by, grease-blackened hands propped on hips.

She pulled into her driveway, let out a breath and dropped her head back against the headrest. The garage door rattled. She snapped straight.

The door rose, opening on an ever larger slice of garage, on oil-spotted concrete and dusty clutter.

The only problem was, she didn't have a garage door opener.

A cup of truly vile coffee sat off to one side of the design sketches on her worktable.

Amethyst didn't like coffee. No matter how much she doctored it, it upset her stomach. Maybe that was why she felt so queasy now.

The door to the utility room was closed and locked now. So was the door between the utility room and garage. Fear was as sharp and vivid as the fragments of glass on her cutting board. Her laptop search bar said *Psychologists*. She tapped an ad with her forefinger. *Anxiety, Stress, Life Transitions*, it said.

She couldn't be crazy, could she? But if everything that was happening wasn't in her imagination, then that meant it had to be real. If she gave into that idea, then she really would be crazy. She lowered her head into her hands. Either way, she'd better get help.

But a blind pick off the Internet? It didn't seem like a good idea.

She pushed away from her worktable picked up her phone.

Three rings, four, five. Melodie answered, and Amethyst let out a silent breath.

"Mel. It's me. Listen, I know you're busy, but I need a big

favor. I remember you told me that Marl talked to a, um, mental health professional after his wife died. You wouldn't happen to know who, would you?"

There was a beat of silence on the other end of the line. "What's wrong? What happened?"

Amethyst scooted glass around the cutting board. "I—I'm having—well, this whole stalker thing is really beginning to…to bother me. I think I'm going to need some coping skills."

"Nothing else has happened?" Asked with the greatest delicacy.

"Oh, nightmares. That sort of thing."

"Mmm. You'd tell me if it were more than that, wouldn't you?"

"I swear on my mother's grave."

"Your mother isn't dead."

"It's just dreams. Really."

"Okay, then. I remember it was a funny name. Wait a minute. I'll be right back."

A click as the phone was set down, then unidentifiable rustling noises. Amethyst arranged the glass into a pattern and waited, phone clamped between ear and shoulder.

Melodie came back on the line. "It's in my Daytimer. Everyone's card seems to wind up in here somehow. I even have one of yours, like I can't remember your address or phone number. The name is Eliot Korhonen, PhD. Got a pencil?"

"Ready." She wrote down the phone number and the address.

"Amethyst." Melodie hesitated, then went on, "Are you sure you're all right? You sound… I don't know. If I didn't know you better, I'd say you sound scared."

She massaged a temple. Scared might about cover it. It was certainly more appealing than 'crazy.' "As well as can be expected, I guess."

Another hesitation. "All right. But call me if you need anything, okay?"

"I will," Amethyst promised, said her goodbyes and hung

up.

She tapped the phone and stared at the writing on the notepad. Dialing that number seemed such an act of surrender.

It was either that, or surrender to the idea of a sentient car and a world where magic really existed.

Amethyst thumbed on the phone and tapped in the number.

Chapter 5

The Mustang was perfectly mannerly this morning, behaving just as one would expect an automobile to behave. Amethyst steered along Rio Grande Boulevard, past the squat adobes of Old Town, the garden pottery place behind its wrought iro+n fence, past offices and condos, all tauntingly ordinary.

She gripped the steering wheel, waiting for it to wrench away under her hands. But that was the crazy part, and she wasn't crazy. She *wasn't*.

Then where had the car come from?

"Well?" she said. "Do you know where I'm going?"

No comment from the car. None of that alone-in-the-park-at-night feeling of being watched, none of those odd, disembodied flashes of amusement or sympathy.

"You've done it. You've wrecked my truck, scared the hell out of me, harassed me nonstop, and finally driven me crazy." She hissed a breath between her teeth. "See? You've even got me talking to you."

Still nothing, when she'd expect at least a vague sense of amused scorn, if not remorse.

Maybe she was already better. Maybe she didn't need to see the therapist. But a cancellation on the day of the appointment would look classically neurotic.

She turned onto a narrow, cottonwood-shaded lane. Gravel crunched under the tires. Water flashed in acequias winding through irrigated acreage. Glossy horses grazed by hidden adobe villas. It was if she travelled an entirely different city, miles and worlds away from the hot and noisy sprawl that rambled from the feet of the Sandia Mountains in the east to the dark jut of the volcanic escarpment in the west. The scent of honeysuckle drifted in through the open car window, soothing, a scent from childhood. A curious burro hung its head over a white-painted fence and watched her go by.

Amethyst made the right onto Calle Encantado. About a block ahead, the little lane ended at a wrought iron gate set in an adobe wall. The brakes wheezed a little. The sun-face in hammered copper that adorned the center of the gate smiled benignly through the windshield.

"May I help you?" a pleasant female voice said from an intercom speaker.

"Yes," Amethyst said. "I have a ten o'clock appointment with Dr. Korhonen."

"Your name?"

"Amethyst Rey."

The gate clicked and trundled to one side. "Yes, Ms. Rey, please drive up. You'll find the parking area to the right of the house. Just come in the front door."

Noble old cottonwoods rained drifts of cotton that floated on the morning breeze like out-of-season snow, lending a dream-like aspect to the gentle curves of the drive.

The gate, the wall, this long, winding drive… The hourly fee she'd been quoted didn't seem sufficient to cover all this. A place like this had to cost…who knew what, but it couldn't be cheap.

Paving stones and gravel suggestive of a dry streambed led from the carport to the entry. Amethyst drew a breath, pressed the bronze latch and pushed open the door.

'Impressive' just wouldn't cover it.

Stacked sandstone walls. Lamps and sconces of wrought iron and handblown glass. Pottery. Paintings. Flagstones in shades of red and orange beneath her feet.

Footsteps echoed. A blonde woman in a short, stylish haircut, a gauzy dress in jewel colors and soft, expensive-looking boots approached along a hallway. She extended a beautifully manicured hand. "This way, please, Ms. Rey."

The woman led Amethyst into a spacious office then closed the door softly behind her.

Across the room, a man sat in a big chair before tall windows. Amethyst was conscious of her hand fisted on her purse strap. She relaxed it.

The man stood and approached, hand extended. "Ms. Rey. I'm Eliot Korhonen."

Oh, no. She was going to laugh.

He looked like Santa Claus.

He smiled brightly, amplifying the effect of wavy white hair, full beard, twinkling, bright blue eyes and round cheeks. She shook his hand and managed to murmur something polite. Thankfully, he wasn't wearing red.

"Would you like to have a seat?" he said, gesturing her forward. "If you care to, we can sit out on the patio. It's a lovely morning."

It was, too. Down here in the bosque, the river valley, the usual spring winds only ruffled the treetops. There was a joke that New Mexico had four seasons: summer, fall, winter and wind.

The door clicked open and the woman who'd greeted her stepped in, bearing a tray.

"Thank you, LaDonna," Dr. Korhonen said. "Would you be so kind as to bring that outside?"

Amethyst drifted along behind. French doors opened onto a walled courtyard furnished with cushioned chairs and a glass mosaic-topped patio table. He chatted, and she managed polite replies.

She perched on the edge of her chair.

"How can I help you today?" the doctor said.

She cleared her throat. "I've never visited a...a therapist before. How do we start?"

Korhonen spread his hands. "However you wish." A sort of staccato lilt was audible in certain words. "Since this is a consultation, it might be helpful for you to tell me what brought you to see me, or what you hope to accomplish in any future sessions."

So, start with the discarded stalker thesis, or go straight to the magic car business? She looked into the teacup between her hands. Too bad there were no tea leaves to spell out an answer.

She took a long breath. "Well, a couple of weeks ago, I started finding things on my doorstep."

She wouldn't tell him everything. Just the more reasonable bits. But Dr. Korhonen remained silent at just the right times, and... Well, inferring a stalker from a parked car and some junk on the doormat didn't seem particularly rational, Melodie's belief notwithstanding, so she had to tell about the five-minute kidnapping. And she couldn't very well create a driver and then explain why she hadn't called the police. Or account for why she was driving that very same car without relating the dream in the garage.

She didn't say anything about the opera program. Or the menu at Double Lightning.

Now she stared at the bottom of her empty cup, trying to concentrate on the way the light glowed through the thin china. Trying as well to ignore the sick squeeze of her stomach that came from the absolute certainty that Dr. Korhonen would politely excuse himself, go inside and call a mental institution.

Instead, he only asked, "More tea?"

"Thank you." Amethyst wasn't reassured.

He poured, offered a muffin, shifted in his seat. "How does all this make you feel?"

She stifled a cough. "Well, it made me feel like I'd better come and see you."

He didn't laugh. But then, therapists probably weren't supposed to laugh at the client's jokes—which might not turn out to be jokes at all, and—damn!—making a joke at a time like this probably revealed something tortured in her psyche.

"Why is that?" he said.

She shifted in her seat, found her hands locked around the cup and put them in her lap. "Cars don't just..." She gave an abrupt little gesture. "...drive themselves."

Or only did if someone had—what?—a few spare tens of

thousands to spend on full-scale RC equipment. Oh, no, that could be delusions of grandeur, and she wasn't going to give him *that* idea. Maybe the magic car theory was actually less crazy than the techie stalker. Delusion still, but on a lesser scale.

"And you have to admit it's pretty, um, strange to find myself going places and doing things I didn't plan, and not remembering how I got there."

Now she'd look like she had split personalities. Much more of that and he'd have her on Thorazine. She glanced around surreptitiously. There must be a gate in the courtyard wall. She could probably make an escape before the white van arrived.

If she weren't driving a car that stood out like a guy with a sledgehammer at an art glass show.

Dr. Korhonen made a considering sound. One hand rested on the table by his teacup, and when he lifted it, he held a deck of cards. Amethyst swallowed hard. Those hadn't been there a moment ago, she knew they hadn't. They curved, popped free of his fingers, fluttering from one hand to the other.

"I would say you've acquired a familiar," he said. "But I must say, I find it fascinating that the spirit has chosen to inhabit an inanimate object. Very unusual."

What?

"Generally," he went on, shuffling the cards in a more elaborate pattern, "the wizard is the stronger of the pair. In this case, however, the situation seems to be reversed. Thus, when your familiar calls, you are compelled to answer."

"*What?*" This time, she said it aloud.

He shook his head. "The modern mindset is woefully inadequate at preparing a young wizard."

She shoved her chair back. "I don't think this will work out." What was this, some sort flaky, fringe-y therapy? "Thank you for your time, Dr. Korhonen. I'll settle the bill with your assistant."

"Running away, Ms. Rey? It won't help, you know."

Cocking her head, she paused. "You know," she said, "Whatever you're trying to do, I don't like it. And I don't feel inclined to stay and find out."

Deftly, with the skill of a casino dealer, Korhonen laid out the cards.

"I often find the cards informative," he said. "Much more so than tea leaves." He gestured at her empty cup. "I must admit, though, I've always preferred bones and entrails, though most people these days are too squeamish for them. Animal rights and all that sort of thing, you know."

Amethyst edged toward the house.

He said, "And auguries involving human entrails are wonderfully lucid, but sadly, have been out of favor for some time." Like a magician, he tapped a card, then turned up a king, a smiling, white-bearded face that looked like Santa Claus.

She stared. He'd had cards made up with his face? He turned up another card, a queen.

The face was hers.

She went hot, then cold, then spun to bolt for the house.

It wasn't there.

She stumbled to a stop, turned, turned again. No house. Nothing but endless, winding corridors between the columns of ancient cottonwood trunks.

No. No. Impossible. This was like finding herself in that parking lot, or in the garage.

Beyond the table and chairs, the flagstones of the patio ended and cottonwoods ranged away, furrowed and enormous with age. In the high branches above, birds called, their voices echoing through the vaults of a wood. Gently, lazily, cotton drifted on the air, appearing and disappearing in shafts of light.

"You see?" Korhonen said behind her. "Magic is quite as real as automobiles and computers."

She clutched her purse before her like a shield. "The tea— You drugged me, didn't you?" This primeval cottonwood bosque couldn't exist. And servos and remote control didn't come anywhere near explaining it. "Or hypnotized me."

"Now, why would I do such a thing?"

"Maybe it keeps business brisk."

He still didn't laugh, but he smiled. "An intact sense of humor can be an excellent coping mechanism. Except when one uses it as a way of avoiding difficult truths."

The house had been over there, past Korhonen's right shoulder, and an adobe wall had encircled the patio. Any direction she walked, she'd encounter one or the other. That would dispel the illusion of the limitless wood. Amethyst walked forward.

"Such as the fact," he went on, "that you are no longer in the pleasant and pastoral North Valley you know."

One hand held out before her, she kept walking. She never would've thought she'd be so susceptible to hypnotism. There had to have been something in the tea. Something that definitely warranted a call to the Medical Ethics board.

Her feet carried her seamlessly from smooth flagstones to uneven earth; her outstretched hand never jarred against an unseen wall. A smell of wild roses came from somewhere in the woods. She stopped before a cottonwood, splayed her hand on its trunk. The bark was cool and rough, as thoroughly bark-like as it should be.

"Stop. It." Each word fell like glass. "Whatever it is."

"I'm doing nothing you cannot do."

She braced her back against the tree. "What are you talking about?"

He still sat in that same comfortable, easy pose. "You're no magic dabbler, half-mad from handling an element she can't control. You're wizard enough to have attracted the attention of a familiar."

"No, I'm a stained glass artist driven half-mad by a car that won't leave me alone and psychologist who's determined to artificially increase his client base. I'm sorry, but the strangest thing I've ever done was to switch from Computer Science to Fine Arts. I don't make things appear and disappear, turn lead into gold, or make stones speak. I do, however, tend to grow resentful and angry when people mess with me."

His smile faded. "I assure you, Ms. Rey, trifling with you is the furthest thing from my mind. But in this day and age, I fear it takes the most graphic of demonstrations to convince people that certain experiences are anything but the product of a demented mind."

This day and age. Like what the voice in the garage had said. The Mustang. Talys. And his "passing centuries" and "immeasurable knowledge and experience." Amethyst closed her eyes as if that would shut out the words. Behind the lids, pictures glowed, images of robed men and silver knives beneath great, twisted oaks, of standing stones crusted green with moss and brown with old blood.

She snapped her eyes open. More images, like when she'd first touched that damned car. Her heart pounded. Her senses ranged outward. The tree behind her was strong, ancient, drinking down power from the sun, pulling up life from the earth. The whole net of life surrounded her—beavers sleeping the day away in their lodge, fish darting in the river somewhere nearby, birds singing, mice scurrying—unbroken, not fragmented as it usually was even in the most rural stretches hidden in the city's heart.

She curled her fingers, driving bark under the nails. What was happening? How could she know those things without seeing them?

Korhonen watched her, interested, intensely curious.

"Okay," she said. "Let's say I'm convinced. *Put me back.*"

He gestured to her chair. "Please, sit down. There is no need to shout at one another across the patio."

Whatever he'd done—magic, hypnotism, teleportation, whatever—she couldn't undo it. Cooperation was the obvious alternative. The patio table sat all small and lonely on an island of flagstones in the middle of the bosque. It seemed like a long walk to reach it.

"Are you certain you wouldn't like to try the magic I just used?" Korhonen asked. "I'm willing to help."

"Oh, yes, please. Who knows when I might want to zip between realities to amaze and impress friends."

He pressed his lips together as if repressing a smile. "Perhaps later." He indicated the chair again. "Please."

She sank into it.

He didn't gesture, wave a wand or speak arcane words. He didn't even click the button on an unseen remote—his hands remained folded over his portly stomach. But suddenly the house was back, and the adobe wall, *flick*, like a scene change in a movie. The distant, subdued hum of the city vibrated the air.

Once more, Amethyst's heart scrambled up, galloping.

"Better?" he said.

"What do you care? Why should it matter whether I believe I'm a—whether I believe you or not?"

"Hasn't the knowledge that you are by no means going mad eased your mind?"

She still wasn't sure about that. The madness, or whether or not her mind was eased. "You haven't answered my question."

He made a little frustrated or surrendering gesture. "There are so few of us left, you see."

"Why?" The car hadn't answered. Maybe Korhonen would.

"No one seems to know," he said. "Perhaps magic dwindled in the face of a mechanistic worldview."

That in itself seemed like magical thinking. But what else should she expect?

"So you met with me to check out the competition? Or was this an initiation?"

"Neither. Both. However, you should be aware of the conditions under which you'll be practicing."

"Excuse me, practicing?" *In a world that mocks magic as madness and scorns sorcery as superstition...* That alliterative little phrase in the opera program had told her that. "What would I do? Set up in some seedy little place on Fourth Street as a psychic? Offer my services in Vegas for a cut of the winnings?"

"There are those who have done both, but that wasn't quite what I had in mind."

"Oh?"

He leaned forward. "Ms. Rey, magic is not like a book one can simply pick up and read, should one have the ability to do so. It is a living, almost sentient force, complex, even unpredictable at times, and takes much practice and skill to master. You have an ability which, unschooled, can cause you and the world at large a great deal of trouble."

Trouble. Right. "That's assuming I have any intention or desire to use it."

He turned another card over, the ace of spades. "Oh, you'll use it."

That single black spade seemed to stare balefully at her, a shovel to dig a grave for the life she knew. She wanted snatch up the damned cards and fling them into the trees. She locked her fingers together instead.

"It's nice to know everyone in the magical world is so concerned about my well-being. Forgive my cynicism, but—"

"Why did I bring you here?"

She was pretty sure she didn't want to hear this. "I came on a referral." It couldn't be anything else. Melodie had given her Korhonen's name, and she of all people had absolutely nothing to do with this craziness. "I could've called anyone."

"You could have," he agreed. "But that is the mark of a truly skilled wizard, to influence chance and circumstance until the desired end is achieved. Bindings, compulsions—pah. Heavy-handed and inelegant."

"So you're not even a psychologist."

"As a matter of fact, I *am* a psychologist." He quirked a smile. "Specializing in the treatment of delusional patients."

Of course. Easier to find desperate and confused proto-wizards that way. Whether they wanted to be found or not.

"And?"

"And when I find someone with rather more than the average show magician's ability…" He flicked his fingers, and the cards were gone. "…I offer an apprenticeship."

Chapter 6

Amethyst stared at the cheerful, white-bearded face, then laughed. The laugh was higher than usual, and it was a minute before she could stop. This was *not* the time to lose it.

"An apprenticeship! Are you kidding? Do you honestly think I'm here talking to you because I enjoy what's been happening?"

Dr. Korhonen leaned back in his chair. "I think the revelation runs thoroughly contrary to your experience. However, adaptation to new situations demonstrates healthy flexibility."

"I suppose wanting power of choice shows inflexibility."

He looked perplexed. "Are you saying you object to the magic?"

"You can hardly expect me to be enthusiastic about having my life turned inside out."

He held up a placating hand. "Of course, your distress is quite justified, but that would be the point of an apprenticeship."

He just didn't get it. "Look," she said, "*I am not a wizard.*"

"I doubt your familiar would make that kind of mistake."

Amethyst covered her eyes. "How can I make you understand I don't, and never have, done anything that could be remotely construed as magic?"

"Of course you wouldn't, given the current environment—"

She lowered her hand. Suspicion prickled along her nerves. "Go on."

"I'm simply speaking of the utter lack of imagination in today's rational, skeptical, technological society," he said briskly. "You could scarcely be expected to test something that isn't supposed to exist."

She was certain he'd been about to say something else. "You know, the voice in the dream kept skating around some subject, too."

"There is so much you don't yet understand."

She eyed him, one finger tracing a pattern in the table's mosaic. "Obviously. And you're asking me to take a leap into the dark."

"Should I tell you enough to do you harm, or merely enough to frighten you?"

"My alleged familiar said that, too. But hey, why argue? It's a moot point."

"Believe that, and no one can help you. Not me, not your familiar. You cannot escape what you are, and what you are will not permit you to live as an ordinary mortal."

She frowned. "What does that mean?"

Lowering his chin to his chest, he studied her. "What will your life be when all those you know and love are gone?"

She went cold. "Are you threatening—"

He overrode her. "Even if you never touch the magic, you are still a wizard. And wizards live rather longer than ordinary mortals."

"Rather longer."

"Friends, loved ones…" He tossed invisible dust into the air.

Die. Her voice wouldn't come. She shifted in her chair. She wanted to walk away again, but then he might do something else to enforce her attendance.

"You see, in the end, we have only one another. Fellow wizards, or the people who come and go in a fraction of our lifetimes. Or solitude."

Somehow, his words still felt like a threat. Or maybe they just hit too close to home. "So I'm supposed to embrace all this wizard stuff because of *loneliness?*"

He sat back as if she'd wrenched open a door to his soul. "No, certainly not. Consider what I've told you informed consent, if you wish. So much is at stake. Would I serve you better by allowing you to cling to a fantasy? I would not do so as a therapist, and I cannot do so as a wizard."

"Except you have yet to prove what's fantasy and what's fact." But he had, hadn't he?

"Consider what I've told you." He no longer looked like a cheerful Santa Claus, but like a grandfather forced to tell his grandchild the puppy had died. "It has been a great deal." He crooked a small smile. "As a therapist, I'd advise you not to make any decisions until you've had a chance to assimilate it all properly. One should never make life-altering choices under duress."

Duress. Interesting word choice. But it certainly fit, didn't it?

"Okay, I'll think about it." *After* she got out of here.

"Good." Korhonen's smile this time was relieved. Almost too relieved.

Was she missing something?

Amethyst put on a polite smile for Dr. Korhonen's assistant on the way out. She didn't grab the woman by the shoulders and say, "My God, woman, do you know what you're working for? Do you know what he just did in there?"

Magic. Wizardry.

Gripping her purse strap like one on a ride at the fair, she wobbled back along the faux dry streambed. The Mustang hunkered where she'd left it, a black blot in the bright noon sunshine. She opened the door and climbed in.

The door slammed behind her—hard. She hadn't touched it. The engine started with a snarl—she hadn't touched the key, either—then gunned hard enough to make the car rock. The shift lever dropped into reverse and the Mustang shot backwards.

Amethyst seized the steering wheel. "What are you doing?"

The car's anger surrounded her, battered her; a turmoil of worry and fear seethed beneath it. The wheel dragged her hands along with it. The car slewed around, shifted into first and lunged down the driveway, spitting gravel.

She stomped on the brake. Through the windshield, the gate at the end of the drive bounced rapidly nearer. The *closed* gate. Sunlight and shadows flashed across the hood; chamisa and sage flicked by on either side in a motion-picture blur.

"Are you crazy?"

The gate was rolling open. Slowly—too slowly. Cringing into the driver's seat, she gritted her teeth and turned away.

The side mirror snicked past the gate and they were through, out, turning onto the paved road, doing 50 in a 25 MPH zone.

"What's the matter with you?" She shook at the wheel. "Will you slow down? It won't be you looking at mondo fines and possible jail time for reckless driving!"

The engine dropped into a grumble. Then the radio came on in a pop of AM static.

"Where did you go?" it said. "I felt magic, and you disappeared from my ken for far too long."

It was the same voice. The voice from her dream Sunday night, the cocoa-and-cinnamon voice. She might've been talking to the car as if it could hear her, but somehow, to have it—him—actually answer...

A slick of sweat rose between her fingers and the steering wheel. She moaned.

"We haven't time for that," he said. "Do you have any idea of my danger in your absence?"

Anger suddenly spurted through her. "Yours! What about me? I was the one snatched into an alternate reality!"

"Oh, better and better. I indulge you in this little soul-searching jaunt and you manage to find precisely what I resolved to avoid."

She spluttered. "Whose fault is that? I was doing just fine before you came along. Why don't you leave me the hell alone?" She snapped off the radio.

It blinked back on. "It behooves you to listen to me, even if you won't hear me in the fashion any reasonable wizard hears his familiar—in his mind."

"I'm not reasonable." She banged the steering wheel. "I'm not a wizard." Another bang. "And I'm sure as hell not gonna let you into my head!" She flipped off the radio again.

Naturally, it didn't stay off. "You most certainly aren't reasonable, I shall grant you that. What do you intend to do? Deny the facts until you meet the next wizard, who may not be so generous as to let you go on your way unmolested?"

This time, she wanted to bang her head against the steering wheel. "You're the one who's supposed to know all about this stuff. Seems you should be able to tell the wizards from the non-wizards."

"Not," he said, "when they conceal themselves." The boil of his emotions settled. "Amethyst. Tell me about him. I must know."

Go to hell was on her tongue. She was reacting like all this was real. But after a point, she had to make the decision as to whether or not she was sane, and she was weirded out enough that she *had* to be sane—if that made any sense.

"The doctor is a wizard."

"Indeed!"

"One who specializes in delusional patients."

The car made a right on Rio Grande, moving like a predator among the Lexuses and BMW's. A peculiar growly sound, a little like one of those Emergency Notification tests, came from the radio speaker. "Clever. What did he want?"

"For me to become his apprentice. I'm sure you know my answer to that."

"Nevertheless, his basic point is sound. You must embrace the power you possess."

"And tell me, why should I do that? To protect *you?*"

"And yourself. Surely this experience demonstrates your utter helplessness in the face of magic. Does it not make sense for you to develop your own magical abilities in order to…what is the term…level the playing field?"

Estates with their vast lawns, irrigated pastures and gated drives gave way to renovated adobes behind coyote fences—cut juniper branches wired together—closely fronting the road. She tapped a fingernail on the steering wheel. Even though the car was doing all the driving, she couldn't bring herself to relinquish the controls.

"Maybe. But this conversation didn't start out about me. You were all hot about some kind of danger to you."

His sigh sounded like a rush of static. "You see, Amethyst, I have little power of my own. Without a wizard host, I, too, am woefully vulnerable. However, despite your inexperience, together we are to be reckoned with."

She narrowed her eyes. "This sounds like the part where I should start worrying."

"Wizards aren't the most sociable of creatures," he said slowly.

"Uh-huh. And?"

"The fact is, they're rather a contentious lot."

"So then why should Dr. Korhonen want me to buy into this wizard business, all the way to offering to teach me?"

"Certainly, wizards once took apprentices," he said. "The practice imposed some order on the system and kept the young and powerful under a degree of control."

"So that's why he wants to keep an eye on me? Because I might be a threat to him?" She waved away the idea. "But I'm not powerful."

"Indeed you are. After my last wizard died, I chose my current habitation and slept, for there was no other with whom I would desire to bond."

Had there been the slightest shade of hesitation on the word 'died'?

"I did not school myself to wake easily," he went on. "Yet you're powerful enough to have awakened me."

Lucky me, she thought. "How? How did I wake you?"

"You touched me one day as you passed, skating. Do not you remember? No, of course you don't."

The Mustang made the left onto the freeway onramp, accelerating smoothly past everything but a guy in a red Dodge pickup who decided to race them. They topped the end of the ramp doing 70.

Amethyst hung onto the wheel. "You have got to quit that. My insurance premiums for something like you will already stink."

The Dodge whipped around them doing substantially more than 70. Good. Let *him* get the speeding ticket.

"It won't be necessary for you to carry full coverage," Talys said. "You'll find me remarkably immune to auto accidents. And I believe I can safely assure you that no one will steal me."

"Too bad."

"Now, now. I thought I had you convinced how much we need one another."

"Uh-huh. What's wrong with Dr. Korhonen? You said there was no one else to partner with, but there is. Him."

His rueful laugh didn't sound quite so rich coming from a 40-plus-year-old radio speaker. "Even had I known of him, I have very specific requirements, you see."

"And those are?"

"I wished for a young wizard."

She snorted. "What else?"

"I needed one adapted to the current magical environment. You have power, yet it hasn't manifested in twenty-eight years, which suggests you possess that adaptation."

Dickens *and* Darwin. He must've been educated abroad. "And that environment differs how?"

The radio hissed and popped. "How can I explain that which you have been taught is no more than the fancy of children and savages? Magic is the energy created by life, by thought, by the possibilities that proliferate by being and doing, wishing and planning. Wizards are intimately intertwined with it. What a wizard possesses is not magic itself, but the power, greater or lesser, to direct and manipulate the force that is magic. With wizards so few…"

"Magic changed somehow," she finished. She hadn't written code for so many years without being able to follow a chain of logic.

"Precisely."

She tapped a foot on the floorboard, thinking. The Mustang growled east on I-40. Uptown's high-rises glided past: the black glass-and-steel structure the locals fondly called the Darth Vader Building, Magus Corporation's green glass pyramid, a pair of sandstone and turquoise office towers. The granite bulk of the Sandia Mountains grew in the windshield, a barrier at the end of the world. Where did magic fit into all that?

"How has it changed?" she said.

"Now that," he said, "seems the sort of thing only a wizard should be interested in. Have you at last surrendered to the fact?"

She scowled at the dash. "Don't push it, Talys. I've had about enough for one day."

Amethyst leaned forward and flipped off the radio. This time, it stayed off.

Chapter 7

The whole situation was like one of those good news-bad news jokes. Hey, Amethyst, the good news is…you're not crazy! The bad news is…

She stopped to think about it. Ugh. Maybe better not.

What was a supposed wizard to do?

Amethyst plunked into the chair in front of her worktable. It gave its usual pained screech. The cut shapes of glass for the DeBaca's atrium window spread across the pattern pinned to the table, their unfoiled edges and the gaps in the pattern accusing her. She rubbed her forehead, then propped chin in hand.

Afternoon sunlight slanted across sketches of design ideas tacked on the wall of her front-bedroom-turned-workshop. The message light on the answering machine just below was blinking. She leaned over and pressed the *PLAY* button.

"Ms. Rey, this is Caroline DeBaca."

"Like I can't tell by the prim, yet assertive voice," Amethyst answered the recording.

"I'm calling for a status update on our window. The decorator is scheduled for a consultation next Friday—"

She hit the fast forward button. "I think I can safely promise the windows won't be done by then, Mrs. DeBaca. Magic, haunted cars and Santa Claus wizards or not."

Message two started playing. "Wiz," Melodie's voice said.

Amethyst buried her face in her hands. "Please. Don't call me that now."

"How'd it go? Call me."

"You don't want to know," she said into her hands. "And I can't begin to tell you."

She pushed the rewind button. Great. It was already starting. The most important, soul-shaking event in her entire life, and she couldn't even talk to her best friend about it. Or her parents, her brother, or anyone else who counted, for that matter.

She could run away. She snorted. Sure. A temporary solution to a permanent problem. Anyway, what was that quote? 'Wherever you go, there you are.'

Amethyst eyed the pattern on the worktable, the bits of scarlet and tan and green glass. With everything she'd been putting up with, magic ought to make itself useful.

Say, for example, by finishing this window for her.

She pushed away from the table, rattling glass. No way. She had the makings of a decent window here. She was not about to ruin three weeks of work for the sake of an experiment that was bound to end with some disastrous application of the law of unintended consequences.

If it ended with anything more than a profound sense of foolishness.

She got up and stalked down the hall. So, what was the best venue for attempting magic? Or rather, for proving that she couldn't do magic. Definitely not outside, where the neighbors might catch her behaving like they'd expect an eccentric artist to behave. The garage would've been perfect, except for the current occupant. Did magic make a mess? Maybe the bathroom, or kitchen.

She stopped in the living room. Everything looked just as it always did: the floral print couch she'd splurged on last year beside the tall Tiffany-style lamp she'd made; the parquet-topped coffee table, bentwood rocker with its antique footstool, the entertainment center with its collection of electronics. At least those familiar, comfortable objects hadn't somehow transformed, disappeared, been destroyed or turned inside out in the last few days.

She was stalling. It didn't matter where she tried it. She slid into the rocker and tipped back. So, what kind of magic should she try to do?

What kinds were there?

She studied the long, mostly-blank wall that separated the

living room from the garage. Three small paintings hung there, a pastel by her mom and two by her friend Jeannie, from her MA program. Those paintings had always seemed so small and lonely on that wall.

She was an artist. If she wanted to try some magic, it might be safest if the attempt had something to do with what she knew best.

Glass.

Last summer, she and Melodie had gone hiking in the Jemez Mountains. They'd followed a little stream, quiet and so clear that every pebble in its bed had gleamed like a polished stone. Eventually, it widened into a pool. She'd been wanting to work that pool into glass ever since.

Amethyst closed her eyes and leaned back her head. Memory conjured an image of summer trees and scowling rock, a glass-green pool that shimmered in a shaft of sunlight, its shore jeweled with wildflowers in lavender and yellow and blue.

She selected glass: waterglass, of course, for the water, wispy opalescent for the leaves of trees, opalescent for the rocks, clear cathedrals for the flowers. She built the pattern in her mind, imagined the whole framed in honey-stained oak.

Squeezing her eyes tighter, she drew a long breath. *Okay. Let's see what happens.*

She reached—to something outside her, or something within. She couldn't tell, like reaching from a dim room toward a shaft of sunlight...

Force exploded through her. Light, color so vivid it was almost a sound, sound that crossed into sensation, a tinkling, shivering, chiming hum that tuned her until she vibrated in harmony with it. She couldn't move, couldn't open her eyes, couldn't turn her mind to anything else—

Something hard slammed shoulder and arm, hip and head. Pain cracked through her, then nothing else.

"Amethyst?" someone was saying. "Amethyst!"

A man. Where would she be sleeping that a man would be there to wake her up?

"Speak, for the gods' sake!"

Her eyes winced open.

The living room carpet stretched away, a fuzzy taupe plain interrupted by table legs and the sofa skirt. The arm of the rocker, overturned under her, jabbed painfully into elbow and ribs. Lights burst across her vision with every heartbeat. Groaning, she dragged herself free of the chair and levered herself up onto her elbows.

Behind the glass of the entertainment center, the stereo was on.

"Ohh," she said, and fell backward onto the carpet. A whistling hum that seemed to come from nowhere and everywhere at once vibrated in the bones of her skull.

"By all the gods of every heaven in creation, woman!" a familiar hot-cocoa voice boiled over the speakers. "What in all the pits of hell do you think you're doing?"

How should she know, when every nerve ending was screaming?

"Are you trying to destroy yourself?" the voice demanded. Talys. "Are you so disturbed by what has occurred?"

The ceiling descended, then rose again.

"I told you I would assist you. But will you accept my aid? No. And then, do you attempt a simple, cautious work? No. You must throw yourself wide and execute a *making*."

"Making?" At least, that was what she meant to say. She only got out, "Mehhh?"

"Beings holy and profane!"

The volume coming from the speakers rattled everything between her ears.

"Get up! Feed yourself, by all that shines! If you don't, there isn't a cursed thing I can do to prevent the consequences. Would that I'd chosen a form more capable of governing such a balky, obstinate, underachieving—"

"*Underachieving?*" That word came out intact.

"Up!" Talys boomed over the stereo.

She rolled over, pulled her hands toward her, tucked up her knees. Her stomach made a threatening lunge. Gritting her teeth, she panted. Okay. Cheek still pressed to the carpet, she pushed up and made a sort of wobbly-colt lurch forward.

When had the kitchen moved several hundred miles from the living room? The pantry, the refrigerator beside it, rose shimmering like a distant mountain above an endless playa. She hauled herself toward them.

The refrigerator door handle taunted, far out of reach. The pantry door was ajar, though. Raising a hand to push it open, she toppled over again. The jars and bottles on the bottom shelf were just in reach. She dragged out a bottle of maple syrup.

Pure, artificially flavored maple syrup had never tasted so good in her life. Not even the entire two thirds left in the bottle.

Levering herself up, she pried open the refrigerator and reached a jar of raspberry preserves in the door shelf. Fortunately, she'd put some on toast this morning, so the lid wasn't glued shut. She slurped gooey preserves, then cleaned the jar as well as she could with her finger.

From the living room, the stereo said, "How are you?" Talys sounded anxious.

"Alive," she croaked and sagged back against the wall.

"Devils and pits of chaos!" he snarled. "Eat! Eat!"

"Will you quit cursing? You're making my head hurt. Worse."

Even feeling like someone had turned her inside out like a sock, she didn't need convincing. She pulled some leftover pasta salad out of the fridge.

"Forgive me." His voice was softer, and he did sound sorry. "You must understand. Your body must be tended to after that performance, else I'll be forced to await you in a hospital parking lot while you languish in a coma."

A *coma?* But she was conscious. Conscious, and seeing things. Something seemed to be there, an invisible yet almost-perceptible density of air.

"What's that?" she whispered. "By the breakfast bar."

"That is I." The words were spoken on an outrush of breath.

She glanced quickly away from that spot of *presence*. He was much less disconcerting as a car. And how could something that didn't have lungs be making all those breath sounds?

"I dislike disembodying myself, but you see what your antics have driven me to do."

She absolutely did not have the wherewithal to argue. She leaned her head back on the pantry door. "What happened?"

A snort. "Magic happened. I would have warned you, but you didn't appear interested. What *were* you attempting to do?"

"Prove I couldn't do anything."

"Alas, I fear you've proved quite the opposite. And demonstrated, once more, my superior powers of discernment."

Talys had gone awfully quickly from frightened witless to smug. She wanted to say, *Hey, I still feel like somebody plugged me into a 440-volt socket*, but didn't quite have the energy. She wished she could somehow levitate herself to bed.

No, she didn't. She might end up connecting to that socket again.

"*That's* magic?"

"That is what magic has become," he answered. Grimly. "Feral, isn't it?" The stereo was quiet a moment. "Happily, I quickly interposed myself and absorbed a portion of the blast."

She lifted her head. Kitchen and dining room made a queasy swoop and roll. Her stomach followed suit. Colors heretofore unknown to human eyes shimmered at the edges of every object. If only she could shut out the garbled sibilance, as if a few thousand people were holding whispered conversations in the next room. Or eliminate the flashes of hot and cold dancing across her skin. She heard a dog whine: Caramela waiting outside the back gate for her meal. Except that it wasn't mealtime, and the whine sounded distressed and worried, like Caramela knew something bad was going down.

"You mean…" She suddenly smelled roses, grass clippings,

fresh dog doo, the stink of a city bus. The contents of her stomach made a lunge for her throat. Amethyst clenched her jaw and swallowed. "...that wasn't...full force?"

"For the instant before I knew what you were about, it was. I beg you, don't surprise me like that again."

She couldn't very well argue with that.

"I earlier said you were a happy adaptation, and this little adventure vindicates me," he said. "Not only have you survived, intact, a first, full plunge into the boil of magic, but you also bent it to your will."

Survived? The news was not getting better. "I think," she said, "it bent me."

He laughed. "Just a bit, perhaps. But you did admirably."

"Thanks." Amethyst tugged at her thoughts like the cord to a cranky lawn mower engine. "Is that why there aren't very many wizards left?" All those words hurt. Better stick to shorter sentences.

For a moment, there was silence from the living room. "Certainly, the nature of modern magic tends to ensure that fewer wizards survive to claim their power."

There was a gap in the logic. "Feral."

"Once tame, but gone wild."

"I *know*. Tell me why."

"Are you certain you wouldn't like to admit me to your thoughts? It would make this discourse a great deal easier."

He was dodging again. She scowled, then quickly smoothed her face. Violent facial expressions did not improve skull-buster headaches.

"Very well," he sighed. "I shall take mercy upon you and spare you the effort, although I could simply pretend to misunderstand you. Why has magic changed?"

"Yes." The smells and whispering had diminished, but that clot of thick air yet hovered. Talys must still be worried.

"Perhaps like any wild thing," he said, "magic must be constantly handled to remain tractable."

And there weren't enough people—*magic-using* people—to

do so? Wait—that was a circular argument. Magic eliminated magic-users because it was wild and it was wild because there weren't enough magic-users.

"You needn't look so perturbed," he said. "I'll submit that a lucky combination of greater-than-usual power and a strong instinct of self-preservation restrained a premature experiment on your part. Now that you know what to expect, it will grow easier with practice, I assure you."

"*Practice!*" That blew through her like the magic had. The kitchen then slowly capsized into a dark and heaving sea.

The phone was ringing. Loudly. Insistently.

Amethyst opened her eyes. The kitchen linoleum stretched away, soft and blue with twilight. Why didn't that seem strange right now?

The phone stopped ringing. From the answering machine in the front bedroom, a voice drifted, faint but familiar. "Wiz, you've got to be home by now. Pick up the phone, will you? I'm getting worried."

Somehow, she was on her feet and stumbling across the kitchen. She fumbled the phone from its cradle, dropped it on the countertop, made a grab at it and sent it skittering. Finally, she caught it and punched the talk button. "Mel, hi, I'm here, sorry."

Pieces of the world fell back into place: Korhonen this morning, magic in the afternoon. She leaned her head in one hand. That was why she felt like she'd been sick with the flu for a week, why her skin felt like it'd been peeled down to the raw nerves. At least her head and stomach no longer felt like they were at war with the rest of her body.

"Jeez, Wiz, I've been calling all afternoon. I was about to drive over there. Where've you been? Are you okay?"

"Sorry, I—" She thought of the variety of floor coverings she'd awakened to. "I've been down with a headache."

"Down? You mean, in bed?"

This was not going to be an easy conversation. "Well…" She wobbled toward the living room, steadying herself on the wall. "I haven't slept well for a week and—"

Her breath puffed out in a little *uh?* Her body stammered to a halt—heart, lungs, gut, brains, everything. She stood in the living room doorway and stared.

The front curtains were still open, admitting a strange combination of purple twilight and orange streetlight. But the strange mixture of light didn't account for…for…*that.*

The entire left hand wall, that long, blank, white, naked one, dressed with only the three small paintings, from the gas heater in the corner to the front window…

Had become that mountain pool in the Jemez. Shimmering with color. Glowing with its own inner light. Except that it was an enormous stained glass window, perfectly matched glass, soldered lines, stained and varnished oak frame, light streaming through and all. And that was an *interior wall.*

"Wiz?" Melodie said over the phone. "Wiz, are you all right?"

She sank down on the couch. "Oh, God, Mel," she finally breathed.

"What? Amethyst, tell me—"

"I think I'm going to faint." Again.

"I'll be right there."

"No!"

Melodie would notice a huge stained glass window that hadn't existed when she visited a few days ago. Amethyst's stomach was in sudden and full rebellion again.

"You can't. It's—I'm—I've got the flu." She had all the symptoms, at least. "I don't want you to catch it."

Silence on the other end of the line for a moment. "I'm coming by anyway. I don't like the way you sound."

"Mel, wait—"

"And oh, if anyone else is there, like your stalker friend, let him know I'm calling my police officer neighbor, and he'll be along shortly, too."

In the middle of the hijacking by magic, she'd forgotten all about the hypothetical stalker.

"No, really, I'm sick. I swear. If it was something like that, I'd talk code, I promise." More silence. "You know I would." *Please, please, Mel,* believe *me*.

"I think you would," Melodie finally said. "But still. I'll be there in a few. Bye." The line clicked into silence.

"Dammit!" Amethyst flung the phone into the couch cushions.

She pressed fingertips to eyes. Maybe she could make the window go away again. Pursing her lips, she gazed at the pure, vibrant colors, the smooth solder lines. It was beautiful, a perfect realization of her idea, with none of the flaws and blemishes that always touched something made by hands. No. If she made it go away, she'd feel like she was killing it. Maybe Talys could tell her how to hide it.

He probably could. If she were inclined to dip her little tootsies into the magical lava flow again.

Soliloquy – First Voice

*H*e leaned back in his chair, gazing out tall windows. The phoenix colors of the New Mexico sunset had dwindled to pale flames of gold and peach, then finally died to ash. Venus gleamed low in the sky, shining with distant promise.

He braced his mind, unsheathed his wizard's power and extended his senses.

Magic seethed and spat, as turbulent as the surface of the sun, as hot to the touch. He winced, resisting the urge to withdraw. How long before it couldn't be handled at all? How long after that until, untapped, unrelieved, it erupted like a solar flare, spewing wild energy across a complacent world?

He pressed his clasped hands to his mouth, seeing in his mind's eye the panic, the bewilderment of people suddenly faced with speaking caves, with crossroads that sent unwary travellers to other times and other realities, with beings that roamed the night in quest of that unique sustenance provided by the human essence. A nuclear war wouldn't upend society so completely, couldn't shatter so many lives and minds.

He dropped the magic. His ears rang, and pain thumped behind his right eyeball. Phantom lights danced and glimmered in his peripheral vision. He blinked them away, gazing upon a room as mundane as any other. The antique oak desk, the bookshelves bearing volumes with bright, crisp covers and those bound with worn, gold-lettered leather, the computer in the armoire behind him gave no hint of his otherness. Yes, this world of technology and science was his as well, and he had no interest in seeing it plunged into chaos. Yet what could he do? What could anyone do now about the cataclysm that approached as relentlessly as a tidal wave or a hurricane?

The magic must be used once more. Frequently, familiarly, as it had once been. But that required wizards who could do so.

Sometimes, he'd sense someone new touching the magic, gingerly, a fragile, tenuous outlet for the rough surge of current that might draw down the least bit of building pressure, delaying the impending explosion by just that much. Then, when he reached out again, a day or week or year later…nothing. Empty static on that frequency, the hand stilled, the mind silenced.

Another wizard gone.

He dropped his hands, drummed his fingers.

How were they being taken? What was the cause?

How was almost irrelevant, no matter the energy he expended on speculation. *Where*, he knew.

Here. In this city. A power that hunted those who could wield the magic and then sucked them away into oblivion.

It hadn't been here when he'd first come to this city in the midst of empty miles of high desert, a place where his senses wouldn't be befuddled by the pressing mass of humanity. But one day he'd turned and found it snuffling in his very dooryard, blind, groping… hungry.

Another wizard. That was the only conclusion he could come to.

What could a wizard gain by so destabilizing the magical currents, by making them so painful and dangerous to tap even by the powerful? Even, presumably, by the unknown hunter himself.

Yet the disappearances continued, nowadays insignificant spoon-benders with little more than a single talent, an unusual knack for finding, perhaps, or uncanny luck. The wizards he'd known years ago, colleagues, friends, enemies… He drew a hand down his face as if that could wipe away remembered faces, voices, his gnawing loneliness. All gone long ago.

And that hunger, lurking so near, once it found him…

He watched. Cast out his senses for the searching mind, the ravenous will, the power around which magic might swirl as if into the mouth of a whirlpool.

He gave a self-mocking smile. No doubt he should quietly decamp again. But after a century or two or three, running grew wearisome. Much simpler, actually, to know where one's enemy laired, the better to watch.

And perhaps that very watchfulness was what had enabled him to survive this long. Nevertheless, he suspected he'd be wise to better his odds.

Like a skipped stone, he skimmed the surface of the heaving ether, touching as lightly and briefly as possible. The room grew translucent, a scene painted on a glass screen. Letting his senses range, carefully shielded, through the howling churn of magic, he searched.

He had long done so carefully, so as not to expose himself. He couldn't see the city, the buildings and streets, the billboards and streetlights and dreadful concrete-lined arroyos. But every life glowed like a gem, refracting light from the soul within: a tourist strolling through Old Town, a pinon pine on the mountainside, a ray swimming in its tank in the Albuquerque Aquarium, a puppy idly chewing on a patio chair leg.

A wizard's soul, the fire of a wizard's power, blazed brightest of all. He looked for it now, eager, incautious, scanning the cityscape of life.

Where was she? When he'd first located her, he'd read the surface shimmer of a mind as clear and glowing with color as the glass with which she worked, so new, so artless that she made no attempt to obscure herself as wizards learned to do. Just yesterday, she'd wielded the magic like a fire-eater, taking it in and blowing it out again in a jet of pure, directed power. Magnificent!

If he'd found her so easily, the other, the devourer, could do so as well. And she would become one more disappearance, one more dawning star consumed by the nameless darkness.

He surged to his feet. Clasping his hands behind him, he paced to the windows, gazed across that ethereal webwork of light, the glimmer of life, the spurts of birth, the pop and wind-blown flutter of death. He found her, a violet beacon wreathed with silver, vigorous, valuable... Vulnerable.

Unless he took preemptive action. Unless he persuaded her to come to him.

Chapter 8

Amethyst dragged the ottoman across the carpet, keeping her back to the living room wall.

Okay, so she was a…a…

A wizard.

Say it, Amethyst. *Look*. You have the undeniable proof on your living room wall.

Not a dream, not a hallucination, because the window had still been there yesterday morning. And still was today.

Wobbling on the well-padded ottoman, she took down the first of the three small paintings, leaving behind a perfect nail hole in the glass. A pinprick of light showed where the nail had been—even though there shouldn't *be* any light coming through that window, since the garage was on the other side of the still-intact wall.

She climbed down and set the painting on the coffee table. She'd be battered to death with iron-clasped spellbooks before she'd give Talys the satisfaction of asking where the light came from.

Someone knocked at the door.

The stereo clicked on. "You have company," his cheerful voice said.

She jumped. She should be used to it by now, but she still jumped. She'd tried unplugging the stereo. It still came on. Maybe she could put it out in the garage, with the Mustang. No, then he'd probably just use the phone, and that would be even creepier.

"It's Melodie, and if you know what's good for you, you'll keep quiet."

"Oh, no, I fear not."

She punched off the stereo and opened the door.

It wasn't Melodie. It was a skinny guy in faded, holey jeans. He wore a greasy t-shirt that said *Jesus Saves!* Jesus wielded a hockey stick and wore arm pads and shin guards. Jesus' jersey was emblazoned with a big cross.

Amethyst debated slamming the door again, then realized she recognized the guy. Caramela's owner. Her hand tightened on the knob.

"I seen my dog in your backyard," he said.

Cold spread around her middle. *Play it cool*, she told herself.

"Me, too," she said. "She looked pretty hungry."

"Yeah, well, it don't do me no good if it ain't in the yard watching my shit."

It? *It?* Amethyst wanted to smack him. "Sorry about that."

"I know you been feeding it. You better quit."

She wasn't cold any more—or even cool, for that matter. "Look, if you—"

"Amethyst, love," Talys' voice called behind her. From the stereo speakers again. "Who is it?"

"One of the neighbors, looking for his dog," she called back over her shoulder. "Do you want me to let you know if I see her again?" she asked the skinny guy. She emphasized *her*.

"Just leave my dog alone." He stomped off down the walk, giving her one, last evil look when he got to the sidewalk.

Amethyst shut the door and leaned against it, shaking.

"Do forgive me, love," the stereo said in Talys' voice. "I know I was supposed to keep quiet—"

"All right, *thanks*, okay?"

"My pleasure. Although I did attempt to warn you."

She swallowed a *shut up*.

"However," he said, "you may now safely open the door. Your friend has timed her arrival quite nicely."

This time she peeked through the front window. Melodie's Insight sat at the curb. Melodie herself walked briskly up the walk.

"How will you contrive to keep her out of the house today?" Talys inquired.

"Shut up." This time, she said it aloud. She'd found excuses so far, but the excuses were fast running out.

"Now, now. You must put on a cheerful face for your friend lest she become suspicious."

Amethyst dived for her hat and fanny pack on the stand by the front door. "I'm telling you with utmost seriousness, Talys, you'd better leave my friend out of it."

"Just take me along, so I needn't worry about you. You're so wont to put yourself in vulnerable situations."

"All right!"

She darted out the door and almost ran into Melodie.

"Sorry, Mel." She forced a laugh. "I didn't realize I was running so late."

Melodie looked at her a little oddly. "No, I think I'm early."

"That's okay. I'm ready. I'll drive, okay?"

Melodie followed her down the walk. "Drive? What?"

"Oh, the—" Amethyst winced and bit her lip. "The Mustang." Melodie stopped and stared, and Amethyst said quickly, "I had to drive it to that doctor's appointment, so I thought…"

The sound of water spraying came from next door. Gary, Oscar Griego's son, sprayed a jet of water at the pansies and primroses his mother had planted last week. He wore shorts that showed more pale, pudgy, hairy leg than Amethyst ever wanted to see. He must've been waiting for her to look his way, because he immediately took his thumb off the end of the hose. The flowers lay half-pummeled in the mud.

"Hi, 'Thys," he called.

Melodie's brows shot up.

"Hi, Gary," Amethyst said without enthusiasm.

"Where you guys going?"

Melodie nudged her and mouthed, *Him?*

Amethyst shook her head in reply. She'd have to lay to rest the stalker theory. It was growing increasingly inconvenient.

"Hiking," Amethyst said. "Wa-a-a-y up on the mountain."

"Whoa!" he said. "I figured with that new car of yours, you'd go road-tripping or something." He gave a much-too-studied grin. "Maybe you 'n me sometime, huh?"

He never got it, no matter how many excuses she made.

"Sure, Gary. Maybe when I don't have so much work."

She stepped from the front walk onto the driveway. The garage door was already open.

Dammit, Talys!

Had the door been open when Melodie pulled up? She bit her lip. She didn't know.

Amethyst tossed her things in the backseat and backed out of the garage, pretending cool. She stopped and Melodie got in.

She backed the Mustang down the driveway and into the street. As she shifted from reverse into first, the engine backfired with a shotgun bang. Amethyst jumped, and through the tinted window, saw Gary jump, too.

The hose went flying, jetting water, twisting as hoses under pressure will. Of course, it sprayed him. He scrambled for it, but it writhed out of reach, soaking him all the while.

Melodie laughed. So did Amethyst—she couldn't help it. Poor Gary. Good thing the windows were rolled up, or his humiliation would be complete. She let out the clutch, pushed the gas—

Except that the clutch stayed down, and the accelerator stayed up. And that hose, always twitching just out of reach, still sprayed Gary.

Clenching the steering wheel, she leaned her full weight on the gas. *Quit it, Talys!* she thought fiercely at the car.

Gary finally broke and ran for the hose bib, squirted all the way. The accelerator popped free at the same moment, engine roared, tires screeched, and they went fishtailing down Flint.

Melodie stopped laughing and gripped the armrest and the edge of her seat. "Jeez, Wiz! What're you doing?"

"Sorry!" Amethyst snatched her foot off the gas. The Mustang lurched slower, dragged down by low gear. She shifted hastily.

The radio snapped on. Amethyst pretended to ignore it. Talys would start talking any minute now, and he'd promised—

No, he hadn't.

Only music came over the radio. An old song, "Tears of a Clown," covered by someone new. Amethyst strangled a wild laugh.

Melodie scowled at the radio. "What the hell is going on?"

Amethyst lugged the engine, and the Mustang bucked to a stop at the bottom of the street.

She tested the brake, clutch, accelerator. Yes, they worked. How nice.

She chuckled—convincingly, she hoped. "I guess I was laughing too hard. I sort of—ah—jammed the gas."

"Oh." Melodie chuckled a little, too. "And what about the radio?"

What about the radio, Talys? Maybe you'd like to explain that one. On second thought, don't.

"I don't know. It keeps doing that to me, too. I turn it off, and it comes right back on again."

"Huh," Melodie said. "Doesn't sound like a very dependable car. I think I'd sell it."

Amethyst choked the steering wheel. "I think I will."

Foreigner's "Cold as Ice" started playing on the radio.

Melodie, cranking down the window, hesitated. "What station are you listening to? Sounds like they dropped their playlist in a blender."

Amethyst resisted the temptation to close her eyes. She was a wizard. Maybe she could rewind this morning. No, make that the whole past week. She sighed, thinking of the last time she'd done magic. Maybe not.

"Must be Radio Free Santa Fe," she answered. "They play everything." You also couldn't pick them up in Albuquerque unless you had streaming, and she didn't.

Saturday morning traffic on Eubank wasn't bad; Amethyst made the right, skimming past offices, a couple of apartment buildings, gas stations, strip malls. The tumbled glass decorating the medians sparkled.

"So," Melodie said.

That wasn't encouraging.

"About the stalker. Are you sure your boy next door isn't him?"

Amethyst snorted. "Gary is thirty-something and still lives at home with Mommy and Daddy. A stalker, maybe. A stalker with the brains and money for the whole car routine, not."

Melodie's brows crooked. "What do you mean, brains and money?"

Oops. Melodie only knew the gift-leaving, Isuzu-wrecking ordinary stalker theory. She didn't know the servo-installing techie stalker theory, now disproved.

"Well…" Amethyst scrambled. "Do you suppose he has enough of a bankroll for a fully restored classic car?"

Melodie shrugged. "How would you know?"

"I guess I wouldn't. But—" Time to get past the stalker. "I haven't gotten any more weird gifts. I think something must have happened to him—the stalker. Maybe the law snagged him for something else. Or somebody else did."

Melodie drummed fingers on the window frame. "What about the car? Last we talked, you didn't want anything to do with it."

This was one question Amethyst had been ready for. "Since I can't find a VIN anywhere on this thing, let's say I decide to go on the offense. Once he shows up—if he ever does show up now—I'll have a chance to nail him."

Melodie gave a broad, delighted smile. "That's the Wiz I know. Get a name, and we can get online and do a little hacking. Let him know he picked the wrong woman for his fun and games."

If only. "How about we stick to conventional channels?"

"Weenie."

"Yeah, well, data security has gotten a little more sophisti-cated since we last romped through hapless mainframes. I don't want to be safe from a stalker because I'm in jail."

Melodie only gave a Cheshire Cat smile and leaned an elbow out the open window. "Still, I think it's too soon to relax."

"Too true," Amethyst sighed.

That seemed to satisfy Melodie. "Since you didn't turn left toward the freeway, I assume we're getting breakfast."

"I was thinking Rocco's Tacos."

"Sounds good to me."

The restaurant's pink stucco exterior blazed amid the humdrum tans of the shopping center behind it. Neon palm trees in yellow, blue and green glowed against the wall, Caribbean-tropical in the bright, sharp high-desert morning. Amethyst pulled into the parking lot and idled along, looking for a space.

She made a turn around the back of the building. The restaurant's garbage bin was nestled discreetly in a Pepto Bismol pink-painted niche, allowing the street person there to dumpster-dive in comparative privacy.

She wouldn't stare—she could spare him that much dignity. But somehow she couldn't keep her eyes away. A blue t-shirt hung loose on his thin frame. His arms and the back of his neck were burned red, his hair bleached pale by the high-altitude sun.

He looked up suddenly as if called and met her eyes—through the dark-tinted window.

They were past the dumpster and around another side of the building. Amethyst kept seeing the man's eyes, wide and startled, meet hers through a window so dark, you couldn't see inside. How—?

"Finally," Melodie said.

A car pulled out of a space ahead. Amethyst turned into the spot (or rather, let the Mustang pull in while her hands rested on the wheel). She wouldn't think about the homeless man. Just walk across the parking lot into the restaurant and pay attention to the bright pink and turquoise and yellow tiles on the restaurant floor, the wispy mustache on the kid who took their orders—anything but that man's eyes, the shock of recognition on his face.

Recognition of what?

She didn't want to know.

They ordered and took the food to a table. Voices filled the restaurant, a babble that rose over too-loud salsa music.

Amethyst slid their drinks off the tray, and Melodie studied the scrawl on paper-wrapped breakfast burritos the size of small logs.

"Egg, sausage and green chile," she said. "That's you."

"Yeah."

"Hey, you okay?" Melodie said. "You look distracted."

She hadn't managed to hide the latest jolt of weirdness then. She began assembling some glib reply.

"Lady," someone whispered behind her.

The hair on Amethyst's neck prickled, but she didn't turn. Melodie lifted her gaze with a look that could make brave men quail.

"Lady," the voice said again, from just behind her left shoulder.

"We already gave at the office," Melodie said in an overly loud voice. Heads turned at a couple of nearby tables, but she only returned her attention to her breakfast.

Whatever force had caught her in the parking lot made Amethyst's head turn now.

The man, the one from the dumpster outside, stood just far enough away to remain unthreatening, but close enough he couldn't be ignored. He looked pretty tidy for a street person, especially one who'd just been investigating the contents of a dumpster. He didn't smell, either.

"Lady, I'm so empty. Give me some, just a little—"

Maybe he'd go away then. She cut off the bitten end of her burrito and wrapped up the remainder. Her hands were shaking. "Here you go." She pushed it across the table.

Melodie shook her head sharply.

The man shuffled a step or two closer, but didn't reach to take the food. "Lady, you shine," he said, still whispering. "You shine, I saw the light shining through you, a rainbow beaming out of your eyes, colors in your footsteps."

She shivered. She wanted to get away, but was somehow frozen.

Melodie's hand plunged into her purse, came out holding

her phone. "My friend gave you what you asked for. Now leave us alone, or I'll call the cops."

"No, give me your gift," he said, still speaking to Amethyst. "Just a little, not much. Where did it go, bubbling and sizzling, I used to fizz like a bottle of soda pop. He touched me, cracked open my top, drank me down, all of it, gone. He stole it, smiling, and now I'm so, so empty, hollow, hooting in the wind."

Amethyst gripped the edge of the table with both hands. She couldn't move away—he blocked her in. A spot of cold congealed in the air beside her, and—

The man *looked* at it. He saw it, Talys's invisible presence.

He should stumble back now, exactly what she'd do if she saw a clump of uncannily dense air suddenly form. But the man only blinked as if trying to decide if what he saw was some new delusion.

Melodie was saying, "Look, I won't tell you again…"

Amethyst lost the rest of it. The cold spot that was Talys reached out, encircled her hand. Where it touched her, it felt warm. Warm as living flesh. Warm as real fingers, but spiderweb-light. The touch eased her grip loose from the edge of the table, coaxed her hand up, toward the vagrant.

She tried to pull away. The man's nail-bitten hand reached toward hers, toward the connection Talys seemed to be insisting they make.

Amethyst wrenched her hand away, flung herself backward into her seat.

"Hey!" Melodie half-stood, hampered by the table.

At a nearby table, a big American Indian man stood up. "You ladies need some help?"

His companion, a little older and with his black hair done up in a traditional knot, also stood.

The vagrant's face twisted. "No, I have to warn her." He turned back to Amethyst. "He sees the light, hunts by the light. Watch out for him! The light's too strong for him. It burns him, bites him, he's too weak to touch it. He'll take your gift, fill up, empty you, get strong enough…for awhile…"

"Who?" Amethyst asked abruptly. Why ask him? The poor guy was obviously mentally ill.

"Him! The light shines in him, too, but it struggles, it struggles, trying to find a way home—"

"Here." Their rescuer dug in his pocket and offered a couple of crumpled bills to the street man. "Go get you a burrito or something. You're scaring these ladies, can't you see that?"

The vagrant looked from Amethyst to the two men and back. Like a mime, his face flicked from emotion to emotion. "I'm not trying to scare them. She should be scared! He'll find her, pop her open, drink her down—"

The big Indian grabbed the panhandler's wrist and thrust the money into his hand. "Okay, you warned her. Now go on before they call the police like they said."

The street man stared at the money in his hand as if wondering how it had gotten there. Distress pinched his face. He drew breath to say something more, but their rescuer gestured toward the front of the restaurant.

Apparently, the guy wasn't so far off plumb that he didn't understand when it was time to go. He wasn't happy about it, though. He sidled, hesitated, then finally shuffled for the door.

Amethyst glanced surreptitiously to the side. No Talys. Having made sure she behaved as bizarrely as possible, he was gone. She rearranged herself in her seat, out of the corner she'd been cowering in.

The two men watched the vagrant leave, then until he was out of sight.

Their rescuer turned back then and asked, "You okay?"

The way she'd acted, they thought the poor guy had done something to her. Amethyst smiled a scared-a-minute-ago-but-no-big-deal-now smile. "Yes, thanks—"

Melodie blurted out, "Thank you, we really appreciate it, he didn't seem to be getting the hint, can we buy you breakfast or something?"

Oh, Melodie. Acting bold but really as scared as Amethyst had been.

The man indicated the table littered with unfinished burritos, soft drinks cups and empty packets of hot sauce. "We already got something. Thanks anyway."

His companion spoke a few lilting, halting words in one of the Indian languages—Tewa or Navajo, most likely. The big man he replied in the same tongue.

"I think that man was…" he spoke to his friend again. The man murmured "shaman," and the older man turned back to Amethyst and Melodie. "He was once what we call shaman," he said in accented English. "You should probably listen to what he says."

And Talys had wanted her to touch him. Why?

"A—a shaman?" Melodie said. "I thought he was crazy."

"Maybe he's crazy," the man said, "but I think you better find out what he was talking about." His gaze, dark and seeing, moved to Amethyst.

Maybe this man would know what all those mumblings about light and soda pop had meant. Maybe she should ask. She cleared her throat. "Thank you. I'll keep that in mind."

It sounded lame and false, but what else could she say? *Yeah, I bet he's a wizard just like me, only instead of ending up with a stained glass window he can't explain, the magic reamed out his brains with a red-hot poker.*

The two men sat down once more to their breakfast. She and Melodie did the same. Amethyst prodded at her burrito with the plastic fork.

Watch out for him, the street man had said. The only problem was, who was she supposed to watch out for?

Chapter 9

The sky arched above Sandia Crest like a blue-glazed pottery bowl, that endlessly deep color only high-altitude skies could achieve. Fresh green aspens did a flirty little fan dance in the spring wind, and across the gravelly slope, wildflowers nodded their pink and lavender and gold heads. And best of all, they'd left the Mustang behind in the parking lot.

Amethyst should have felt better, but she didn't. Magic was beginning to show an alarming potential to ruin her life. She resisted the temptation to say so.

Maybe she should talk to Dr. Korhonen again. He could probably teach her some wizardly jujitsu…just in case. If nothing else, she should probably ask a few not-so-casual questions like, is anyone out there doing something terrible to wizards?

"What a great day," Melodie said.

"Yeah," Amethyst said.

Melodie shot her a glance. "Still bothered by our encounter with the homeless gentleman?"

"You're right, it's a great day," Amethyst said.

Never one to abandon an unanswered question, Melodie arched a brow.

Amethyst sighed. "Yes, I'm still bothered. I'll be fine in a while."

The paved portion of the Crest trail gave way to rock and gravel and snowmelt-saturated soil. Melodie stepped over a particularly soggy section.

"I have to admit," she said, "he was a little scary."

"A little." The less said on the subject, the better. Melodie had a real talent for wringing every last drop of information out of her when she was inclined.

"D'you want to hear something else strange?"

Amethyst bit the inside of her lip. "What?"

"Remember that morning you called me and I looked up

Dr. Korhonen's card in my Daytimer?"

"Yeah," Amethyst said, cautious.

"After you mentioned that he wasn't the type you could picture Marl seeing, I looked for his card again." Melodie gave a nervous little laugh. "You won't believe this, but it wasn't there! There wasn't even an empty slot where it should have been. I almost called you for his number." Another of those laughs. "I thought I must need it."

Amethyst knew the feeling. "It was probably on top of some other card and fell out. Or you put it away underneath another card. What else could it be?"

Melodie's brow puckered. "You're right. What else?" But the frown didn't smooth away.

"Hey, come on. It's a great day, remember? Let's make a deal—I'll stop thinking about the street person and you quit worrying about Dr. Korhonen's card." Amethyst swept a hand toward the sheer plunge not far from the edge of the trail. "Look at that view."

Beneath a haze of windblown dust, the city sprawled some five thousand sheer feet below. To the south, an airliner, rising toy-tiny from the airport, flashed in the sunlight.

"We're above everything here. And of course you know worries can't survive thin mountain air."

Melodie grinned. "Just like lowland tourists, right? Okay. Let's see how many of those we can find to pity on this trail."

Amethyst rolled her eyes. "Spoken like a true transplanted Californian. Should I remind you of your pale, dewy face, your shortness of breath upon first coming up here?"

"Yeah?" Melodie said. "I'd like to see how you cope with 580 traffic at five-fifteen on a Friday night."

Amethyst blew through her lips. "Oh, please. Try being single, childless and even boyfriendless at an eighteen-year-old cousin's wedding."

"Ouch. Okay, I concede. I've met a couple of your aunts."

"Do you think we can make it to Cienega trail and back?"

Melodie hitched up her fanny pack. "Nothing to it."

Almost ten miles at 10,000-foot altitude, half of it mostly uphill, was a little more than nothing. By the end of the afternoon, Amethyst's thighs and calves burned. Between the spiky tops of the pines, the sky was the color of sapphire.

"We should have turned around earlier," Amethyst said. "It'll be dark before we get back to the parking lot." It wasn't an appealing thought, groping their way back across the dimming mountainside.

Crack.

She whirled. "What was that?"

The trees stretched away, endless dusky columns rising from a bare, root-knotted floor. The wind had fallen into the calm of evening, and silence spread like ripples across a still pool.

Pausing, Melodie brushed back damp hair, propped hands on hips and breathed hard. "What?"

Amethyst strained, listening. "Didn't you hear it?"

"All I heard were your plodding feet and puffing breaths."

"No, there was something…" Watching. Hunting.

A little alarm bell went off in the back of her head. She opened her senses. As when she'd been with Dr. Korhonen, more information came than could be accounted for by the usual five. She almost snatched herself back, but that feeling of something lurking just out of sight wouldn't let her.

She touched melting snow hidden in shadow, deer waking for the evening. An owl swept over the forest floor in search of unwary mice— Maybe that was all it was. That owl, waiting for two noisy humans to move on so it could get on with dinner.

But still…

She shivered. "Let's run. I don't want to get caught on the cliffside part of the trail in full dark." She brushed past Melodie.

"Wiz, wait!" Melodie said, then called, "You're gonna fall flat on your face!"

The roots were full of life. Amethyst could sense them, and her feet avoided them in the deepening dusk beneath the trees. Melodie came behind her, feet thumping the dark, damp ground, breath chuffing in the thin, cool air.

And beyond eyesight, beyond the finest discernment of listening ears, something glided shadowlike through the forest, closer to imagination than perception.

To the side, trees, logs, snarls of branches. Nothing more. That man this morning had spooked her, with his talk of light and emptiness and hunting—

A sense of eyes prickled her neck, of a crafty awareness watching prey run through the trees. Amethyst sucked in a breath and ran faster.

The black network of tree limbs and needles scrolled across the ultramarine sky. A breeze teased a strand of hair across her face. She hooked it away.

The trail made a sharp right turn and plunged down a flight of steps cut into the rock. Then the world opened, gulfs of sky ribboned with mauve and turquoise and ocher, the city below a net full of sparkling diamond and topaz fishes.

Melodie scrambled down the steps behind her, panting. "Whew! Ever think about trying the La Luz run? And here I thought you wouldn't run to save your life."

That sounded too much like a bad omen. Ahead, behind, the trees lay silent, still.

It didn't make her mind any easier.

Hands braced on knees, Melodie paused to catch her breath. "Half a mile more, at most. And with that sky, we won't have to worry about slithering over the edge."

Amethyst panted, too. Sparks popped and flashed across her vision. Rock loomed to the right, crowned with wind-twisted trees. A waist-high pipe guardrail fenced off the sheer drop to the left. If there ever was a rock and a hard place to be caught between, this was it.

She grabbed Melodie's elbow. "Come on."

"What's the hurry? We're okay now."

"Let's not take any chances."

Ahead, the wall of granite gave way to a slope covered with wind-flagged aspen and pine. And between, black against the fading shapes of the trees, a twisted shape stood.

Amethyst stopped. It might have been a bear or a mountain lion crouched on that trail, the way every instinct screamed against it. She knew it was a lightning-blasted tree stump, but every muscle seized up. The cold, after-sunset air suddenly got a lot colder.

"What's wrong?" Melodie said behind her.

Something inside her shouted, *Be still! It'll get you!*

Melodie stepped close. "Do you see something?"

"I—" Nothing else would come out.

"There's nothing there, Wiz." Melodie eased past. "Come on, before it gets dark."

Amethyst consciously took hold of her muscles. What else could she do? Go back? Try to bushwhack her way around, through the dark, close woods? Stand here frozen on the trail until—

Until darkness conveniently fell?

Melodie walked ahead, ponytail bobbing, coming ever closer to the dead tree that wasn't. Wasn't dead, and wasn't a tree. Amethyst didn't know how she knew it, but she did. She bit her lip and plunged after her.

"Mel, wait—"

Melodie kept walking. Her movement trailed through twilight as blue and clear and still as glass. She didn't stop, didn't turn, didn't give any indication she heard Amethyst at all.

"Melodie!"

Gravel popped and crunched under her feet, loud as in a cement mixer. Something was wrong, as if the twilight really were glass, a pane separating her and Melodie. On Amethyst's side, time moved differently, dragging dreamlike at her feet. The sharp, high sound of her shout died unheard.

She gulped a breath and pushed her tired legs as fast as they'd go. Something so barky and still and treelike couldn't possibly move quickly, no matter its grasping, twig-fingered branches, its staring knothole eyes, the grinning crack of a mouth. Look how the roots gripped the rocky soil like toes—

toes embedded in the earth. It wasn't moving anyway, not even a flutter of the dead leaves clothing the limbs. She was almost in reach of the thing, and it remained as still as…as a bump on a log.

Wind gusted up the sheer face of the mountainside. It tore damp tendrils of hair loose from her ponytail, flicked them across her face. The stump's branches rattled, the sound of death's fingers tapping.

Twiggy fingers *reached down* (oh no no) and brushed her arm. She dodged to the side, gravel slid and one foot dropped off an edge. The thing made a sound, a sort of strangled screech—

No, she made the sound, it came from her throat. She felt it there, like hot liquid swallowed too fast. And then a hand locked around her ankle.

It pulled—no, yanked her back. Her head and shoulder smacked the guardrail, her hip cracked on stone, and for an instant, everything drifted on dazed pain.

She'd slipped, and someone had caught her. Oh, good. Might have slithered right under that guardrail, otherwise. She only wished they weren't dragging her by the ankle across the gravel—

Amethyst wrenched up. Oh, God, not a hand, that wasn't a hand around her ankle. It was a root. A root, hard, wooden, cold as stone, wrapped all the way around, like a shackle, still dragging her toward that tree. That grinning tree, with the green light coming from knothole eyes. It creaked and rattled as it bent down, reaching for her.

She braced her free foot, tore at the root with her fingers.

Branches caged her arms, pinned them to her body. She couldn't move, couldn't breathe. The coldness of earth and stiffness of wood seeped into her. Everything reeled horribly, dreamlike.

This was no dream.

Do something!

She reached—inward, outward, she didn't know. The magic would explode again, burn again—

It did, like a volcano too long dormant, plugged with megatons of rock and ash and dirt, overgrown forest. All vaporized, flung into the stratosphere with careless, terrible force, by the flow of power that burst from her.

Light blazed on the leering face that bent over her, on the smooth knobs of cheeks, on the wooden slab of forehead. The knotholes winced, the fissured mouth twisted and turned down. A hiss like a wet pine log thrown on a fire came from it. Twig fingers flinched, released her.

Magic coursed through her like adrenaline. Crabwise, hands braced behind her, she scrambled away. The tree-thing shook its branches, and hands bristling with fingers stretched toward her again. Stone ground on stone, bunched up, tumbled away. A—a *foot*, black, many-toed, uprooted itself,.

Oh God, oh God, the thing could *walk?* It couldn't, it wasn't alive, it was a thing, impossible!

Power blasted through her again, but this time she directed it. A fireball purple as the twilight hit the stump, the tree, the monster, knocked it backward.

The thing keened like a burning pitch-soaked log. Green light seeped like sap—or blood—though bark, bubbling, oozed pitchlike down the trunk. Limbs creaked and groaned. The mouth gaped wide, wider, and the keening rose to the shriek of overstrained wood.

The thing cracked like a branch in a storm, that awful, drawn-out rending sound a big, old tree makes just before an enormous limb crashes down. A phosphorescent fog wreathed the head in green tendrils—what was that, its soul?—then streamed outward, flayed by her magic. Rotating, it coalesced, a green galaxy twisting itself into tighter and tighter spirals, then streaked away over the valley and plunged into the greater galaxy of lights there.

The magic switched off, disconnected. Amethyst fell back, like air rushing out of an inflatable toy. Above her, halfway down the bank now, the thing stood, split from top to bottom. A dead, blasted stump.

Blasted by magic. Dead by her hand.

Chapter 10

"Oh my God, Amethyst, are you okay? What happened?"

Fear and alarm shook Melodie's voice.

Amethyst lay crumpled across the trail, her feet against the slope. The guardrail barred her view of the darkening sky. Her head throbbed, and her shoulder and hip. Melodie knelt beside her, touched her. Her face was only dark smudges of eyes and mouth in a pale oval.

Where had Melodie come from? What world, what reality, there on the other side of that pane of blue glass in gathering night.

A bit of the past clicked into place. That's right. She'd slipped, and banged her head. She'd been unconscious, that was all.

Except that wasn't all. She'd slipped because she'd jumped away from that thing. And she'd been unconscious because she'd had to use magic to—

She jerked her head up. The stump stood above her, just visible in the last glow of twilight. Still. Dead. Ripped from top to bottom by some elemental force.

By *her*, Amethyst.

The breeze on her skin felt like licks of flame—or ice. She tried to lever an elbow under her. Her muscles shook too much. A ghost of red light swirled against the dark trees, like shadow-colors that played on the retinas after looking at a bright object.

Melodie caught hold of her and began whispering. Except she wasn't whispering, because she said in a normal voice, "Can you get up?" Emotion rolled off her in heat shimmers: concern, upset, fear.

"I—slipped. Hit my head on the railing." Queasiness rolled over her, just like last time she'd used magic, and that dreadful dizziness, like some sadistic amusement park ride. She remembered the hundred-mile crawl from the living room to the kitchen. "God, I don't know if I can get back to the car." Had she said that aloud?

"Sure you can." Melodie sounded like the losing team's coach. "It's not that far now. Here, I'll help you." Melodie hauled her up, murmuring encouraging words at odds with the fright emanating from her.

The world reeled, darkening. No, she wouldn't, couldn't faint again. She couldn't do that to Melodie. And she'd have to eat. Talys had told her last time, eat, or go into a magic-induced coma. She fumbled at her fanny pack.

Melodie whispered, *God what happened to her she must've really hit her head hard she's so weak what if she's got a concussion is there a ranger at Crest House why didn't I bring my phone dammit will it even work up here—*

"Mel, I'm—I'll be all right," Amethyst broke in. "Please don't call the ranger. I just have to—to eat. Rest a little."

She couldn't see Melodie's face. But she felt her alarm. Melodie was unnerved. Why?

Because Melodie hadn't said any of that aloud.

Amethyst couldn't think. The tree-thing's voice screamed in her memory so loud it didn't leave room for thoughts. She had to keep quiet. She couldn't say anything strange. The green light in its eyes had gone out, bled away. Red ghosts had replaced it, swimming against the dim, colorless shapes of rock and tree and mountain.

"Here are the steps," Melodie said. "We're almost to the parking lot."

Up the steps then. Melodie should just let her down, so she could crawl up them. Every step was higher than the last, and her fumbling feet tripped on each one. Her heart pounded, and the blood in her ears sounded like words, like someone shouting her name, but the someone didn't have a voice.

Her head began to resonate to the shouting, a jab of pain with every pulse. "Stop yelling!"

"Wiz, I'm not even talking." *Shit she's in really bad shape there's still lights on someone can call an ambulance—*

"I don't need an ambulance!"

"I—I didn't say anything about an ambulance." Melodie's voice shook, shook like the emanations of fear coming from her.

No, be quiet, she'd done it again, said something wrong. There was the car, gleaming with silver light, radiating intention like words written in glitter on the deep purple velvet of evening: *Amethyst! I'm coming—*

She bit her lips to make sure her mouth stayed closed. *No! Don't, please!*

The silver gleam shivered. Amethyst hurried, stumbling on the asphalt. Silver with a black core, the car grew like sunrise.

Melodie's hand made a flat black shadow in front of the silver. It fumbled at the door handle, the door opened, the dome light blinked on. Melodie pressed her backward, and Amethyst fell into the passenger seat.

"Wiz, I really think—"

"No. No doctor."

Thoughts, emotions pounded her, Melodie's, Talys'. Amethyst blinked at the red ghosts, pressed her temples to squeeze out the echoes of screaming wood. The movement of her arms burned a fiery rill across her skin.

"Melodie, I swear I'm—I'll be all right." There. Her voice sounded normal, reasonable. "It—it just scared me. Rattled me. I thought I'd go over the edge, then I hit my head—"

"That's the part that worries me. Here. Let me see."

Amethyst turned her head.

"Ow. There's a lump there, all right. Crimeny. What happened to your sock?" Melodie's fingers touched her. "And your ankle, jeeze! What'd you do?"

Amethyst squinted. Even in the wan yellow glow of the dome light, her ankle looked awful. Maybe particularly in that yellow light: red and raw and ribbed with friction burns from her sock. The sock itself was in tatters. "I—must've caught my foot on something. That must be why I tripped."

Here in the car, her mind seemed clearer. The desperate, brittle drained feeling ebbed, as if she'd stepped from a blowing, frigid night into a warm room with a cozy fire. As if warmth, energy were pouring into her from some outside source.

From Talys.

She wanted to jump up—well, tumble out again. But it felt so…so comforting. Like she wouldn't disintegrate into a messy puddle of fluids after all. A skin formed once more between herself and her companions' thoughts and emotions. They were still there, but outside now, no longer slamming against Amethyst's magic-flayed psyche.

"Okay, get your fanny pack off," Melodie said. "Give me the keys."

The car could drive itself, but Melodie might object. *If* it could drive itself while it was trickling energy into her like a battery charger.

"Here, I'll get 'em." Melodie whisked away the pack, unzipped it. Keys jingled. "Are you sure you're hungry? Here's some dried fruit."

Melodie slid into the driver's seat. Amethyst ate—devoured—the dried fruit. The engine started, quaking the car. The warm, friendly energy coaxed her sputtering neurons into firing properly, forming thoughts.

What had that thing been? Why had it gone after her?

Her stomach made a cold, queasy knot around the fruit she'd eaten.

The headlights swept pines and tight switchbacks, back, forth, down the mountain. At the bottom, Highway 14 led to the freeway, then the freeway slid by in headlights and taillights and the rush of cars and semi trucks. Melodie talked and so did Amethyst. *See, Mel? I'm fine. Nothing to worry about.*

That cold lump sat in her middle, sending frost crackling across her whole life. She suppressed a shiver. Melodie mustn't know anything was wrong. She couldn't know an earthquake was going on inside Amethyst's head, sending walls groaning inward, the ceiling crumbling down.

An offramp led to Eubank, and Eubank to Flint. The car climbed her street, rumbling, and turned into her driveway. Amethyst talked, laughed with Melodie, her regular, old self, just with a little bump on the head and a sore ankle. What an adventure today! Haven't had one like that in a while. Thank god for small favors.

In her mind, foundations buckled and heaved. A water main broke, spewing everywhere.

The garage then, and the house, comforting, familiar rooms. Close the curtains, turn on the lights. Drink some tea with Melodie at the dining room table, share a package of cookies. Her hands weren't even shaking. Amazing.

Melodie left, and Amethyst leaned on the utility room door. At last, alone. She didn't want to be alone. She had to be. A little bump on the head wouldn't explain it if she slid to the floor, sobbing hysterically.

In the living room, the stereo clicked on. "Amethyst—"

"Shut up!" she shouted. "Leave—me—*alone!*"

Her fists clenched. That was wrong, wrong. She should thank him—shouldn't she? Go out into the garage, look him in the—in the windshield and say, Thanks for your help, when I was sliding off the edges of myself.

She stomped into the utility room, flung open the door. It rebounded with a bang.

The car took up almost the whole garage: only a couple of steps from the door to the front bumper. She slammed her fists on the hood. The metal gave a musical *plonk*, distorting under the blow, then sprang back again.

"This is all your fault! My life was *normal* before you came."

"Of course it was." His voice came tinny but gentle over the old car speakers. "But—"

"Do you know what happened up there? Do you?"

"I sensed a great power—"

"It tried to kill me! A tree stump. It walked. It grabbed me by the leg, dragged me to it and started squeezing."

"But you're here. You're quite safe. It must have been a golem, an inanimate object driven by magic. You repelled it—"

"I killed it!"

She was screaming. Mr. Meadows next door would hear and call the police. *That crazy artist next door is talking about killing someone!*

"Whatever it was, it was merely an artifact of power. Nothing you could—"

"I don't care! I've never even killed an animal, anything with a face, and a voice, that—that *screamed.* Is this what I have to look forward to? Well, I won't be that kind of person!"

She wanted to hurl paint cans, the tool box, anything heavy she could get her hands on. She wanted to collapse right here on the garage floor, after an hour of pretending that nothing more had happened on the trail than a little slip and a little scare. She didn't want to do either, to humiliate herself in front of him, though he wasn't even human.

Amethyst blundered back into the house and into her bedroom. The bump on her head throbbed, vicious. Hip and shoulder ached, and the wrung ankle sent silver spears of pain up her leg. She threw the phone and clock radio out into the hall and slammed the door. If she heard Talys' voice again, she'd—

She didn't know what she'd do.

Chapter 11

There was a four-foot-tall letter "F" in neon pink on the left hand side of the garage door. Amethyst glared at it, grinding her teeth, then hauled up the door. It rattled and clattered, just like always.

Inside, the sharp smell of paint filled the air. Neon pink spattered the floor, the workbench, the wall. Judging from the pattern, the paint should have been all over the Mustang, too. Its black body was pristine.

A spray paint can lay on the garage floor. She bent and picked it up. Pink Flamingo. The can was split down one side.

"What happened here? How the hell did this get in here?"

"Your caller from yesterday made a little midnight visit with the intent of advertising his disapproval," Talys said, sounding smug. "I opened the door for him. I fear the fate he had envisaged for me befell him, instead."

Her hammer was on the floor, too. "And this?"

"Alas, ineffective. He grew marvelously frustrated. We had a little chat, and I ushered him out."

She picked up the hammer, hung it back on the peg board and started laughing. The laughter went on too long, though, and she had trouble catching her breath.

"What next? A little arson, maybe, just for variety?"

"Amethyst," he said. "I sincerely doubt he'll return."

She sagged against the workbench. "I can't take this." She walked out, down the driveway. The car started. She stabbed a finger at it. "Stay. Here."

The engine abruptly cut off. She stormed along the sidewalk, not caring that she had to pass Caramela's house on the way to Eubank. Not caring that, after yesterday's ordeal on the mountain, it was probably incredibly stupid to take off by herself.

The sun was already diamond-brilliant and intense, stinging

her back and shoulders through the fabric of her t-shirt. Her ankle stung, too, and ached. She didn't care about that, either.

She rubbed her eyes. Her head still hurt. Her shoulder hurt, too. She was *scared*, and she couldn't even talk to anyone she trusted without getting committed to a psych ward.

Morning commute traffic, much of it doubtless headed for Kirtland Air Force Base and Sandia National Labs, streamed by on Eubank, a dull seethe of tires and engines. Normal people with normal lives beginning a normal day of designing nuclear weapons or maintaining fighter jets or developing the next generation of supercomputers.

What had happened to *her* normal life?

She turned down a side street onto a quieter residential street. Another older neighborhood, but the homes were larger, nicer than those in her own. She came to Indian School, half a mile or so. Snow Park was just ahead. She checked traffic and jogged across the street.

The park had an arched bridge that spanned Embudo Arroyo. She crossed it to the grass and trees beyond, sat down in the shade and leaned her head on her knees.

She had to do something. She had to get control again somehow. The whole horrible mess had started with Talys. It would have to end with him, too.

Talys' attention fell on her, heavy and somber, but he didn't say anything. Not even when she opened the trunk and tossed in some AutoZone bags. They clanked, loud as that stick's crack in the woods. She wouldn't think about what was in them. If she did, Talys might suspect—

No. She wasn't thinking about it.

For the sake of verisimilitude, other stuff had to go in: the boxes of scrap glass she'd never gotten around to doing anything with (remember Dr. Korhonen's beautiful glass mosaic table—? She didn't want to think about Dr. Korhonen, either.), an old CRT monitor she hadn't been able to find a home for but couldn't bear to throw away because it still worked, boxes of her first set of mismatched dishes, which had been taking up space in the spare bedroom. A few lengths of maple moulding and some metal channel went through the window and into the back seat for good measure.

Back the car out, oh-so-casual, nothing worse going on today than a mood black as the burned stuff on the bottom of an untended pot. She moved to get out and shut the garage door, but it rolled smoothly down on its own—no rattle, no clatter. Talys, being helpful again.

She clamped her jaw. Did he really think that would make everything better? That seeing how *useful* and *convenient* magic could be would make her change her mind?

Over the growl of the engine, the radio came on softly. She tensed, but only smooth jazz, harp music—maybe Andreas Vollenweider—came over the speakers. Dammit, now he was trying to soothe her.

Don't bother, she wanted to snap, but then he'd know something was up.

Don't think about it.

The harp music ended and the DJ said, "Are you feeling better?"

It took her an instant to realize the DJ was Talys. "Just dandy," she said.

"Where did you go?"

She bit back another sarcastic remark. "For a walk. To the park. To the store to pick up some things." It had been a long, hot walk. Longer and hotter on the way back, carrying those heavy bags. But with a Westerner's devotion to the auto, she didn't know the bus routes, and didn't want to waste time finding out.

"When you are ready, we can speak of what occurred yesterday."

"Sure."

Silence from the radio for a moment, then, "Where are we going?"

She flashed on *2001: A Space Odyssey*—What are you doing, Dave?

Amethyst said, "Doing some housecleaning."

What had Dave told HAL, before he started removing memory banks? She couldn't remember.

The music came back on. It irritated her more than before.

The procession of strip malls, gas stations and fast food joints slid by. Talys let her drive today. She was impatient, but she kept to the speed limit. No point in risking a traffic stop that would make this drag out even longer. She stopped at a light, turned right. Now apartment buildings lined the street, and rental houses, ill-maintained, cars parked in yards of packed dirt fringed with kochia and the emerald green shoots of tumbleweeds. A sign up ahead on the left announced her destination. She turned into the driveway and faced a rolling chain-link gate topped with razor wire.

She took a deep breath, turned off the engine, climbed out of the car and walked into the little office outside the gate.

She wouldn't look over her shoulder, wouldn't slink. Why should she? She was just clearing out some junk that had accumulated.

The middle-aged woman behind the desk smiled.

"I called earlier about a storage unit," Amethyst said. "You suggested a ten by twenty."

"Oh, yes." The woman put half-glasses on her nose and rummaged in a drawer. "I'll just need you to fill out a little paperwork, then I'll need payment."

"No problem." Amethyst glanced outside. The Mustang waited, long, low and sleek, exuding power.

It was also a storm of chaos that had sucked up her life and spat it back out in mangled pieces.

She signed the rental agreement and handed her debit card across the counter. The woman drew on a map with a pink Hi-Liter, wrote "D-7" and the gate's access code.

Back to the car. The gate jerked, jingled, then began to roll slowly open. Rows of storage units slid by like concentration camp barracks, encircling fence, razor wire and all. She turned at the block labeled with a big, white "D," spotted unit 7, backed the car.

Calm, she told herself. Her heart wasn't beating hard, her breath wasn't shaking. Get out, roll up the storage unit door.

Now back in the car. There was just enough room.

Talys didn't say a word. The driver's door banged against the wall when she opened it. She squeezed out, edged around to the back and opened the trunk. Any minute now he would suggest that it would be simpler to unload the boxes if she pulled forward a bit. Or worse still, do it himself.

She hurried, not enough to make it look like she was hurrying. Just lifted out the boxes. They were heavy, shifting, and glass chimed as it slid, plinked when she set down the boxes. She shoved them with her foot, making sure they were right in front of the wheels. The AutoZone bags remained. Her heart galloped. She had to settle down, feel the calm she pretended.

She pulled out the bags. They went *clink* as she carried them around to the front of the car, *clank* when she lowered them to the dusty concrete floor of the storage unit.

She was glad she'd backed the car in, otherwise she'd be trapped between the car and the storage unit's back wall.

She popped the hood release and raised the hood. Smells of gasoline and hot oil unfurled around her.

"Amethyst. What are you doing?"

She wedged a length of two-by-four between the open hood and the engine and kept her mouth shut. She took a wrench out of the bag and attacked the battery cable clamp.

"Amethyst!" The engine thundered to life.

She jerked back. The hood banged her head. No, she'd hit it, not the other way around. She took an unsteady breath, leaned back in and twisted at the nut on the clamp again.

The Mustang gunned and roared. The fender shuddered against her thigh, hood shook over her head. The two-by-four fell, bounced on the valve covers and through the engine compartment with a clunk and clatter.

"Going to run me down, Talys?" In one savage handful, she yanked the spark plug wires off the distributor. The engine spluttered and died.

In the sudden silence, his voice went from hot cocoa to thin, bitter coffee. "Have you gone mad?"

She cracked a laugh. "Damn near, thanks to you." She went back to work on the battery cables.

"I'm your *familiar!* I've done nothing to deserve this!"

"Let's see. I guess that night in the alley and the destruction of my Isuzu don't count. But how about my life? I kind of enjoyed it up until recently. You know, little things like my friends, my art. Uneventful breakfasts at restaurants, peaceful walks in the woods. But since you came along, all that seems…" She pursed her lips. "How shall I say it? To have become an unfortunate casualty. Collateral damage, I suppose."

"I'm sorry! I'm sorry about your car, about frightening you. But yesterday—"

"Yesterday was the last straw!" She got the positive cable loose and flung it aside, then one by one, jerked the wires loose from the spark plugs.

"I would help you, but you refuse to tell me what happened!"

"You want to know? That—that—*tree thing* hunted me through the woods. Just like you hunted me before. Is that how it goes? Whoever grabs me gets to keep me? I'm not a toy, and I'm not a prize!"

"Never—*never* have I considered you such."

"That thing wanted me, and it did some kind of weird timeshift thing to separate me from Melodie. And then it caught me, and it dragged and shook me, and squeezed and squeezed—"

"Amethyst, listen." He spoke quickly, breathlessly. "This is precisely why you need me."

"Oh yeah? But you weren't there, were you, Talys? It didn't grab me, crack your head, try to twist your foot off and damn near break your ribs. No, you don't even *have* a head or feet or ribs to injure, do you?"

"I have had. I understand your vulnerability. Why do you think I wish to remain close?"

"So it's my own fault now, huh?"

"No. No, of course not. But what you're doing now will not end what is happening."

She popped off the distributor cap.

"I've walked that trail a hundred times, and nothing ever happened before. Then you come along. Don't you find that just the least bit coincidental?"

She stuffed both cap and wires into one of the bags and pulled out a hydraulic bottle jack and set of jackstands.

"Perhaps...perhaps I am to blame. My presence..." He stopped, then went on. "Yet it was only a matter of time before your power manifested, with or without me. You must understand, I am not the cause of your troubles."

"Keep telling me that. I'm sure to believe it sooner or later."

She pulled a star wrench out of the bag. Amazing how she'd schlepped all this stuff for blocks. The things a person can do when there's a will.

"You don't know how to conceal yourself," he said. "And when you evade me, I cannot obscure you. Do you not see, Amethyst? In your ignorance, you are incapable of protecting yourself. I can teach you."

"Interesting. Then how come you never bothered to?"

She cracked the lug nuts loose first. She'd changed enough tires to know that. Slip the wrench on, lean into it, *crack!* and do the next one.

His voice rose. "I would have, but you—" The sound of a breath taken came clearly over the radio speaker. "You had no desire to learn."

"Funny, I remember asking an awful lot of questions you declined to answer."

"I had no wish to frighten you."

She gave an incredulous laugh. "Really?"

"If I'd told you—" Another breath. "Wizards have been disappearing. Others have attempted to discover how, only to vanish as well. The homeless man yesterday—he was empty of power. Damaged, but not destroyed. Not totally."

She braced her hands on the fan shroud. "And you wanted me to *touch* him? Why?"

"From him, we may have discovered the source of the danger."

"Oh, sure, and what else? 'Give me some,' he kept saying. Give what? Magic? My lifeforce, maybe?"

Damn, the bump on her head pounded. She hoped it wasn't swelling like the balloon it felt like, pumped up with every beat of her pulse. And the shoulder she'd cracked on that guardrail—it was objecting strenuously to the wrench-twisting and jack-cranking. It would have to hold out a little longer.

"I would let no harm befall you," he said.

"Harm! You? Thank God you're not out to do me real damage." She propped a knee on the tire to keep it straight and spun off a final lug nut.

"I am not your enemy!" he said as if through gritted teeth.

"I can't imagine what leads me to believe you're anything but *my friend.*"

That last bit came out nasty. She hadn't realized she was quite that angry.

"I *am* your friend," he said. "Or would be, would you allow me. Possibly one of the few you'll possess as a wizard."

"Good thing I don't plan to be one, then."

She shoved a jackstand under the car, let down the jack and scooted the wheel underneath, too.

"You *are* a wizard. And no other wizard you meet will believe differently, no matter what you profess."

"Don't give me that crap. You keep telling me wizards are gone."

"You met Dr. Kohonen."

"Who's been decent enough to *leave me alone.* And I didn't hear you warn me about *him*, either."

The tire thumped to the floor. Amethyst moved to the last wheel and pumped the jack.

"Until he used magic, I had no way of knowing." Amazing how calm he could sound while she dismantled him. "One will not realize a wizard's true nature until he chooses to reveal himself."

"Then what the hell good are you?"

"Please," he said. "I beg you. Allow me to stay, even if only as a simple automobile."

"Too late. I'm rebooting my life. Restoring conditions to their original state."

The wheel fell off, wobbled into stillness on the concrete floor. Planting a foot on it, she shoved it underneath. She twisted the handle on the jack and the car eased down. It settled on the jackstand with a bump.

"Certain transitions once made, cannot return to an original state," he said. "Allow me to help you through this one."

"Kind of like a shaman, helping people on to the other side? Thanks anyway, I think I'll pass, no pun intended."

"What can I say?" His voice rose. "What can I do to convince you?"

She scraped the jack out. The handle weighted her hand like a murder weapon. So maybe he was telling the truth now. The truth—but only part of it, never all. What else was missing?

"Believe me, Talys. You've already convinced me."

She stood, dusted off the knees of her jeans and removed the battery. It was heavy. She set it on the floor. She should've thought about getting one of those plastic used oil receptacles to drain the engine oil into, too. But with everything else she already had to transport home on foot, she probably couldn't've managed to lug that, too.

She slammed the hood, *whang!* the last word of an argument.

"Sorry. I wish we could have parted on better terms."

"Amethyst..."

The Mustang filled the storage compartment like it did her garage. Sitting wheelless on jackstands, though, it didn't look quite so formidable. Like a vigorous man in a wheelchair with broken legs. She hesitated.

No, no, no. She would *not* relent now. How stupid could she be, feeling like she was betraying someone. Someone devoted, patient, in the face of all her upheavals.

Devoted. Patient. Sure. And he'd make a perfect boyfriend, too. Please.

She gathered up the bags, wrenches, jack, spark plug wires, distributor cap and all, set them clinking on the pavement outside.

"I wouldn't bother yelling for help, by the way. You might get someone to come open the door, but I don't think you'll be able to convince them to put your wheels back on and buy you a new ignition set."

Amethyst caught the knotted nylon rope dangling from the door and pulled. It came rattling down, settled with a thump. She pulled a padlock out of her pocket, slid it into the latch and snapped it shut.

Chapter 12

"**W**iz, no," Melodie said, hands on hips and facing the pickup. "Tell me you didn't buy that."

Amethyst crossed her arms. "I had two thousand bucks to spend. Yeah. I bought it."

The little Chevy pickup was old. Ugly, a chalky, oxidized red. But it ran, and it even had a camper shell.

She allowed herself one last, longing glance at the rows of new cars and trucks gleaming in the afternoon sun. The salesman she'd talked to was nowhere in sight. He was probably inside, cursing his lack of commission. Or hiding.

"But—" Melodie spluttered. "I thought we were going to get you a new car." Her lips thinned in distaste. "At least something newer than that."

"I only asked if you wouldn't mind driving me to a few car lots. Believe me, if I could afford a new car, I'd love to get one."

Now Melodie crossed her arms. "Are you kidding me? You could sell that Mustang and have more than enough money for something new. Hell, for two or three new somethings. But you stick it in storage—and buy *this*." She gestured at the awful old pickup. "Why?"

"I told you—"

"It'll take too long to sell the Mustang for what it's worth," Melodie broke in. "You don't want anything to happen to it in the meantime. Fine. Another flimsy excuse. I'm not going to argue with you here."

"Mel, I need something that can haul—"

"Forget it." Melodie waved in irritation. "I'll follow you home. Maybe this thing runs, but I don't want to trust how well. Even if you do."

She stalked to her Insight, parked in one of the visitor spaces by the showroom.

Amethyst took a step to go after her, then turned back to the truck and flung herself in. All this crazy business was still—*still*—messing up her life. For ten years, Melodie had been her best friend. And Amethyst couldn't tell her what was really going on. Why the car was really locked up.

And Melodie knew she was being lied to.

"Damn." Amethyst slammed the door. It shut with a tinny clap. The little four-banger engine started with a clatter. "Damn, damn, damn."

The cab smelled of stale cigarettes and spilled beer. The transmission clacked when she put it in gear. The laces on the steering wheel wrap hung half-unraveled. The dealership hadn't had time to go over it (and probably dispose of it), but that was why she'd gotten it so cheap, even if she did have to lean pretty hard on the salesman to consider it a serious deal.

She toyed with new excuses. Melodie was right. They were flimsy. Pretty soon she was going to have to decide which would lose her a friend more quickly—the flimsy lies, or the crazy truth.

She still hadn't decided when she pulled into her driveway. She turned off the key, leaned her head on the steering wheel a moment, then got out.

Melodie was already on her way up the driveway, and there was still—dammit!—that stained glass window on the living room wall.

Amethyst hurriedly dug keys out of her purse and cut off Melodie's path to the front door, heading for the garage door instead.

"Come in. I'll make us—" At the same time, Melodie said, "I'm sorry, Wiz. I—"

She stopped, Melodie stopped. Amethyst looked down. The apology somehow made it worse.

"No, don't be sorry," she said. "You're my friend, for godsake. Aren't friends supposed to watch out for each other?"

Melodie tugged the hem of her jacket. "Yeah, but not tell each other what to do. It's just that I've been so worried—"

"Worried!"

Melodie threw up her hands. "Jeez, Wiz, you've been acting like a mob witness. The whole thing with the car…okay, I can understand that. But first you're driving it because you say the stalker stuff has stopped, then suddenly it's in storage. Then you buy this heap." She jerked her chin at the Chevy.

Amethyst popped the lock on the garage door and rolled it up. "That car just…it creeped me out, Mel. I couldn't stand waiting for the other shoe to drop." She wasn't lying this time.

"And what's in your house you don't want me to see?"

Amethyst swung around. "*What?*"

Melodie planted fists on hips. "Every time I come over, you either meet me outside or keep me in the kitchen. Did you think I didn't notice?"

"I—I—" Amethyst raked a hand through her hair and gusted a noisy breath. "All right. Come on."

She led the way into the house, still through the garage. Melodie frowned, but the extra doors and distance gave Amethyst a little time to gather her courage. She paused again to put her purse in its usual spot on a dining room chair. Melodie did too, then glanced at the patio door. Caramela stood outside, her pink mouth open in a welcoming grin, wagging.

"There's a pit bull in your backyard," Melodie said.

"That's Caramela."

"I thought she belonged to the terrorist neighbors. The ones who'd trash your house if you crossed them. And I noticed a freshly painted patch on your garage door. Plus pink spray paint inside your garage."

Amethyst would have squirmed, but was more than happy to be sidetracked. "The neighbors are more polite these days."

"Uh-huh. For how long?"

Amethyst sometimes wondered the same thing. "There are a couple of loose boards in my gate. I can't help it if she likes it here better."

"Meaning you improvised a doggie door, and since this is where she gets fed…"

Amethyst grinned. "You can't even see the hinges from the outside. Want to meet her? She's really sweet, and she's had a bath."

Melodie made a disgusted noise. "Later. After you show me what we came in here to see."

Damn.

Through the kitchen then. Amethyst's stomach twisted into knots. This was it. She'd have to tell Melodie...what she was. And what she could do. She set her jaw and took a long breath.

Melodie stepped into the living room and gasped. "Oh my god, Wiz. It's beautiful!"

She walked fully into the room, her face rapt. "It's that place we found hiking, isn't it? The one you said would make such a great window." She turned round, hazel eyes on Amethyst. "This is what you've been hiding from me? Why?"

Amethyst twisted her fingers. "Well..."

"You even installed lights behind it. It must've taken months! When did you do it?"

"I—I— I did a little here and there, when I had time." She dropped onto the couch and slumped. She couldn't do it. She couldn't say, 'I used magic. I held the image in my mind and willed it into existence.'

"And you've been keeping me out of here until it was finished," Melodie said on an outrush of breath. She laughed, plunked onto the couch beside her and hugged Amethyst. "God. I thought it was drugs or something."

"Drugs!" Amethyst almost laughed, too.

"Or blackmail or abuse or—I didn't know what. Sometimes I thought the stalker had moved in somehow. You have no idea."

The skin between Amethyst's shoulder blades prickled. Melodie had no idea how close to the truth she was.

"No. No drugs, blackmail or abuse. And like I said, the stalker seems to be gone." All true.

"But you got rid of the car? Without selling it?"

"I didn't want to deal with it anymore. I thought I could drive it like it was any car, but…" Amethyst shrugged. "It isn't, and I can't."

Melodie hugged her again. "Okay. I've seen your secret project, and the car and the stalker are out of the picture. Everything is back to normal."

Someone was following her. The absolute certainty touched the back of Amethyst's neck like the brush of a hand. Talys' voice kept buzzing in her head—*Please! I'm not the cause of your troubles!* If not, then who was?

She glanced at the rearview mirror again, remembered again there wasn't one and looked into the pickup's side mirror. Behind her, Highway 522 wound between the Taos Mountains and the Rio Grande Gorge, a wake through a grey-green sea of sage. It had been harder to tell in the strings of traffic on I-25, even on the hills and curves of 285 north of Santa Fe. But here, on a two-lane road the middle of the sagebrush flats north of Taos, it was obvious. Nothing was back there.

But she was sure someone must be.

"Stress," she muttered.

But that wasn't exactly what was bothering her, was it? More like guilt, beating like a telltale heart in the sudden quiet at her house. Exactly why she was headed to the family home in San Cristobel instead of staying in Albuquerque where she should be, working on the DeBaca's window.

Locking up Talys was the only thing she could've done. If she'd relented then, she'd never have had another chance.

Amethyst's pickup pinged, knocked and slowed. Great. Besides being old, ugly and smelly, it was also underpowered. She downshifted and tromped the gas to the floor. The engine yowled but didn't provide Mustang's acceleration.

Okay, Amethyst. So turn around, go back and get the car out of that storage unit. Start the craziness again. Is that what you want?

The mountains loomed larger. The monotonous expanse of sage seemed to conceal spying eyes. Those eyes couldn't belong to anything worse than a coyote or raven or bobcat. They *couldn't*.

The homeless man's rambling warning came back to her: *watch out for him*. Sweat suddenly prickled along her sides, vague panic cramped her throat. It followed her off the highway, onto a gravel road. Irrigated pastures replaced sage. Cottonwoods arched over the road, sheltering, familiar. There was the old adobe ruin, slumping back into earth with each year of summer rains. And there, the Romero's ancient tractor standing like a monument to procrastination. Everything perfectly normal, exactly like it had always been.

She wasn't comforted. Happiness didn't well up in her, anticipation of home. She pulled into the driveway, around its curve into the shade of the cottonwood by the side of the house. Gravel crackled under the tires. She turned off the key and the engine dieseled, then clattered into stillness. The truck's door creaked when she opened it. Amethyst stretched, twisting out the ache of a couple hours spent in the pickup's sprung seat.

The storm door squeaked and Mama came out onto the porch. "Violita!" Even in what was more or less a housedress, she was shapely, a long way from Amethyst's wiry angles.

Dad's blue heeler dog, Caballero, came yammering out. Dad had gotten him after she'd left for school, so Caballero didn't know Amethyst well. Each time she visited, she had to soothe the dog's suspicions anew.

"Hi, Mama." Amethyst hugged her mother in spite of Caballero's protests.

She held Amethyst away from her. "You look tired."

Amethyst shrugged. "A little."

Mama cocked her head. "More than a little."

Tears tried to wrestle their way past Amethyst's throat. Then Dad was there, and she flung her arms around him. He wasn't a tall man, but he was stocky and solid. His strong hug made the worry finally go away.

"How you doin', Thistle?"

"Oh, Dad," she whispered into his shoulder.

"Come inside," Mama said. "I have chile verde and posole."

Amethyst stepped out of the hug, but Dad draped an arm around her shoulders and turned to Mama.

"We have time to stretch our legs a little?" he asked.

"Go on, Alejandro." Mama made a shooing motion. "Show her your new gadget."

Amethyst grinned in spite of herself. "What new gadget?"

Dad returned exactly the same grin. "A radio control helicopter."

She followed him around the side of the house. He glanced at the pickup, then at her, but didn't say anything. She was glad. She didn't want to talk about the truck.

Dad opened the door to his workshop. The cars parked in the adjoining garage were different now, but the workshop was the same as when she'd lived at home: a not-so-secret hideout full of fascinating clutter, tools and projects in various degrees of completion. Its familiar smell, a delicious combination of oil, paint, metal and sawdust came between her and the weight of worry like a shield. She might have been in high school again, eager to help build a compost tumbler or wind harp or home weather station.

Greenish light filtered through a window, but Dad flipped on the overhead fluorescents. A scale model glider hung on the wall, graceful and pristine white. A thin, blue stripe ran the length of its fuselage. The helicopter sat on the workbench. Dad put it on the floor, turned on the RC controller and thumbed the joysticks. The little helicopter whirred, tilted forward on its skids and lifted into the air.

"Oh, that is so cool!" she said.

The 'copter spun on its axis, swooped forward, stopped, then rose again, tracking slightly backward.

Dad landed it on the dusty concrete floor and offered the controller. "Want to try?"

"I'll crash it."

He angled her a glance, one that conveyed skepticism better than raised brows ever could. "Since when have you been afraid to try new tech?"

"It's not that, it's just…"

"What?"

Amethyst shrugged in frustration and leaned against the workbench. "I feel like…I keep making mistakes."

His lips twitched. "If you're talking about that truck out front, I'd have to agree. The business going okay?"

"I'm getting a few more commissions, but I still can't charge for the time it takes."

He grunted. "Gotta make that name first. No commissions right now?"

"One."

This time the look he gave was straight-on. "Then what're you doing here?"

She resisted the impulse to squirm. "I need to talk to you."

He put the controller on the bench and leaned beside her. "So what's going on?"

She glanced at the remote control unit. Thank god she'd never said anything about the stalker. She drew a long breath. She *still* couldn't tell the truth—but she could tell a version of it.

"I think I haven't been fair to someone."

Dad just waited.

"Someone—someone I met when my Isuzu was wrecked." Technically, she'd met Talys *before* he wrecked her Isuzu, but no way would she get into that. "He, uh, lent me his car for a while. We sort of became friends. Well, not friends, exactly, but kind of close in a way."

Dad's sideways glance had a sparkle to it. "In a way."

She picked up a washer, slid it over her finger. "Well, we fought a lot."

"I get the feeling I'm missing part of the story here."

"I'm not telling it right." She puffed out a breath. "This guy was—was with us—Melodie and Marl and me—that night, at the opera. The night somebody wrecked my car. He got...I don't know. Sort of protective, I guess."

"Okay. Protective how?"

"He wanted to hang around all the time. He wanted me to learn how to watch out for myself." She snorted.

"Hmm. He a cop?"

Amethyst twisted the washer on her finger. What had Talys been to her? Besides an annoyance, that is.

"A teacher."

Dad gave a surprised grunt. "Pretty paranoid for a teacher. Or did you have more trouble after that night?"

Now why did he have to go and ask that? "None he didn't invite," she muttered.

He frowned. "What's that mean?"

This was still dangerous ground. She trod it carefully. "He insisted what happened wasn't random. He kept hounding me about it."

"Oh yeah?" His tone was ominous.

She really, really didn't want to lie to Dad—not flat out like that. She waved her hands. The washer flew off and rang on the floor. "It doesn't matter. I got rid of him."

"A good thing, if he was messing with your mind," he said. "A bad thing if he had a reason to worry. I guess you're wondering the same thing."

"Not exactly. I don't think he was messing with me, but..." She gave a frustrated sigh. "Everything was different with him around. I got scared. I felt like my life was out of control. Like I was becoming someone I didn't even know."

He nodded thoughtfully. "You can't always be in control, Thistle. Things change. Life happens. You gotta live it, or what's the point?"

"That's not the kind of life I want to live."

"Well then, I guess you did the right thing."

"But I'm not *sure*." She rubbed at the black ring the washer had left. "I think he really was trying to help me. I didn't for a long time, but now..." She trailed off.

He slid an arm around her shoulders. "You're smart, Thistle. You've got a lot of talent. But sometimes you get it in your head the way things should be, and when they aren't, you bail. If you do that every time something gets too hard, you'll never get anywhere."

She stirred under his arm. "You know I don't do that, Dad. I—"

"Sometimes, I said. Brain stuff, practical matters, no problem. You're stubborn as a pit bull. But when it comes to people... Well, then you're your mother's little violet and not so much my sturdy thistle."

She wanted to argue, but couldn't. After all, that was why she liked to work alone. Why dating scared her silly. Too hard. Too many chances to get hurt.

Talys technically wasn't 'people.' But what he wanted—

"It wasn't just that," she said. "It— He— I have to make my own choices."

"Yep, you do. Don't ever let anyone else make 'em for you. Not even me."

"I never had problems with my choices before," she grumbled.

He laughed. "Oh, that was because you were a kid before. Now that you're all grown up, you get to grapple with the hard ones."

She leaned away to look at him. "Dropping computers for stained glass wasn't exactly an easy decision!"

"Easier than this one, right?"

"I guess."

"There you go. All I can tell you is there's tradeoffs to everything. You have to decide if the minuses outweigh the pluses—or vice versa." He jiggled her shoulders. "No matter what, I want to know if anyone's giving you grief. I won't put up with that, no matter who—friends, dating, married, whatever. Hear?"

She took the hand, square and firm and comforting, on her shoulder. "Nobody," she said, "is going to give me grief."

He grinned. "That's my Thistle. Are we good to go in now? You know your mom'll be worried. You do look tired."

She sighed. "Maybe something to eat and a quiz about my love life will perk me up."

Dad laughed. "Your mom just wants you to find as good a man as she did."

Amethyst made a face and punched his arm. "Gosh, you're modest." She could laugh with him this time.

They left the garage sanctuary and headed for the house. Inside, the savory smell of food filled the air. Caballero trotted over to greet Dad, then gave Amethyst's jeans legs a thorough sniffing, probably smelling Caramela. She had to do something about that dog. Caballero glanced up at her with a huffy "wuff" and flopped onto his bed by the wood stove.

The living room invited with Mama's tasteful decorating. A few of the details had changed, but the warmth hadn't. Indian baskets and soft watercolors decorated the walls. Pillows on the sofa and chairs and silk flowers in vases picked up colors in the paintings. Dad's copies of Scientific American and Popular Mechanics lay in neat fans on the coffee table.

Mama poked her head around the kitchen doorway. "Come in! Get something to eat."

Amethyst sat at her old place at the dining room table. She picked up an agate napkin ring. "I love these. The swirls of translucent browns and golds…" She slid the napkin out and replaced the ring on the table. "I bet I could make something like it in glass." She frowned. "Maybe more along the lines of glass mosaic, though. I could probably fix the glass to an acrylic ring."

Mama put a bowl of chile verde in front of her. "They'd make good Christmas presents. You're smiling now. Did your papa figure out your problems for you?"

The change of subject was so seamless, Amethyst still had her mouth open to talk about Christmas presents.

Dad pushed plump white kernels of posole onto his fork with a piece of tortilla. "Nothing a good pep-talk couldn't cure."

"Mmm," Mama said.

Amethyst's face went warm, and not from the spicy tang of green chile in the bowl in front of her.

She stirred her stew, chunks of potato and tomatoes and tender pork. "It wasn't a mom-problem," she explained.

"Mothers care about all kinds of problems."

"I know. But they're best for problems with guys, and I don't have many of those."

Dad slid her that look again.

She coughed, and this time she told herself it *was* the chile. "I don't!"

Mama's nicely-shaped brows went up.

Amethyst scowled at Dad. "It was nothing. Just…this guy, and he's not around anymore."

"So that's why you looked sad," Mama said.

"I am not sad!" Amethyst blew through her lips. "He was arrogant, overbearing, and he thought he had all the answers. I'm glad I— I'm glad he's gone."

"If that's what you say."

"Mama!"

"All right, Violita. But when my daughter suddenly comes home looking tired—" she emphasized *tired*, "and then I hear about 'this guy,' what am I supposed to think?"

"Well, you don't have to think there's any romance involved, because there wasn't, believe me."

She choked back a wild impulse to explain that the guy in question was a spirit inhabiting a car. Definitely kinky if romance was involved, not to mention utterly hopeless.

Mama sat down and shook her napkin into her lap. "Maybe no romance, *mija*, but if he was as bad as you say, you wouldn't be here with that face."

Amethyst dropped her head in her hand.

"I don't think you're helping, Tonia," Dad said mildly.

"She's helping, Dad," Amethyst said into her hand. "You know how."

He chuckled. "Yeah, I do." His hand fell on hers where it rested on the table. She raised her head. "She cuts right to the chase and makes us be honest with ourselves," he said. "Why do you think we've been married thirty-five years?"

Amethyst gave a wry twist of a smile. "Great for a marriage, tough on the kids."

Mama cupped her cheek. "But look what kids I have. They can do anything."

"Yeah," Amethyst sighed. "Anything."

Anything except decide if locking up Talys had been the best decision of her life—or the worst mistake.

Soliloquy – Second Voice

Darkness surrounded him, broken only by a knife-blade of light. During the day the light was white and crept from the wall behind him, across the wall beside him, finally falling angled upon the floor until it shortened into nothingness. Now it was the orange of sodium vapor, and did not move. The metal shell of the building imprisoning him ticked, cooling, quiet after rattling in the day's winds.

He did not mark time as a human would; he should not feel impatience. Impatience was a symptom of mortality. Nevertheless, he did feel it, as well as desperation…yes, even fear. Not about the door, or the lock upon it—laughable, irrelevant. Even with his slight abilities, he could open the second and raise the first. Yet even were that insufficient, the power and imperviousness of this form could bring him through with little consequence. But the rest—

By the cursed gods' cruel jests! That damage was more problematic.

What could have driven the woman to such extremity? Too much, no doubt, in a short time. But to jump to such a self-destructive conclusion! To cut off her greatest advantage, as if a soldier decided to meet a coming battle by discarding his sword.

He roamed in and out of his metal skin, quivering, a vulnerable thing venturing out of its safe burrow.

Hurry! Hurry! Why must it all take so long? He'd once thought this shape a fine idea, faster and stronger and tougher than any beast, capable of roaming most anywhere without attracting undue human attention while evading the frailties of a living creature.

But living creatures were made to repair themselves. This form was not. It forced him to gather what he needed to rebuild himself. It forced him to expose himself, his fragile essence, that could be blown out by a breath of magic. Why else had he turned down the fire of his consciousness for so long, but for the same reason a fawn, alone, lies flat and still on the dappled forest floor.

He gave a silent, bitter laugh. So it came to nothing more than self-interest. He was no more than a dog shut out of the master's house, abandoned and starving out in the cold. He'd been honest, at least. He'd told her he needed her. But not why.

Oh, the danger, the danger! He hadn't counted it so near, so imminent, before some wizard set a golem upon her. And to what end that attack? To destroy, or merely capture?

Yet she attributed it to him. He was to blame for that. He, from the beginning, when he'd frightened her, when he'd obfuscated rather than enlightened her. She'd told him, but he'd not listened. He'd been blinded by delight of her: her power, the freedom, life and hope she represented. He'd wanted to rush forward like a foolish mortal painfully cognizant that tomorrow brings death one day closer.

So now, if she ended before he did, he would know it was his eagerness that had doomed her. His selfishness. His conceit. And what could he do to undo it? Nothing. Nothing but watch while the wolves circled closer. O Amethyst, hear me, heed me! You must free me! *Please...*

But he'd said all that before, and she'd not heeded.

He built, fit another molecule into place, like an ant building its hill grain by grain. Forcing his magic to feats he'd not attempted before. He did not possess her power. But he possessed knowledge, experience she lacked—to her great vulnerability. Somehow, he must find a way to undo his mistake, find a way to protect her.

If he could escape this very effective bondage under which she'd placed him.

Chapter 13

*A*methyst. Talys' voice, distant, tenuous, echoed down the corridors of her dreams.

She couldn't get away from the damned car. She'd locked it up…

So how could it be that she was locked up with it? The closed metal door was behind her, and her shins almost touched the bumper. She could barely see it—him—there in front of her in the darkness, still, silent, aware, yet unconscious of her presence.

She hugged herself, but couldn't feel the pressure of her fingers on her arms, the warmth of her skin through the fabric of her nightshirt. It was a dream. Another dream. *Please, let me wake up. I don't want to be here.*

She squeezed her eyes closed. That might put her back in bed, where she belonged. Still she smelled dust, a faint scent of oil, a stronger one of rubber. Somewhere in the distance, a truck rumbled by. Nearer—much nearer—something scraped on concrete.

Her eyes sprang open again. Another scrape sounded from under the car, like the dragging step of something undead. Something large moved in the deeper darkness there, something round-headed, that crept out from under the car… A tire.

The hair prickled up her spine, down her arms. The Mustang was trying to fix itself? She shuddered. If she opened the hood, would she see spark plug wires regrowing themselves, pink and shiny like new flesh?

Amethyst.

She froze. That wasn't Talys' voice this time, that insidious whisper like a thin, gleaming thread. It snaked lazily through the soft dark waters of sleep, seeking, coiling as if to snare some unsuspecting prey. She ebbed away from it, becoming dark in the darkness, silent in the silence, a dream within the dream.

The new whisper followed, not a snare she could evade, but a fog that surrounded her, pressed into her nostrils, wound down into her lungs, seeped into her bloodstream.

Out of the fog, Talys's voice now spoke: "I'm not your enemy!" Not the tinny AM radio voice, but the rich one she'd heard before in another dream. "One will not realize a wizard's true nature until he chooses to reveal himself."

The beat of her name filled her, tugged at every cell in her body, molding her will to another's thoughts, another's wish. A door opened in her mind. The unknown whisper drew her through it. She took a step—

Light blazed up before her, bright as a magnesium flare.

"I had hoped to have you a bit further along before meeting other wizards," that silver sun said in Talys' voice. "You must understand that you are in danger."

She flinched back, into herself. She jolted upright.

Dim streetlight filtered through the bedroom curtains, casting a vague square on the ceiling and one wall. Her comforter stretched away in a rumpled topography. The mirror reflected the vase of pinwheels on the dresser and an angle of wall.

She fell back onto the pillow and curled up tight.

Why did she keep having these dreams? Was it still guilt about what she'd done to Talys? Still uneasiness and uncertainty?

No, it couldn't be. Nothing had happened since she'd locked him up. Nothing… Except these dreams.

So whose voice had that been, that second, compelling whisper? She pulled the covers up tight to her chin. Like dreaming of being chased, but your feet only…drag…so…slowly. A dream of powerlessness, of being utterly overcome by a superior force.

She raised her head to look at the clock. The glowing green numbers showed 3:27, a long way till morning.

Sleep didn't seem like such a good idea now.

◇◇◇

"Ms. Rey?"

Amethyst blinked. Caroline DeBaca came into focus, tastefully made-up, dark red hair swept back in a style that looked like it must take at least an hour to do, her large, blue-green eyes regarding Amethyst with wary perplexity. The contractor was eyeing her, too—what was his name? Leffler? Lenard. That was it. She hoped.

"I'm so sorry." Amethyst glanced a little desperately around the DeBaca's atrium—or soon-to-be atrium, anyway. Right now it was a collection of unplastered adobe walls, bare beams and unadorned concrete floor. Of course, no glib answers were stenciled on any of them. "I was…" Zoned out due to nearly a week's worth of sleep deprivation? "…just thinking."

"Do you see a problem?" the contractor asked.

No problems yet, but give her another day or two of that voice chasing her out of sleep, and she might start having hallucinations.

"Ah…no," she said. "Just, um, evaluating how the window will fit into the overall design. This is the first time I've seen the room…well, in the flesh, so to speak."

Mrs. DeBaca's immaculate brows pinched together. "Does that change anything?"

"No." Amethyst put on a smile. "Not at all."

Amethyst. The whisper came from nowhere, everywhere.

"Ms. Rey, are you quite all right?"

Who had asked that? Amethyst rubbed her forehead. Something had happened, a gap, a film jumped off its sprockets. The contractor was holding her elbow. God, they were going to think she was drunk—or on drugs, like Melodie thought. She'd better get it together, or she was going to lose this job. In spite of Mrs. DeBaca's words of polite concern, that was perfectly clear on her petite, elegant face.

"I'm so sorry," Amethyst said. Again. "I've been—" fighting a psychic assault every night. You know, kind of like the Twelve Dancing Princesses. Except instead of being drawn down into the fairy world, I'm being drawn to a certain storage unit. "I must be coming down with something."

Mrs. DeBaca opened her mouth to say something—probably like asking why had she come, if the only thing she was good for was to spread germs around. The contractor spoke first.

"I think I've found out what I need to know. If I have any questions, Ms. Rey, I'll call you."

She gave him a relieved and grateful smile. "That'll be fine."

"Will your...illness impact the schedule?" Mrs. DeBaca asked.

Amethyst wasn't about to admit how far behind she was. She nodded at Contractor L-something. "The window will be ready when this gentleman is."

She managed to shake hands then and take her leave like a rational person.

She stepped through an open French door with the manufacturer's label still on the glass. Gravelly soil crunched under her feet like tiny bones. Granite in odd, rounded shapes stood around the house, like trolls petrified by the sun's rays. The mountain rose just beyond, boulder piled on boulder, massive and looming.

Amethyst hunched her shoulders at a sudden memory. The Sandias no longer seemed a friendly constant against the eastern sky, turning watermelon pink at sunset, crowned with lightning-spiked clouds during the summer monsoons, streaked with snow after a winter storm. Instead they'd become the place where an impossible monster had tried to kill her. She had nightmares now, about the tree-thing, and last night, something about rocks, tumbling down on her, pressing out the will to struggle.

A voice murmured her name.

She snatched herself back into the here-and-now, clenched her fists so hard the nails dug into her skin. She scrambled into her truck, backed into the street. Exhaustion, fear, desperation clawed at her. What did the damn voice want?

She knew what it wanted. She was supposed to go back to that storage unit. Except it wasn't Talys' voice.

Watch out for him, the homeless man had said. Who?

A street curved by, fringed with Apache plume and chamisa, bordered with rocks instead of sidewalks. Throttling desperation, she drove on, down the hill, down.

"I can't!" She thumped the seat. "I *won't!* It's my life, and I'll live it the way I want to!"

The architectural-showcase homes, the street winding among the hills and boulders and spiky desert vegetation of the Sandia foothills blurred as if she watched through a filter: muted, dampened, dreamlike. She rolled along streets, past a traffic signal, along a wide boulevard thick with afternoon traffic. Mount Taylor floated on the western horizon, vague blue and still snowcapped. Peaceful. Lulling. Far from noise and worries and struggle, why struggle? Simply drift like the mountain, come—

"No!"

Her throat felt as if the word had been ripped out of it. She scrubbed her forehead with the heel of one hand. Friction-heat tingled the skin. She was on the freeway—which one? I-40, westbound. There was the Juan Tabo exit. How had she gotten—what? Five miles down the road? Ten? How many intersections had she blown through? And navigating the onramp, merging with 65-plus mph freeway traffic—

Her throat closed, her heart raced. Her fingers went cold and tingly.

She eased across to the right lane, steering the truck onto the Eubank exit.

"What do I do?" she asked aloud, and her voice sounded thin and scared.

Amethyst passed Flint, her street—didn't decide to, just drove past. Under-maintained four-unit apartment blocks and neglected rental houses slid by. She turned right onto a side street. Spiky shoots of Russian thistle sprouted from the cracks between curb and sidewalk. A chain link fence topped with razor wire came into view. Behind it stood the ranks of storage units, blue corrugated metal with white-painted letters. One was painted with a big, block letter "D". She pulled into the driveway, braked in front of the gate. The keypad that would open it waited. She reached through the open window to enter the code.

Her hand shook. She couldn't do it. She couldn't let Talys out, let him take her away from everything she valued.

"Are you going to drive me crazy, Talys?" she said to the rows of storage units behind the fence. "You tried before. Might as well go with what's successful. I won't be much use to you then, though, will I? Although maybe I'll lose it bad enough to set this place on fire one night—"

No. She didn't do things like that. She wasn't that kind of person.

She set her teeth, gripped the steering wheel and *pushed*. A fiery rill went through her, twisted her stomach, the flaying touch of magic. But this time the cacophony of smells, voices, impressions did not assail her. This time there was silence. Every foreign influence ricocheted off the shell of her will. No whispers would reach her. Dreams wouldn't torment her.

Her hands still shook—weakness this time. She might not suffer that horrible exposure to the external world, but magic still seared along her nerves.

Magic. She had to use it to escape it. She laughed, an angry, exultant chuckle.

"Looks like maybe I learned a little too well, huh, Talys?"

Chapter 14

The mail lay scattered across Amethyst's dining room table, a mixture of bills, car sales ads and solicitations for donations. And one opened, empty envelope containing something that made no sense whatsoever.

Amethyst's hand shook on the check she'd found inside. It was so unreal, she'd almost thrown it away. But somehow, tearing up a check made out in her name in the amount of $137,843.77 didn't seem like a great idea. So now she was on the phone, working her way up the food chain at Capital Title Company, trying to find out what the hell was going on.

It felt like part of some kind of setup, like any minute guys in ninja-chic would bust down her door and haul her off to some black site, and…

Her imagination failed her there. Or maybe she was afraid she *wasn't* imagining things. Maybe someone really *was* after her. She leaned her head in her hand to push out the thought.

"It's a mistake," she said into the phone. At the tone of her voice, Caramela sat up, perked her ears and wrinkled her forehead. "I didn't buy any property. I didn't sell any, either. Trust me, nobody owes me this kind of money."

She'd thought that magical *push* she'd given Talys would solve all her problems. The dreams, the insidious whispering. The creepy feeling of being watched. A problem like this one should be a relief. It wasn't. It felt like more of the same.

"I'm sorry, Ms. Rey," the woman at the title company said. "Everything was in order on the escrow statement. The seller signed the disbursement statement, on which you were listed."

Amethyst put the check on the dining room table and rubbed her eyes. "Fine. But I'm telling you, this money isn't mine. I'll return the check to you, or shred it, but I'm not going to deposit it."

"It's already been wire transferred. The document we mailed you is only a voucher."

Amethyst dropped her hand. "You mean it's already in my bank account."

"Yes, Ms. Rey."

Maybe, *maybe* someone had gotten a name mixed up—but a name like "Amethyst"? And how the hell had they gotten her bank account number? She didn't like it. It was weird, and she'd had enough weirdness over the last few weeks.

"Okay, listen. I need to get this money out of my account. I'm going to get a cashier's check and bring it over there, then you can file it or whatever until this is straightened out. How do I get to your office?"

The woman gave her directions to an office off Louisiana, in Uptown.

Amethyst thumbed off the phone and tapped a fingernail on the voucher. It could still be a mistake. A big one. If her bank balance was where it should be when she checked it online, she could stop worrying.

She headed through the house to her office-slash-guest bedroom. Her laptop still rested on the futon, nestled in the corner with a couple of patchwork pillows. Amethyst tossed the voucher aside, plumped into the pillows and fired up the machine.

Her balance showed $137,843.77, plus a few hundred.

"Damn."

Carmela had followed her into the room and was now intently sniffing the check.

"Yeah, it stinks, doesn't it?"

The fur along her back bristled from skull to the base of her tail. She didn't growl, but her tail did the stiff wag of a pit bull getting ready to rumble with an enemy.

Amethyst pulled into the Louisiana exit lane. The geometric patterns on the freeway sound wall blurred by on one side, the mid-morning I-40 traffic on the other.

She let up on the gas. The pickup hardly slowed. She frowned and raised her foot a little more, then finally let off the throttle entirely. The truck kept barreling along at 60 mph.

She cursed, foully.

She pressed the brake, then stood on it. The truck slowed reluctantly, engine racing, pulling against the drag of the brakes. Her heart raced too. Her hands on the wheel went slick with sweat.

A glance in the rearview mirror showed cars on the exit ramp close behind. The light at the top was green. The car ahead made the right onto Louisiana. Amethyst turned after it, tires screeching. Cars ahead, stopped at the light. The light she'd just come through had changed, and vehicles surged toward her in all four lanes. No place to get out of the way— No, wait. One of the left turn lanes was open. She steered for it.

She couldn't put the transmission into neutral—the engine freewheeling at full throttle would tear itself apart. If she turned off the key, the steering wheel would lock. She got the truck down to a bit-in-the-teeth few miles per hour. A car crossed the intersection ahead. She eased off the brake and made the left— against the light—through the intersection.

The smell of hot brakes and unburned gas filled the cab. Traffic on the side street was less. Office driveways zipped by, none with lots big enough or empty enough to accommodate a too-fast turn. Ahead and on the right, Magus Corporation's green glass pyramid reflected its own enormous parking lot. Amethyst's legs ached, stiff on the brake. She steered for the wide driveway, her breath shaking. The truck jolted up, across empty spaces. She pried a hand off the wheel and threw the shift lever into neutral. The engine screamed. She shut off the key.

The truck went silent and jammed to a stop.

Amethyst leaned her head on the wheel and breathed hard. Okay, she told herself, calm down. She hadn't crashed or burned—

The smell of gasoline was thick. She jerked her head up,

fumbled for the hood release.

The hood went up with a creak when she opened it. Gas was everywhere, dripping down the engine block, onto the pavement. She couldn't find the little rod that held open the hood. Bracing the hood with one hand, she popped the cover off the air cleaner. Gas fumes almost choked her. Gas swam in the carburetor.

Amethyst dropped the air cleaner cover and the hood and backed away. All that gas on a hot engine—

Her purse was still in the cab. The cashier's check for the title company was inside. She flung open the door and dived for her purse, then scuttled back again, waiting for flames to leap up around the hood.

Nothing happened. She let go a breath, half in relief, half in disgust. Melodie was right. The pickup was a mistake. Now she'd be out more money. A tow truck first, then a mechanic. She heaved another sigh, and this time it was all disgust.

She pulled out her phone and did a search for tow companies. She got a fast busy signal when she dialed the first one. She tried again, and again. Same thing. A bad feeling settled around her, the same one she'd had when she'd pulled out that $137 grand check.

Okay, some network must just be down. She dumped the phone back into her purse and trudged toward the Magus building, past row after row of cars. *Nice* cars, late models in every make, shiny and spotless. She could've had a nice car, too, if she'd stayed in the computer field. But oh, no. And the one nice car she'd had, she locked up—

She throttled that thought fast and took a long breath. One problem at a time. First, a phone.

The building's tall, Coke-bottle-green glass doors reflected her own image: a thin, jeans-clad woman with wind-tangled dark hair. That reflection might've been a systems designer returning from lunch on a windy spring day, heading back to lines of code and LCD screens in windowless, air-conditioned rooms. Her hand met the reflection's on the clear acrylic door handle. She pulled and the image disappeared.

The lobby inside was like stepping into a fairy cave, all green light and murmuring water and echoing voices. The floor was pink and grey and green stones—terrazzo, but not the cheesy, institutional-looking kind you saw in old government buildings. This looked like water-smoothed pebbles. On the far side of the space stood the fountain that made the water-noises. It was raw granite, at least ten feet high, like a natural waterfall somehow transported into an Uptown lobby. Water sheeted down and seemed to disappear into the floor.

Amethyst caught herself staring and started walking again. People in business dress waited by the elevator banks. Two young men in long t-shirts and baggy pants sat on a bench, talking animatedly. Programmers, Amethyst thought and smiled. The Suits were probably sales reps. Standing here and there like spellbound souls were sculptures—a crane made entirely of stacked sheets of glass, a massive polished stone with a hole piercing it, a dragon made of junkyard castoffs.

The patter of the fountain and the liquid light soothed, easing her upset and discontent. She took a few steps toward the dragon with its round washer eyes. No, she thought and stopped. She had more important things to do than admire art.

A security desk faced with brushed brass sat tactfully to one side. Amethyst ran fingers through her messy hair then headed that way.

The guard, a woman with a frontier face and graying blond hair tied back in a ponytail, smiled. "May I help you?"

Amethyst realized suddenly that she stank of gas. "Do you have a phone I could use? My pickup is broken down in your parking lot and my cell isn't working."

"There's a phone in the small meeting room next to the elevators. You're welcome to use it."

Amethyst hesitated. Most places would just offer the desk phone. But then again, this was a security desk. They probably didn't want to tie up the line.

"Thanks," she said and walked toward the door the guard

pointed out.

Voices, footsteps, water echoed strangely, combining until they almost sounded like a single voice, a subliminal murmur. She strained to hear words in it, then shook herself. She didn't have to worry about weird voices any more. She'd taken care of that.

The meeting room door swung open noiselessly, closed behind her with a solid thump. The lobby echoes fell silent, replaced by the hush of an air conditioning vent. An oval table in pickled oak and four chairs seemed to float in the underwater green light of the window. The cool air smelled vaguely of citrus and herbs. All soft, lulling, as if she swam in a peaceful green pool far from runaway trucks and money that wasn't hers.

She sat in one of the chairs and rubbed her eyes. She was so tired of problems. Tired, period. It had been one thing after another ever since Talys had shown up in front of her house. She wished the universe would give it a rest.

She leaned her head back and closed her eyes on the slim phone at her elbow, on her latest difficulties. The cool, tangy air swirled around her, smoothed the wisps of hair around her face, stroked her forehead. Worry ebbed, then thought. Her arms and legs grew at once both heavy and floating. She was comfortable, content, like sinking down into soft snow on a cold, clear night.

An image of a winter sky slid into her mind: black, scattered with points of light, a vast bowl of stillness, of silence. It cupped her like a hand trapping a butterfly. She lay beneath it, a bright fluttering in the beguiling night.

The black began to fray at the edges. The unraveling was shapeless at first. Lights winked out, others merged and brightened: highlights on a gleaming surface, two round, staring globes. An uncertain, unsettling shape began to form, one long and low and lean. A hood. Tires. A grille. A glittering chrome smile of bumper.

Amethyst jerked forward and snapped her eyes open. Her pulse raced again, but she was only in the little meeting room, alone with the table and chairs and phone. Had she fallen asleep?

Here?

Under the fluid caress of air, her skin burned as if with the residue of magic. But she hadn't done any magic. Only dreamed—imagined, whatever—the damned car. Again.

She rubbed the back of her neck. The watching tickle was back. She glanced up at the ceiling. She hoped the meeting room didn't include surveillance cameras, a definite possibility in a computer security firm. Embarrassment heated her face. The best thing she could do now was call her tow truck and get out of here.

Melodie snapped the menu shut and put it face down on the table. "God, Wiz, you look awful."

"Thank you, Ms. Jarrett, for that vote of confidence." Amethyst slid into the opposite side of the booth. The lunchtime crush was in full swing. Even with the restaurant divided into a series of small dining nooks, the din of voices was like the rush of a freeway.

Melodie wrinkled her nose. "And what's that perfume you're wearing? Eau de Texaco?"

Amethyst swallowed a snotty reply and said instead, "Sorry I'm late."

"Okay, what happened? Somehow I suspect it's more than splashing gas on yourself when filling up."

Amethyst pulled a second menu toward her. "Let's see. Where shall I start? The check? My truck? Or the sleep deprivation?"

"Oh, boy. I told you that truck was a mistake. Might as well start with that."

"The damn thing ran away with me. The throttle stuck wide open on the freeway."

"*What?*"

Amethyst waved a hand. Melodie was right—the smell of gas wafted to her even though she'd scrubbed. "The tow truck driver popped it loose—he showed me what to do if it happens again." He'd also suggested she get the hood-holder replaced. She put on a fake smile and said cheerily, "Didn't even have to take it to the shop."

"Jesus, Amethyst! Are you okay? Did you wreck it?"

Amethyst looked down at the menu. "No, I'm fine."

"You don't look fine. You don't act fine, either."

Amethyst puffed out a breath. "I'm behind on a job and the customer is getting mad. Then I have to deal with some kind of bank mixup."

"And you're worried and not sleeping. That explains it then."

Amethyst lowered the menu. "That explains what?"

"Everything." Melodie counted on her fingers again. "Your pale, hollow-eyed appearance, your short temper and your feeling of being overwhelmed."

The waitress brought water and took their orders.

What the hell made Melodie think she felt overwhelmed?

"Yeah," Amethyst muttered. "Maybe it even explains falling asleep in public places."

Melodie slipped the paper off her straw. "Of course it does. And don't look at me that way. My sister has terrible insomnia. I've learned a little." She took a sip of water. "I read a case study about this guy who went something like a month without sleep. He started hallucinating after a week or two. Then he got paranoid. He thought the doctors observing him were doing diabolical experiments on him." She rubbed her hands like a melodrama villain. "You know, watching him, out to get him. Bwa-ha-ha-ha-ha!"

Amethyst sat up straighter. "Really?"

"Yep. And it took him *months* to recover."

"Months." Amethyst slumped in her seat.

The waitress brought rolls and soup, and the air was suddenly full of the aroma of warm bread and onions and toasted cheese.

"A few good nights' sleep and you should be fit for company again," Melodie said. "Maybe then I can convince you what a bad idea that truck is. If it doesn't do the job itself before then."

Amethyst gave an exaggerated shudder. "Don't say things like that. I don't need any more trouble."

Chapter 15

Sunlight sparkled in the tumbled glass that ornamented the Eubank median. Trees tossed their boughs in the wind like teenaged girls tossing their hair. A young woman dressed as the Statue of Liberty stood in front of a tax preparation business and waved at the passing traffic. Amethyst grinned and waved back.

No more sleep deprivation. The title company had accepted the check. Even the awful Chevy pickup acted like it wanted to be reliable. Life was back to normal. So suddenly and completely, in fact, that "normal" felt really, really strange.

The finished sidelights for the DeBaca's atrium rode in the back now, all snug in Styrofoam and board frames. Amethyst still had the fanlight to finish, but it was foiled up, pinned down and ready to solder.

She stopped behind a line of cars. The light changed, the cars ahead accordioned out, and she pushed the gas.

The truck died.

She took a long, slow breath through her nose. She would *not* curse. She glanced in the rearview mirror. At least no one was honking. Yet.

She twisted the key in the ignition. *Ruh-ruh-ruh*. She cranked the engine again.

The *ruh-ruh-ruh* changed to *uhn. Uhn. Uhn*. The dreaded click and whirr of a dead battery was next, she just knew it.

"Dammit!" She banged the steering wheel. It gave a distressed *pong*. The cars behind were pulling around now, good Samaritans all.

She swung the door open. Well, it was a small truck. It was probably light enough to push. Even with the camper shell and stained glass windows. Maybe. Hopefully.

She put the gearshift in neutral, got out, braced a hand and shoulder on the doorpost and heaved.

The Chevy rocked an inch or two forward, then rocked back. She leaned into it, and it lurched forward a sullen foot or so. Her foot slid on the grit on the street. She reset her feet and shoved again.

The truck gave another reluctant lurch then rolled, as if it had suddenly become lighter. Amethyst snatched a glance back to see if anyone was behind, helping push, but couldn't see around the camper shell. And she had to pay attention to where she was going.

The light turned, and cars eased around her through the intersection. She kept pushing, steering left, the downhill direction, with one-handed jerks.

She finally began to feel the downhill grade. The truck picked up speed. She jogged alongside then hopped into the cab, steered across the street and into an Applebee's parking lot. The truck's momentum carried it out of the way. She set the parking brake, leaned back and panted.

"Are you all right?" a man's voice said.

Amethyst jumped.

A slim man stood beside the window. A—ah, well, *yes*— very good-looking man. She stared, realized she was staring but couldn't stop right away.

He had black hair and a pale face with uneven eyebrows— one had a little quirk to it. Eyes as black and deep as a backcountry summer night. He wore a tieless dress shirt of pale green with the sleeves rolled up, and he, too, seemed to be breathing hard.

Breathing hard… Like she was.

"Was it you? Helping me push my truck?"

He smiled and the entire Rio Grande Valley depressurized. It felt like it, at least—breath seemed suddenly hard to draw.

"No one else seemed to have any intention of doing so," he answered. "And you didn't appear to be getting far by yourself." He blinked as if a thought had just occurred to him. "I beg your pardon." He stuck a hand through the open window. "I'm Jas."

The handshake was on the friendly, this-is-a-woman's-hand-I'm-squeezing end of the scale, not like some men (and women, for that matter), who scrunched like they were in an arm wrestling match.

"Jazz?" she repeated. So far, she must sound like she had the IQ of a ham sandwich.

"Jas. With an *S*."

"Pleased to meet you." That was better. "I'm Amethyst."

The smile deepened and little crinkles appeared at the corners of his eyes. "Amethyst." He said it the way a prism splits sunlight into rainbows. "I suppose that makes us even."

"It—it does?" She had yet to get beyond single-syllable words.

"Name-wise, in any case. You see, we're both named for semi-precious stones."

Maybe there really was a lack of oxygen going on here. That would explain her lack of coherent thought.

"My name is actually Jasper. Thus Jas, for short."

"Oh! As in chalcedony, the green stone." She closed her mouth and bit the inside of her lip to keep it closed.

He made a face and laughed. "*Chalcedony*, ouch. Glad I didn't end up with that."

But he wasn't leaving yet. She might yet have a chance to prove she was an intelligent form of life. She cleared her throat. "It would be nice if I were to thank you for helping me." She smiled. "Thank you."

He bowed his head, a gesture that seemed somehow old-world and regal. "My pleasure. Do you think you'll need a tow?"

She was going to break her budget on tow trucks. "I'm hoping it's just flooded." She pulled the door handle.

He stepped back to let her out, then followed her around to the back of the truck. "That doesn't sound encouraging."

"It's not so bad. This has happened before. Or something like it, anyway." She could deal with the carburetor as long as she hadn't killed the battery. No way was she going to ask him to help her push-start it.

She raised the hatch and dropped the tailgate. Should she explain why she went to the back of the truck to deal with a flooded carburetor? *Well, Jas, you know that metal rod that flips up to hold the hood open? It's missing. If I can only find this stick I use…*

No, probably not.

Amethyst put a knee on the tailgate and clambered in, careful of the windows in their packing, bracing her feet on the wheel wells. Of course, the official hood-propping stick was at the front of the bed, on the difficult side of the windows.

She was conscious of Jas back there. Nothing like giving a man a view of one's backside to make a good impression. She snatched the stick and slithered back out. Jas was off to one side, so maybe he wouldn't have had that particular view. One could only hope.

He did, however, continue peering curiously into the back of the truck. "Is that a stained glass window?"

"Two of a set of three. I'm on my way to deliver them."

"May I take a look?"

She gestured a reluctant be-my-guest. Great. Here was a potential client, and she'd be embarrassed to tell him she was the artist. The truck didn't say much for her level of success. She gently rapped one knuckle with the hood-propping stick. With any luck, he'd think she was just the delivery girl.

He put a knee on the tailgate and leaned in. "This is tantalizing. I wish I could see more, but—" Ducking back out, he dusted off his trousers. "Are you the artist?"

She hesitated a moment, then said, "Yes." Oh, well.

"I don't suppose you have a business card with you."

Of course she did, and he shouldn't have had to ask. Any rational businessperson would have offered a card straightaway. She resisted an urge to rest her head in her hand.

"They're in the glove compartment…"

It never failed. Her apparent intelligence changed in inverse proportion to the attractiveness of the man. This one was very attractive.

"Would a portfolio, as well, be asking too much?" he added.

She opened the passenger door and fumbled in the glove compartment. "I have a flyer with photos of my work." But he'd asked for more than a flyer, hadn't he? "My complete portfolio is at home. I wasn't expecting to need it today…" She trailed off. She was blathering.

He turned, shading the flyer from the sunlight. A serious line appeared between the mismatched brows, almost as captivating as those crinkles at the corners of his eyes had been.

"Very nice," he said. "This one," he tapped one of the images with a graceful finger, "has a strong Art Deco influence, while the window in the back of your truck…" He caught her gaze. "….I thought saw some Art Nouveau curves there. You must be quite willing to indulge your clients' tastes."

Wow. And he knew art, too.

"Actually, I do prefer Art Nouveau, but…" She shrugged. "You know what they say—the customer's always right."

"Ah, but then where's the pleasure of working for oneself?"

She fiddled with the stick. "Oh, well, there's still, ah, a lot of satisfaction to it."

He folded the flyer into a neat little packet around her business card and tucked it into the breast pocket of his shirt. "By the way, I don't consider my rescue complete while you remain stranded."

"Oh. Yeah." She popped the hood, propped it up with the infamous stick and popped off the air cleaner cover. Once again, gas fumes came shimmering out. Not nearly as bad as last time, though. "Phew. Yep, it's flooded."

Now was her chance to demonstrate what a competent woman she was. She got her tools out from under the seat. Stuck a screwdriver into the carburetor to hold the choke open, just like her brother had shown her on that precious Toranado of his. Climbed into the cab, held the accelerator to the floor and cranked.

The truck started with its usual death rattle, then the engine blatted through the open choke. Jas disappeared behind the upraised hood and the blatting abruptly ceased. The hood went down next, and he reappeared carrying the damned stick. The screwdriver, too. She scrambled out of the truck and he handed both to her. His hands showed no trace of the oily grime that smudged hers. It was probably on a handkerchief now befouling the inside of his pocket.

"Thanks," she said again. Well, that was it, then, she supposed. Whatever fluttered under her breastbone suddenly fell. "Um... I appreciate your help. Can I buy you lunch?" Was that presumptuous?

"I'm glad to be of service." Again, that gracious nod, that dizzying smile. "And lunch is an excellent idea, but I'm afraid I'm on my way to a meeting."

She turned away and looked around. Hopefully, her face wasn't showing embarrassment and disappointment, but why take a chance? "Your car..."

He nodded cattycorner across the street. "I pulled into the gas station just over there."

He held out his hand again. She took it automatically, but he didn't shake it this time, just held it, a gesture that seemed somehow more intimate than it should have.

The noise of traffic, the truck's clatter, the smell of exhaust, the glare of sunlight on cars in the parking lot—all faded. There was only Jas, slim, not too tall, with his deep dark eyes, the feel of his fingers curved around hers, the bright tingling running up her arm to bubble in her middle, percolating up to fizz in her brain.

"I'm pleased to have met you, Amethyst," he was saying.

Polite. Gracious. Gallant, but that was all, wasn't it? What more interest could he have a woman so plain and unendowed—in more ways than one?

She clamped a lid on all the bubbling and fizzing, regained her hand. It was as if an electrical connection broke.

"Me, too." She gave a light laugh that sounded quite natural. "Definitely."

There was nothing left to do but get back into the truck, put it in gear, and continue on her errand. Nothing that wouldn't make her look like a moony idiot, anyway. She looked in the side mirror. Jas stood, hands in pockets, watching her drive off.

Probably making sure the miserable beater didn't conk out again. She stuck a hand out the window and waved. Stupid thing to do, like a school kid. But he waved back. She pulled out into the street and lost sight of him.

Her damp hands stuck to the tacky fake leather steering wheel wrap. Jeez. How pitiful. And she'd never even see him again, either—she recognized that fold-up-the-brochure gesture. A brief stop in the pocket before the ultimate destination of the trash can.

Amethyst sighed. Oh, well. It was interesting while it lasted. And a lot more pleasant than most of what had been going on lately.

◊ ◊ ◊

The phone rang. Amethyst eyed it, lifting her soldering iron from a joint between stained glass clouds. Talys had always shown a preference for radios, but...

Well, she couldn't get out of her head a ghost story in which a dead man kept calling his wife—and when the woman went to the cemetery, she found a phone line had fallen across her husband's grave.

Eeek.

She didn't like the suspicion that Talys would somehow find a way out of that storage unit. Maybe it was still guilt, maybe it was paranoia, maybe it was the knowledge that someday, she'd have to do something more...permanent. What, she didn't know—or want to think about. It was too much like planning a hit on someone—perhaps a persistent ex-boyfriend.

She slipped the soldering iron into its stand, braced one hand against her worktable and picked up the phone.

"Ms. Rey?" a woman's voice said.

Amethyst relaxed her grip on the edge of the table. "Yes, speaking."

"My name is Sylvia Liotta, with the Magus Corporation."

Magus Corporation! Amethyst flashed on her pickup, so recently dripping gas on their parking lot.

"Yes?" she said cautiously.

"We're interested in installing some stained glass in our building here in Uptown. You come highly recommended, and we'd like to invite you to submit a proposal."

"A proposal," she repeated, wrenching her mind away from the truck.

Was this good news? Could it be possible? The colors of the fanlight on her workbench suddenly brightened. She wondered who might have done the recommending. Not that she felt she didn't deserve it, but she was curious who had that kind of connection.

"I'd be delighted to," she said. "When would you like to meet?"

"You're welcome to come down anytime during business hours for a site inspection and to obtain a spec sheet," Ms. Liotta said. "After we've had a chance to review the various proposals I'll contact you again and set up a meeting with Mr. Harker, our CEO. He does all our acquisitions of this sort."

Amethyst deflated a little at that. Other artists would be trying for the job. But if she could get it…

It was likely a big job, paying plenty of money. Even better, something like this could make her reputation. No more quoting jobs on the cheap just to get them.

"Thank you, Ms. Liotta. If I can't make it this afternoon, I'll be there tomorrow."

She thumbed off the phone and gazed across the reds and oranges of the window in front of her.

Wow. When things decided to change, they *changed*. Hell on earth for a while, and now… Now who knew what could happen?

Chapter 16

Amethyst glanced at her reflection in Magus' eight-foot-high glass doors. Just like the last time, only now she wore a broomstick skirt, concho belt and long-sleeved black top. A silver clip inset with turquoise held her hair back, so she only had to smooth a few strands the wind had flicked over her shoulder. She was as ready as she'd ever be for this meeting with Mr. Harker.

She found herself clutching the portfolio containing her proposal and sketches and forced herself to relax. Her heart beat fast. She couldn't do anything about that, so she concentrated on her breathing, on keeping it slow and calm.

The lobby still impressed her. Intimidated her, too. The sculptures took on a whole new significance. Someone here liked art—and knew art, too. This was the big leagues.

She crossed the grey, green and pink terrazzo floor to the elevator and pushed the call button. Above the elevator was one of those big, old-fashioned dials with a needle that showed what floor the elevator was on, like those in fancy buildings in old black-and-white movies where the men all wore hats over slicked-down hair and the women wore chunky shoes and foofy blouses. The dial went up to 25, a tall building for Albuquerque. Maybe even the tallest.

The elevator opened, disgorging a young woman dressed all in black with blunt-cut black hair and a ruby eyebrow stud, arguing earnestly with a heavy-set young man who looked like he had no concept of "outdoors." Amethyst waited, pretended not to notice when they eyed her and stepped in after they exited.

Techno music played over the speaker—of course. The elevator glided up. And up. She flipped open her portfolio and dug through it for the name of the person who'd arranged the meeting. It was right on top: Sylvia Liotta. The same woman who had invited her to submit the proposal.

The door opened to a short corridor carpeted in pale green and with dawn-peach walls. A brightly-lit reception area waited at the end. Paintings adorned the walls. She wet her lips, smoothed her hair again and tried not to think about how good those paintings were.

She was good, too, she told herself. Otherwise she wouldn't have been asked here.

A skylight illuminated the reception desk's glass blocks and polished granite top like a beam from Heaven on Saint Peter's rostrum. If an old, bearded man in white robes had been sitting behind the desk, her intimidation would have been complete. Fortunately, it was a pretty Spanish woman who sat there, and she was actually dressed in a blouse and slacks. Maybe the Doc Martens and skater gear she'd seen on the pair in the elevator were only for the technical staff.

Amethyst offered her business card. "I'm here to meet with Mr. Harker to discuss my proposal."

"Yes, Ms. Rey. Will you please come this way?"

'This way' turned out to be another corridor that led to a small conference room. Her guide paused at the door. "Can I offer you anything? Coffee? Chai?"

"Chai would be nice, thanks." No ordinary tea here.

Not just chai, either. The receptionist returned with a plate of pastries, as well. "Mr. Harker will be in shortly." She left and the pickled oak door shut behind her with a quiet and yet impressively solid thump.

Amethyst couldn't just sit and drink chai. She put her portfolio on the table and paced to the window. It faced east, looking down on Uptown, the shopping mall with its glittering skirt of parking lots. The curve of I-40 crawled with traffic toward the wall of the mountains. There, houses crept up the foothills, finally giving way to rock and junipers.

The door opened again and she turned. A man—dark hair, less than average height—stood in the doorway, speaking to someone outside; she could see only the back of his head, a shoulder, his hand on the doorknob. Mr. Harker, no doubt.

Amethyst quickly sat down and folded her hands on the table. He turned, stepped in, and shut the door.

No *way*.

He smiled and offered his hand. "Amethyst. How nice to see you again."

Mismatched brows. Dark eyes with those crinkles.

Jas.

"Mr. Harker?" she said.

Jas was—CEO of Magus Corporation? Oh. My. God. She fought the urge to crumple in her chair.

He slid into the seat beside her. "Since we'd already met, I didn't realize formality was necessary. Shall I call you Ms. Rey?"

"Uh… No. Sorry. Amethyst…Amethyst is fine."

"Good. Then so is Jas."

She thought of how they'd met. The awful, ugly red Chevy seemed to crouch between them like a troll. She was here to convince him that she was the artist to create a window for his awesome lobby, and she drove a vehicle that would embarrass the paperboy. Damn.

"Well." She fumbled in her portfolio. "What did you think of my design ideas, ah, Jas? I've brought photos of several of my installations…"

She looked up. His eyes were on her, not the photos.

"Still so formal!" he said. "Here, have a pastry." He pushed the plate toward her. "That way I can eat and not feel ill-mannered about it."

She smiled—actually, the smile just happened, like a sneeze. "Thank you."

One looked like it might have a cream-cheese-and-pineapple filling. She took it.

He chose a scone and took a bite. "Now that we're in no danger of a board meeting's gravity, let's take a look at those designs."

But haven't you already seen them, in my proposal? She kept her mouth shut and slid the sketches over.

He studied them, then tapped one. "Printed circuit boards? Clever. A thematic tie-in that appears at first glance to be an abstract. As for the Southwestern scheme, I appreciate the Pueblo motifs as an alternative to the all-too-popular Navaho rug designs. But I confess myself disappointed."

"Disappointed?" she repeated faintly. That word felt like a misjudged step in the dark—*ulp*.

"Where is the Art Nouveau you favor?" he said. "The flowing lines, twining vines, rippling water, koi in ponds?"

"I'll be happy to sketch out those ideas." She shuffled through the photos on the table. Her hands were shaking. Great.

She managed to find the pictures she was looking for without much fumbling. "Here's a series of clerestory windows I did for a remodel down in the University area. Is that closer to what you had in mind?"

He took the photos from her fingers, laid them in front of him and rested his chin in one hand. "Yes, I like this very much. As I do the idea of koi in a pool."

She always brought graph paper and colored pencils to these meetings. This sort of give-and-take wasn't unusual. Why on earth was she such a knot of nerves this time?

Jas rolled his chair closer as she sketched. That prickling in her fingers was surely sweat—yes, the pencil suddenly went slippery. Stop that, Amethyst!

"Exactly," he murmured. "Bodies gracefully curved, just so, the ripples of the water all shades of jade, as in a Japanese garden. Simple, very Zen, to harmonize with the other pieces in the lobby."

That musing murmur was terribly distracting.

"Except for the found-objects dragon." It just popped out, like the smile had.

He laughed. "Yes, I saw that up in Madrid, and couldn't resist."

Not Madrid, Spain, but the ex- coal mining town on the other side of the Sandias, with its old board-and-batten miners' houses transformed into shops and galleries. Their unfinished, unlevel wooden floors and seedy-paned, mullioned windows only added to the charm.

"I think I saw other sculptures by the same artist," she said, struggling to recover. "They're cute. I've always enjoyed them."

"Ever had that ice cream they serve at the general store there?"

His blunder-skirting skills were absolutely incredible. "Oh, yes."

"Still good?"

"Still great."

"It's been a long time since I've visited the town," he said, then studied her, much as he had studied the pictures.

Amethyst held her breath. Or more like, her lungs seemed somehow to forget what they were doing.

He turned back to the sketch, and her lungs suddenly recollected their function. "Yes, good," he said. "I'd like another fish here, though, in this corner. The composition looks almost too balanced otherwise. Too Western, don't you think?"

Amethyst drew another fish, curled as if to dart off across the pond. It did make the design look better. She'd have to get a book on Japanese art before she worked up a presentation design. He seemed awfully well versed.

"Did you select the rest of the artwork I've seen here?" she asked.

"Most of it, yes."

"It's very nice." Did that sound ingratiating?

He inclined his head in that same, vaguely noble fashion she'd seen before. "Thank you. I run a technology firm here, but technology needs a leavening of..." He made a vague gesture. "Humanity? Soul?" He gave a wry laugh. "That sounds pretentious, doesn't it? Actually, I just enjoy looking at beautiful things," he said. Looking at her.

She let her gaze fall to the drawing and sketched in a water lily. Her lack of reply sounded loud as a shout.

"What do you think of this, rather than another fish?" she finally said.

He reached across her, covered the fish with a thumb. His arm rested on hers, and she held perfectly still.

"That's even better, as a matter of fact." He removed his arm and gave a smile that did the same thing to her insides that the warmth of his arm had. "I think we'll make a good team."

Grinning like a delighted thirteen-year-old would probably not be the best reaction to that comment.

"Great!" Hopefully, it came out with just the right amount of professional enthusiasm. "Do you have any other ideas for me to work with?"

He leaned back again, elbows on chair arms and fingers laced. "Mmm. Not at present. What's our next step?"

He surely didn't mean that to be the provocative question it seemed. "I'll work up a design that includes break lines and color, then we'll meet again to refine and finalize it. At that point, if you decide to accept my proposal, we'll get into the selection process. You'll look at glass samples and decide what types and colors of glass you want to go into the finished window."

"Endless possibilities."

She swallowed. She really had to stop reading things into his words that weren't there. Glass. He was talking about *glass*. "It can be an intimidating process, but I try to make it as easy as possible."

"Of course," he said.

She slid sketches and photos back into her portfolio. "When would you like to meet again? I should have this done by Friday, at the latest."

"Shall we say Monday, at two?"

He didn't even consult his phone for his schedule. Was his time that flexible, or was he willing to make it flex?

"I'll look forward to it," she said.

She gathered her things. He stood, extended a hand.

As before, in the Applebee's parking lot, he simply held hers with that courteous yet somehow intimate grip. "As will I." He relaxed his fingers.

◈ ◈ ◈

A good song was playing on the radio, Tears for Fears' "Head Over Heels." Amethyst sang along with the chorus line. The paintbrush glided along the door trim as if she simply unrolled the paint. She loved the colors Melodie had picked—melon orange with cream trim. She wouldn't mind painting her own walls that color. Too bad it would clash with the magic stained glass.

"You seem pretty happy," Melodie said.

Amethyst glanced across her friend's drop-clothed, masking-taped living room. Melodie slid her roller back and forth in the paint pan, a picture of perfect casualness.

Amethyst dipped her brush and smoothed off the excess on the lip of the can. "Do I?" she said at her most innocent.

"Um…" Melodie put a finger on her chin as if pondering. "Well…yeah. You're singing. Unless painting my living room is a lot more fun for you than it is for me."

Amethyst grinned and touched her brush once more to the angle of woodwork and wall. "I might have a job. A really good one."

Melodie's roller smacked the wall then squeaked up and down, laying down a broad swath of melon-orange paint. "Mmmm. And here I was hoping you were in love."

"Oh, please."

"Okay, so tell me about this job."

"It's for Magus Corporation."

"Magus, as in the computer security company?" Melodie's roller drooped. "Wait a minute, are we talking about a get-dressed-up-and-go-somewhere-every-day-type job?"

Amethyst snorted. "Are you kidding? No, a stained-glass-commission-type job. A big one."

"For a minute there, I was going to be jealous of you."

"Let's not get started on that again." The excitement that had been bubbling in her slid, as always, into nervous uncertainty. "Anyway, I don't actually have it yet."

"How did you get in on this job, anyway? Magus has a reputation for some pretty tight security. Not the sort of company to publish a public request for bids."

"Believe it or not, I owe it to my truck."

"Uh-huh." Melodie paused. Paint dripped from the roller and made orange drizzles on the dropcloth. "This I gotta hear."

"You were right," Amethyst said. "It broke down again, in the middle of the Eubank and Mongomery intersection this time." Melodie gave a disgusted snort, and Amethyst went on. "A guy stopped to help me push it. When we were trying to get it started again, he saw the windows I was taking to the DeBacas. Well, guess what? Turns out he's Magus' CEO."

Melodie put the roller in the pan and turned to face her, hands on hips. "The CEO of Magus Corporation helped you push your P-O-S pickup? And you *let* him?"

Amethyst ducked her head. "Well, I didn't know who he was at the time. And I didn't exactly let him. I only realized he'd been back there when this man appeared beside my truck asking if I was okay."

"Ah-ha! Don't think I don't see that big, silly grin. What's he like?"

"I am *not* grinning." Amethyst concentrated on the trim in front of her. "His name is Jas Harker. He's friendly, charming, and good-looking enough to make me act like a complete idiot. Hopefully he finds my artistic abilities more interesting than my social skills."

Melodie's brows crooked. "I'm missing something here. Hiring the help doesn't exactly seem like part of the normal CEO job description."

Amethyst shrugged. "He said art is his hobby. There's a lot of it in that building."

"Huh. Art. That's not something in the rumor mill."

Amethyst lifted the brush. "Yeah? What is?"

Melodie picked up the roller again. It went *squish squeak* on the wall. "That he keeps a very low profile. That Norton supposedly had a lawsuit against Magus that suddenly just went poof, and no one quite knows why. That Magus' competitors have suffered some, shall we say, convenient setbacks. Bankruptcies. Firewalls that let mean, evil, nasty viruses in to play on the mainframe."

"Oooh, conspiracy theories." Amethyst rubbed her hands. "Nobody makes up better ones than computer geeks."

"Yeah, I know. And it's pretty hard to engineer a financial meltdown. At least one that won't get picked up on an audit."

"Pretty hard to sabotage a competitor's software, too. Too many people scrutinizing it at too many different phases."

"So, what now?"

Something quivered in Amethyst's middle. Hadn't Jas asked that very question? "Now I wait to hear if I get the job."

Melodie gusted a sigh. "No, dear. I meant, 'what now' with Mr. Jas Harker, the good-looking CEO of Magus Corporation."

Heat prickled Amethyst's face. "What do you think? If I get the job, I'll probably work with him some. If I don't…" She hitched one shoulder. "He'll go back to doing his CEO thing, and I'll make Christmas ornaments and window hangings until my next commission comes along."

"You have *no* ambition." Melodie raised a paint-spattered finger. "Examine the possibilities. You're an artist, he's into art. You're a tech whiz, he owns a tech firm."

"*Was* a tech whiz. Past tense."

Melodie went on as if she hadn't spoken. "He keeps a low profile, you only come out of your workshop to buy groceries and deliver windows. Oh, and help paint living rooms."

"I'm not *that* bad—"

"It has all the signs of a promising relationship."

Amethyst's brush went *splat* on the plastic drop cloth. She scrambled to pick it up again.

"Come on, Mel, get real. This is a man who owns a multi-million-dollar corporation. He's going to have zero interest in a struggling artist."

"Whatever you say, Wiz. But when a guy arranges to see you again after an accidental meeting, it's a little more than zero interest in my book."

Amethyst bit her lip. *Do you think so?* she wanted to say. But no, that was silly.

She sighed. "It's just business." Melodie opened her mouth to argue, but Amethyst held up a hand. "And if you get me thinking it's anything more, I won't even be able to do business right."

Melodie held out the roller as if fending her off. "Okay, okay. Time will tell, anyway. Like you said, you haven't even gotten the job yet, right?"

Amethyst nodded once.

Melodie turned back to her painting. "But somehow, I just bet you do."

Chapter 17

Mrs. DeBaca looked apologetic for a change. And awkward.

"I don't know how you've done it, Ms. Rey."

"I'm sorry, I don't understand," Amethyst said. "Done what?" She'd been getting a bad feeling the last few days that she was in over her head. This was beginning to sound like she had a reason to worry.

"Your windows." Mrs. DeBaca gestured at the installed stained glass sidelights with a manicured hand.

Amethyst studied them. The panels depicted mirror image trumpet vines twining up a crooked juniper post, all in scarlet and green and desert tan. They looked good. The atrium was wasn't far from finished. Saltillo tiles covered the floor in warm, organic shades of orange with blushes of red. The French doors had been stained and clear-coated. She wondered what Mrs. DeBaca had found to complain about now.

Outside the open doors, workmen slid the fanlight out of the back of Amethyst's pickup, calling instructions in Spanish to one another.

Mrs. DeBaca swiveled and watched them. "Will—will that be going in today?" she asked abruptly.

Amethyst followed her gaze. "Um…I'm not sure." She shifted her weight. "Shall I ask Leo?"

Leo was the foreman, a big Mexican guy with a bristle of greying black hair. He made sure the workers didn't cuss in front of the customers, kept the jobsite nice and tidy and was smart enough to pretend he spoke less English than he did so the contractor had to deal with the clients. The wrinkle in this tactic was that Mrs. DeBaca spoke Spanish, but it was New Mexican Spanish. He pretended he couldn't understand that, either.

Mrs. DeBaca fluttered a hand. "No, no. That isn't necessary. I suppose it'll have to go in sooner or later."

What the hell was going on? "Mrs. DeBaca, I'd like to help, if I can."

The woman actually fidgeted. "You see, it's the most remarkable thing." She paused again.

Amethyst waited. She kept from chewing her lip with an effort.

"The windows..." She gave a nervous little laugh. "Well, they seem to glow even at night!"

Amethyst's stomach made a small, cold knot. "They must be picking up a streetlight somewhere. Or maybe reflecting light from inside the house."

Mrs. DeBaca laughed again. "My husband pointed that out as well. But the doors face the mountainside, as you see. And I was out here last night, when no lights were on in the house."

Damn. "Moonlight?" Amethyst said hopefully. "Cityglow?"

"No, not moonlight," Mrs. DeBaca said, but she suddenly seemed relieved. "I hadn't thought of the city's glow. That must be it."

Amethyst forced a smile. "I'm glad we figured it out."

"Yes, me too." She smiled back, and for once the smile seemed genuine. "Actually, it's quite a lovely effect, the colors of the glass muted and shimmering, almost dreamlike."

"Sort of magical," Amethyst said, trying hard to keep the irony out of her voice.

"Yes, exactly! Although I must say I'm happy to have found an explanation. That glow was quite unsettling at first."

Amethyst resisted the impulse to pinch the bridge of her nose. A customer finding one's work unsettling was *not* a good thing. Especially now that someone at Magus might be calling for references. She'd been trying not to think about that. One thing at a time.

"Then I'll just get out of your way now. Call me, please, if there's anything else I can do."

She made her escape, but paused to check on the window. It was fine. Nothing looked strange—yet. Still, she hovered, peeking under the boards and foam insulation that protected it.

"Cuidado de ella." *Take care of it*, she asked Leo.

He grinned and gave her a thumbs-up.

She grinned back, but her heart wasn't in it.

She got in the Chevy and slammed the door. The bad feeling was stronger than ever. Like she walked the tracks of the Doom Express, and the rails had begun to vibrate.

"Magic," she muttered and pulled out of the driveway. "Again!"

How had she managed to put magic into the DeBaca's windows? Especially when she'd explicitly decided to stick to old-fashioned, built-by-hand construction. Her stomach churned.

What next? If Magus—*Jas*—decided he wanted those fish on his window, would they suddenly start swimming? Or maybe the water from the stained glass pond would run down the walls; another fountain, this one horribly misplaced.

"Dammit, dammit, dammit!"

She couldn't, *couldn't* let magic leak into her work. But obviously, she didn't know how to stop it. She chewed her lower lip, winding her way down out of the foothills to Tramway Boulevard.

They might not be able to explain it, but people knew weirdness when they saw it. She'd lose referrals. She'd lose commissions. Hell, someone—someone like Mrs. DeBaca, if she didn't stay convinced—might want the window removed and payment returned.

Maybe that was what rode the Doom Express—financial ruin first, then the ruin of her career. The sun blazed through the windshield, but her fingers on the steering wheel went cold. And not just this career. Any career. If she had to go back to computers, what would code laced with magic do? How would magic-infused databases work?

Dr. Korhonen had warned her. He'd said she wouldn't be able to live like an ordinary person, that without learning what magic could do, she'd run into trouble.

And he'd offered to teach her.

She pulled to a stop at Tramway. Traffic rushed past at 50, 55 mph. Not something you wanted to pull into in an undependable vehicle without a substantial pause.

A car behind her honked. She jumped and hurriedly made a right onto Tramway, heading the wrong direction because it was easier. She'd just make a U-turn.

Okay, she told herself, she was panicking prematurely about this magic stuff. Think this through. She'd been working on those sidelights when Talys was around. In fact, she'd been working on them when she magicked up that damned window in her living room. Magic might be like an electromagnetic field, affecting nearby objects. She sat straighter. In fact, she wouldn't be surprised if that was exactly what it was like. The few times she'd deliberately touched it, it had seemed like an ether, something "out there," like air or charged particles. So a little of the magic that made the light behind her own stained glass window could have been transmitted to the DeBaca's sidelights.

She let out a breath. It was a reasonable theory. The problem was probably an isolated one. It had to be. If she had to replace—or worst-case, remove—one pair of sidelights, she could manage. Barely.

In the meantime, she had Jas' koi pond design to finish. Thinking about that pushed away the sense of disaster long enough to get home.

Something was going on at Caramela's house. An old Ford pickup hitched to a pickup bed converted to a trailer were backed up to the door. Appliances, beat-up furniture and box springs piled helter-skelter in the back of the truck. Mounds of garbage bags, weight-lifting equipment and something that looked like either a welder or an air compressor filled the trailer.

Moving? Amethyst's stomach turned over. *Caramela!*

She parked, unlocked the door and, distracted and heartsick, went inside.

Caramela stood outside the patio door, wagging. Joy and relief washed through Amethyst. At least she'd get the chance to tell the dog goodbye.

Keys still in hand, purse on her shoulder, Amethyst popped the lock and slid open the door. Caramela came in, butt and head happily swinging in opposite directions.

Her tail quivered to a halt. Her head came up. She looked past Amethyst, into the house, and the fur bristled down her spine.

The hairs on the back of Amethyst's neck rose, too. She clenched her fingers around the keys and turned.

Nothing. The chairs around the dining room table were straight, the appliances, the few breakfast dishes on the kitchen countertops unmoved.

Caramela stalked stiff-legged into the room, black nose twitching. Amethyst flared her own nostrils, drew in a slow breath. A faint whiff of cumin and garlic from dinner last night overlay the musty, sweetish smell of old house. She held her breath, listening. The refrigerator hummed. Nothing out of the ordinary. But still…

Caramela definitely picked up something. Amethyst did, too. The powerful sense that someone had been here in her absence breathed cold across her skin and coiled in her middle.

She lowered her purse to the floor. "Come on," she murmured to Caramela.

The dog went ahead, making a soft noise somewhere between a growl and a whine. Amethyst took a firm step after her, toward the kitchen, then another. The next few weren't quite so firm. By the time she neared the door to the living room, she was tiptoeing.

Caramela moved around the room, sniffing the art books on the coffee table, the Tiffany lamp, snuffling along the wall with the stained glass window.

A narrow strip of dust-free tabletop showed alongside of one of the books, as if it had been moved then replaced.

A trembling started in her. Amethyst forced it still and listened again. Except it wasn't exactly listening. It was more like opening senses she didn't know she had. Like she was a photographic plate exposed to every ambient glimmer. The sense of…invasion…grew stronger, but it didn't feel live, present. Something that had happened, wasn't still happening.

She set her teeth, fisted the keys with points protruding through her fingers and stepped into the living room. Caramela followed her nose down the hallway and into each of the bedrooms in turn, but didn't erupt into barking.

The living room looked okay. TV on its stand, stereo still in the entertainment center. She obviously hadn't been burglarized. Or vandalized. She moved toward the hall, following Caramela.

Behind her, something popped, then hissed. Amethyst spun. Her heart hammered, almost drowning that unidentifiable hissing sound.

No—not unidentifiable. Static.

Red and blue lights glowed on the stereo receiver. It had been turned off when she'd looked at it a second ago, she was sure of it. Billows of static came over the speakers. A voice whispered at the edges, as if the stereo was tuned to the very edge of a station. She couldn't pick out any words. But the voice was male, and sounded urgent.

"Talys?" Her voice quavered.

She caught snatches of syllables now: "oo," "dayn," "must." The voice could've been a DJ or talk radio blowhard. Or not.

"God *damn* it!"

She stormed into the living room, yanked open the glass doors that protected the stereo and punched the power button. The speakers fell silent.

"I don't want you," she shouted into the silent house. "I don't need you! Do you understand?"

The stereo stayed off, and nothing replied.

The Doom Express grew closer. Amethyst could hear the whistle now off in the distance.

What a stupid idea. Things were going great—fantastic, in fact. Why was she neurotically trying to ruin them? But the nagging, uneasy feeling made her pace to Melodie's dining room window again. Parting the curtain, she peeked out.

The street was still quiet, bluing toward night. Older homes, most remodeled and enlarged, sat well back from the street, yards landscaped with jointed cholla cactus and feathery desert willow. The enormous old Spanish broom on one corner of Melodie's property blocked much of the view that way, but she could see almost to the curve of the street the other way. A few nice, unthreatening late-model cars parked on the street, and those were the same as the last time she'd looked.

Headlights came around the curve. At first she couldn't see anything else, then a streetlight outlined something low and sporty. She tensed, then relaxed. The orange sodium vapor made it impossible to tell colors, but for sure the car wasn't black. It wasn't the right shape, either, and looked way too new.

"Everything okay out there, Amethyst?" Marl said from the sofa.

She dropped the curtain and turned hastily. "Oh…fine. Just…" She shrugged. "Restless, I guess. Sorry."

His lips curved in a quirk half amused, half understanding, he lifted a page of the document Amethyst had brought. He leaned an elbow on the sofa arm. "I'll be finished here in a minute."

"Okay. I'll set the table."

Amethyst opened doors and drawers in Melodie's antique buffet and forced herself to be quiet. Paper whispered as Marl turned over a page. Amethyst glanced over her shoulder, but he was still reading.

"Marl," she said, pretending calm. "Do you know where Melodie keeps her placemats and napkins? I can't find them anywhere."

"In the bottom drawer on the right, in the Pier One bag."

"Oh. Yeah. Thanks." She should have known. Everyone kept placemats and napkins in the store bag they brought them home in, didn't they? The drawer squeaked when she opened it, and a smell of old hardwood unfurled.

The smell reminded her of when she was little, exploring

the drawers of the handmade dresser at Nani's, her grandmother's, house. Of how once she'd found strange little packets of herbs, pale and powdery with age; a snakeskin; a tiny, unidentifiable figure carved from agate.

Amethyst suddenly gripped the edge of the drawer. She'd forgotten. Family history said that Nani's mother had been a *curandera*—a folk healer. A shaman. Amethyst had dismissed the tale as old ladies' superstition. Now—

She sat down hard on the rug. Stories said that some *curanderos* did more than use herbs to treat ailments. Some warded off curses or *mal de ojo*—the evil eye. They sang spirits to help them in their work. They interacted with the supernatural.

She clutched the bag in her lap. Mary Mother of God. *Her great-grandmother—*

Paper rustled again. Amethyst scrambled to her feet, shoving down the stunned realization so it wouldn't show on her face. Marl was folding the document.

"This is a fine contract," he said. "Congratulations, Amethyst."

She let out a slow breath and put the placemats on the table. "It's a bigger contract than I've ever signed. And more complicated."

"Corporate contracts are like that." He laid the papers on the coffee table, clearly in lawyer mode in spite of his polo shirt and jeans. "Don't worry about it. This one is on the up-and-up."

She nodded slowly. "Good."

She set out the placemats and napkins. He watched her. "Something has you worried?"

Oh, just this little matter of possible magic leaks. And an inheritance I didn't realize I had. "Higher stakes, I guess."

She crossed to the living room and picked up the contract. With a fingertip, she traced Jas' signature, a series of bold, indecipherable loops beneath the description and location of the job. Just seeing that signature somehow quieted her jangling nerves. It seemed to say, *Relax. All is well, nothing to worry about.*

"And the stakes are higher than she's letting you know,"

Melodie said from the kitchen door.

Marl shot Amethyst a concerned look. "How so?"

Melodie leaned a hip on the door frame and smirked. "You mean she hasn't told you about Jasper Harker, the good-looking CEO of Magus Corporation?"

Amethyst hunched her shoulders. "Mel…"

"The one who signed that paper she's hanging over?"

A look of interest replaced Marl's concern.

Amethyst snatched her fingers away from the contract, but she knew better than to rise to the bait. "Marl, will Bree and Jenna be joining us tonight?"

He took the hint without even blinking. "Jenna was invited by Sophie next door for dinner and an overnight. Bree, being seventeen, would consider it a punishment to spend a Saturday night with the geezers."

"You remember those days, don't you, Wiz?" Melodie said. "Acting goofy with your friends, hanging out, ogling boys—"

"Hey," he said. "Don't even *say* that."

Apparently she'd decided to tweak Marl for his misplaced gallantry. In fact, what Amethyst mostly remembered was coming home, doing homework and chores, reading and poking programs, two fingered, into her two- or three-generation-old DOS-based machine. Any ogling she'd done had been mixed with too much hopeless longing.

Melodie arched a brow. "It's something you'd better come to grips with, Papa. Sooner or later, girls and boys get interested." She slid a wicked glance at Amethyst. "Take, for example, our own dear Wiz."

"You know," Amethyst said, "I was under the distinct impression I was invited here for a celebratory dinner. If I'd known it was a roast, trust me, I'd never have come."

Melodie took amber-colored Mexican glass plates from the buffet. "And a celebratory dinner it is. But perhaps there's more to celebrate than the contract." She arranged the plates around the table. "Perhaps there's a budding romance, too."

Amethyst's face heated. "Oh, *please*. A business lunch is

hardly a romance."

Melodie nodded significantly at Marl. "Two hours. At The Gastronome."

"Whoa," Marl said. "That sounds like pretty serious business to me."

"Serious enough that he took her on a personal tour of the facility, too," Melodie said.

"I'm never telling you anything again!" Amethyst said.

Marl *tsked*. "Above and beyond the call of duty."

Amethyst huffed an exasperated breath. "Not you, too!"

"Tell her, sweetie," Melodie said to Marl. "Tell her men don't go to that kind of trouble without a reason. Especially men who run large corporations."

"I think I just did."

"Well, he's not buying flowers yet," Amethyst muttered. "I must be safe."

"Safe!" Melodie squawked, then flung back into the kitchen. "You're hopeless!"

Amethyst looked at Marl. He only held up his hands helplessly.

She sighed. "Excuse me," she said and followed Melodie.

Melodie stirred a pan on the stove. She didn't look around when Amethyst walked in.

"C'mon, Mel. Don't make it such a big deal."

"Okay, fine, whatever," Melodie said. "You're not interested in the man. Anyway, it's none of my business."

Amethyst sighed again and leaned on the edge of the countertop. "I *am* interested. I'm *too* interested. But there's no way he can be interested in me, don't you see? We're not talking about some nice, ordinary guy—somebody you'd meet at the grocery store, say—"

"Wiz, you met him when he helped push your truck."

"A guy who owns a big-gun computer security conglomerate. Let's be realistic here. People like that do not fall for members of the laboring class. Whatever Jas is doing, I can be pretty sure that it won't be going anywhere serious."

"So you're already planning to marry him, or what?"

"No," Amethyst spluttered. "But—" She picked at a line of grout. "What happens if I start to really like him, and all he's interested in is a fling. Or even worse, what if he's only the kind of man who's friendly when he does business?"

Melodie put on oven mitts, opened the oven door and slid out a casserole. Savory steam unfurled into the kitchen. "If he wants a fling, you say, 'Oooh, let's have fun,' or, 'I'm flattered, but that's not my style.'"

"God."

Melodie put the casserole on the stovetop then a mitted hand on her shoulder. "It's not that bad, Wiz. People survive worse every day."

"That's not what I'm worried about. No matter what I feel, the man has just given me a very lucrative job, one that could get me other lucrative jobs. I *cannot* afford to screw it up."

Melodie pushed out a breath. "Okay, granted. But try to trust yourself a little. How many major, horrible, life-ruining mistakes have you made?"

Amethyst pushed out her lower lip. "Not many. So far."

"So what makes you so sure you'll make one now?"

Amethyst grinned suddenly. "Unreasonable hope and sheer terror."

Melodie threw up her hands. "I knew it."

"Okay, have I bared my soul enough for one day? Can we sit down and eat dinner like civilized people?"

Melodie picked up the casserole. "Get the salad and dressing out of the refrigerator."

Marl had moved into the living room. He put down the magazine he'd been reading and ambled into the dining room. "I feel like I'm in the waiting room of my therapist's office."

Dr. Korhonen? Amethyst wanted to ask. Then she remembered that Dr. Korhonen didn't have a waiting room. She wondered again how exactly his business card *had* gotten into Melodie's Daytimer. Or if it had really been in there at all. It was beyond creepy that a wizard could arrange circumstances that way, and no one ever knew he was doing it.

A vague worry, a sense of wrongness flickered over her. No, not wrongness, that was too strong a word. More like someone whispering, trying desperately to attract her attention, but she couldn't quite hear.

Amethyst picked up the contract Jas had signed, lying folded on the table. She didn't open it, but only slid it through her fingers. The nagging dissonance faded. It had to be fear of success, that she wouldn't be up to the job. Nothing more than that.

Marl passed the salad bowl. She tucked the papers under the edge of her place setting, safe and close.

Chapter 18

Traffic humped and wavered past, a distorted reflection in Glass Attack's storefront. Amethyst caught herself watching it—again, and pointlessly, since she didn't know what Jas drove, anyway. And since he was supposed to meet her here, it wasn't like she was going to miss him, was it?

Damn Melodie, anyway! It was her doing that Amethyst was surveying the street—in the reflection in the glass—like a teen-aged girl hoping for her crush to drive by in his hopped-up, low-ered-down ride, take your pick depending upon era. Her face prickled. Not that Jas was her *crush*, thank you very much.

Late afternoon sunlight glittered on fenders and windshields and wheel rims. She caught a flash of chrome, black paint on something crouched low over its wheels.

She whipped around, scanning the traffic. No, she didn't see it now.

Forget it, she told herself. Unless the damned Mustang re-appeared in her driveway, she had more important things to worry about, like getting this project beyond the design stage.

Cars were leaving Kirtland Air Force base, and even the early throes of rush hour traffic were never any fun to drive in. Maybe this wasn't a good idea, having Jas meet her here. But…

She sighed. Well, Jas preferred greater involvement in the design process than the average client, to put it delicately. An endless series of meetings wasn't going to get the job done.

A car pulled into the driveway at the far end of the strip mall. Amethyst didn't let herself zero in on it like a cruise missile. She just glanced as if she had no reason in the world to be nervous or impatient.

Idling back down along the parking lot, the car, a deep emerald green, came toward her, pulled into a space. An Infiniti of some kind, judging from the grille emblem, but no kind of Infiniti she'd seen before. This had all the attitude of a Jaguar, announcing to the street, 'Not only do I have money and taste, but style, too.'

The door swung open and Jas climbed out, dapper as always in slacks and a shirt of dove grey with a pale green tie.

"I almost missed the place," he said. He hit a button on his keychain and the car's locks snicked and the alarm bipped on. "Fortunately, I caught a glimpse of your truck down at the end of the lot."

The Chevy was good for something, then—other than a constant source of embarrassment.

"I appreciate your taking the time to come—"

He waved her words away. "Don't think I don't realize your extra effort on my behalf. I appreciate *your* patience." He stepped forward and opened the shop's door for her.

Her heart did the conga. Come on, she told it, don't be ridiculous. Men do still open doors for ladies in this town. She stepped through the door. Okay. Mind on business. In this case, choosing glass.

She was glad, after an hour or so, that she gave the shop much of her business. Otherwise, she'd be embarrassed at the number of sheets of glass dragged out and scattered across the countertops and light table. Even Deb, the woman who owned the shop, looked somewhere between amused and amazed, and she'd been in this business a lot longer than Amethyst had.

Jas glanced at his watch. "This is enough for today. I don't want to keep this lady past closing."

"Would you like to take any glass samples?" Amethyst asked.

He tugged at his lower lip a moment, then deftly separated several sheets. "These are promising. Let's see how they look beside those you showed me already, then we'll go from there."

At least she could put away some of the glass while Deb rang up and wrapped the foot-square samples.

"Here," Jas said, taking the parcel. "Let me have that."

It wasn't right for the client to carry the glass, but arguing about it would be worse. And it didn't help that Jas also walked her to the truck. She pretended there was nothing strange about having parked at the far end, partially hidden behind the dumpster.

He put the glass on the floorboard, straightened and dusted off his hands. "I'd like to repay you for your patience. Will you let me take you to dinner?"

Dinner?!

She really needed to remember that breathing was not optional, no matter how many acrobatics the rest of her insides were doing. Besides, one needed to breathe to make a proper reply, something along lines of, *I'd love to, but let's finish the project first.*

"I'd love to," was what came out. She closed her mouth a little too quickly.

Jas beamed. "Excellent. How about Giannini's?"

Oh, yes. That would be the place where the valet would curl his lip as he took the keys to her truck and held them at arm's length, even if he didn't suggest that she might instead wish to patronize the Pizza Hut down the street.

"Great!"

His glance flicked over the horrible Chevy. "Why don't we ride together?"

This was beginning to look like a date. In fact, if she wanted to flatter herself, the whole situation had all the earmarks of a set-up: the late afternoon appointment away from the office, the lengthy process of choosing glass. If it was, she had to admire Jas' style. He'd inveigled her into it with a minimum of protest.

But she still had to answer, and the pause was reaching uncomfortable proportions.

"I don't want to make you go out of your way…"

He made an inviting gesture toward his Infiniti. "Not at all."

He also opened the car door for her. Amazing. Hardly anyone did *car* doors. It closed behind her with a *thunk* of precision-crafted steel, unlike the Chevy's tinny clap.

She studied the cockpit around her, all leather and burlwood accents, with a GPS system.

Jas got in and turned the key. The engine started with a well-tuned purr that scarcely vibrated the car. He hooked an arm around her seat as he backed out of the parking space. Amethyst folded her hands in her lap and swallowed. How had she never noticed how snug the interior of a car was? And sitting in these soft, leather seats was like…like being cradled in the palm of a hand. His hand.

She cleared her throat. "I see you have an onboard computer system."

The GPS system got her through a few miles of street and several traffic lights. She didn't have to pretend to be interested and enthused, and she even got to play with it.

The sun slanted their shadows long across the restaurant parking lot. Really, she thought, it was far too early for a romantic tête-à-tête. Then she stepped inside.

Uh-oh. Cloth-covered tables, flickering candles, low violin music in the background. Her cotton blouse and chinos felt instantly grubby. Smoothing her slacks, she followed the waiter with his spotless apron and elegantly bound menus. Only two of the tables they passed were occupied.

Jas pulled out her chair. She made a bumpy business settling into it. She folded her hands under the cloth-covered table with its napkins folded like little Napoleon's hats, a formidable array of silverware, a candle glowing in a glass globe. Okay, she wouldn't be intimidated. It wasn't like the waiter was going to give her a quiz on which fork was for what.

Amethyst opened the menu. Scanning the prices, she made an effort not to wince. She also managed not to gasp anything like, *An entire third-world village could eat for a month on what they charge here!*

"See anything interesting?" Jas said.

"Hmmm." He'd invited her to dinner, so she likely wasn't expected to pay. Nevertheless, good manners dictated that one not order more than when footing the bill. "The Caesar salad sounds good."

He lowered his menu. "Too early for dinner?"

"Ah…" Good manners weren't improving matters. "Actually, I haven't heard of most of these things. I was expecting spaghetti and ravioli and—" She glanced around and lowered her voice. "Pizza."

He laughed. "Well then. I can definitely recommend the chicken Marsala. And spaghetti does come with it."

"I'll give it a try."

The waiter returned, and Jas ordered for them both. He also ordered wine. The waiter gave a little bow and departed.

Wine. Oh, dear. It suddenly became much easier to study the silverware than meet Jas' gaze across the table.

"Did you know I intended to hire you once?" he said.

She looked up. "Hire me?"

"Seven years ago. I thought your name sounded familiar, and discovered I was correct when I saw your security profile."

"My *what?*"

He reached out a placating hand. "I'm sorry. No one mentioned it? It's routine—required of contractors as well as employees. I'm sure you understand."

"Oh…yes, of course. I hadn't thought…" Damn! She hadn't. But what could he find? A traffic ticket. A few lates on bills, no big surprise there.

What about that time she'd hacked into the university's mainframe? All just to prove she could do it. But no one had caught her…

Had they?

"Your marks in the CS program caught our eye back then," Jas went on. "I can't speak for anyone in Human Resources, but I was personally disappointed when I heard you intended to pursue other things."

What did she say to that? Fortunately, the waiter arrived with the wine, and Jas paused to inspect the label, inhale the aroma and swirl a sip across his palate.

Gosh, the things a girl was exposed to, hobnobbing with the upper crust. The art of wine tasting. Superb automobiles. Men with the kind of manners you mostly only saw on PBS programs. She took a sip of wine and thought, *I could get used to this.*

He twirled the stem of his glass. "Quite a change, from IT to stained glass. Have you ever had second thoughts?"

In the low light, his eyes seemed deeper and darker than ever, but his expression was open and interested.

"Certainly the pay would've been better if I'd stayed in the IT field," she said. "But…"

She fiddled with her own wine glass. "It seemed something was lacking. Programming, even systems design, is so…lifeless. No, that's not quite it. One-dimensional. If reality were a Renaissance painting, with computers, the most you can get is a few lines on newsprint." She took a hasty sip of wine. Great. She'd just insulted the man's livelihood. "Don't get me wrong. I still enjoy working with computers. And let's face it—the world would probably fall apart without them."

"They simply didn't fulfill your creative instincts," Jas offered.

"Exactly," she said on a relieved sigh. "When I was finishing up my bachelor's coursework, I felt like there was something in me that if I didn't let out, I'd explode—"

That made it sound like she had issues with repressed impulses. Why couldn't she just carry on a conversation like a normal person?

He picked up the napkin-covered basket of bread the waiter had brought. Pondering how to respond to the lunatic across the table, no doubt. Maybe considering that he still had dinner to get through, and afterward, share the close confines of a car with her.

"Believe it or not," he said, "I understand what you're talking about."

He offered bread. The fragrance of sourdough wafted out. The distraction of knife and butter kept her from blurting out, *You do?*

"My outlet is managing my company," he went on, "prodding here and tugging there to ensure its success. You might be surprised how much creativity that enterprise requires at times."

"It's a competitive field."

He paused on the way to taking a bite. "Ah. So you *do* still keep up with it."

"I try to. My best friend went through the IT program with me, and… Well, she's always accusing me of wasting my talent. I mean," she said quickly, "that's what she calls it, my 'talent'…" She stuffed bread in her mouth and chewed.

Jas propped chin on fist. "I'm afraid I happen to agree with her."

Amethyst didn't actually choke on the bread. It was more a muffled snort. A startled muffled snort.

"I should qualify that by saying, *one* of your talents. Have you ever considered returning to the field? Part-time, perhaps? We're always looking for white hats to prove the applications."

White hats. As in hackers who broke into computer systems at the owner's request—or tried to. Did that mean something was buried in some datafile somewhere about that hacking incident?

"I read the trade magazines and play around at home with my own system, but any more, the most I'm competent for is programming databases for small offices," she said.

Was this whole dinner thing set up for that—a job offer? No, that was crazy. He had access to people with technical skills far more current than hers. Which left the option that he was trying to do her a favor.

Why?

He took a sip of wine. "I doubt it would take you long to get up to speed."

Thinking about that *why*, her face started going hot. She ducked her head and gave a laugh. "But then who would make your window?"

"All right." He sat back and devoted attention to his bread. "I won't push. But please, do consider it. And remember, the offer stands."

"Thank you. I appreciate it." She did. He might have ulterior motives, but it was still a kind offer.

"Mmm. You've gone formal again. Have I scared you off?"

"N-no. Not at all."

"Good. Because that certainly wasn't my intent." Idly turning his wine glass, he studied her a moment. "I've enjoyed working with you a great deal."

Try to trust yourself a little, Melodie had said. The problem was, though, was Amethyst reading Jas' signals right? She'd rather die than make a fool of herself in front of this man.

"Me, too," she said.

There. That couldn't possibly get her into too much trouble, now could it?

Soliloquy – Third Voice

*H*e mustn't take it. He mustn't. This time, it might destroy him.

He paced. The carpet whispered beneath his bare feet. The vague shadows of bed and dresser and nightstand loomed against the paler blur of walls and curtains. Orange city light glowed around the edges of the blinds.

So much had gone wrong, so much he'd never expected. Oh, not in the beginning, of course. He remembered the first he'd taken, the warm rush of vitality that had filled him, strength, *power*. The feebleness, the pain, the weariness, all gone as if the long, wearing years had wound backwards. Each new day brought triumph and fierce joy, not dread, not death approaching with withered flesh and sunken eye.

He hadn't taken the first deliberately. No, he'd been forced to. What else could he have done, faced with that vicious young man? He could still remember that grin, the front teeth chipped so they looked like a dog's bared teeth. And once the deed was done, why waste what was offered?

What a revelation that had been! That a wizard with the knowledge, with the power—himself—could pluck such a jewel of impossible enrichment! How easy it had become—after all, so many used what they had for selfish or evil ends, and really, he did the world a favor by removing their ability to act.

He hadn't known there would be a price to pay. He hadn't known he would come to require those jewels, that rare and precious elixir within. And the greater effects…

He shuddered. He'd looked around him one day and realized that he was alone. Any of his peers who remained had hidden themselves so thoroughly, he could detect nothing more than presence, as if entering a seemingly empty room that held an elusive scent. Worse still, he couldn't deny now what he'd wrought, not when those consequences wracked him every moment of every day, awake or asleep.

Shaking, he hugged himself. He mustn't take the power. It wasn't helping any longer. It was, in fact, worsening the situation. How could he have guessed the paradox involved? The more he took to strengthen himself, the more strength required—

"I can't continue like this." In the darkness his voice shook as if on the verge of tears. "This is no way to live, this bare survival." And the magic gave him so much pain, always more pain.

But there hadn't been much power to take these last years, so little to find. Perhaps if he availed himself of the bounty now offered—

He clenched his fists behind him, one inside the other. He'd taken so many already, the entire structure was crumbling. It tottered and groaned around him even now. Only his restraint could save it.

Save it, yes. With his death. What did a corpse care what came afterwards?

"Idiot! I'll be a corpse either way, whether I fade or whether the magic burns me alive!"

But was he so sure those were the only choices? He'd only been sipping strength lately. Clearly, it hadn't been enough. Now that he'd found a wizard bred to survive this brutal, savage environment—

He twisted his fingers in his hair. "No! I cannot!"

Faces reared up before his mind's eye, mouths stretched in pain, eyes wide with terror and betrayal. He pressed the heels of his hands against his eyes as if that could drive out the images. Blood pounded in his ears, but not loud enough to drown the memory of agonized and despairing wails.

He shouted and flung out his hands. Light bloomed everywhere. Walls glowed, the dresser mirror shone like a sun, the design on the bedspread glittered like a constellation.

The faces and cries faded. He held his hands clenched to his mouth.

"I couldn't help it," he pleaded, with himself, with the memories. "I couldn't simply let myself die, not while I had the means to prevent it. They—they would have done the same, had they known how, anyone would. And…I've never killed… No. I would never do that, of course not, that would be unforgivable."

Perhaps he hadn't killed. But could he say the same if reality imploded?

Would it truly? Surely reality was sufficiently robust to withstand the actions of one man.

But that was the essence of magic: its far-reaching and not always predictable effects upon the ordinary world. And he had been tampering with, if not magic's underpinnings, then the keystone species of its ecosystem. Certainly, there was evidence enough in the natural world to demonstrate the disastrous results of such tampering.

"Every system has self-correcting mechanisms," he scoffed.

Unless the system has been so badly damaged that those mechanisms can no longer function.

"Very well then. The situation must require intervention. Who better than myself to intervene?"

With more of the same? Another power taken. Another face to haunt him.

He paced again, knotting and unknotting his hands behind him. "I'll admit magic's instability, but to be corrected, it must be managed. I know what has gone wrong, none better. This has gone beyond simply my own survival. The survival of far more is at stake, now."

But he'd spent time with Amethyst, heard her laugh. She was a gentle, pleasant young woman. How could he possibly do this to her?

He walked to the window, parted the blinds, peered outside into the night. "She has refused the power. I will be taking nothing she values."

But…the consequences! To her, to the magic…even to himself—

Turning back, he shut off the argument, the quivering fears.

"I have no other choice," he said to the room glowing like the interior of the jewel that was his own soul. "And very little more time."

Chapter 19

Amethyst rolled up the stained glass pattern. She caught herself humming. Humming, for godsake!

"Back to Earth, Amethyst," she told herself. "You're way happier than you should be."

The phone rang. Something danced around in her middle. She scowled, tried to calm down and snagged the phone. It was only Melodie.

"Hey, Marl and Jenna and I are going to play miniature golf at Cliff's," she said. "Wanna come? We're going for dessert afterwards."

Amethyst clamped the phone between ear and shoulder and tied a length of twine around the pattern. "Thanks, Mel, but I can't tonight. I'm meeting with Jas."

She could almost hear Melodie's brows go up. "Another *meeting*, huh?"

Amethyst rolled her eyes despite a stubborn bubbly tickle inside. "I'm hanging the full-scale pattern tonight. I can't do it during business hours. I'd be in the way."

"Oh, yeah, sure. Look, why don't you call when you're finished. Bring Jas. We'd love to meet him."

Would she dare? Jas had taken her to enough lunches over the last month. She could tell him she owed him. "I'll see how things go."

"Great!" Melodie sounded honestly delighted. "And don't you dare chicken out."

◇ ◇ ◇

The aluminum extendable ladder banged on Amethyst's hip. Echoes racketed around the Magus Building lobby, overwhelming the fountain's liquid voice. At the reception desk near the elevator, the security guard, the large Hispanic woman who worked the evening shift, glanced up.

"Wassup, Amethyst?"

"Hi, Lena," Amethyst called back. "I'll be taping up the pattern so Mr. Harker can see what it'll look like. Let me know if I'm in the way."

She schlepped a couple more loads from the back of the little Chevy and arranged everything out of the way. The lobby was empty. She extended the ladder and braced it against a crossmember over the door.

A telephone's discreet chirp sounded at the reception desk. The guard answered it, then rose and rounded the desk. The utility belt around her middle bristled with a two-way radio, Mace, handcuffs and nightstick. "I gotta step away. You got everything you need? I'll need to lock the doors."

Amethyst checked. Tools, tape, purse, pattern for the new window, sample window on a stand near the doors... "Yep, I should."

"Okay. Mr. Harker said to tell you he'll be right down, but if you need anything, just call the security office."

"Thanks," Amethyst said.

The woman nodded and ran a card through the scanner by the doors. It beeped and a light turned red. The back of Amethyst's neck prickled.

That was silly. So she was locked in. A phone call, and she'd be out again.

The guard made her way to the elevator, her businesslike shape a contrast to the fairy cave lobby.

Amethyst slid the roll of tape over one wrist, tucked the pattern under an arm and climbed to where the finished window would be installed. Outside, the parking lot was nearly empty, a handful of cars stretching shadows across the asphalt. She taped one edge of the pattern to the window and began unrolling it, masking the view.

The elevator chimed. Her watch showed 8:12. Across the lobby, the elevator door slid open and Jas stepped out.

She ignored the quiver in her middle. Actually, she was getting used to it by now, because no matter how often she told herself how hopeless it was, the anticipation, the pleasure of his company didn't go away.

She concentrated on smoothing down the last piece of tape, then hurried down the ladder. Jas was in a hurry, too. The heels of his shoes snapped even above the fountain's splash. He glanced aside at the empty reception desk.

"Hi, Jas," she said.

"Amethyst. I'm late, I apologize."

"No problem." She slid the roll of tape off her wrist and gestured to the pattern taped above the doors. Now that she saw it up there, it looked pretty damned good: a swirling collection of black lines depicting swimming fish and rippling water. "What do you think?"

He studied it, then the sample section of window propped on its stand. It was a four-by-four square of a koi head in white and vivid orange, a few circular ripples and an edge of water lily in green opalescent. He folded his arms and frowned.

"The sunset doesn't show the true colors," Amethyst explained quickly. "And of course, the installed window won't have the green tint you see now from the windows behind." Damn. "I'll bring back the sample at your convenience during the day, take the section outside so you can get a more accurate idea of what it will look like."

He cocked his head, then smiled. "I like it," he said. "I like it very much indeed."

She let go a breath.

His brows flicked up. "Surely you didn't have doubts? Not after all the work we've done."

"A scale drawing and some sheets of sample glass don't adequately depict the finished piece."

"You've gone formal on me again. You *were* worried."

"It's important that you're satisfied with the work." For more reasons than usual.

"I have been, I am, and I intend to be. But since you're still formal, that must not be the problem."

Fiddling with the roll of tape, she put on a smile. "There's no problem. Really."

He studied her. "Amethyst," he said. "Do I make you uncomfortable?"

"You? Me? No! Of course not!"

"Because from time to time, I catch a glimpse of a smart, funny woman I'd very much like to know better..." He stood very still. "If you'd let me."

She was turning and turning the tape in her hands. She stopped.

"I—you..." She realized how tight her fingers were and forced them to relax. "You don't do anything to make me uncomfortable, Jas."

Under level brows, his dark eyes regarded her.

"It's...just..." She put the tape down abruptly on the stand and gave an angry shrug. "Me."

He touched her shoulder. She flinched, but he took her other shoulder, too, turned her to face him.

"And what is wrong with you?"

Where should she start? With the fact that she was an oddball geek with the social skills of a box of Pop Tarts?

"Oh," she said on a laugh, "I could give you a sample, but you don't want that."

"I do," he said, "indeed want that."

She opened her mouth, but nothing came out. His hands were still on her shoulders. Warm. How could hands feel like that, as if they were the source of some rich liqueur spreading through her?

The sunset's red light had faded, and his eyes were twin wells of darkness in blue twilight. She wanted to look down, to step away; she didn't want anything of the kind.

He touched her cheek. "Is that so impossible to believe?"

Finally, her voice came. "Not when you say it."

"Good." His fingers slid up and back, into her hair.

Fire followed his touch—or chill. A shiver rippled through her. Her fingers encircled his arms—how had that happened? And when had they moved so close? His shirt felt cool and slippery, like silk, the flesh beneath warm and solid, muscular.

Okay, wait—wait a second. She had to think, there was something—something she had to pay attention to, a frantic whisper at the far edge of consciousness.

"But—"

His face wore a quizzical combination of frown and smile. "But what?"

The whisper grew less vague; something like, *Amethyst, wait...* "What if there're problems with the job?"

He gave a breath of a laugh. "The job is the farthest thing from my mind."

He bent his head and kissed her. She spun, or the world spun, a whirlwind that swept her up, down, inward—she couldn't tell. She closed her eyes. The echoes of the waterfall dimmed until she heard only the beat of her own pulse.

Jas' lips on hers, the warmth of his encircling arm, the tug of his fingers in her hair were all, all the world, the axis of her rotation. His hands gathered her up, pulled her in. The rest of her went along, thoughts, emotion, will; like being drawn down by warm, caressing quicksand. The urge to struggle came and went, smothered by some outside force.

He drew back. "There." He smoothed her cheek. "That wasn't so bad, was it?"

There was only his voice. His face, his eyes were all existence, the sensation of his body against hers the singular touch of reality, the faint scent of him the very air.

He undid her barrette, combed his fingers through her hair. She stood unmoving in his arms, couldn't even think to move.

"I was beginning to think you'd forever keep me at arm's length." He gave a smile that might've been indulgent. "What a surprise you've been! I'd never have expected you to be able to resist me as you have."

Darker than the gathering night, his eyes gleamed, forming her out of nothingness. Blocks of light fled across him, illuminating the sweep of black hair across his forehead. Somewhere far away, a voice called—not his.

He stepped back, releasing her, then traced the line of her

jaw with one forefinger. The other voice went away.

"I'm truly sorry to manhandle you like this, but as they say, desperate times call for desperate measures. I can't allow you to bolt this time."

Light shifted across his face, throwing the angles of nose and cheekbone and chin into high relief. The curve of his lips, the dark stubble of the day's growth of beard, the sketching of crow's feet at the corners of his eyes—consumed all her awareness.

"You see, Amethyst…"

Her name echoed in her mind in another voice.

"I need your help to solve a very serious problem."

Another sound impinged upon the words. She strained to hear him over the noise, a sort of howling roar, growing—

Jas' head jerked up. Light, bouncing and quivering, glared on his face. His brows snapped together; his arm around her waist, his hand on her collarbone tightened.

His lips shaped, "What the hell—"

The roar filled her ears, shook the floor on which she stood. He spat a single word that exploded in her mind in a searing knot of green sparks. Closing his arms around her, he lurched into her, then the breath was slammed from her body.

Thunder filled her ears, a terrible, rending, glittering crash, a yowling screech. Jas was on top of her, shielding her—she felt him, smelled him, then finally, saw him, a slim shadow against jumping light.

Glass blew inward, a scintillating rain, behind it a low, black shape with two blazing eyes. Jas threw up a hand. Glass bounced and slithered down all around as if off an invisible dome that covered them. He sagged on his elbow, then scrambled up and pulled her to her feet.

Her heartbeat shuddered in her throat with all the will she lacked. He spun and slung her behind him.

She was lost, cut adrift. His eyes were turned from her, the howling took his voice. Two lights, like eyes round and white and glaring, turned him into a shadow, a cutout flat and undefined. Smoke, stinking of rubber and exhaust, drowned the scent of him.

She gasped, groped after her own thoughts, her will, her *self*, but met only drowning emptiness.

An alarm wailed. Snarling, screeching, the black thing lunged forward. Shards of glass, twisted lengths of metal flew from under it. Jas jabbed his fist as if punching, and a knot of writhing green fire shot out, struck the attacker, splattered. The thing shuddered, coughed. Its eyes flickered, dimmed to dull yellow.

Something like a desperate, panicky hand reached inside her, wrenched at her innards. She staggered. Glass bit at her. A fiery tide of magic surged, rushed through her like erupting lava, then burst out. The wavering light of the thing's eyes blazed once more, its voice rose in fury and it leapt forward.

With a gesture Jas swept up a wall of glass daggers and steel spears, hurled them and sprang aside. He landed sprawling in wreckage, struggled to his feet again. The black shape of the monster rushed toward Amethyst. Spitting glass and stinking blue smoke, it howled, screeched, then slung itself sideways, showing curves of chrome, planes of gleaming black metal and glass. The glare of its eyes swept away, cutting an arc of light through smoke-filled air, across shattered sculptures, shards of glass, crumpled metal—across Jas.

He reached out to her and his eyes, wide and horrified, locked on hers. His voice was back, harsh and frantic, filling her mind where her own thoughts and will should've been: *Move, Amethyst! MOVE!*

His fingers closed and a disembodied force gripped her—

Fire blazed through her again, battering it away. Thunder filled her mind, drowning Jas' voice. The black shape swept nearer, slowly, so slowly, a galaxy's ponderous whirl. A crack appeared in its side, grew, became a door opening onto a maw glowing with dim green light. The petroleum stench of the thing's breath engulfed her, hot and choking. The door struck her, swept her forward and sideways at once.

Pain: chin and chest and shins, exploding in the back of her head. Her elbow rammed her ribs, her head cracked sideways against her shoulder. Lights burst across her vision, pain blanked out the lights and darkness swallowed the pain.

Chapter 20

"**W**ake."

The voice came through a dark fog.

"Amethyst, you must wake."

Sick weakness buffeted her on a heaving sea of pain. She knew that voice, ragged and frightened, like a radio DJ reporting some disaster.

No, she answered. *No*.

Silver light dawned through the fog, shining on her, shining within her. The cold dwindled, the weakness. The pain contracted and found nesting places: her head, ribs, arm, legs, foot.

Amethyst groaned and opened her eyes.

Tangled shapes rose very close to her face: a rod sticking out of a…a cave?

No, not a cave. The underside of a car's dash. There were the pedals, and the rod was the steering column.

She jerked upright and banged her head on the steering wheel.

"At last!" the voice said on an outrush of breath. "Speak to me."

She clutched her head. "Talys? Where—?"

She squinted at the windshield. Shiny, dark green leaves and twigs pressed against it. Same on the side windows. Last she remembered, she'd been standing in the Magus lobby, talking to Jas—well, not *talking*, actually. And then he'd…he'd—

Her stomach twisted. She fumbled at the door handle, or tried to, rather; her hands only flopped. The door opened anyway. She spilled halfway out and retched. Nothing came up but a little bile.

"I am sorry, love," Talys said. "I had to borrow your power in order to extricate you. You must eat," he said. "I bought you a hamburger, though I fear the restaurant employee may currently doubt her sanity."

Still fumbling, she found the burger bag on the passenger seat. A smell of cold grease hit and her stomach lurched again. She swallowed hard and crammed a rubbery French fry into her mouth before she had a chance to think about it.

"There," Talys said.

She shuddered and almost threw up again—this time it wouldn't be just a little bile. That was what Jas had said, when…when…

"He's a wizard!" She crumpled the hamburger bag. Tears pushed up and fell. "I couldn't do anything! Not even think! And I thought he— I really liked—"

She, too, crumpled. Every throbbing bruise on her body was nothing compared to the feeling in her chest, in her gut.

"Why?" It was more a wail than a word.

"I do not know," Talys said.

She gulped back tears. He sounded hollow—dangerous. He spoke like a human being, often seemed like one, but he wasn't. He was something unguessably old, something that glided above the warring plains of human life like a raven with eyes of polished black stones.

"No doubt it was he behind the attack on the Crest," Talys said. "Then I sensed your distress while we were parted. I assume he put you under further duress."

She didn't want to remember, didn't want to think about it. She'd been wrong, wrong…

She sniffed, raised her hand to wipe her face. Her hand glittered with glass dust. Her tank top did too, and tear-splotches muddied the streaks of dirt there.

"Dreams, scary ones. You were in them." She unwrapped the hamburger and stared at it. "I thought it was you, trying to wear me down," she said in a low voice.

"No," he said gently. "I attempted to warn you."

"And then…" Memory and realization rushed in. "My truck's throttle stuck one day. I ended up in the Magus parking lot, and when my phone didn't work, I had to go inside…"

It suddenly seemed so clear, so obvious, she couldn't believe she hadn't made the connection before. But how could she have?

"That was Jas, too, wasn't it? When I went into that room to use the phone, I felt weird. Hypnotized. Like...like..." Like she had after he kissed her. Tears spilled out again, but silently, as if they were blood from that awful pain in her middle. "What—what did he do to me?" Her voice came out very small.

"He spellbound you—took your will and subsumed it to his own. You would have done as he wished," Talys said in that same icy voice. "You would have had no thought of refusing him. And you haven't knowledge enough of your own power to break the binding. Perhaps, when he was certain you were tamed, he might've released you..."

Amethyst's stomach twisted again, and not just from magic's aftereffects. She felt again the glide of Jas' fingers through her hair. She swallowed a desire to cut it all off, then peel off her own skin.

"None of it was you. I thought you made those dreams and everything else happen, but you didn't do any of it."

"You had no reason to think otherwise," Talys said in a more normal tone. "Now eat, love."

She took a small bite. The bun had a dry edge to it and the lettuce was like a piece of wet Kleenex. She had to chew a long time before she could get it down. "Where did you get this?"

"Winslow, I believe. I'd hoped you'd wake a good deal sooner."

"Winslow! Arizona?" How many shocks could a nervous system stand before it shivered apart into sharp little pieces? The leaves pressed against the windshield looked like oak, but in the Southwest, she'd never seen oaks big enough to park under. "Where are we now?"

"Somewhere in California's northern coastal mountains."

"*Calif—!*"

Amethyst shoved at the door again and tumbled out. Twigs snatched at her hair, raked her skin. Dry grass stems pricked one foot. She hissed and jerked it off the ground. Her sandal was missing, and dried blood caked the sole and between the toes, like she'd stepped on broken glass.

Hopping on the foot that still wore a sandal, she pushed through the branches. Beyond lay a rumple of golden hills, towering dark green mushroom shapes of oak trees and grass taller and thicker than the best, wettest New Mexico summer could ever produce—except the grass was lion yellow and dry instead of proper summer green. Not to mention that hot, heavy air certainly wasn't any mile-high atmosphere.

She sat down hard. The musk of oak and dry grass curled around her. Afternoon sun pressed down on her shoulders. Wind ruffled the yellow grass, showing and then hiding the tire tracks that wound around a shoulder of hill.

"Are you well?" Talys called.

She folded arms on knees and pressed her face to them. It should be impossible for one person to be so scared and confused and disappointed and badly hurt all at once.

"Amethyst, come. Sit down and talk to me."

She *was* sitting down, and she didn't want to talk. Her ribs hurt. Really hurt, like something was broken. Well, something *was* broken, but it was more than just her ribs.

Behind her, the car's engine started with a rumble like a waking beast. Twigs popped, dry grass crunched, but she didn't turn. The engine sound grew nearer until it was at her shoulder, until she felt the buffeting of air from the radiator fan. The engine died again.

"What can I say to ease you?" Talys asked quietly.

Why couldn't he have flesh and a heartbeat? Arms to hold her with.

She rolled up the hem of her top and wiped her face. "Tell me you forgive me. Tell me you aren't going to chew me out as soon as I look like I'm not likely to dissolve into a puddle. "

"Forgive you!" The words came out on a disbelieving snort. "I should ask forgiveness of you! Would that I'd paused to consider…"

"In one fell swoop, I think you've made up for all that." She pulled a handful of grass and brushed at her shirt and arms. "Why—why are we in California?"

"Distance was necessary in order to break the binding that wizard placed on you."

Jas had tried to hang onto her all that way? "Is he— What if he's following us?"

"I've shielded us." The tone of his voice suggested a smug smile. "He shan't find us by magic."

"Shielded…like I did that day at the storage yard?" The dreams had stopped afterward. But she thought she'd been pushing Talys away. "So then how did *you* find me?"

"I'm your familiar, love. I always know where to find you."

Apparently Jas had known where to find her, too. The convenient breakdowns of her Chevy. That afternoon she'd been so sure someone had been in her house…

She pictured Jas roaming her rooms, touching her things. Once, the thought of him in her home would've given her a pleasurable thrill. Now, she went cold again.

"What are we going to do?" she asked.

"I have ideas."

"What kind of ideas?"

"Not now," he said.

She drew breath to argue.

"No, later. Now, I must ask that you get in and finish the food."

She really didn't feel up to arguing, anyway. Much easier to simply get up, limp around to the driver's door and ease herself—carefully—into the seat.

The door whumped closed and the car bounced through the grass, following its own tracks to the road.

She leaned her head back, closed her eyes and trusted the driving to Talys. She wanted to tell herself the past day was a dream, that Jas was still the ideal guy he seemed to be, and these steep, wooded hills and that strangely pale sky were conjured from memory of a trip to visit Dad's side of the family when she was a teenager. But she'd never seen those years-ago woods gradually change to this dim, gothic forest, or the two-lane strip of blacktop winding like an intestine between moss-grown trunks.

But it *wasn't* a dream, and Jas *was* a wizard. One, in fact, substantially less forthright than Dr. Korhonen had been. She had to stop blubbering over a promising romance gone bad and decide what to do now.

For the last however-many miles, Talys had been discreetly quiet. She gently rubbed a lump on the back of her head.

"Talys, California is a long way from home. I'm still hungry. I look like hell and I really, seriously need a dose of ibuprofen and probably some antibiotic ointment and Band-Aids, too. And my purse is buried somewhere in the lobby of the Magus building."

"The location of a lady's purse being a matter of all-consuming importance, of course."

Her lip quivered, but she smiled a little. "Well, it does contain a few minor things like my ID and phone and credit card."

"Ah. That is a problem for which I may provide a partial solution." The glove compartment fell open.

A car came around the curve ahead, headlights sweeping twilight-blurred ferns and trunks. Amethyst waited until it slid past, then leaned over and explored the glove compartment. Her fingers brushed a stack of loose papers too small for a map.

She pulled out a fistful of… No, not dollars. Twenties.

"Holy Mary mother of God. Where did you get this? Did you drive up to an ATM machine somewhere and whisper sweet nothings in its ear?" She shoved the bills back into the glove compartment. "Never mind. I don't want to know."

"Very well. I shan't explain it to you then. Suffice it to say, you'll suffer no repercussions in spending it."

If that was true, then her money worries were over.

They rounded a few more curves and time seemed to slide backward a half-hour or so. Blue twilight of open air replaced the trees' deepening night. A sort of picket fence of weathered grey boards divided the road from an empty stretch of grass. The road sloped down to a stop sign, and beyond that…

She gripped the steering wheel. Across the road and beyond an old building, a gulf went halfway to forever.

Ultramarine shaded through every tone of blue, lightening until it met an unbroken plane of deepest midnight. Dividing the two was a seam of fiery orange.

"Wow," she breathed. "What a spectacular window that would make!" She wondered if glass came in that many shades of blue.

"The Pacific Ocean," Talys said as if he were personally responsible for that view that disappeared into the curvature of the horizon.

The clutch came up, the accelerator depressed, and the Mustang idled across the road and up into a parking lot. A single light illuminated a lonely pair of old-fashioned gas pumps and the front of the building beside them. The headlights swept the side of the building. Faded letters read, *STEVEN'S POINT STORE*. The car pulled into a parking space before a flight of wooden steps.

The engine died. "You may be able to meet some of your needs at this establishment," Talys said.

Amethyst wadded up the greasy burger bag. She still felt weak and shaky, although that might have been attributable to Talys' use of her magic.

She climbed out of the car. The breeze off the ocean smelled strange, tangy almost, and so full of moisture she could almost feel the water molecules sticking to her skin and hair. The tall, narrow steps, cool and splintery under her bare feet, seemed way steeper than they should have. She shivered in the cool air. Trying not to limp too much on her cut foot, she pushed the door open and stepped inside.

A woman with John Lennon glasses and dressed in a sulfur yellow caftan manned the cash register. Amethyst smiled at her, but the woman only looked her up and down with some alarm.

Two huge, purple knots and a red sort of almost-gash stood out on her shins. God, she must look like a victim of domestic abuse. And the abuser had wielded an iron pipe.

Amethyst hurried across the sloping wooden floor into the shelter of an aisle and started grabbing things: juice, granola bars, string cheese, a California Republic hoodie and a pair of screaming lime Crocs knock-offs. She pulled the sweatshirt carefully over sundry bumps and bruises on her head and shoulders. At the register, she added the tag for the sweatshirt, a bottle of Advil and some disinfecting wipes to her pile on the counter.

The clerk kept snatching glances at Amethyst while she scanned her purchases. Amethyst studied the newspapers in a rack by the counter. *San Francisco Chronicle. Santa Rosa Press Democrat.* Then the date leapt out at her: June 13. But— It was the *twelfth*, wasn't it?

No, of course not. How could it be? It had to take at least a day to drive to California, and besides, she'd been with Jas at twilight and found herself with Talys in the afternoon. If she'd bothered to think about it—

"Are you all right?" the cashier asked. "I can…" She paused delicately. "…call somebody for you, if you need."

"Oh," Amethyst said, scrambling. "Thanks, I'm fine. I…I was in a wreck." Yesterday, but she didn't say it. Jeeze, a whole day and then some? And—dammit! She'd promised to call Melodie! "Ah…" She looked around. "Do you have a payphone?"

"The one outside, but it's out of order." The woman hand-ed her a bag with *Thank You!* in blue letters. "Which way are you headed?"

"Um…" Amethyst shifted weight off her cut foot. "Wherever I can find a phone."

"You'd better go north, then, up to Ranch Bluff. That's clos-est, about ten miles up the highway." She studied Amethyst over her small, round glasses. "I can let you use the store phone. If you really need to."

This wouldn't be the sort of conversation she particularly wanted overheard. "I think it'll probably end up being a long call. Plus it's long distance. But thanks anyway."

She grabbed her bag. Things were starting to *loom* again. She limped to the car as calmly as possible. The engine started as soon as the door closed.

"Talys," she said. "We need to get to a phone. The woman inside said the nearest town is north—"

"I believe you shall find one at our destination for the evening."

Cracking the plastic cap on a bottle of orange juice, she paused. "Where?"

"My, you're suspicious. Have I not proven myself trustworthy?"

"I didn't mean—" She scowled down at the bottle. "Of course you have. I'm sorry. But if you'd just tell me—"

"One thing at a time, love. You've been through a great deal, and I'd prefer to discuss strategy when you're better rested. If you'll forgive my saying, you aren't at your best at the moment."

◇ ◇ ◇

'Better rested' at least entailed a motel. It looked like it had been built in the 1950's or '60's, with little carports adjoining each room. The owners had apparently decided to go with the era, with square-cornered furniture in a blondish tone, a pole lamp with egg-shaped plastic shades and a pink Princess phone on the nightstand. The décor was in pink, lime and aqua—the sort of colors Amethyst saw after using magic. But the room had a bed, and she'd be able to take a shower—later.

Amethyst plopped down on the edge of the hard mattress and punched in the numbers off the calling card she'd bought.

The phone rang on the other end. "Hello?"

"Hi, Mel, it's me."

"Wiz? I almost didn't answer. The caller ID came up weird. What happened? I thought you were going to call last night."

"I—I—" Tears erupted unexpectedly. Why couldn't she stop crying? It was disgusting!

"Amethyst, what's wrong?" A pause. "Where are you?"

She'd planned on telling Melodie that she'd gotten into a wreck, had to get the Mustang out of storage and had forgotten to call. She hadn't even thought about what caller ID would show.

She forced herself to breathe normally and cleared her throat. "I'm in California."

Melodie took an audible breath. "California!" Another pause. "What're you doing *there?* Are you all right?"

"I'm…I'm okay. I'm sorry. This is so stupid—" Her voice went shaky again.

"Calm down. Tell me what's going on." A little of Melodie's own calm cracked there.

Amethyst gulped and sniffed. She couldn't think of any more lies. The truth was hard enough. "I…I went to Magus, like I told you. I think Jas sent the security guard away. We were talking, and…and he kissed me, and then…then he…"

Her throat closed. How could she possibly begin to explain, after everything that had happened in the spring, after everything she'd been hiding… And do it over the phone two or three states away?

"Then he what?"

Amethyst struggled to push the words out, but still couldn't.

"Are you saying what I think you're saying?" Melodie said in an ominous tone.

That freed up her voice. "What?"

"You can't stop crying. You're a goddamn helluva long way from here, and you got there after driving all night. I can't think of a lot that would send you tearing off like that, and what I can think of, I sure as hell don't like."

"What are—"

Wait. Melodie was thinking…that Jas tried to rape her? Amethyst was doing nothing but playing catch-up tonight. If she weren't so beat up and upset, she would've realized that's exactly what it sounded like. Yes, Jas was a bastard, but she couldn't do *that* to him.

"No, Mel, he—" Amethyst stopped again.

But he *had* tried to rape her. Maybe not in the physical, legal sense. But was overpowering her psychically any better? He'd taken away her ability to think, to choose—to do anything. He'd taken her *self*.

The memory made her sick. "I got away," she said, reminding herself, reassuring Melodie.

If she hadn't... She felt again his arm around her waist, holding her body to his. She shuddered.

"Oh, that makes it so much better," Melodie said. She sounded more relieved than sarcastic. "But Wiz, why didn't you call me?"

"I—I didn't even think of it," she answered truthfully. "All I wanted was away, where he couldn't get to me. I know it was stupid—" A bad thought scratched at the edge of her mind.

"You were traumatized," Melodie said. "I doubt you were in a condition to think things through."

Amethyst twisted her fingers in the bedspread. "No," she admitted.

"Okay." Melodie paused. "I have to ask... What do you want to do now? Do we smear his fine name all over the papers? Do we call the cops?"

"And tell them what?"

An image of breaking glass, of the Mustang screeching around the Magus lobby flashed through her mind, all no doubt captured on security feeds. What story was *Jas* telling right now? It was suddenly hard to breathe.

"Mel, I'm scared."

"No doubt."

"No, listen. This is a powerful man. What'll he do to keep me quiet?" Amethyst asked the question that was really bothering her. "What'll he do when I go home again?"

"What can he do? I think you're overreacting—not that I don't understand why."

"Yeah, maybe, but remember the rumors we were talking about? The funny things that happen to his competitors?"

"Things we decided had to be coincidence, because it's impossible for someone to *make* them happen."

Amethyst rubbed her eyes. She couldn't argue. Not under the circumstances.

"Just come home," Melodie said. I know you're scared—I'd be scared, too. But you can stay with me. Or I'll stay at your house, I don't care. Once you're here, we'll figure it out."

I can't, Amethyst wanted to say. *I can't come home*. Then another thought. "Caramela!"

"I'm sure she'll be fine at her own house for a day or so."

"Her owners moved," Amethyst said. "They left her behind. Like the rest of the junk in their yard."

"I'll take care of her, then. Don't worry."

"No!" Amethyst did *not* want Melodie anywhere near her house. "No, just call the Griegos, next door. Oscar won't mind putting some food out for her."

"I'll call him as soon as we hang up," Melodie said. "Are you okay for now? Do you need money?"

"N-no. I'm all right."

"Listen, I know how long that trip is. Get some rest before you try to drive home. Everything will be fine."

"Right." She hung up, tucked up her knees and pressed her face to them. Oddly enough, she didn't feel like crying any more. Throwing up, maybe.

The phone rang. Amethyst jumped, grabbed it and said, "Hello?"

"Amethyst," Jas said. "How are you?"

She dropped the phone. The receiver hit the floor. She grabbed the cord, reeled it up and slammed it back into the cradle. Shit! How had he found her? Talys said they were shielded—

It rang again. She sat on her hands. Every blare of the bell sent a shot of adrenaline through her. Six rings. Seven. She scrambled up, tracked the wire to the wall and unplugged it.

The phone kept ringing.

Damn him. *Damn him!* Hadn't he done enough? She snatched up the receiver. It was slippery in her grip, and the back of her neck prickled like her hackles were rising.

"*What?*" she snarled.

"Don't hang up on me, Amethyst," he said pleasantly. "You won't find my next means of communication more natural."

"Go to hell, Jas." She banged down the receiver again.

The television snapped on, a little pop and whine of electricity through the set.

She spun and there he was on the screen, dressed in a black shirt and dark green tie, just as good-looking as ever. His hair and the shirt blended into a dim background, making his pale face and dark eyes more compelling.

She really, really wanted to put a foot through his smiling face. She didn't trust the cheap Crocs to hold up against shattered plastic, though.

"What do you want?"

"We parted rather abruptly. I was concerned." His gaze flicked up and down. "I see I had good reason to be. You look rather the worse for wear."

Nothing would come out for a moment except outraged splutters. "Concerned!" she finally choked. "After you—you—"

"I do apologize about that. And speaking of apologies, who was the rash individual with so little respect for my property?"

There had to be a word for that kind of attitude. 'Audacious' was the nicest that came to mind.

"That was my familiar." The nasty snarl came out exactly as she'd intended.

His brows shot up. "Indeed! And here I was deceived into believing you were determined to carry on your life as an ordinary mortal."

"I don't think you should be talking to me about *deceit*."

"I suppose not, but would you have had anything to do with me if you knew what I am?"

"You have an explanation for everything, don't you?"

His lips thinned a little. He suddenly looked like what you'd expect a wizard losing patience to look.

"I didn't call to argue with you, Amethyst."

She sat down on the end of the bed and crossed her ankles. "Then why did you call, Jas?"

"It's important we talk."

"I don't think so, because quite frankly, about the only words I want to say to you are the kind that aren't allowed on TV."

She slid off the end of the bed and stood.

He laughed. "I've always loved your sense of humor. Sit down. Please."

Oh, yeah, he was laying on all the old charm. The disgusting thing was it worked. Besides, she was sort of morbidly curious as to what he could possibly have to say.

"So. Talk."

He kept smiling, but his eyes had a glint. "I don't think you realize your position."

"I guess you're going to enlighten me."

"You don't know what you're doing, and as a consequence, you're vulnerable."

She clapped her hands to her face. "Gosh, am I? I'd just better go tell my familiar right now so he can make sure to protect me from any unsavory characters I might run into."

"You might," he said, "have encountered far worse than me."

"You're right. I forgot about the nightly dream assault and the tree-monster on the Crest." She gave an exaggerated shudder. "I wonder *who* could've sent that?"

His black brows quirked. "Dream assault?"

"Oh, please. Don't try to tell me you had nothing to do with any of it."

The smile disappeared, leaving only the glint in his eyes. "Your attitude is not at all productive."

"*My* attitude?" she said on a disbelieving laugh. "Excuse me, but I'm not the one forcing myself on people."

His voice rose. "I have not forced myself on you. I'm trying—"

"You know, Jas, don't even bother, because at this point, I don't care what you're trying to do." She stood again. "As far as I'm concerned, you're one damn despicable excuse for a human being. Even if you are a wizard."

"That's all very well. Nevertheless, you'd be wise to listen to what I have to say."

"Or what? I can leave. I can get another room."

He gave a smile very different from his usual humorous crinkle. "Do you think I won't be able to follow you?"

"In the words of a certain famous leader, 'Bring it on.'"

"Bravado does not at all suit you."

"Fine," she said. "Then I'll tell you straight." She poked his TV-screen chest with a forefinger. "You got me once, but you try again and you'll have the chance to discover first-hand if I'm as clueless and vulnerable as you think I am."

"Amethyst—"

She wadded up the bedspread with its little pink and aqua rounded rectangles and threw it over the TV.

From under it, his voice said, "This is absurd."

After everything else, he was going to make her do it. Well, she didn't care right now.

She reached for the magic and got the usual horrible jolt, as if someone had flipped the garbage disposal switch while her hand was inside groping for something that fell down the drain.

"Shut up, Jas. And *leave me alone.*"

Magic pulsed out like a curtain of broken glass and twisted mirrors, something equal parts aggression and diversion.

Her knees buckled and she dropped onto the bed. The TV had fallen silent, but she could still feel something—someone—fumbling around the edges of her consciousness, as if it knew about a back door she'd forgotten to bolt.

Chapter 21

Amethyst shoved to her feet. The motel room reeled, the stripped bed and sharp-edged Fifties furniture tilting at a queasy angle. She swallowed hard and teetered for the door.

The Mustang sat just outside, gleaming black and forbidding in the wan yellow glow of the porch light. A few cars occupied the carports, and lights shone from behind curtains. In the rooms nearby, lives breathed; voices murmured, thoughts flickered, emotions glowed. Under the concrete walkway, the earth's memories of wave-whipped cold seeped into her feet. The ocean breathed. Beneath its churn and surge, a shark hunted a young seal.

She shook her head and leaned a hand on the fender. Touching it was like soothing ointment spread over raw nerve endings. The intrusive impressions receded, but she felt Talys stir questioningly. He would've felt the magic she'd used.

"Talys," she whispered. "I messed up. I did something really stupid."

The driver's door clicked open. "Tell me," the tinny radio voice said.

Still limping, she slid into the car. "I—I called Melodie."

She waited, but he didn't say anything. Between fear and magic's sledgehammer aftereffects, she couldn't get it out.

"Yes?" he finally prompted.

"After I hung up, Jas called."

"*What?*" It was the first time she'd ever heard Talys surprised. "How? The shielding—"

"The phone," she explained. He didn't reply, and Amethyst realized he still didn't get it. "Jas owns a computer security company. He doesn't need magic—just technology. All he had to do was monitor the right phone lines…"

She was still playing catch-up, missing obvious things. "Oh, Mary mother in heaven," she breathed. "My purse—it was in his lobby. He knows—" But he probably hadn't even needed her cell phone call log or calendar by then. "He knows everything about me. My family, my friends, who I do business with. If he can't get to me, what'll he do—?"

"Has he contacted them?" Talys interrupted.

Amethyst put the brakes on where her thoughts were headed. "No. I don't think so. Melodie didn't say anything."

A white-noise hiss came over the radio for a moment. "Did he make any threats when you spoke?"

"No, but—"

"I suspect your fears are premature. If he has determined where you are— Is that possible?"

"Yes." It seemed strange to be answering such an obvious question when Talys usually had all the answers. With another cold splash, a new thought occurred to her. "He talked to me over the TV. Can he get to us? Can he come here—magically?"

"He can, but he must still contend with the shielding I— we—erected. No easy task, particularly at such distance."

"Talys, I know tech, and you know magic. Jas knows both, and he obviously knows how to make them work together. You and I—don't. And this is a really bad time to be trying to figure it out."

Again, that thoughtful pause. "Indeed. Yet I feel he must prefer a sly approach to a bold one. He beguiled rather than confronted you. I believe he will try the same again. He wants something, and he requires your cooperative to obtain it."

"He said—" Her jaw tightened with the memory. "He said something about a problem."

"Yes."

She ran her thumb along a seam in the seat. "You know what it is."

"You do as well—the toxic state of magic. How he intends to approach that problem, that I do not know. Nor where you fit in as a solution."

If only Jas had done a classic villain's monologue when he had her in his clutches. She pushed away the panic plucking at her gut. "So what now? I can't go back, and I sure as hell can't stay away."

"I did not bring you here arbitrarily, nor do I intend to deliver to your enemy unarmed and undefended. But my purpose requires magic. Which, I might add, you are scarcely in a state to use."

She folded her arms on the steering wheel and rested her head on them. If things had loomed before, now they seemed impossible. She was filthy, she hurt inside and out, and she was hanging onto rational thought by a fingernail. She just wanted to take a shower, crawl into bed and sleep until everything was over. Except that if she did that, everything *would* be over.

"Maybe I'm not at my best and brightest right now," she said. "But I don't see how we have a whole lotta choice. While I'm recuperating here, we don't know what Jas is up to there. And I'm pretty sure he won't just be sitting by the phone, waiting for me to call."

"Nevertheless—"

"You said you had an idea. What is it?"

"To gain aid, of course, but—"

She straightened. "What about Dr. Korhonen? He offered to help before."

"You said he offered to teach you. Not to become embroiled in a wizard's war."

Her breath suddenly wouldn't come. "Is that what this is? A wizard's war?"

"Forgive me," he said. "I spoke too hastily. Nevertheless, if this Jas intends to control you, and you intend to resist his control, the potential for conflict remains."

"Potential for conflict," she repeated. Talk about understatement. Maybe she should've talked to him when she had the chance—

No. Never once had he been open with her, tried to explain or persuade rather than overpower. Whatever he had planned, it had to be something she wouldn't like.

"I still think I should call Dr. Korhonen," she said. "He could always say no."

She thought hard. She wasn't sure how safe even an old-fashioned payphone would be. Payphones weren't exactly plentiful anymore. There couldn't be that many of them in the area, and there'd be a database somewhere of which numbers belonged to which payphones. Tap the local phone system, plug in voice recognition software to screen calls from those numbers, and bam! She was caught again.

"I could get one of those pay-go cell phones," she said. "Jas shouldn't have any reason to connect me with Dr. Korhonen, so he wouldn't be keeping tabs on him. As long as I don't call anyone else with it and give Jas a way to pinpoint the signal, it might not show up on his radar."

"I must defer to you on that. However, I would argue that the closer we hold our intentions, the less likely they are to be thwarted."

Amethyst chewed the end of her thumb. "Okay," she said. "Then let's go find your help first. You can tell me what it is on the way."

The radio hissed, but with his annoyance, not static. "You need time to—"

"Talys, *Jas knows where I am.* Are you really suggesting I stay the night here?"

"Another inn, then."

She restrained the urge to knot her fingers in her hair in frustration. She'd already been through this calculation.

"One winding road with few outlets. An easily estimated speed of travel. Few choices of lodging. It won't take much effort to pin us down. Hell, he won't even need to get fancy with the computer. Just get on the phone and call a few motels. Plus I don't want to give him too much time to start thinking of ways to bring me in out of the cold."

Talys didn't reply. She tugged at her fingers. He could easily exercise veto power—she wouldn't be going anywhere without him.

"I promise—"

"Very well," he said. "The points you've made are valid. Not that I'm pleased with the option."

She rested a hand on the dash. "Neither am I," she whispered, because her voice wanted to shake. "But the ball's in our court right now, and I want to keep it there."

Amethyst sat curled in the seat, her head against the car window. Soft New Age music played on the radio. The engine's vibration transmitted through the glass, a soothing purr marred only by the occasional shifting of gears. A full moon shone on asphalt like a black satin ribbon. Past silvery, grass-clothed bluffs, the ocean was a shimmering darkness. She tried hard to let the beauty seep into her thoughts and chase other things away.

"Close your eyes," Talys said. "You're supposed to be resting."

Amethyst shifted, sliding a hand between her head and the window. The vinyl seat made a soft noise. "How can you see they're open?"

"The same way I see anything."

Which, of course, was no answer at all. She suppressed a sigh. "I could rest a lot easier if I knew what the plan was."

He did sigh, a crackly whisper over the radio speakers. The music snapped off. "I suppose you won't until I satisfy you."

"Nope."

"Very well. I spoke to you once of my last wizard."

"The one who died."

"Yes." He paused as if gathering his thoughts. "Meredydd, his partner—also a wizard—had vanished. He was greatly distraught, and searched for her long, but could find her nowhere. At last, he discovered something that excited him greatly, something he felt might be the key to her disappearance."

"What was it?"

"I don't precisely know. 'I think I've found her,' he said, but would tell me no more. He determined to investigate, and forbade me to accompany him."

This sounded uncomfortably familiar. "But...wasn't that dangerous?"

"Of course it was," he snapped. He seemed to catch himself, then went on as if calm once more, "I rued my obedience when our bond broke."

She hesitated. His emotions roiled around her: upset, recrimination.

"Bond," she repeated. "You mean, the same thing that lets you know where I am?"

"Among other things, yes."

Those other things apparently being whether the wizard was still alive or not. "Sounds like he didn't want anything to happen to you, too," she said gently.

"No," he sighed. "I suppose not. I've come to realize I was to be a fail-safe. A message in a bottle, if you will. Yet I did not accept my role with equanimity. I, in my turn, searched for what had befallen him."

The road curved inland and down, into a small canyon full of evergreens and shadow and wisps of fog that wreathed and glowed in the headlight beams. They made the hairpin turn at the bottom and started up again and out of the trees. The fog remained, even when the road climbed once more to the bluff tops. It seemed Talys' explanation was just as curvy.

"Did you find out?"

"No. But I did find a place that reeks of power, layer upon layer of binding, blinding, barrier and bafflement. I haven't the ability to penetrate it—"

"But I do," she finished for him.

"Precisely."

She eyed the dashboard, the big, round tach and speedometer gazing at her like eyes. "This is where I get to repay you for that spectacular rescue, isn't it?"

His laugh was rueful. "Upon my honor, that wasn't what I

had in mind."

She blew through her lips. "Okay, so I punch through these layers—providing I even can—"

"You can," he said.

"How does this tie in to the help we're here to get?"

"Such spells are consistent with prison walls for individuals with power," he said. "If we free them—"

"They'll be eternally grateful and agree to back us in our wizards' war? Please."

"My, you're young to be such a cynic."

"Well, yeah. 'Here ya go, the door's open, and by the way, would you mind getting my back while I fight it out with this guy you don't have any argument with?'"

"Ah, your last assumption may be mistaken."

She flapped a hand. "Wait, wait, you've lost me."

"Are you so sure that your enemy and that of those imprisoned behind the spells aren't one in the same?"

That stopped her. "You mean Jas—" The thought made her queasy again, just when she'd gotten over being queasy.

"I find his actions worrisome."

She cracked a humorless laugh. "Worrisome! Yeah, I guess you could call them that." She gripped her arms, hugging the cold spot in her middle. "I can't believe I—I'd let someone like that get close to me." That *she* would want to get close to someone like that.

"Clearly, others have allowed their attacker to draw close. Wizards aren't easily overcome when on guard—not without a great deal of untidiness."

She wondered what wizardly untidiness consisted of. Maybe about like what the Magus lobby must look like right now. Her bruises throbbed willfully again, and the queasiness wouldn't go away.

She touched the sore place where her chin had connected with the steering wheel when Talys had scooped her up. "So how far to this prison place?"

"Not much farther, I think—ah, yes. Just ahead here."

On either side, grass stretched grey and ghostly in moon- and headlight. The car slowed, angled left across the road and bumped off the shoulder.

An overgrown track stretched ahead, barred by a sagging metal farm gate. The Mustang bounced and squeaked to the gate and stopped. The padlocked chain rattled and slithered off. With a howl of disused hinges, the gate swung open.

"Cool," Amethyst said with little enthusiasm.

The fog seemed to press claustrophobically close.

"Do you see it?" Talys said.

A palisade of black and twisted trees resolved itself ahead. Something large and pale loomed against the trees, two-dimensional in the fog. A house.

It had two stories, with added wings sprawling like after-thoughts within a drooping, gap-toothed picket fence. The steep roof sagged like the backbone of an old horse. Moonlight bleached the weathered clapboard siding to monochrome silver.

The car fishtailed a little in the tall grass. It stopped by a little picket gate hanging askew by the bottom hinge. Amethyst's arms prickled.

"Looks like the kind of place you'd find a whole family grue-somely murdered," she muttered.

"Is that what you sense?"

She took a shuddering breath and concentrated. "No. More like the whole place is screaming 'Keep away!'" She chewed her lip. "I'm not sure if this is a good idea."

"That will be the spells," he reassured her. "This, I think, will be the most difficult part—the approach. After all, a prison must be proof against potential rescuers, as well."

It was hard to think past that gut-twisting compulsion to *leave, now*.

"Talys, wait. If your old master—"

"Chauncey was alone." He sounded distant and dangerous again. "*You* will not be."

The black hollows of the house's windows seemed to stare at her through the windshield. Splintery shutters hanging askew gave them a scowling look. The glass, however, wasn't broken, which somehow made the whole effect more menacing.

Her fingers and feet were tingly. She rubbed her hands up and down her thighs, but it didn't do much good.

"I appreciate the sentiment, but there's a slight problem. You're a car. How do you plan to get in?"

"Never mind that. Simply be assured that I will."

She had visions of the Mustang crunching up the steps and through the front of the house, bringing the whole decrepit thing down on them. But then she supposed if he could do that, he wouldn't have needed her.

Amethyst pushed out a shaky breath. "Well, let's get it over with, then."

The car door swung open. A smell of decay, of rotting wood and moldy plaster swirled in. Dry grass crisped under her feet. A whisper of waves muttered on the air.

She trailed her fingers along the Mustang's fender, cool and misted with droplets from the fog. She shivered, from night cold and fog dampness, from nerves, but the engine's warmth breathed on her legs. She took a breath and squeezed through the broken picket gate and across a weedy yard. Fog swirled and parted as she moved.

The porch steps groaned and shuddered. The porch itself made sounds like a pack of angry rats—or maybe it really was rats. She curled her toes in her Crocs. She had a horrible thought that if she were to peer through the windows, she might find herself eye to eye with *something* peering back.

She suddenly couldn't take another step forward. "Talys?" she whispered.

Warmth, like the warmth from the car's engine, curled around her. Close beside her, the mist thickened, formed a shape taller and broader than she. She flinched back, then sensed its un-mistakable Talys-ness and frowned.

"I thought you said you don't like to...to disembody yourself."

The warmth simply wrapped her shoulders like a shawl and urged her toward the door.

She didn't know who reached for the magic, her or Talys or both. It came wrenching through her, hot and caustic as dragon's blood. Color flooded her mind: yellows, blues intertwined with deep, vibrant purple and glittering silver, like an inspiration for a new window. The urge to *keep away* vanished as if cut off. Then she saw the spells that surrounded the house.

Shapes moved, sharp and angular and aggressive, whirling kaleidoscope-like against a pulsing wall of energy, ether, magic, whatever. She reached out with the lovely stained-glass colors of her own power and sheared through it. The edges of the spells sizzled back, leaving a cool, moonlit gap.

Biting her lip, she reached into that gap and touched the old-fashioned doorknob.

The colors disappeared and the door dragged open as if she'd put a shoulder to it. The smell of rot and mildew wrapped her in a puff of cold, sweetish air. She coughed. The sound echoed. Bright moonlight sifting through the windows showed a high room with a dusty, water-stained plank floor and walls shedding yellowed wallpaper. Each of the walls held a door, all closed.

She wished they weren't. Then she wouldn't have to worry about what might be behind them. Her mouth tasted like the contact of a battery, but she stepped in. She definitely did *not* want to shut the front door.

"Hello?" she whispered.

Why did she have to say that? It was what people always said when entering creepy old houses in scary movies. And immediately afterwards, something awful always happened.

The room whispered back. Somehow, it didn't sound like her voice—at least not *only* her voice. Talys stood behind her, somehow solid even though he wasn't solid at all.

"I'm—" Her voice came out in a breathy creak. She cleared her throat. "I'm here to help, okay?" That sounded even stupider.

She looked from door to door. Someone was standing behind each, listening, she'd swear it. She set her jaw and plowed through fear toward the door on the opposite wall. The some-one receded. She put her hand on the knob. It felt warm, like someone had been holding it.

Talys was still beside her, a silvery nimbus. His warmth en-wrapped her hand. She turned the knob and opened the door.

This room was dimmer, cooler than the last. Empty, too. Disintegrating curtains veiled a single window. Two more doors faced her, one ahead and one to the left. Whispers came faint, like a memory of people in the room.

"They're here, Talys. Why are they hiding?"

She crossed to the left-hand door. The floorboards squeaked under her feet.

Another room, dimmer, colder still, more closed doors. Also empty— No. She whirled, breathing fast. What made those shadows, flitting around the corners of the room? She backed toward the door she'd just come through, turned—

Something filled the doorway, large, dark, a shape like a man in a cloak. She made a short, sharp sound like a breaking stick and the shape swept down on her.

Eyes, pupilless, bottomless, a face blank and masklike. Pain, pain, emptiness, hunger, *anger anger anger.*

Amethyst screamed and flung up her hands. Purple light shot with silver webbed a face, shaped a man's large form out of shadow. The sense of invasion, of another mind ripping into hers stopped. She staggered back, thumped into the wall behind her. The shadow shifted, swelled. Fingers of darkness reached, groping toward her—

She fumbled along the wall. Her fingers bumped a door-knob; she turned it and tumbled through.

More shadows, oh God, rolling toward her, clots of rage, coagulations of pain. Magic coursed lava-like through her, spilled out in a swirl of incandescent violet, Talys' molten silver. The shadows recoiled, eyeless, snuffling things scenting warm life in the dark.

Get out! Get out now! a voice called—her own or Talys'? There was no help here, only mindless, destroying hunger. There was the door, open, half visible through the storm of shapes pouring in— no, no, she couldn't go that way, how many were there?

She burst through another door into blackness. Voracious shadows tore through the nebula of shielding magic surrounding her, seized her, flayed her, drained power from her. Vision darkened, changed; she peered at herself through another mind.

Hands grasp a young woman, dark-haired, glowing silver-edged against darkness, eyes the violet of her power. Warmth where there was only cold, life when there has been limbo, power in emptiness, wholeness in the grip of what was crippled, ravaged, mutilated. Power is there, within, throughout, permeating her. What was broken must be mended. What was lost must be retrieved.

Pain then, the tearing of herself out of herself. Her eyes could see in the darkness, see the leprous walls, the floor of buckling black and white tiles. There were no doors, none. The shadows were no longer shadows, but people. They massed around her: a boy reached out pleading hands; a sad-faced woman plucked at the hole under her heart; a man twitched like a broken puppet; a girl in a hoop skirt turned round and round, groping for what was stolen.

But the pain—it wouldn't end. It seared like fire, dragonfire, the dragon's wound, never-healing, never killing, a bloodless gash where a soul once resided.

Silver blazed. Someone was screaming—

Amethyst came back to herself, leaning against a wall that seeped cold and damp through her shirt. Her throat was raw, ragged-feeling. Her whole self felt ragged, worse than the magic usually left it, like something that didn't fit had tried to squeeze inside, pouring in thoughts that weren't hers.

She scrubbed at her face to erase the memory and raised her head. No shadows. Just that flat magnesium glare that came from nowhere and everywhere, black-and-white floor squares, mildewed walls—

Oh.

Oh, God.

No doors.

She couldn't breathe. She turned, turned—*no door, no door, no door—*

The light went out and phantom flares jerked and bobbed across her retinas.

"Talys!" she gasped, a half-strangled wail.

No reply, no warmth, no comforting sense of presence. Like reaching out and finding only a stump at the end of her arm. She whirled, groping with her hands, with magic-sharpened senses.

A thin streak of light appeared. Another retina-ghost? No. It was growing longer, a thin, silver line glimmering through the room's darkness. It turned a corner, then another, and now two knives of light sliced downward, outlining a tall rectangle about where the wall must be—

The door! It had to be! She lunged for it, fumbled at waist height, found the doorknob and was through.

More darkness, as if the room were so full of shadows they'd left no room for light. Whispers, like a pot boiling over on the stove, a sense of hands snatching at a morsel too hot to touch. Magic lay thick, burning on her skin, scalding her mouth and lungs and innards with each breath, a spitting, half-wild defense against the assault.

Silver gleamed to her right—Talys' silver, showing the outlines of the next door. The magic pushed ahead like a bow wave, thrusting those almost-material shadows aside. Her hand found the knob this time as if she could see it.

The next room was the one with the tattered curtains. Except now those curtains seemed to frame a space of blank wall, just cracked plaster with a glimpse of lathe boards behind. Where were the crowding shades? What were they doing?

That shadow, shade, whatever, in that last and darkest room, had wanted her—they all had, horrible, mutilated, pitiful things. She shuddered and groped for Talys, but still couldn't touch him. He must be keeping ahead of her, finding the doors. Another long rectangle defined itself on the adjoining wall. God, how many more rooms? This was awful, worse than the tree-thing on the mountain, worse even than Jas, like a nightmare.

She grabbed hold of the fear, shoved it back. If she just kept following those silver lines, kept opening doors, she'd get out. The shades weren't trying to get at her for the moment. They were behind, all around, following—or stalking.

Her hand hit another invisible doorknob. She made grab for it, missed, tried again and spilled through the door...

Into a furnace.

Magic blazed in sheets of red and orange and yellow. She smelled the stench of burning flesh and crisping hair, gasped a breath that seared her throat, shriveled her lungs—

No! She wrestled terror, clung to logic as if threading bug-riddled code. This was magic, like the darkness before, like the doorless rooms. She muscled aside illusion to see what was real—the water-stained floor, peeling wallpaper, the two tall windows flanking the door.

The door was still wrong. It opened onto hell, a void dotted with fiery eyes and howling mouths. Shaking with effort, she struggled to replace the fire with cold, rot-smelling air, to put a sagging porch and moonlit yard outside that door.

The barrier spell crumpled like flame-eaten paper and she stumbled forward again, sweat cold as fog on her face and neck and arms.

Talys stood silvery, mirage-like between her and the half-open front door, lighting the way. The room was empty of fire, of darkness, empty of shades. He glided through the door ahead of her, then drifted down the porch steps toward the waiting Mustang, its curves etched in moonlight. She hurried after him before anything else had a chance to go wrong.

A wisp of hair stirred against her cheek. Cold air breathed on her back. She refused to look. Two more steps and she'd be through the last door, safe.

But the spell walls were all gone. She'd broken them down.

Her pulse rushed in her ears, throbbed in her throat. She turned her head. A lightless wave filled the room behind her.

Strips of wallpaper flew past, out the open door. Her hair whipped across her face, half-blinding her. The front door scraped on the floor, an inch, a sudden six inches, then caught on a buckled floorboard.

She dived for it. Dark wind roared down on her. She threw out her arms and shielding magic, panting with effort and fear and exhaustion. The tumble of shadows buffeted her and howled past, flattening the sagging picket fence, plucking at the porch roof until the whole structure shrieked. Amethyst clamped her fingers around the edge of the door. She shoved a shoulder between jamb and door, squeezed through and out. The wind sent her hair writhing around her. She scraped her face clear.

A knot of shadow seethed and twisted around a brilliant silver core, like blood-frenzied hounds on a mountain lion.

"Talys!" she screamed. He'd said he was vulnerable outside his chosen form.

Vulnerable—

She flung magic blindly, something, anything to protect him. It disappeared into the swarm, swallowed up.

She was down the steps and across the yard. The fallen gate cracked under her feet, weathered old wood giving way beneath her weight. She snatched at the magic again, wrestled it into a form hot and dense, as furious and desperate as she was. She didn't care about her own shielding. Talys was the only thing in this deadly, helter-skelter mess she could trust. The air compressed around her and the shadows were on her again.

She grew thinner, lighter, torn out of herself. Darkness bled into the edges of her vision, then it was all she could see. She struggled, clinging to her power, her *self*, against the hunger trying to drain it away. The shadows, the shades screamed in her ears and pain blazed again in every nerve.

Pain, pain, anguish, loss, anger, horror, misery, bewilderment, hatred. Thoughts, memories pummeled her, tore at her, carried her away into other minds, other lives.

She was a young boy in a dusty village of mud houses, talking to beasts. She was an old woman walking a pig on a leash through a forest, seeking healing mushrooms. She was a blind man whose eyes saw the future; a beautiful, pale-haired woman with the power to raise empires, or send them crashing into ruin…

She was going insane. Where was she? Who was she? A wizard, yes, that she knew—hadn't she worked every kind of magic, snuffed the great prairie fire with rain, brewed subtle poisons for the ruling family, set the flux on the enemy's troops before battle, laid the goddess' blessing on children and pregnant women? She bore so many names she was nameless, existed in so many times and places she was spread thin to nothingness. The wind would blow right through her.

Stillness descended, silvery, foglike. She faded into the night, the moonlight, into the damp, misty air. Something in her struggled, desperate with fear, but the silver warmth soothed her as it had months ago in the seat of a strange car. Beyond the calm place shadows whirled, flurrying away in scraps of darkness. The comforting sense of warmth faded, and she slipped back into herself.

Amethyst panted, dizzy. Cold and damp seeped into the front of her shirt, her cheek, the skin of her arms. She was half-sprawled across the Mustang's hood. She pushed herself up, dragged straggling tendrils of hair off her face with trembling fingers. Her throat was raw again, but she didn't remember screaming.

"Talys?" She still leaned on the car. Her hand on the fender felt only cold metal.

She wrenched upright, staggered and almost fell.

"Talys!" Her voice cracked, climbing to a frightening note. *No, please. Not now.*

She started shaking. She stumbled away from the car, turned, slipped in the damp grass. Her breath came short. He couldn't be gone. He couldn't be. Her throat closed, and the breath whistled through it, tattered. She fumbled for the magic, but her power, battered, unraveled by panic and exhaustion, wouldn't answer.

She clenched her fists. "Stop. This isn't helping."

She took a breath, pushed it out. Slow, easy. The next one was a little better, not quite as tight. She squeezed the panic into a small, hard ball in her middle. She slumped and braced a hand on the fender, staring down at her reflection in glossy black paint. It wavered a little, as if still not quite sure who it was.

"Think," she told herself. "What happened?"

It had saved her, that thinning and fading. No, *Talys* had saved her—again. He'd shaped magic to hide her, to make her disappear into her surroundings. She hadn't managed to return the favor. And the shades had—

She didn't know what they'd done to him, when he'd made himself a target instead of her.

She hurt inside like she'd been in a terrible fight, a brutal screaming match with a cherished friend, the kind that leaves you sick and weak and wanting only to crawl into bed and stay there for the rest of your life, wishing the memories would quit swirling like vomit in a toilet bowl.

She bent and pressed her forehead to the car's windshield. The smell of rot reached her from the house, the sea tang, an herbal smell of some unfamiliar plant.

She owed it to Talys not to fall apart. She had to think, had to follow this through logically. They'd miscalculated once, expecting to find help in that house. So what had they found instead?

Wizards' shades. The thought popped into her mind as if from some outside source.

She straightened. The memories still careened around her mind, a chaotic whirl of thoughts and knowledge and experience. Of magic. And over and over, the anguish of betrayal, of the agony of being torn out of oneself.

"That's what happened to them?" she said aloud. Power ripped out, like the filling sucked out of a Twinkie. The will stolen, the self annihilated—

Like Jas had tried to do to her.

"No," she whispered. "It can't be."

Yes, Jas had put that spellbinding on her. But all the time she'd spent with him, she would've known—*sensed*—something as repugnant as what had happened to those wizards.

Power suddenly prickled her skin, bubbled in her blood, seeking outlet. Spells flicked through her mind: stealthy spells that would creep through the earth to drain an enemy of joy until he ended his own life; dark spells that would call man-eating spirits from worlds beyond this one; fiery spells that would blast everything in their path—

She pressed hands to temples, pushing the knowledge away. No. No. *That wasn't her.* That was someone else—one of those wizards who'd tried to push her out of herself, who'd tried to rob her of what had been stolen from them. Okay, fine, they couldn't help it, their humanity had been drained out of them leaving nothing but blind hunger. But she *could* help it, and she didn't do things like that—to anybody.

Amethyst shivered—she wasn't used to this damn damp, and she was beat up and overwhelmed, too. She pulled the car door open—no help this time—and fell into the seat.

"Well, Talys." Her voice was steady now but too high. "We got something out of it. I know what magic can do now."

The Mustang, being only a car now, didn't reply.

Chapter 22

She was alone. Talys was gone—snatched away, snuffed out, gobbled up—Amethyst didn't know. She couldn't even stand to think about it. Jas was some kind of serial soul-killer, and he was still back in Albuquerque, waiting for her. And now she couldn't reach Melodie. Not a particularly unusual circumstance on a weekday afternoon.

But right now, she had a very bad feeling about it.

Amethyst hung up the payphone receiver and stared at the graffitied walls of the booth. She cursed, but there wasn't a swear word bad enough to come near what she felt.

She gritted her teeth. "Think, Amethyst."

She still felt sick and shaky. Added to the throb of day-old bruises was magic's internal second-degree burn sensation. Wisps of thought, strange images floated through her mind; echoes from the night, she guessed. Magic that would conceal her from enemies. Songs to keep a battered ship from sinking. A pattern of lines scratched into the bottom of a cup to turn the drinker to one's will. The kinds of things experienced wizards might be expected to know.

She had no idea how to put them to practical use in the current situation.

Well, it wouldn't to do any good to just stand here, feeling desperate and hopeless. Amethyst straightened and pushed back her hair. Traffic moved along the highway, in and out of the gas station, with perfect indifference. People in another little town on the California coast going about their business, truckers making deliveries, tourists on their way to the next destination.

The Mustang, parked a few feet away in the early morning sun, was nothing but an inert mass of metal and glass, rubber and plastic.

Oh, Talys.

The payphone rang, a shattering, old-fashioned jangle. She jumped and her heart lurched into high gear as if she already knew who was calling.

She picked up the phone.

"Amethyst," Jas said. "I see you're taking the long way home."

She clenched the receiver to her ear and wished she hadn't lifted it. But what else could she do? She couldn't afford to push him into doing something drastic.

"Am I?"

"Oh, yes. Gualala last night, Fort Bragg today… You're certainly taking your time. What have you been doing?" It was his usual pleasant, friendly tone.

She fought down sudden rage. "Maybe I should ask you the same."

"Why? I'm not the one setting off fireworks for half the country to see."

Of course he would've been able to sense what she and Talys had done at that house, the way a seismograph could detect an earthquake a thousand miles away.

"Is that so?"

"Indeed it is. Personally, I recommend subtlety."

"Subtlety!" she exploded. "Do you call what you—"

"Calm down," he broke in. "We'll have no chance at all of successful negotiations if you allow your emotions to get the better of you."

The muscles of her hand hurt, they were knotted so tight. "Look, if you're going to threaten me, say what you mean."

"Threaten you? I wouldn't dream of it."

"Tell me what you want, Jas. For once, just come out and say it."

"You." He said it like a jaguar dropping out of a tree onto prey.

She clutched the phone and wrapped her free arm around herself.

"But you already know that," he went on.

"How about what I want? Or does that matter?"

"I think I can convince you that our interests coincide," he said, just as smoothly as ever.

Her stomach turned over. She didn't want to hear how he planned to convince her, but she had to know. "So let's hear it."

"Not like this," he said. "Come home. Get in touch with me then."

She leaned her head against the side of the booth. It was cold, hard and probably dirty, but she just couldn't care right now. "Right."

"And, Amethyst? Trust me—you really don't have another option. Don't waste more time trying to find one."

"Yeah. Thanks." She hung up.

The breeze blew cool and moist off the sea, smelling of salt and fish, a foreign, far-away smell. She couldn't hear the waves here, just the rush of tires on the highway, the squeal of brakes, the rumble of trucks. The phone booth walls imposed their obscenities on her.

He had access to Melodie, and they both knew it. Along with Dad, Mama, and everyone else she cared about. He was right: what other options did she have?

Just one. And she'd damned well try it before she went slinking back to Jas.

She slid into the car and picked up the pay-go cell phone she'd bought at the Walgreen's down the street. There'd still been enough money left in the glove compartment to cover it. She only hoped there'd be enough for gas back to New Mexico. With Talys gone, the needle had been doing an unprecedented fall toward empty.

She called information, burning through precious minutes. At last, a woman said, "Good afternoon, Dr. Korhonen's office."

"May I speak to Dr. Korhonen? This is Amethyst Rey. It's—kind of an emergency."

"I'm sorry. The doctor is with a client right now, but I can have him call the moment he's free."

Amethyst pressed her temples. "I'm on a cell phone, and I'm not sure what kind of signal I'll have—" Her voice was going higher and she stopped. "Will you please tell him I called and it's important I talk to him? I'll call back—"

"Thank you, LaDonna," a man's voice said. "I'll take this call."

Thank the blessed Virgin for whatever wizards did to screen their calls.

There was the click of a line disconnecting and Dr. Korhonen said, "Amethyst. I'm so glad to hear from you. Are you well?"

"I— No. I'm in California, and—I'm in some trouble."

He was silent a moment. "California! Please, tell me what happened."

She told him—most of it, anyway. He didn't need to know about the kissing.

"Talys—my familiar—brought me here. He thought we might find help—"

"Where are you now?"

"Fort Bragg."

She thought of where she had to go, what had to be done, and couldn't continue.

Talys had been right. How could she ask Korhonen to help fight a wizard who'd destroyed so many others? It was impossible. Korhonen hadn't replied yet. Probably saw where this was going.

"Dr. Korhonen, I'm sorry. I shouldn't have called."

"On the contrary," he said quickly. "You were right to do so. I'd sensed the magic used—now I know what happened. You say your familiar was looking for help? I take it you didn't find it."

She rubbed her forehead. "No. We found…something else. Not what he expected."

There was another short silence. "Very well," he said as if reaching a decision. "Listen carefully, Amethyst. This man may try to bring you to him, as a wizard can do."

More scraps of knowledge came churning up like wreckage in flood waters: words whispered into a cup of water and then poured into the stream that ran past the door of the one called. Wizardry that could reach across the miles to pluck up objects— or people. A trap laid in dreams. She knew first-hand how that one worked.

"You must not go to him," Dr. Korhonen said. "And you mustn't allow him to reach you. Your familiar will show you what to do."

Except she didn't have a familiar any more. She couldn't stand to say the words. They'd make it real, irrevocable.

"I know what to do," she said instead.

"Good. Contact me when you arrive. We'll put an end to all this."

"Thank you." She pushed the button to end the call.

She knew she should be grateful, but was only lost and scared, drowning in events too wide and deep for her.

Jas knew exactly where she was, but she couldn't make it easy for him or he'd get suspicious.

She grabbed magic like a polished shield that would blind an enemy and flung it up, It hit her like a bad case of flu, making her feel sicker and weaker than she already did.

Melodie still wasn't answering the phone. Not when Amethyst had called from Flagstaff, or Gallup, or Grants, sixty miles back. Not anytime over the fifteen hundred-and-some-odd miles between the Pacific coast and Albuquerque.

She hadn't slept since awakening slumped under the Mustang's dash back in the California hills, what? Day before yesterday? She'd lost track.

Her eyes burned. Her head buzzed. Taillights and headlights spangled, refusing to quite come into focus. She almost missed the University exit. She suspected magic was the only thing that kept her going.

It didn't help her emotional state. She was so scared she

couldn't think. And when she could, all that went through her head was, *First Talys, now Melodie. It's all my fault, if I'd just listened to Talys to begin with and not wasted all that time*—

She thumped a fist on her thigh and stopped the thoughts. Recrimination didn't help a goddamn bit. She'd better start plotting out if-then scenarios like her life depended on it, which it probably did. She only hoped Melodie's didn't, too.

Amethyst downshifted and made the right onto Melodie's street. Streetlights cast pools of sickly orange light over yards and parked cars, sapping the life out of every color. The darkness between seemed blacker, as if every terrible possibility lurked there.

She steered the Mustang around the curve of the street. The porch light was on at Melodie's house, a wistful gleam. Amethyst pulled to the curb and turned off the ignition. The engine's bass rumble died and silence spread all the louder.

"Well, Talys…"

She didn't bother finishing, didn't know what she would've said if he'd been there. But talking to him kept her from remembering he was gone. Until he didn't answer.

She gripped the wheel for a long moment. Her pulse beat too fast, and she had trouble catching her breath. At last, she climbed out of the car and started up the walk.

On the doormat, she raised her hand to the bell. Her finger hung there, an inch from the lighted button. She had to push it. Waiting wasn't going to make anything better.

She rang the bell.

Nothing. Nothing. Fear fluttered under her breastbone. She struggled with an impulse to burst open the door with magic. She could do it easily enough, but there probably wouldn't be much of a door left when she was done.

The door jerked open so suddenly she flinched. But it wasn't Melodie standing bemused in the spill of light from within. The fluttering in her middle turned to a cold knot.

"Marl," she said.

"Amethyst. Thank God!" He snatched her inside. "I just got in. You're lucky you caught me here. Have you heard from

Melodie?"

She already knew it, it wasn't a surprise, her legs shouldn't be trying to dump her on the floor. She had to catch herself on Marl's arm.

His face, so full of hope and abject relief a moment ago, closed in on itself.

"No," he said. "How could you? You just got back into town. You came straight here, didn't you?" He ran a hand through his hair. "Amethyst, I'm sorry. I'm not thinking— After what you've been through—"

She took his arm again. "Don't worry about that. Just tell me—" Her voice disappeared. Somehow, they were walking, past the newly-painted living room and into the kitchen. "Tell me what's going on. Where are Bree and Jenna? Are they okay?"

"They're with my mother, they're fine," he said with a distracted wave. "They don't know anything about this yet. Melodie never went in to work. I've looked everywhere—her car's in the garage, her purse is here—" This time, he ran a hand down his face. "I don't know what to do. I can't lose another—" He stopped.

Funny how she could bawl for hours on end about a love affair gone bad, but when it came to her best friend facing some unknown and possibly dire fate, it seemed like her soul had been ripped out of her the way those shades' had been. The way Talys had been.

The kitchen's fluorescent light cut the appliances, the counter tiles, the stainless steel sink sharp and clear. A spell rose out of the mire in her mind, equally clear. Something cold and quick went through her, like mercury, bright and slippery.

"I'll find her."

He swung around on her. "No," he said. "I have friends in APD. They're already working on it."

She couldn't look at him, not with the pain and fear so clear on his face. "Okay," she said and turned.

He caught her. "Wait. What are you planning?"

"She's been my best friend for ten years. I know a few

places to look."

His eyes narrowed. "Like where?" He was too much the lawyer not to recognize evasion.

"Favorite hikes, favorite restaurants, friends' houses."

"You're not surprised," he said. "Upset, but not surprised. You knew she's—" He seemed to struggle. "She's missing."

"I've been trying to call her all day," she said, trying to sound patient.

She could see his mind working. "Amethyst, if you know something, tell me. Please."

She folded her arms tight over her chest. A thousand years worth of wizards' experience had shown her that words were powerful, but she couldn't—wouldn't—tell him the truth.

"It won't do either of us any good if I told you all the stuff that's going through my mind." She gave a breath of a humorless laugh. "I'm pretty paranoid right now. All I know is, I'll feel a lot better if I'm doing something." She touched his arm. "Do you understand?"

Marl paced away, braced his hands on the kitchen counter. "Better than you know." His voice sounded thick and unsteady. He straightened, turned back. "All right, tell me where you plan to look. I'll help."

She said the first thing that came into her head. "Did you try the CS department at UNM?"

"This afternoon."

"How about...how about Fajitaville?"

"Where is it?"

She told him. He nodded and fished his car keys out of his pocket.

She crossed the kitchen, laid her hand on his arm. "We'll find her."

She left before he could muster more questions.

Amethyst paused by Melodie's patch of lawn, an island of rough-coated buffalo grass surrounded by rocks and spiky desert plants. A single dandelion raised its head there, a perfect, silvery globe of tufts. Clouds veiled the moon. Amethyst held up the dandelion to the vague glow. An uncomfortable combination of foolishness, fear and instinctive confidence buffeted her.

She decided to go with the confidence.

"Dr. Eliot Korhonen. I'm back. I'll let you know where to find me soon." When she knew where Melodie was.

She blew on the dandelion head. Tiny parachutes bearing her message spun away. With a flick of the hand, she called up a small wind to carry them to their destination.

Chapter 23

The spell was simple. Whatever wizard contributed the memory had used a slab of mica, but the magic worked just fine using the Mustang's mirrors. If Melodie was straight ahead, Amethyst saw her image in the windshield mirror. The left and right hand mirrors showed when she needed to turn.

She had three advantages going into this Jas didn't count on. First, he had no idea she knew such spells. Second, she'd have backup. And third, she'd have her best friend safe before she even confronted him. She should have felt confident. But worry and fear chewed holes in her hopefulness.

The streetlights had petered out about two blocks ago. So had the pavement—the Mustang bumped over packed and puddled earth more appropriate to the suspension of contractors' pickup trucks than to forty-year-old muscle cars.

The spell now tugged behind her eyes like a tension headache. Melodie was here. Amethyst rubbed a suddenly damp hand on her sweats. A construction site didn't seem like a place to hide or imprison someone—someone *alive*—

No. Don't think it.

The headlight beams flickered over cranes and earth moving equipment like monsters hulking in the dark. Ahead, the skeletal steel of a building rose maybe ten stories.

Amethyst sent her senses ranging ahead. What exactly was she sensing for? Melodie's terror? Jas gloatingly rubbing his hands like a melodrama villain?

She touched nothing, which in a way was even worse.

Wait—not quite nothing. Something flitted, faint, faraway. Magic? It had the right queasy, turbulent feel, but somehow, felt more like…an echo of magic. Something Jas was doing, or maybe Dr. Korhonen? No, it was too scattered, like it had many different sources. She hunched her shoulders. Please, not something *else* to worry about.

She steered around a pile of construction debris: knots of wire, slivers and chunks of metal, rubble from the washing out of a cement truck. A construction trailer resolved itself out of a tangle of equipment and building materials and chain link and banded stacks of sheet metal.

She braked beside the office trailer. The mirror showed Melodie straight ahead, eyes closed, lying down as if asleep. Yes, *asleep*, she promised herself.

She ignored the dread in her stomach and got out of the car. She touched the fender, but the dead metal didn't lend her any strength.

The traffic noise from the freeway nearby sounded like a rush of wind through trees. A cool breeze carrying a scent of rain and wet juniper came out of the east, down off the mountains. If she turned, she might see lightning playing on the Crest.

She didn't turn. She stepped around a puddle—silently, as a wizard can. She threaded around bits of metal decking, over rucked earth where a vehicle had driven through the mud.

Up close, the building girders were huge: dark columns rising from a plain of concrete into the night sky. City light painted the cloud bellies so it looked like the girders held up a billowing tent canopy of lurid orange.

"Amethyst," a voice said.

Something moved among the steel columns, a pale flicker in the orangey dark. She held still, held her breath, and a figure emerged.

White hair, Santa-Claus portly. Not Jas.

She let go a breath and lowered her hands (when had she raised them?). But when she moved toward him, her legs trembled. Her mouth tasted metallic and her heart whapped against her ribs. She couldn't understand why.

Dr. Korhonen was wearing a windbreaker and jeans, looking totally un-doctorish.

"You got my message!" she said. The feeling that something was very, very wrong still squeezed her chest. She glanced around again at the unlikely setting. "Melodie is here somewhere. The mirrors led me here."

She felt silly saying it, like a kid pretending to believe in magic.

"Yes," he said, flat, unsurprised.

She felt tiny, overshadowed in the vast, hollow space. Melodie might be hidden behind the framework for the building's elevator, or maybe in the crane cab on the other side of the structure. She paced across the concrete, searching.

"Jas doesn't know I can do this kind of stuff."

Korhonen followed. "No doubt he'll be greatly surprised. I take it you finally accepted your familiar's aid?"

Her jaw tightened. "Yes."

She wished she had Talys' aid now. She wished she had *Talys*.

He walked beside her. "Have you considered…" Korhonen paused. "Your familiar might be a point of vulnerability in the coming contest. It might be prudent to remove him from the equation."

Her head drooped, but she resisted the impulse to hug herself.

"I'm here now," he said quickly. "You won't be alone."

"Yes," she said. "Yes, of course. I'm very grateful you are, especially since there's no reason for you put yourself in the middle of my mess. I was just thinking of something my familiar told me…" She swallowed and plowed on. "Something he told me yesterday, about his old master."

"What was that?" The question was the therapist's, a gentle drawing-out.

"That he'd obeyed a command then to stay behind—and how he wouldn't do it again."

A knot appeared and disappeared in Korhonen's jaw. "That is unfortunate."

She briefly pressed fingertips to eyes. "More than you know."

"What do—" He stopped, glanced back toward the

Mustang, then pivoted slowly toward her. "Something has happened with your familiar." He searched her face. "Where is he?"

It wasn't fair to keep holding back, not if she was asking him to stand with her against Jas. He deserved to know what he could count on—and what he couldn't.

"I…I don't know where he is."

He abruptly turned away, hands clenched hard behind his back. "You bring only your native power, and what knowledge you've been able to glean over a short time."

"Yes, I'm sorry." Stupid, stupid! Why hadn't she told him from the beginning? He deserved to be angry, she knew it. She'd be on her own again, and it was her own damn fault. "I wasn't thinking about anything but…" Talys. She couldn't say his name. "I'm sorry," she whispered again.

"No, no, my dear." He turned and took her hands. "You mustn't apologize. This makes it all a great deal simpler."

He wasn't consoling, he was…relieved.

"How?"

"I fear your familiar wouldn't allow you to do what is necessary."

She pulled her hands away. "Wait. Do you mean, kill Jas?"

Jas was a problem, but— Killing people to solve problems wasn't something she intended to start doing.

His features contracted then relaxed again so quickly she couldn't identify the emotion. "Have you been in contact with him?" he asked.

She hesitated. "Not since I've been back."

"Good," he murmured. "Good."

She didn't like where this was headed. "Look, once Melodie's safe, we can reason with Jas. We don't have to do any-thing…drastic."

"Not yet," he said.

Something felt *so* not right. Like expecting a step in the dark, yet not encountering it. Something that should happen but didn't, a word that should be spoken but wasn't—

Then it occurred to her. Korhonen was worried about Jas, about Talys, about everyone *except* Melodie. Why? Because she was an ordinary human being, beside the point in the conflicts between wizards?

The compass needle of some internal truth swung around, pointing toward… No, not quite that. Yet something to do with her best friend.

"Look," she said, "Right now, I have to find Melodie."

"Of course," he said. But he didn't offer to help.

He never had. He'd known she was here—he'd said 'yes' when she told him Melodie was here. But then he'd talked of Talys, or Jas.

He was saying something now, but she couldn't pay attention. She ran back through everything that had happened since she called him, what she'd told him. Her stomach twisted, and it was suddenly hard to catch a breath.

"Dr. Korhonen. How did you know I was coming here? I didn't know where Melodie was until I got here."

He stopped whatever he'd been saying. "Ah. So quick."

"I didn't even tell you she was missing."

He shook his head. "No."

She took a step back. Her ears rang, and her heart beat way too fast.

"Where is she?" The words came out as if her mouth had formed them without her brain's direction.

"She's right here. Your knowledge remains woefully incomplete. You should have considered illusion."

He gestured. The darkness within the building's steel skeleton rippled, wavered, turned itself inside out like a leaf unfurling.

Melodie lay a few yards away on a folded tarp, slack, eyes closed as if sleeping. Amethyst went cold, then hot.

"What did you do to her?" she shouted and dived for her friend.

Magic shoved her back.

She whirled, fists clenched, ready to do serious damage.

"Don't," Korhonen said and pointed at Melodie.

The muscles of Amethyst's arms quivered. She willed herself to stand still, closed her thoughts to the spells that seethed through her mind: seal his eyes and ears and mouth; gouge the thoughts from his mind like melon from its rind; turn the concrete under his feet to molten lead or liquid nitrogen. She couldn't do any of those things. Not with Melodie there.

"It never was Jas, was it?" Jas had said she might've encountered someone worse. She hadn't wanted to listen. "*What the hell do you want?*" she grated.

In the distant gleam of sodium vapor light, his face wore the psychologist's practiced expression of calm, of compassion.

"I'm not an evil man, Amethyst, but one grappling with hard choices. Surely you feel the instability of the magic. I must soon take steps to set it right, or disaster will ensue."

Tremors ran through her like a prelude to earthquake. Her voice wanted to shake, too, so she kept it low. "What kind of disaster?"

Part of her mind ran through scenarios, searching for a way to get Melodie out of this.

"One beyond imagining," he said. "One that might tear the world apart. Magic teeters on the brink of explosion, you see. Should you…contend with me, you might push a delicate situation over the brink."

"Contend?" The tremors abruptly turned to shivering—no, shaking. She couldn't understand why for a moment, then she knew. Of course she knew.

He took a slow step toward her. "Amethyst, the difficult fact of the matter is, I require your power."

Everything was glazed in unreality, distant and cracked and muffled. "Like the shades?" She didn't want to know. "Like the wizards in that house?"

His fists clenched, then relaxed. "Yes." As if by saying it gently, regretfully, he could make it less horrible. "I had—have no choice. I've waited too long. I'd considered—" He stopped, then began again, "This is the only reasonable option."

When had it gotten so cold?

"You didn't think of asking for help?" Her voice came out too high. The house by the ocean came back to her, the pain she'd found there, the same pain the shades themselves had suffered. "You left those wizards in agony! So many of them! All that knowledge, all their power—mutilated. Destroyed!"

"You know nothing," he flared suddenly. "Nothing about wizards, what they're like. What they'll do. They're predators."

"*They're* predators," she flung back. "What are *you*?"

"I did what I had to survive."

She wrestled anger and revulsion and fear. He was so calm. He'd completely rationalized atrocity.

"That includes assaulting my friend?"

That cracked his calm a little. "I've done nothing to harm her."

"Oh, no, of course not. She's lying unconscious on the concrete while her boyfriend is home going nuts with worry. What about him? How will they explain to each other what happened when you're done playing with her?"

"It doesn't matter."

She took two long breaths. "After the other things you've done, I guess not. Hey, they're only regular people."

"In the scheme of things—"

She waved her hands. "Yeah, yeah. The ends justify the means and all that, right? What are a few gruesome maimings and deaths to the guy who's more important than everyone else?"

"Damn you!" he shouted, taking an aggressive step toward her. "This—isn't—about—me!"

"Then prove it. Quit eliminating potential help and use it instead."

He hesitated, then began pacing. "That isn't possible now," he said. "I don't have the luxury to take chances. You must understand."

She watched him, calculating. "I'm trying to, but it's hard to think with my best friend lying on the concrete. I don't even know if she's okay." She kept her voice even.

Another scrap of knowledge arose: a translocation spell. She could snatch up Melodie and send her away.

"As long as your friend is here, you aren't likely to do anything rash."

She slid a foot, shifted her weight, one step closer to Melodie. The spell was pretty straightforward.

"But I can't trust you," she said. "What will you do to her if I'm not here?"

His face spasmed again. "I'm not a murderer. I have no reason to harm her."

"Huh," Amethyst said. "Except you've harmed other people. You're going to harm me. And what have *I* done? I've offered to help you."

He closed his eyes. "I-I-I can't—" he stammered. "I don't—"

She threw a bright, hot knot of magic at him and lunged for Melodie. Korhonen snarled a curse and shaped some spell of his own. It struck her, wrapped like a shock wave around the shield she tossed out. She didn't know what the magic would do, but she gathered her own and flung out her arms as if throwing a net.

Korhonen's spell struck, knocked her to her knees, vibrating painfully into her bones. Magic set every nerve afire. Her ears whined. Her insides ached. But her spell held.

She crawled across the concrete, shoulders hunched, head down, gathered Melodie into her arms. "Mel. Mel. You're okay, right? Please be okay."

Melodie moaned and opened her eyes. "Wiz?" she said. She rolled her head and plucked at Amethyst. "Wha's going on? Where are we?"

Amethyst gusted a shaking breath and resisted the urge to clutch Melodie and burst into tears. Another of Korhonen's spells rammed her shields. She didn't have much time.

"You're in bed. Go back to sleep, Mel." She called up a smile and brushed a few strands of hair off Melodie's face. "You're dreaming."

She shaped magic some wizard had once worked to get an assassin into the shah's very bedroom.

"Go home," Amethyst whispered. "Be safe."

And Melodie was gone. Just like that.

Magic slammed down like a landslide. She gasped—tried to gasp against the pressure crushing her to the concrete—wrenched over and shoved back, but the magic flaming through her felt worse than usual, thick and hot and foul. *Wrong.* Like some kind of toxic sludge escaping years of confinement.

"Go on," Korhonen snarled. "Keep fighting me. Let the consequences be *your* doing."

He crooked his fingers and thrust out his arms.

Another spell, powerful, subtle, lanced through her protections. She cried out and scrambled to turn it aside. It burrowed into her, a parasite with acid-tipped jaws. She screamed and crumpled. The spell sank hooks into her and pulled, tore her out of herself.

Bright bubbles of thought spun away into a confusion of light and darkness. All around magic coursed, a fiery field that swirled and pulsed to its own rhythms, to the texture of the material world.

Hot knots like cancer swelled under a thinning fabric of reality, throbbing pustules that would spew corruption and chaos. Swirls of darkness like miniature black holes sucked in power, life, being, tore at what was already fragile, circling inward as if drawn by some incomprehensible gravity.

Power flowed out of her like blood, that potentiality that let magic flow through a wizard. When it was done, the power would be gone. Only a shadow, a memory would remain.

Shadow. Emptiness. Hunger. Pain. Pain. Pain.

Screams filled the emptiness, the darkness. Thought, power rushed back in, self, soul...

Amethyst pushed herself up. She retched, trembling and aching in a body that had taken way too much abuse over the last few days.

She was alive. How?

Screams still echoed in a big, empty space. The eerie, cloud-reflected luminosity of city light was gone. It was dark, like a choking-thick dust storm—no, like a cloud of bats. Something immaterial brushed past her, shadowlike—

She squinted, trying to see past a ripsaw headache. The shades? *Here?*

The scream came again, male, hoarse, terrible and terrified. Light blazed a hot, fiery orange.

At the heart of it, Dr. Korhonen flailed at the twisting knot of shades, as overwhelmed and terrified as Amethyst had been in that house by the sea. They circled, growing larger, smaller, thinning almost to invisibility, thickening to black clots of rage, vague almost-shapes outlined with sunfire.

Magic heaved. Shades rode the swells like scraps of ash. The fabric of the world bulged and twisted. *Something* was shaking loose. Amethyst could feel it, like dust sifting down from a ceiling of mortared stones.

She hissed a curse. Korhonen hadn't been lying about the magic. It really was tearing itself apart.

The space between the steel columns looked like the world's biggest car fire. Reddish-orange light leapt and clawed two stories high, and around it shades roiled like curds of black smoke.

But her breath plumed white on the air. The building's frame groaned, cracked, and a white fur of rime crawled up the beams. Ice crystals fell out of the air in a fine, glittering dust.

The fiery light coalesced, no longer just a conflagration, but a shape with mass. Something enormous.

Even the shades seemed darker, thicker, more solid than they had, now a surging crowd of human shapes. As they'd tried to draw from her in the house by the sea, the wizards' shades did now to Dr. Korhonen, sucking leech-like at his stolen power.

At the power that had once been their own.

The huge hot shape that was Korhonen screamed, but that was no man's scream this time. It was high, harsh, metallic, the way a hawk must sound to the rabbit before it strikes.

Amethyst shivered so hard her teeth chattered. No shade-memory bubbled up to tell her what to do. This magic, vicious and violent, was nothing they'd known. She hugged herself against a summer night gone so cold the moisture inside her nostrils froze.

The magic around her shivered too, then shattered, spraying fragments of itself like hot shrapnel.

The concrete under her feet moved, not heaving or buckling, but…flowing, changing. It was rock now, sharp and rough and pale as tuff. The steel girders wailed, hunched, erupted into enormous iron pyrite crystals flashing in magic's fires. The cables on the floor uncoiled themselves, raised ends bristling with wires that groped like tentacled mouths. They slithered off, seeking…God knew what.

Magic surged outward like the shock wave of an explosion. On the ground beyond the building, puddles hissed into vapor, mud split and cracked like eggshells, birthing wet, rounded things that mewed and struggled to free themselves. Chain link rattled and rippled, and thin, vaguely sweet-smelling winds keened through the diamond-shaped gaps between the galvanized wire.

The construction trailer became a squat, boxy lighthouse. Greeny-blue light shafted from its windows. Images flickered and moved in that light: a city of soaring, featureless spires; a churning surge of pure light washed away melting rock; a storm raged in the depths of a vast clear orb before a curtain slid over it, closed and then open again—

No. Not a curtain. An eyelid.

Amethyst jerked her gaze away. The frontage road, and the freeway—they were only a half mile away. Maybe less. Ordinary truckers hauling loads to ordinary destinations. Ordinary people driving to homes and jobs…

That after tonight would probably no longer exist in any recognizable form.

She'd saved Melodie. But what good was it now?

Korhonen. He'd said he could stop this.

She took a step and met a wall of shades. Of *fleeing* shades. She gritted her teeth and braced to fight them off.

They were formed enough now to jostle her like a stiff wind. She could see their faces now, the clothes they remembered wearing a hundred, two hundred, five hundred years ago: top hats and homespun and starched ruffs.

And beyond them, blazing with its own fire-hot light…

For a moment, her eyes couldn't make sense of what they saw. Then she sucked in a breath that burned her lungs with cold. Dr. Korhonen was gone. In his place—

It was horned and winged and clawed and spined. Eyes like twin bonfires, open mouth glowing with inner fire. Scales like burnished brass and copper.

Her mouth went dry and bitter. *A dragon.*

She fell back. The dragon whipped its head around, like a snake spotting prey. Every instinct screamed at her to run. Running was stupid.

She couldn't help it. She bolted. The space around her was huge, empty. The Mustang was too far away. The steel columns of the building's skeleton might be something to get her back against, at least. Junk the magic hadn't changed cluttered the concrete floor. A length of rebar lay there, just a few yards away.

She made a stumbling dive, snatched it up and kept running. The metal freeze-burned her hand. It was hopeless, she knew it was. Terror throttled her.

She might've had half a chance if Talys were here. She could almost imagine the sense of him, that bodiless warmth, the energy he poured into her, the way magic became almost tolerable through his medium. Even his voice seemed to speak at the edge of her mind, beyond the din, beyond the wild heave and surge of magic.

Work a transformation! the familiar hot cocoa voice said, boiling frantic this time.

"Talys?" She couldn't hear her voice over the roar and howl around her. The lurch and shudder of the world was all she could feel. Almost all.

Because she could feel him. He was here—somewhere. With her. Impossibly.

"Talys!" Where the hell was he? "How—?"

Not now! His voice came from all around her—or in her head. She had to be imagining it. The shades had devoured him.

The shades...

The dragon screamed and went down on all fours. It stretched out its neck and hissed, lashed its tail like a hunting tiger.

Do as I tell you, Talys shouted again. *Now!*

The searing pain in the hand holding the rebar ceased. Strength poured from the hidden wizardly parts of her, down her arm to her hand.

Magic ripped through her as if someone had reached into her and yanked it. Magnesium-silver glare blinded her. Heat surged out of the metal in her hands, like a campfire in the icy air. Heat flushed her face, warmed the front of her clothes, breathed through her hair. The dim air shimmered, rising.

The rebar blurred around the edges, bled color and shape in a crackle of energy like static electricity until it became a transparent imprint. Yet her hands still gripped...something. Something long and thin.

A...a sword?

It was like a samurai weapon, all slim, wicked, slightly curved blade and plain, black-enameled hilt.

She stared at it, disbelieving. A sword? Against—*that?*

The dragon gave a coughing, rumbling noise horribly like a chuckle. The sword swept up, jerked her around as if someone very strong and very determined had seized her by the hand and pulled.

A thick petroleum smell engulfed her. The dragon lunged and was *there*, a gleaming, two-story-high wall of scales and heat and oilfield stench that made her eyes water.

The sword cut an arc through the air, humming with magic. Talys' silver and her own deep purple and some flickering color all its own crawled up the blade like an electric arc.

Whang! The blade struck the dragon's outstretched claw, jolted her arms in the sockets then rebounded.

The dragon snatched back its claw and bellowed. The building's steel skeleton vibrated with the sound. The sword swept around again. She went with it, shocked and deafened and in pain inside and out.

The dragon struck again, snake-like this time, and the sword rang on its rhino-horned nose. The joints and tendons of her shoulders screamed. The dragon's wings flicked wide, two vast, jeweled sails, and thrust downward.

The sword wouldn't let her fall under the blast of wind, but the downdraft blew grit, bolts, scraps of sheet metal, wire. She flung out hand and spell. Debris whipped around her. The downdraft still pummeled her.

Amethyst squinted up. Above the building's fretwork of beams and girders, wings spread, spined tail lashing, the Korhonen-dragon glowed blazing orange like a heraldic flag rippling in a beam of light. He—it—screeched, folded its wings and plummeted.

Magic laced the swordblade like blood. Incredibly, she felt calm and clear.

"Talys, Korhonen is the least of our problems. The magic is about to—"

I know what has happened, what to do, his voice came again. The sword hung before her, upheld in her hands as if in salute. Threads of silver crawled up the blade. *We must defeat him!*

"But—"

The sky was full of wings, claws and a belly the size of a city bus armored with red-hot brass.

She raised the sword, pitiful little toothpick. The dragon circled, its bulk weaving through the building's beams like a fantastic hang glider. Its wing- and tail-tips slithered and rattled past the steel columns. She shifted her feet on the rough surface of stone.

No, it wasn't enough. She kicked off her shoes. The power was there, God, more than she'd ever need, like she'd knocked on the door of a nuclear power plant in search of a watch battery. She threw the main breaker.

Magic poured through her. It was still hot and foul, but the relentless flood that surged outward, past the construction site to the freeway and homes and stores, threatening to drown the ordinary world in impossibilities ebbed. She ceased to be flesh and fluid and bone, became only mind and will and magic, a floodgate cranked wide open, sluicing away disaster.

The sword flashed silver and purple, flickered upward toward onrushing destruction. The dragon screeched its glee, a sound of rending metal. It had faced great power before, yes, and prevailed, grown stronger, she heard that in its voice.

She and the sword moved like a partners in a dance, circling as the dragon circled. A step forward, one to the right, another back. Graceful, balanced.

The sky was paved with dragon scales. Dragon's jaws gaped wide. Light grew like the rising sun at the back of the throat. First red, then orange, shined on teeth and a pointed, bright red tongue and corrugated palate.

Amethyst adjusted the sword in her hands, angled it to point at the soft back of the throat. Heat hit her and that hot oil smell. Flesh, cartilage, bone struck the tip of the sword, crumpled her arms and drove her down.

A streaming jet of something thick and hot as oil from a racing engine blasted over her. Pain blazed through her.

She screamed, or a scream tried to tear out of her, but her lungs were already seared away. Skin and flesh peeled off her bones. She was dead even before her mind had a chance to stop working.

But her mind didn't stop working. Magic surged through it, suspended each thought, each pulse of will, the spark of being. Magic traced her shape, held it whole, rebuilt the idea of it. Not the wild magic she'd been using, but a living, conscious force, power that knew what it was to be itself, to be a wizard.

This must be what it was like to die, or to be born, this timeless moment of light, of totality, of perfect acceptance, complete knowledge—spells, languages, a hundred cultures, a thousand ages of time, the minds of beasts and birds, the ways between worlds beyond this one...

The moment ended and she was herself again, alive and whole.

Impossible.

She levered herself off the concrete. The dragon was crumpling around her. Like an image painted on an over-inflated balloon, it dimmed, shrank. The bright scales dulled, the wings shriveled away. It hissed, turned, reached out a claw as if to rake her. The power that filled her shrugged, and the claw scraped past, dwindling, shortening.

The dragon was dull now, brown, no larger than a horse, than a dog, a rat. It shrank into a squat, dull, spiny thing no more than the length of her hand.

Transformation. The huge, powerful, impossible-to-defeat dragon—Dr. Korhonen—turned into...a horned toad. The lizard's wide, ugly little head swiveled one way, the other, then it scuttled away.

She could have reached out with a thought, snatched it up, snuffed it out. She let the little creature go, an insignificant thing.

The power in her held magic like a tiger on a jeweled leash, a wild, savage, beautiful force capable of...anything. Life. Victory. Order. Anything, no matter how impossible.

Her mind felt like a vast library once dim and shuttered whose doors and windows had been thrown wide, its endless corridors of knowledge opened, hers to explore.

Amethyst stood, arms extended, head thrown back. Power filled her, buoyed her up, more power than any wizard had ever owned.

Well. *Almost* any wizard.

She laughed. No wonder Korhonen had taken those wizards! The power felt *good*, like the best day of her life had only been a shadow, but now was full and bright and clear and would last forever.

She could put everything back the way it was.

She closed her eyes and raised her hands. Magic spilled through her, washed outward, re-forming the building and everything the rampaging magic had damaged, as it had reshaped her body.

Simple. Perfect. Beautiful.

She let go the magic and opened her eyes again.

To living, seething darkness—bottomless hunger, draining emptiness, mindless fury.

The shades! But they'd fled!

She scrambled, called up a wind to blow them away, coils of sleep to bind them, a flurry of lights to confuse them.

They came on, leeches drawn to the scent of warm life. So many of them, too many to affect all at once. She hurled magic, but they only absorbed it, growing thicker, more material.

A head full of knowledge, all this power, but how could she fight a black hole—except to release all the magic she'd just contained?

"Talys!" she cried and raised her hands.

Where was the sword? She swung wildly one way, then the other, scuffing among the trash and debris scattered across the concrete. Then she saw it.

Or what was left of it.

Cracked black hilt. Melted stump of blade. She dived for it, scrabbled it up. No silver light came from it, no friendly energy glowed. She tried to call his name again, but couldn't get her voice past the tightness of her throat.

A voice, a presence fluttered at the back of her mind, like a faint tapping under rubble. She reached for it, desperate, not caring about anything else.

The shades descended on her, a wall of voracious darkness, snatching, devouring.

And then nothing at all.

Chapter 24

Lights. Red and blue and white, flashing. Sounds—bleeps, squawks, voices. And cold. Cold to numbness, cold to death.

Amethyst tried to raise her head. It was like winching a great, heavy theatre curtain. Legs moved around her. Feet walked across a smooth plain. Hands turned her over.

"Lie still now, miss. You'll be just fine."

"Get a BP cuff on her," another voice said. "She's shocky. Lactated Ringer's I.V., fourteen gauge catheter…"

Where had they come from?

Her head was turned a little. Her arm stretched out, her fingers clenched around something.

"What's this?" A woman's hand touched hers. "I can't— Miss, open your hand for me. Can you do that?"

No. No. She couldn't. If she did, he'd drift away, lost, gone forever.

"Here…"

The hand gently plied at her fingers, opened them. A black cylinder, a handle, the hilt of a melted sword, rolled out, rocked, fell still.

Amethyst gasped, a great, terrible, shuddering gasp. How could she hurt so much? She'd *won*, she was alive, alive, alone, she'd failed. Talys…

She'd felt his life flicker out, and *she hadn't been able to save him*, no matter how many times he'd saved her.

"It's all right. You're going to be fine," a woman's voice said. "Just calm down. It's all over now."

It was, he was.

Finished.

Done.

❖ ❖ ❖

The curtain beside Amethyst's hospital bed stirred. She thought about pretending to be asleep. She couldn't stand any more fuss. Nurses. Doctors. Mama. Dad. So many questions, plausible stories to be made up. She was beginning to think Jas or the shades would be a relief. But neither showed any sign of putting in an appearance.

Melodie's face peeked around the curtain. "Are you up to visitors?"

Amethyst dredged up a smile and lifted a hand. "Come in."

Melodie came to stand by the bed. Marl was right behind, looking grave. They both settled into chairs, the tubular-steel-and-nubby-fabric kind hospitals provided to make sure visitors didn't overstay. The TV chattered on the other side of the curtain, offering privacy just as thin.

"How are you?" Melodie stared into Amethyst's face as if there were some disfiguring wound there. Of course there wasn't. Nothing Melodie could see, anyway.

"Fine," Amethyst answered. "See? Not even a bruise." She lifted her arms to show them.

Try Dr. Korhonen's Magic Bruise and Laceration Remover! One splash of scalding dragon's blood, and every unsightly spot will disappear!

That, at least, was convenient. The multiple bruises and contusions she'd acquired in her escape from Jas would've required even more torturing of the facts.

Except she didn't feel fine. She felt desolate, diminished. Everything was gone. All that glorious power that had poured into her, power that had made anything possible. What good had it been? Not enough. Not for Talys.

Talys.

She swallowed and stared hard at the ceiling, trying to ignore the clench in her middle.

"You don't sound fine." It wasn't the tart tone Melodie normally would have used.

"Suffice it to say the doctors can find nothing wrong with me. In fact, they're quite irritated I'm in perfect health. They're certain they should find *something* amiss in someone who's been insensible three days. But alas, not even a bruise."

Melodie's brows drew together and she shot Marl a look.

Amethyst frowned, too. "What?"

Melodie's face smoothed. "Nothing." She looked down, picked at something invisible on her pants leg. "So. Does that mean you're well enough to tell us what happened?"

Amethyst had been through this already with Dad and Mama. They were a little easier, though. They didn't know as much as Melodie did. "I was driving around, looking for you. You were missing at the time, remember?"

Melodie dodged that. "But, Wiz..." She put her hand on Amethyst's where it rested on the covers. "At a construction site? A *deserted* construction site? At night?"

Amethyst held in a sigh. After so many repetitions, the story—the lie—came easier.

"I took a wrong turn. I thought I could cut across to the next road, but I got stuck. I started walking."

Dad had driven the Mustang home. All he'd said was, "New car, huh?" Something *else* she'd have to explain. She hoped the fact that the car hadn't been stuck wouldn't come up in conversation.

Melodie sat back. "Please, please don't tell me someone else attacked you."

Amethyst winced. Melodie's knack for getting close to the truth obviously hadn't been impaired by her ordeal.

"I saw a flash of orange light, as if from a fire," Amethyst said. "A boom next concussed the air, then I was hurled to the ground." She shrugged. She hoped she wasn't overdoing it. "I awakened to the paramedics ministering to me."

Melodie opened her mouth to say something, then shut it. "There were no signs of a fire," she said.

Amethyst had the impression that wasn't what she'd first intended to say.

"Other people saw a fire, too, hon," Marl said. "The crew of the truck that responded to the calls were the ones who found her, remember?"

"I know," Melodie said. "But there was no fire." She frowned. "Weird. Just like…"

Marl slid his arm around her shoulders. "Just like what happened to you."

Amethyst held her breath. How much did Melodie remember? "Where were you?"

Melodie frowned down at her lap.

"She doesn't remember," Marl answered.

"I don't," Melodie burst out. "I went to bed the night you called from California and woke up in bed. I didn't even know it wasn't the same night until Marl—" She took his hand and squeezed it.

Marl had a very set-jawed look about him.

Should she ask when the wedding would be? No, probably not right now.

"But it's strange," Melodie went on. "I dreamed—I dreamed I was lying on a concrete floor. It was cold, and there were metal columns all around. And—" She hesitated. "There was a big fire nearby…" She hurried on. "And you were there, talking to me. You told me to wake up—or go to sleep. I don't remember." Her fingers locked together. "Do you think I was driving around without knowing it?"

"Your car was parked in the garage," Marl said. "First thing I checked."

Melodie picked at the invisible something on her pants again and laughed, but it wasn't a happy sound. "I've probably had as many tests as you have the last few days," she told Amethyst. "Maybe I should get Dr. Korhonen's number back from you. I don't like this lost weekend business."

"I really doubt anything like that will happen again," Amethyst said.

"I'll be sure it doesn't," Marl said.

Provided Jas behaved himself, not at all a given. Sure, he hadn't been the real source of the problem, but he still wasn't exactly trustworthy, either. And what about the shades? The way they kept turning up—

Could she just go back into a coma now?

Melodie picked up her hand. "Wiz, everything's okay now."

Yeah. That was what everyone kept saying.

"Listen," Melodie said. "After everything—do you need to talk to someone? I mean, someone besides us and your parents. I'm sure the hospital has a—a professional on staff."

Hadn't she heard that before? Amethyst meant to laugh, but a strange, strangled sound came out.

"I'm not trying to say—" Still holding her hand, Melodie scooted her chair closer to the bed and peered hard into Amethyst's face. "You just don't seem yourself."

Marl murmured, "Of course not."

"No, I mean, yes, but…" Melodie wet her lips. "Wiz, your eyes… I mean, you're even talking strangely." She turned to Marl. "You noticed it too, didn't you?"

Eyes? What did her eyes have to do with how she was talking?

Marl only shrugged, avoiding her glance. "Amethyst, when will you get out of here?"

Thank god for men and their blatant tactic of changing an uncomfortable subject. "I believe they wish to keep me long enough to ensure I won't wink out again for inexplicable reasons." She wasn't talking strangely. Was she? "Maybe another day or so, unless I can frighten them with my indigent status."

He made a grunt as if to say that was the least of her worries.

Melodie was studying her again.

Amethyst stared back. "For someone who just disappeared for two days, you're asking an awful lot of questions about what happened to me."

Melodie held up her hands. "Okay, okay. If you're tired, just say so. I won't pester you now."

The image of Melodie lying helpless on that cold concrete floor popped into her mind. "Pester me all you want." A few hours ago—no wait, it was days, wasn't it?—she'd been terrified she'd never see Melodie again. Like Talys. Her throat felt thick.

"I'll never complain—" Her voice stopped and the tears started. The tears, however, didn't show any indication of stopping.

◈ ◈ ◈

"This is perfectly humiliating," Amethyst said. Wheeled around in a wheelchair, like an invalid. Miles of hallway where everyone could stare at her.

"It's hospital policy, ma'am," the orderly said. "Every patient gets a ride to the front doors."

"No wonder a hospital stay is so damned expensive," she muttered.

After five days, she was going to have to declare bankruptcy.

Melodie patted her shoulder. "Come on, Wiz. You're supposed to be happy. The tests are all good and you're on your way home."

CAT scans. EEG's. So many blood draws she'd begun to wonder if they didn't have a party of vampires in the basement asking for free refills. She should've just told them, *Look, what do you expect when someone who just finished battling a dragon is attacked by about sixty-seven hungry wizards' shades?* But then they would *really* have kept her.

She just grunted.

Melodie patted her shoulder again. "Um, I should probably tell you…"

Amethyst took a long breath. "I'm about to find out why Mama isn't here clutching her rosary and praying about a hundred miles an hour, aren't I?"

"Well…yes. We convinced her it would be easier if we picked you up—"

"But she's at my house, plumping up the pillows, hanging a picture of the Virgin Mary where I can see it from my bed in case I die abruptly. Right?"

They rounded a corner. Amethyst caught a flash of metal, put out a hand and bounced away an oncoming gurney.

"Hey!" both she and the orderly shouted at once. Then suddenly Amethyst was hanging over the arm of the wheelchair, her own arm slack and tangled in the gurney supports.

"Wiz, what's wrong?"

"Ma'am, are you all right?"

She retrieved her arm and pushed herself up. "I—I'm fine. Just—must've startled me, I guess." Wonderful. Now she was swooning in front of an audience.

Except…it hadn't been quite like that. It was more like… What? Having the breath knocked out of her?

The young nurse behind the gurney looked shaken and mortified. "I'm so sorry, ma'am."

Amethyst put on a smile. "Really. I'm okay, no harm done."

There was some jockeying of gurney and wheelchair and then they were rolling along the corridor again, past patient rooms and waiting rooms to the elevator and down.

She still felt…weird. Light. Not light-headed, just *light*. Like in the moment just before you realize you've lost or forgotten something.

And then they were across the lobby and through the automatic doors. Marl's Volvo was parked by the curb, and of course everyone made a big fuss getting her out of the chair and into the car's back seat, no matter how many times she said, "I'm fine," and, "I can manage." Solid, practical Marl and sassy Melodie, anxious? She'd never have guessed it. They must've really been worried.

Marl got in, started the car and finally, finally they were on their way.

Melodie sat in the back seat with Amethyst. She fished a newspaper from the seat beside her and handed it across. "Here's something that'll cheer you up."

Amethyst took the papers. "Do I look like I need cheering?"

Melodie half-turned and propped an elbow on the seat back. "As a matter of fact, you do."

Yeah, she supposed so. Too bad she couldn't tell anyone why she was so glum.

Melodie was still studying her. "Your eyes—"

"What is it about my eyes?" Amethyst said, exasperated. She craned up, trying to see her face in the rearview mirror.

"You said yourself, it was probably only tears, hon," Marl said from the driver's seat.

"I know, but since when have tears been silver?" Melodie said.

Marl only shrugged and shook his head.

"Mel," Amethyst said. "What are you talking about?"

"Nothing, I guess. Nothing now, anyway." Melodie gestured at the papers. "Go on, take a look. They're guaranteed to make you laugh."

It was a supermarket tabloid, and the headline screamed, **WOMAN WATCHES ANGRY PEDESTRIAN LEVITATE TRUCK!** The accompanying picture obviously owed a good deal of its sensational nature to Adobe Photoshop. Amethyst didn't laugh, but she smiled.

"The others, too," Melodie said.

Amethyst put the tabloid on the seat between them. The rest were folded-back sections of the *Albuquerque Journal*. Maybe there was something about Local Computer Magnate being arrested for Lewd and Lascivious Beha—

Oh, no.

911 Swamped with Calls of Mysterious Light Show.

When was this? She unfolded the paper and scanned the article—*last night?* In the vicinity of the mesa south of the airport…

Except she hadn't been doing battle with any dragons last night, and the South Mesa was a long way from where she had. She picked up another section.

Vagrant Vanishes from Back of Patrol Car.

Damn. Damn, damn, damn.

Rats Swarm Local Restaurant—*Owner Says He's Cursed.*

Magic? She shouldn't be surprised. Just because her power was gone didn't mean Jas' was, too. But somehow, this didn't feel like Jas' style. Hadn't he said himself, he preferred subtlety? So who—?

"Must be a weirdness epidemic, huh?" Melodie said. "But it kind of puts things into perspective. What happened to us can't possibly be any stranger than this stuff."

"No," Amethyst said. "No stranger."

"Here we are," Marl said, pulling to the curb. "Home sweet home."

Amethyst looked out the window. Somehow it seemed her house should look different, blank-eyed and abandoned, or overgrown with brambles. It looked as if she'd just left. The grass wasn't even much longer than she'd last seen it. She didn't see the Mustang. That was a kindness. She didn't know what she'd do when she did see it, just a lifeless chunk of metal now. The horrible old pickup was in the driveway. She wondered if Jas had seen to that.

Mama's Sentra was parked in front. As soon as the Volvo's doors slammed, her mother was in the doorway, graceful and elegant as always.

Everyone was talking, hands took Amethyst's elbows and guided her up the walk as if she couldn't make it from the curb to her own door. Mama hugged and kissed her, and—was she?

Yes, she was. Crying, for godsake.

"Mama," Amethyst said. "Why are you crying *now?* I'm fine, really, I swear I won't die on you anytime soon."

Mama sniffed and wiped her eyes. "I'm just so happy to see you home!"

They went inside. Amethyst wished for Dad, too, but he'd had to go back to work.

For a moment it looked like they'd let her stand on her own, but Caramela barreled into the room and almost bowled her over, whining and licking. Mama seized Amethyst's arm as soon as Melodie let go and steered her into the kitchen.

"Violita, see what's here for you!"

Amethyst looked.

Flowers. Purple irises, spurs of lavender and lupine and what looked like hundreds of lavender roses, all spilling out of a beautiful bowl of cut glass the color of...amethyst. Enough to occupy one full place setting at her dining room table.

The damned thing must've cost about what the average retail worker made in a month. Which strongly suggested—

Marl gave a soft whistle. Melodie regarded the arrangement with narrowed eyes.

"Such a polite young man!" Mama said. "So handsome! So well-dressed! I told him you'd be home soon, but he wouldn't stay." Her hand tightened on Amethyst's arm. "And his car, Violita! Ooo, you should've seen how fancy."

"Let's see *who* could've sent you such a *lovely* bouquet," Melodie said and strode for the flowers.

This was going to be train wreck, Amethyst just knew it. She scrambled for a diversion. "When will Dad be back?"

"Saturday, maybe Friday night," Mama said. But her eager gaze followed the card from Melodie's hand to Amethyst's. "Open it!"

The envelope was larger than the usual little square of paper that came with flowers. She turned it over and slid a finger under the flap. Would whatever was written within be like the opera program, like the menu at Double Lightning, where everyone saw something different than she did?

One could only hope.

She lifted the flap and pulled out a folded sheet of pale green paper and a smaller slip, also folded.

Dear Amethyst, the note read in Jas' loopy hand. *Excellent job. I look forward to working with you in the future.*

Well. Presumptuous, yes, but not as bad as it could've been.

"I don't believe this," Melodie said. She was holding the other slip by one corner the way a housewife holds the tail of a mousetrap-squashed mouse. "A check! What does he think, he can buy you—"

"Hon," Marl interrupted.

Mama looked like she was about to hear some earthshaking revelation on one of her *novelas*.

"Yeah, well, okay," Melodie spluttered. "So what does he say?"

Amethyst read the note aloud.

Melodie snorted. Marl gave a startled laugh.

Mama had the check now, and she looked even more disapproving. "But why should he give you money? And so much!"

Amethyst retrieved the check, folded it up with the note and slipped both back into the envelope. "Because I was making a stained glass window for him, Mama. He owed me a payment for the design."

"Oh." It was almost a sigh of relief.

"Who brought these?" Marl slid a vase out from behind the massive arrangement. The vase was one of Amethyst's own, the green fluted one that didn't show the hard water stains too much. At least it didn't overwhelm the poor grocery-store carnations it held.

Mama gave them a dismissive glance. "Oh. I forgot. Another young man came by. I think he said he lives next door." Poking at the slightly wilted flowers with a manicured fingernail, she added, "He wanted to stay, but I told him my girl would be too tired, just out of the hospital."

Amethyst gave a relieved smile. "Thanks, Mama. You're absolutely right."

Mama gathered herself out of the chair. "You two go sit in the living room," she said, shooing out Marl and Melodie. "Lunch will be ready in a little bit." But she came back to the table and sat next to Amethyst. "The flowers are from the boy you argued with?"

The flowers. Obviously, only one offering here counted.

Belatedly, horror shot through her. How did Mama know what Jas had done?

Oh. Of course. She was thinking Jas was the one behind Amethyst's troubled visit home, when Amethyst had actually been feeling guilty when she'd locked up Talys. It was getting hard to keep the stories straight, especially when people started concocting their own explanations. But even if Mama was talking about the wrong argument with the wrong individual, the story worked.

"Jas. Yes."

"He must really care about you, Violita."

Sure. About the way a man cares about a good tool.

Not like Talys had. Her eyes filled. Dammit! Not now. Not again! Why was she doing this? He'd been a *car*, not a person. Not something she could ever care about in more than an abstract sort of way.

Mama put her arms around her. "I know he did something very hurtful. But you give it time. Things might work out better than you think right now."

Amethyst shook her head against Mama's shoulder. She couldn't see how they would. She couldn't see how anything would ever be better.

Chapter 25

You can mope around and cry into your pillow every night, but after Dad and Mama have gone home and you've thrown the dried-up flowers in the trash, everyday life has a way of reasserting itself. You've got to pay the bills and go to the grocery store, and work so you *can* do those things. Pretend everything is normal long enough, and you'll convince even yourself.

Yeah, Amethyst thought. *Right*.

So why did normal feel so un-normal?

Amethyst paused at the door into garage. Purse, keys, phone, portfolio—everything she needed to meet the new client. The front door was locked. The dryer beside her was off. So was the oven. The slacks and blouse she had on had been ironed yesterday, the iron safely unplugged and put away. There really was no reason for that little alarm bell to be going off in the back of her mind.

Outside, Caramela exploded into barking.

She slid her purse and portfolio off her shoulder, lowered them onto the washer and eased open the door into the dining room.

Sunlight glanced through the sliding glass doors, sheened on the table. The chairs all sat drawn up and straight at their usual places, empty.

But Caramela's hackles were up, her ears back, and she paced in front of the glass door like she'd find a way in somehow. Amethyst took a step toward the door to let the dog in—

She stopped. No. Whatever was prickling Amethyst's own hackles, she was pretty sure she didn't want Caramela in the middle of it.

Amethyst's feet crossed the old vinyl silently—unnaturally silently. Shade-memories flicked through her mind—magicks of distraction, invisibility, a shield of mystical crystal that would turn away both an enemy's weapons and his ill-will—

She'd better stop thinking like that. She hadn't used magic since Dr. Korhonen, didn't even know if she still could. Didn't *care* if she could. If she were smart, she'd just fade back into the laundry room, grab her purse and get out. The kind of thing any sensible woman would do.

Then again, sensible women didn't feel like beating possible intruders about the head and shoulders. Especially not when dressed to meet a new client.

She snagged the heavy glass blender carafe off the counter-top and took the last two steps to the living room door.

A man sat in her rocking chair, his feet up on the ottoman like he was prepared to stay a spell.

Not Jas, no. This was a stranger, a curly-haired man with a hard, lined face, wearing jeans and boots and a blue check flannel shirt.

Amethyst wanted to knock over the chair and kick him all the way out the front door. Maybe slam the door a time or two on some stray portion of his anatomy.

"Who the hell are you?"

He smiled, an expression like the slash of a dagger blade. "What wizardry has come to in these latter days, that you must ask such a question."

Wizardry. So he wasn't an ordinary house-breaker.

"Let's try again. What the hell do you think you're doing in my house?"

"I've come to see you." His mouth moved strangely, not quite in synch with the words, like watching a badly-dubbed foreign movie.

"You've seen me. Now get out."

"Or what, *bambina?* You haven't even set wards around your home. Now that I'm inside, will it be so easy to make me leave?"

Would that be using the blender carafe or the magic she might not have any more? Amazing. She wasn't scared. She wasn't even quite so overflowingly angry anymore.

The carafe probably wasn't particularly useful. She dropped

it onto one of the sofa cushions.

"What is it with you guys?" she said. "If you want to talk, pick up the phone like you have some manners and I'll see if I can fit you in."

She almost had the feeling she'd met him somewhere before. But she couldn't have. She only knew two wizards. Unless—

What wizardry has come to in these...*latter days*, he said.

All that lovely power she'd had, that was now gone... No way. He *couldn't* have been one of those damned shades.

He raised a finger. "I have questions, and we'll talk now."

I bet, she thought.

She sighed. "Okay. Ask. Then leave."

Another smile, one that said, *Perhaps*. He folded his hands over his middle and tipped back in the rocking chair. "You have power enough to defeat what devoured so many others, yet then release the power. Why? What purpose is served by such an action?"

She stared at him. "You think...you think it was part of some twisted plot? What was I supposed to do while you people, for lack of a better word, were on me like ravens on roadkill? Set the magic loose again so it could turn the world inside out?"

He scowled. "You're speaking nonsense."

"No, you've dropped into a situation you don't remotely understand. In case you haven't noticed, things have changed in the last however-many hundred years. I don't have all the answers, and I don't appreciate your trying to bully me. You've got your power back, you're whole again—you should be happy. Now leave me alone."

He slid his feet off the ottoman, braced hands on thighs and stood. He was kind of skinny and not a whole lot taller than she was. But it was suddenly like having a mob enforcer in her living room, one reaching for an inside coat pocket.

"I think you will come with me. Others are also interested, and this must be settled."

Her stomach shriveled into a small, hard knot. This definitely wasn't a good time to be uncertain if her wizardry still worked. Could she make it to the door and start screaming before he put the evil eye on her?

He raised a hand.

Damn you, no! she thought and reached for the magic.

The air in front of her went thick and strange. Magic cracked it as if shattering tempered glass. Except that this glass just absorbed the force he'd flung and turned clear again; impervious, self-healing crystal.

"Bastard!" she spat. Damned if he'd attack her in her own house! "You—get—the hell—out!"

With each word, she shoved at the air. He jolted backward, looking more shocked with each shove.

He hurled something and for a moment, the whole room went white. The self-illuminated stained glass window still glowed, though. Magic shivered across it, jarring ripples and dark absorption lines, two different magical frequencies.

Different—

It wasn't just a matter of who knew best how to use magic, who was more powerful than whom. It was who could use *this* magic.

And if nothing else, she could.

She stabbed a finger at him, pinning the shape of him to the window behind. *Go away!* she willed. *Go there!*

The power felt like it had when she'd conjured the window, the way it had when she'd rebuilt the magic-ravaged world.

The blinding white disappeared. Her living room returned, just like always. Except for a whiff of ozone, and the spinning wisp of air that fluttered the pages of a magazine.

The wizard was gone. The only question was…where?

Wincing, she glanced at the window. What if she saw a little stained glass Mafia gangster wizard there, maybe standing in the woods, maybe up to his knees in the stained glass pool?

No. No little man figure. Either she'd whisked him away to the real pool in the real Jemez Mountains, or—God, what a horrible thought—he was behind the stained glass trees where she couldn't see him.

She was suddenly out of the house and down the driveway in the awful old Chevy. She must've been scared after all, because she didn't remember the steps between the living room and the truck. At least her purse and portfolio were on the seat beside her, so she hadn't bolted like a brainless rabbit.

The transmission clattered when she shifted. The neighborhood looked the same as always: the little flat-top stucco houses, their yards summer-green and shaded by big trees in full leaf. How strange that they could look so innocent and normal when the world was now apparently full of wizards who could just pop in whenever and wherever they wanted.

And she was all alone now.

Her throat didn't seem to want to open wide enough to breathe properly. Her hands on the wheel were cold.

She took a long, shaky breath. Okay, time to end the pity party. Korhonen was gone, Jas was apparently on good behavior. She'd thought all the drama was over.

It wasn't. She'd have to learn to deal with it. Wards? Fine. She'd figure out how to wire a magical bug-zapper that would keep those pesky wizards out of her house. Preferably something that would keep them out of her life.

In the meantime, she was a stained glass artist who'd better get some commissions lined up. The big one at the Magus building was obviously out of the question.

She made the right onto Eubank and headed north, past the series of strip malls, through residential neighborhoods whose concrete block back walls fronted the street.

Confidence, she told herself. An upbeat attitude. Was she grieving? No! Terrified of what might happen next? Uh...

She turned into the restaurant parking lot, scanning for a spot somewhere in the lunchtime crowd. Surely hostile wizards wouldn't pitch a battle in the middle of all these civilian witnesses. Somehow, the wizards she'd met so far didn't strike her as that tacky—subtlety and privacy seemed the preferred approach. No, this would be an ordinary meeting with an ordinary client.

She hoped.

The fountain in front of the restaurant splashed cheerfully. A couple of men in shirtsleeves and ties sat on the flagstoned rim, talking.

The restaurant's tall faux-adobe front and walled courtyard looked just as pretty and welcoming as always. She pulled the chile-pepper-shaped door handle and stepped inside.

"I'm to meet Mr. Aturj," she told the hostess.

The girl consulted her clipboard and picked up a menu. "This way, please."

The inside was as packed as the parking lot had been. Voices wove in and out of the chatter of the fountain in the dining area. The hostess in her puffy blouse and long, full skirt led the way past wrought iron tables laden with chips and salsa, enchiladas and sopapillas, past the savory smells of chile and grilling meat at the buffet, out through a pair of French doors.

Professionals in suits and skirts lunched under green-and-cream umbrellas; cell phones chirped tunes. A party at a table nearby sang "Happy Birthday" to a blond woman whose face showed equal parts pleasure and embarrassment.

A dark man in a suit and sunglasses sat alone a couple of tables past the birthday party. That had to be him—Mr. Aturj, the client. He had that look of waiting for someone.

Amethyst checked her watch—she wasn't very late, under ten minutes. That tussle with the wizard hadn't taken nearly as long as it seemed.

The hostess laid the menu at the empty place across from the man.

Amethyst hitched up her purse and gripped her portfolio. She smiled and extended a hand. "Hi. I'm Amethyst Rey. I'm a little late, so sorry—"

He stood. Wow. He was *big*. His hand swallowed hers, but gently.

"Ms. Rey," he said in a deep, rich voice. "I'm Thomas Aturj." He handed her into her seat.

"Thank you, Mr. Aturj."

Oh, dear. Another gentlemanly client. But she certainly wouldn't entertain the kinds of thoughts she had with the last one. She just hooked her purse on the chair back and arranged her portfolio on the table at her elbow, perfectly professional.

His blackout sunglasses lent an appealingly mysterious air to that broad, dark Native American face. And the black ponytail with that black suit, no tie, made him look quite the artsy type.

"I generally answer to Tom," he said, resuming his own seat. "But I actually prefer my middle name."

He had a trace of an accent. He looked like he might be Navajo—he had that barrel-chested, slim-hipped build—but his accent didn't have the lilting Navajo sound. His voice seemed awfully familiar, almost like...

"Do you?" She had to make some reply, not just sit there eyeing him.

"Indeed," he said, bending his head and raising a hand to remove the sunglasses. "In fact, I'd be pleased if you would use that instead."

What was going on here? "Of course," she said. "What is it?"

He raised his head. He was smiling, a half hopeful, half mischievous expression. His eyes weren't Native American-dark, but as bright as polished steel.

"Please, Amethyst. Call me Talys."

Those eyes held a warm, silver flicker, like looking into a shadowed doorway and finding instead a mirror: familiar.

Her familiar. Talys.

Somehow Amethyst was around the table, her arms tight around his neck, laughing or crying or jabbering or all three, she didn't know. He was big and solid and warm under the suit jacket and smelled like a man who'd taken a shower and dabbed on a little cologne before an important meeting.

The arms that came around her felt strong enough to hold her through any storm.

Epilogue

Talys stopped three paces from the vile little pickup. Starred windshield. Oxidized red paint. Cracked rubber. The Plexiglas windows on the camper shell were yellow and opaque from the effects of the high-altitude sun.

She couldn't possibly have been driving *this* in his absence. Yet she must have been—she was opening the driver's door.

"Hop in," Amethyst said.

The passenger door creaked when he opened it and the odors of drunkards, vagrants and possibly dirty dog wafted out. He supposed it would be impolite to curl his lip.

"May I ask what has become of my former habitation?"

"It's at home in the garage." She fiddled with her car keys. "I don't—I haven't wanted to drive it."

"I see." He didn't—not with the confusing churn of emotions he sensed from her. He eyed the bench seat. "However, I must drive. I shan't fit, otherwise."

She grinned suddenly. "No. I guess not."

They exchanged positions, he slid back the seat and started the engine. Beside him, Amethyst fastened her seatbelt.

How peculiar, to shift the transmission, tread on the clutch, turn the steering wheel. Conscious acts, all, no longer simply a matter of deciding to move in one direction or another.

They drove along the tree-lined street in silence for a time.

"I thought you were *dead*," she finally said. "Twice!"

Direct, as always. He sighed, but not so she could hear.

"'Dead' isn't an accurate term in my case. Nevertheless, it was a near thing. The first time, by the sea, when I cast camouflage over you, the wizards' shades were drawn to the power I used. I haven't the sort of power they might drain, but disembodied as I was, they swept me along with them when they went in search of another source."

Her brows quirked. "But what about when we fought

Korhonen? You were in the sword, weren't you? I felt you there. When it was destroyed, I felt—I thought I felt you die, then the shades were all over me. And when I woke up, I couldn't sense you anywhere."

"No. You wouldn't." He'd do best to steer this conversation in another direction. Any direction. "Yet as you see, all is well now. Or I presume it is. What has passed with you over these last weeks?"

She rubbed her forehead. "Did you know the wizards are back?"

"I gathered as much. I take it you've spoken with them?"

She gave a soft snort. "Yeah, talking was in there somewhere. Just before I met you. That's why I was late."

"Not a cordial visit?"

"No."

He smiled. "Ah. I see I've reappeared at the right moment."

She turned toward him. "Then…are you still my familiar?"

Long and long had it been since he'd worn human form. He'd forgotten how emotion could take the voice.

"If—if you're not," she said, "I understand. I mean, I'm sure you can go anywhere you want now…"

"Amethyst—" He drew breath, adjusted his hands on the steering wheel. They weren't entirely steady. "I didn't know if you would wish me back. I failed you abysmally, first drawing you into battle with the very force from which I'd sought to protect you, then—retreating at your weakest moment. I—"

"Excuse me, how many times did you save my bacon? And then when I should've saved you…"

She closed her mouth and rolled down the window. Tendrils of hair escaped her ponytail and flicked in the wind. Over the smell of automobile exhaust came a whiff of honeysuckle.

So much had passed. And so much more would come about now, with the world so changed. But those facts could await a more fitting moment.

"I assure you," he said. "You needn't dwell on it. Now tell me, if you will, of your little tête-à-tête prior to our meeting."

"That. Yes." She compressed her lips. "He wanted to know how I did it—how I managed to defeat Korhonen. Hell, *I* want to know how I did it. Okay, yes, I know the magic put me back together after we skewered the dragon, but I can't be the first wizard who pulled steel on the good doctor in a moment of extremity. Isn't dragon-skewering pretty traditional?"

He inclined his head. "Indeed it is, to the detriment of dragons as a species. However, you may be the first wizard to face him who held a properly enchanted sword."

"Enchanted swords not being the weapons of choice against dragons?"

He smiled, braked for a traffic signal. Oh, those earnest violet eyes, the dark arch of brow, those mobile, expressive lips. She considered herself unlovely, yet how could she?

He replied, "How long do you suppose it has been since a wizard last confronted a dragon?"

"Well—"

"Longer than any wizard alive can remember."

"But—"

"I, however, remember," he went on. "I may not have a wizard's powers, but I have a wizard's knowledge—and more. I molded your powers to a certain transformation. That sword was ancient, forged by a people long forgotten, but created and ensorcelled for the task to which we put it. Of course, a sword is made to kill, but this sword, being an artifact of transformation, could only transform." The signal turned green.

Amethyst squeezed her eyes shut. "At least I didn't kill him. I wasn't thinking about that when he was circling down on me. But a horned toad…"

"Isn't apt to have a lengthy tenure on this plane, no. But that wizard was old—very old. He'd far outlived his own lifespan. Thus was he taking others' essence—others' wizardry."

She sighed and opened her eyes. "You know that's a band-aid for the conscience, don't you?" She shrugged. "Forget it. I've just gotten into the habit of feeling sorry for myself lately, that's all." She smiled. "I'll be back to my old self now."

His voice deserted him again.

She didn't appear to notice anything untoward in his silence.

"There's something else that doesn't make sense," she said. "The shades attacked Korhonen before he transformed himself into a dragon. And they sure didn't seem to have any reservations about attacking me. So why am I still in one psychic piece? I didn't—couldn't—do anything to protect myself when they went after me."

He waited for a pause in traffic. Those marvelous violet eyes rested on him insistently. This time, however, he'd prefer not to meet them. He turned left onto Flint.

"Ah. Yes. That was my doing."

"Your doing. I thought you said you'd left—retreated."

"And so I had."

"Talys," she said. You're trying not to tell me something again. Don't think I don't recognize it by now."

"And I have had a taste of your temper on that front, thank you. Very well. I can only hope I'm choosing the lesser of two evils."

"There's got to be a straight line in there somewhere," she muttered.

He cleared his throat. "Would it ease you to know that you did save me?"

She eyed him. "How?"

He'd chide her for suspicion, but she had good reason. "You know now how very vulnerable I am without shelter. As the dragon was destroyed, and the sword, as the wizards' power he'd stolen came pouring out of him, I found the safest possible shelter." He touched her hair. "You."

Her brow rumpled. "In—me?"

She opened her mouth, closed it again, clearly thinking.

"Your eyes are silver," she finally said. "That's why Melodie said mine were—"

Still frowning, she fell silent. He was certain she didn't see the—well, the polite term would be 'modest'—houses and parked vehicles passing by.

"Well," she said at last. "With everyone who's been in my head lately, I guess I should be used to it." She smoothed one leg of her trousers. "And I'd rather it was you."

He let go a breath and said quietly, "That means a great deal to me."

"To be perfectly honest, it means a lot to *me* that you were there to keep those shades from ripping me to pieces when they took back their power."

Her brow remained kinked, however. "You took shelter in me, and then... That was why I felt so weird when we ran into that gurney, wasn't it? You went from me into the gurney. And now you're human. So whose—?" She shook her head hard. "No, don't tell me. I don't want to know."

He felt like laughing, though the topic wasn't particularly humorous. "You needn't worry, love. I'm no bandit."

"Oh. Good." She paused. "I think."

He turned the wheel and the truck bumped up onto the driveway. How strange to gaze at the familiar garage door through the limited medium of mortal sight.

"This brings to mind the night of our first meeting."

She winced. "Don't remind me."

"No, I shan't, because there is something I've wished to do for some time now."

Propping an elbow on the window frame, she said, "Oh?"

He leaned across, scooped her into his arms and kissed her. He might be turned to a toad for his troubles like the unfortunate Korhonen, but he couldn't say he minded the cost.

He released her. She rocked back in her seat, steadied herself against the door.

"Wow," she said shakily. "That gives a whole new dimension to the term hit and run."

He laughed, a sound that came out as unsteadily as her voice had. "I do hope this means I can move out of the garage."

Amethyst favored him with a long, level glance, then opened the door—*crronk*—and climbed out. She leaned an elbow on the door. "I don't know. Will you drip oil all over the carpet?"

He grinned and unfolded himself from the seat. "Oh, I'm better bred than that."

She arched an eyebrow, straightened again and led the way to the front door, passing between the bright rows of marigolds and petunias that lined the walkway.

Still grinning, Talys followed close, close behind.

Do You Believe In Magic

A Land of Enchantment Short Story

The hardest thing about being a wizard was telling your best friend. Amethyst Rey still hadn't managed it. Sooner or later, she'd have to figure out a way to splice the unbelievable and the ordinary parts of her life together. Just not right now.

Melodie Jarret, the best friend in question, took a bite of her huevos rancheros and chewed thoughtfully. "Speaking of Talys…"

It seemed like the clear Albuquerque sunlight should hang quivering, that everyone dining on the patio should pause, forks and glasses halfway to their mouths, breathlessly awaiting the rest.

Of course, people just kept eating and talking, their dogs lying under the mesh patio tables waiting for whatever tidbits might come their way.

Amethyst sighed and slipped Caramela, her pit bull, a chunk of home-fried potato from her plate. "Go on."

"Don't take this wrong," Melodie said. "But aren't you moving a little fast? I mean, how long have you known the guy?"

A sparrow dropped from the shade lathe onto the abandoned plates on a nearby table, clearly familiar with making feasts of toast crusts and bits of potato. Caramela looked up, her wide, pink mouth open in a pit bull grin.

Whose side are you on, anyway? Amethyst wanted to ask her.

Amethyst mentally scanned her notes for the story she'd prepared when the subject came up—as she'd known it inevitably would. She'd been having to make up enough stories over the last few months, since magic became part of her life. It should've been getting easier. It wasn't.

"I've known him a while. I met him while all that stalker stuff was going on."

Perfectly true. Except the stalker had been Talys. And what he'd been doing wasn't stalking. Well, not exactly. But try explaining *that* to anybody.

Melodie reached across the table, suddenly serious. "You went through a lot, Wiz." Melodie's nickname for her since their UNM days. Short for 'whiz kid' then, but Melodie had no idea how appropriate it was now. "But..." She hesitated. "Do you really think it's a good idea to have him move in with you?"

She shrugged. "We get along." Mostly. "And he's been there for me when I needed it."

Melodie's brows climbed. She could see Melodie processing that. That was the bad thing about having a computer geek for a best friend: you couldn't sneak any flaws in logic past her. Like, *Funny how you never mentioned him, then.*

"He was just a friend for a long time," Amethyst said quickly. "Things only got serious recently."

"Don't get me wrong," Melodie said. "He's seems like a nice guy. And damn, Wiz." She shook her head and gave a low whistle. "He's bodacious." Every once in a while, Melodie's California-girl upbringing peeked through. "I'd let him move in with *me* before someone else had a chance to grab him."

"If you weren't engaged," Amethyst pointed out.

Melodie grinned. "Yeah, that too."

"But?"

"But I'm afraid you might just be feeling vulnerable. And having a man in the house seems like the best cure."

Amethyst had to squelch a wild laugh. *But Mel,* she wanted to say, *he isn't even a man.*

He's my familiar.

❖ ❖ ❖

Amethyst gave a flick of magic, and the garage door rolled open. Cheaper and easier than a garage door opener. And no maintenance. She pulled her Outback into the garage and sent the door rattling down behind her.

Caramela hopped out of the backseat and trotted into the house when Amethyst sent a wisp of magic ahead to open the doors.

She dropped her purse in its usual spot on a dining room chair. Through the patio door, she saw Talys, sitting in one chair of her second-hand patio set, a paperback facedown over one knee. He wore bicycle shorts and a tank top—both black, as usual. And as usual, he looked damn good in them, with all that muscle and black ponytail and Indian-brown skin.

Amethyst smiled and stepped toward the door. Then stopped. A woman's voice drifted through the screen. Amethyst gritted her teeth, rolled open the screen door and stepped outside.

There was Heather. Hanging over the concrete block wall that divided their yards, smiling with that adorable dimple, flipping curls the color of good whiskey.

Thank God the wall wasn't any lower. The most she could hang over it now were her chin and elbows.

"Hello, love," Talys greeted Amethyst. Behind his ever-present sunglasses, one brow and a corner of his lips lifted in an amused quirk.

"Oh, *hi,* Amethyst," Heather said, smiling like halogen beam headlights.

"Hi, Heather," Amethyst said. "What's up?"

"I was just talking to Tom, here. Don't you know, honey, he reads the most *fascinating* books."

Tom. Or occasionally, Thomas—Thomas Aturj. Talys liked to see how many people got the joke: Tom Aturj. *Thaumaturge*. Magic-user. Heather, of course, never had gotten it. To be fair, only one person had, and he was an English major.

Talys held up the book: *The Dancing Wu Li Masters*. "I am attempting to convince her that quantum physics supports the existence of magic."

Amethyst produced a grin. "Oh, I bet there are better ways to convince her."

Like Heather's hose suddenly rearing up and spraying her. Or the flock of pigeons down the street deciding to have a little target practice.

Talys cocked his head. "Perhaps so, but likely few that would sit easy on the conscience."

That left out the pigeons. She'd have to mess with their little pigeon brains. "Huh," she said. "Too bad."

Heather laughed. "Oh, you two! Always teasing me. You'd think I'd lived here all my life, instead of only a few weeks." She thrust out her lower lip in a considering pout. "But do you realize we've never gotten together for some socializing yet? It just doesn't seem possible."

And in a just world, Amethyst thought, *it wouldn't be possible.*

Talys tossed her a malicious grin. "Perhaps a barbecue might be in order."

Amethyst shot him a look of baffled outrage.

"Oh, honey!" Heather said. "You know just how to gladden a girl's heart. That's a *fine* idea."

"Well, I—" Amethyst began, fumbling.

"What do you think about inviting the Griegos, as well?" Talys asked her, then turned to Heather. "Have you met Gary

Griego yet? Our neighbor on the other side." He nodded to the right, where the Griegos green fiberglass patio cover showed over the block wall at the other end of the yard.

Heather looked doubtful. "The chubby one?"

"Don't let appearances fool you," Talys said. "He's a real sport."

Amethyst almost choked. "I think—" she started to say.

"We could make it a block party, invite all the neighbors." Heather squeezed her eyes closed in delight. "How fun! I've got to call my momma, get her beans and mudbugs recipe."

Mudbugs? "How about—" Amethyst said.

"We'll figure out a date. Talk to y'all later!" Heather waved and bounded for her back door, her flip flops flapping.

"Gah!" Amethyst said and stomped into the house.

Caramela trotted at her heels, a worried wrinkle on her forehead. Talys came up behind and wrapped his arms around her. She stiffened.

"You," Amethyst said, "are not my friend right now." She tried to disentangle herself, but he only held her tighter.

Talys bent his head and said in her ear, "Now, now, love. Don't you trust me? I'm your familiar. The young lady's blandishments are like a sprinkling of water on hot iron."

He knew perfectly well she wasn't talking about *that.* Well, not entirely.

"I'm talking about Heather Purdy. And Gary Griego. At my house. At the same time." She shifted her jaw to one side. "After you do something like that to me? No, I don't trust you."

A laugh rumbled in his chest. "Pity. And it was such a good plan, too."

She turned in his arms, braced her hands on his biceps and scowled up at him. "What plan?"

Talys had dispensed with the sunglasses. Eyes the silver

of polished steel gleamed with mischief. "Gary, your importunate suitor."

Amethyst made a gagging noise. Gary was 30-something, still living at home with Mommy and Daddy and had been chasing Amethyst since she'd first moved into her house.

"Heather, a most determined flirt," Talys went on. "Should we not endeavor to bring the two together? Ah, think of it, love. What poetry it would be!"

"Yeah. It's also not particularly likely."

He smiled, an irresistible crinkling of his broad Native American face. "With magic, anything is possible."

"Why?" she demanded. "Why do you say things like that to me? Are you *trying* to tempt me? Offhand, I can think of, oh…" Counting on her fingers, she riffled through the jumble of secondhand spells in her mind, courtesy of possession by several dozen wizards' shades. "…at least seven spells that will make them fall madly in love with each other—whether they want to be or not." And not a single love potion in the bunch.

"Do you really believe I'd afflict your delicate conscience? Such things can be accomplished with nary a compulsion or bewitchment."

She drew breath to protest, but he laid a finger on her lips.

"In addition," he said, "hosting a party is the neighborly thing to do."

"Who says I feel like being neighborly?" she muttered.

❖ ❖ ❖

Heather stood beside Amethyst, arms folded across her enviable bosom. She scowled at Amethyst's gas grill. "*This*," Heather said, "is a barbecue?"

Amethyst stuck her hands in the back pockets of her jeans. "I always thought so."

She'd gotten it at the Smith's grocery store a few

summers ago. It wasn't anything fancy, just the grill, a propane tank and a couple of plastic side tables, but as long as you kept the heat on low, it didn't burn anything.

Heather shook her head. Her Glenlivet curls bounced. "I'm sorry, honey. It might be fine for grilling hamburgers and weenies, but for the ribs and links and chicken breasts we'll be having, you need the real thing."

We? Amethyst thought. "Well, since this is what I've got, I guess we'll have to make do."

Heather patted her arm. "Never you mind. Just leave it to Miss Heather. Do you have a mailing list for me?"

"Mailing list?"

"For the invitations. I made up a gorgeous email to send out to everyone."

Amethyst coughed. "There're a lot of older people in the neighborhood. I think most of them would appreciate a personal invitation."

Heather looked thoughtful, then brightened. "You're right. A beautiful invitation card, hand delivered. That'll be lots better. Do you have tables and chairs lined up? And you'll need a tent. You've only got the one shade tree." She gestured at the locust tree that overhung the patio. "Let's take a look at your menu, see if we've got all the bases covered."

Amethyst took a long, silent breath. "Heather, it's just a backyard barbecue. I figured it'd be potluck."

"Well, sure, hon, but you still need a menu. Can't have everybody bringing Jell-O salad and apple pie. Let me see what I can come up with."

Caramela had greeted Heather with a butt-wiggling wag and a thorough sniffing. Now she sat in front of her with her pittie smile, hoping for attention. Amethyst slapped her leg and Caramela came wagging over.

"You know, Amethyst," Heather said and hesitated.

Amethyst patted Caramela's muscular shoulder and looked up, wary. "What?"

Heather shifted from one foot to the other. "Well, it's just that pit bulls scare some people. It'd be a good idea if you can find somebody to take care of her for the party. In fact, she could stay at my place."

Amethyst straightened. "Look at her. This dog is not going to hurt anyone. She's not going to sit all alone on the other side of the wall and listen to everyone talking and laughing and having a good time. She already lived that life. I won't make her go through it again. If people don't want to be around my dog, they don't have to come to my house."

Heather had the grace to look uncomfortable. "I understand, believe me."

"Thanks."

"But you don't want her to see people afraid of her, do you?"

Amethyst grunted. She'd seen that reaction often enough: women pulling their children close, people giving poor Caramela evil looks, when all she was doing was walking happily at the end of her leash.

"No, I don't want that." A spell nudged at the back of her mind. She pulled it out, studied it and smiled. "I'll see what I can do about it, Heather."

"Okay," she said with real relief. She hugged Amethyst around the shoulders. "This is so exciting! We'll have a do that'll have folks around here talking for years!"

"I bet," Amethyst said.

❖ ❖ ❖

Amethyst sat on the carpet beside Caramela. Well, 'beside' wasn't the right word. Whether she was on the floor with Caramela or Caramela was on the couch with her, the dog had to snuggle.

Right now, her big, blocky head rested heavy on Amethyst's thigh. Her short, caramel-colored fur was soft and fine under Amethyst's hand.

The clutter of Amethyst's workroom-slash-front bedroom surrounded them. A worktable stretched along one wall, scattered with bright fragments of stained glass, glass cutters and breakers, rolls of copper foil and solder. Her soldering iron rested in a coiled stand, cooling. The acrid scents of flux and hot solder lingered in the air.

She'd sent Talys to the grocery store for party supplies while she theoretically worked on the Sandia Pueblo commission. It probably wasn't fair to him. He *was* her familiar. He was *supposed* to help her with magic. But having officially been a wizard for a grand total of five months, she often felt like a kid asking Daddy to help with homework.

Though the human form he now inhabited looked maybe thirty or so, he was a lot older than that. A lot. And even though a wizard's lifespan was several times longer than an ordinary person's, Talys had been around long enough to partner with a number of wizards. How many, he'd never told her. She was pretty sure if she knew, she'd be totally intimidated.

Besides, half the time she did magic, she felt stupid. Magic wasn't even supposed to exist. The rest of the time, she had to run any given spell through the Internal Ethics Examiner to make sure it checked out. She'd finally gotten over being disappointed by how many didn't.

This one, though, seemed okay. It was a glamour, a jaunty, lively little spell that just wanted everyone to be happy.

Exactly what she wanted people to feel when they saw Caramela.

"Okay, Caramela. Ready?"

The dog looked up at her out of eyes exactly the same color as her coat and gave her an adoring, ears-back puppy face.

Amethyst braced herself and reached for the magic. It seethed just beyond everyday reality, a fiery ether that burned through her, just short of painful. She shaped it to the spell.

A few months ago, it would've been like grabbing a plug by the prongs while it was in the electrical socket. The magic wasn't as bad now, but it was still a wrestle, like it was a little too big for the spell. Magic kept squirting out in odd directions. Amethyst crammed it back into the spell, waited until it looked like it was going to stay and do what it was supposed to and set the spell on Caramela.

Caramela jumped and scrambled to her feet. She spun in tight circles like she did right after a bath, spun the other way, then plunked on her butt and scratched furiously with one hind foot.

Amethyst stiffened in an instant of panic and reached to snuff the spell, but Caramela twitched her skin, shook herself and lay back down.

Amethyst felt her all over with hands and wizard's senses. Both told her the dog was fine. The spell itself was barely perceptible, just a shimmer of love and attraction like bright fishes swimming in sunlit water.

She cupped Caramela's face between her hands and looked into her eyes. "You okay?"

Caramela gave her an earnest gaze and thumped her tail. Amethyst sensed only her happiness with the attention.

She let out a relieved breath. "Good. Now everybody will love you as much as I do."

❖ ❖ ❖

"*What*," Melodie said, "the hell is that?"

Amethyst stood on the sidewalk with her and Marl Odham, her fiancé, eyeing the monstrosity backed into her driveway.

Marginally, it was a trailer. It was all black with

inexplicable pulleys, chains, levers, a menacing smokestack and doors that looked like they were designed to swallow whole carcasses. A propane tank perched atop the trailer hitch was tied down by jaunty red straps.

A blond guy in a do-rag and barbecue apron swung open one of the doors. Smoke belched forth, and out of it he produced something that was presumably edible. Caramela, by Amethyst's knee, hopefully sniffed the air.

"It looks like a cross between a steam locomotive and some kind of S and M apparatus," Melodie said.

"Shh, hon," Marl said. "If you say much more, we'll have to show her..." He leaned down and stage-whispered, "*The Room.*"

"Ew," Amethyst said. She made a 'T' with her hands. "Too much information."

Marl chucked, then also sniffed the air. "Whatever that thing is, it smells good."

"*This*, I'm told," Amethyst said, "is a proper barbecue."

Marl's brows rose almost to the sweep of his reddish-brown hair. "Whoa. What happens if it's just Mom, Dad and the kids on a Sunday afternoon?"

"You'll have to ask Heather, the barbecue expert."

As if on cue, Heather poked her head around the gate to the side yard. "There you are. I wondered where you disappeared to."

Melodie shot Amethyst a look.

Deadpan, Amethyst said, "Heather, these are my friends Melodie and Marl. This is our neighbor Heather Purdy."

"Hi! Come on back. Billy's slicing up the brisket now," Heather said with a wave and disappeared.

"What happened to the grumpy old guy who was always threatening to call the pound on your dog?" Melodie said.

"Mr. Meadows went into assisted living. Heather is related somehow, so she moved in when he moved out."

"Ah." Melodie tilted her head. "Not an improvement, I take it."

Amethyst headed for the gate, Melodie, Marl and Carmela in tow. "She has the hots for Talys."

"Oh, are we going to hear another verse of 'Nobody Wants Smart, Skinny Women'?" Melodie said.

Amethyst rounded on her. "Hey, I'll tell you what. Let Heather ogle Marl awhile and let's see how you feel."

Marl held up his hands. "Uh-uh, you two. Leave me out of it."

Caramela, that worry wrinkle between her ears, sat in front of Marl and looked up at him. He gave her ears a reassuring rub.

"I would, if it were up to me," Amethyst said. "But I can't make any promises for Heather."

Melodie caught his arm and tucked hers through it. "She can ogle all she wants." She kissed Marl's cheek. "I'm not worried."

"So when do I get to meet Talys?" Marl said.

Amethyst grinned. Marl had a real knack for changing uncomfortable subjects. "Come on. I'll introduce you."

Amethyst's backyard had been transformed. Magic had absolutely nothing on Heather.

The locust tree that overhung her patio dangled paper lanterns. A rented canopy shaded chairs and tables covered with red-and-white-checked paper tablecloths. The aroma of grilled meat filled the air. An iPod player belted out a song about friends in low places while more people than Amethyst knew what to do with talked and drank beers and ate the food that loaded the tables against one block wall.

"Ack," she said.

Large groups weren't her style. She did much better with two or three good friends she trusted enough to be herself with.

Melodie put a hand on her shoulder. "Courage, Wiz. Look, there's Talys."

Talys must've sensed Amethyst, because he'd turned and was already heading their way, looking impossibly cool in his black polo shirt and hiker shorts and sunglasses.

"Melodie," he said in his hot-cocoa voice. "So pleased to see you. This must be Marl, of whom I've heard so much about."

The two men shook hands.

"Tom Aturj," Talys introduced himself. "But please call me Talys." He gestured toward the tables. "Get a plate and help yourself. What would you care to drink? Alien Ale? Wine? Or a soft drink?"

He took their drink orders and slid through the people as smoothly as a killer whale.

Caramela was in heaven. All these new people to make friends with. Amethyst watched her, hoping she'd forget to greet Talys. And hoping the spell was just as hard for him to notice as it was for her.

The dog trotted from one guest to the other, offering up her big grin and wagging tail. People looked down at her and smiled. Liz, a woman from a few houses down, crouched and petted her. In the past, Liz had always seemed a little nervous when meeting Amethyst with the dog. Perfect.

"Nice guy," Marl said, nodding in Talys' direction. "Interesting accent. It doesn't sound Navajo."

"Um, no," Amethyst said and grabbed Melodie's arm. "Let's get something to eat."

Marl was smart enough she'd have to come up with a whole new mythology to explain Talys. Like maybe some foreign couple had adopted a little Navajo boy and he'd grown up—

She didn't know where. His diction was straight out of Jane Austen, but he didn't quite speak with an English accent.

More like someone who'd learned English from a Brit.

She arranged fruit salad and tortilla roll-ups and chili and a hot link on her plate. Talys brought her a strawberry lemonade.

"Exactly what I wanted," she said, smiling up at him.

He stroked her cheek with the backs of his fingers. "Of course it is, love. After you've eaten, remember to mingle."

"So, Talys," Marl said. "What do you do for a living?"

The two drifted away, chatting.

"Woo." Melodie fanned herself then mimicked Talys' gesture. "That little cheek thing he did would've had me dribbling out of my chair."

"Not you, too!" Amethyst said.

"*Kidding*, Wiz. He's a little exotic for me. I'd be worried that any day, he'd reveal his secret identity as a spy or assassin or something and leave me heartbroken."

Sometimes, Melodie was uncanny.

"I don't know about the secret identity," Amethyst said with a straight face. "But I trust him with my heart."

Unexpectedly, Melodie hugged her. "Good. It's about time you found somebody like that."

Amethyst hugged her back and swallowed the tight feeling in her throat. She couldn't ask for a better friend.

More people came into the backyard—Oscar and Angela Griego, her next door neighbors on the other side. Their son, Gary, trailed behind them carrying a crockpot. He looked around, spotted Amethyst and tipped his head with a grin.

Amethyst waved and sighed. "I guess I'd better go help him find a place to plug that in. You're coming, right?"

"I'd love to see what you'd do if I said 'no'," Melodie said.

"No, you don't. Trust me."

She stood, hauled Melodie up and headed for Gary.

"Hi, 'Thys," A name like 'Amethyst' begged for nicknames. He shifted the crockpot to one side and gave her a one-armed hug, but held on a little too long.

Amethyst stepped back and saw Melodie watching with a small smirk.

"What did you bring?" Amethyst asked Gary.

He bent and patted Caramela, who had apparently made the rounds. "My mom's famous chile verde. Where should I put it?"

Amethyst swept the crockpot out of his hands. "I'll take care of it, Gary. There're drinks in the coolers. Go ahead, get whatever you want." She made her escape.

Melodie, following her, shook her head. "What will Talys think? And so soon after you got together."

Amethyst only growled.

Melodie laughed. "You got railroaded into this, didn't you? I know you well enough to know that you wouldn't volunteer to host a party like this. So what's going on?"

Amethyst opened her mouth to explain Talys' plan, but Heather sidled up.

"Isn't this great?" Heather said. "I just knew we'd make a splash. But I wanted to ask a favor. Could you introduce my cousin Emily around?" She patted the hand of the young woman hovering behind her. "You know way more people here than I do."

Emily didn't have Heather's looks or figure, but she was pretty and looked sweet. Amethyst held out her hand and introduced herself and Melodie. Emily smiled and made eye contact only for a moment. *And shy*, Amethyst added to herself. She felt a sudden rush of sympathy for her.

"Just let me take care of this," Amethyst said and set down the crockpot. "Then we'll walk around and say hi."

"Thanks, Amethyst," Heather said. Caramela stood beside her looking expectant. She gave her a quick pat on the head. "You were right about her," she said. "She's a great dog. Everybody loves her."

Heather dived back into her element. Emily seemed to find the dog easier to look at than two unknown people. She didn't attempt to pet her, though.

"I love dogs," she said. "I wish I wasn't allergic to them."

Amethyst had begun to worry that Emily was one of the people Heather had mentioned who were afraid of pit bulls.

Melodie's eyes had a malicious sparkle in them. "You two go ahead, Wiz. Caramela and I will hang out here awhile."

Amethyst sighed, put on a smile for Emily and struck off into the sea of people.

Actually, it wasn't as bad as all that. Yeah, it was a crowd, but she did, after all, know most of them. She caught glimpses of Talys' dark, sunglassed face here and there, laughing and talking with this person or that. Considering he wasn't human, he made a gracious, easygoing host. The smell of barbecue hung in the air, and the iPod thumped out "Everybody Have Fun Tonight." Several women had kicked off their shoes and were dancing. Emily bopped a little, too.

It made Amethyst more optimistic. She'd labored through small talk until she discovered that Emily was interning at Albuquerque Studios as a sound engineer. Conversation after that went a lot easier. They stopped to talk gardening with Angela Griego for a while. Amethyst left Emily comparing recipes with Darla Wesley.

Caramela lay panting under the tree. A guy Amethyst vaguely recognized from the rental house three doors down crouched to pet her. Caramela, of course, ate it up. The guy looked up as Alex, the Martin's oldest daughter, sauntered past in a pair of Daisy Dukes and a cami top designed for exactly the effect they produced: the guy unfolded himself and strolled after her.

Amethyst looked for Talys again. So far, she hadn't seen any sign that he was maneuvering to get Heather and Gary Griego together. No, there was Gary waving a chicken leg to the beat of "Funky Town." Heather, one of the few women who'd managed to get a man to dance with her, was now wiggling and hip-shooting to the music.

If Talys was waiting for people to get a little more lubricated, he shouldn't have to wait long. The volume was going up. And people were definitely beginning to act uninhibited.

A man—she couldn't tell who from the back—had a woman pressed against the block wall, his hands braced on either side of her head. The woman's arms were wrapped around his neck. Another couple pretzeled around each other at one of the tables. It wasn't even five in the evening. And Amethyst was pretty sure the party supplies hadn't included *that* much booze.

Three young guys in knee-length shorts came in and shouted, "Where's the beer?"

"Damn," Amethyst muttered.

She didn't recognize them. She also didn't see Talys. She steamed for the party-crashers. Caramela must've sensed something, because she fell in beside her.

They were already chugging beers by the time she reached them. She stuck out her hand.

"Hi. I'm Amethyst. You must be new to the neighborhood."

All three grinned. "Yeah," said one, an Anglo guy with a narrow goatee that extended two or three inches past his chin. "Real new."

I bet, Amethyst thought, trying to figure out how to get rid of them. She glanced around for backup, but still no Talys in sight.

"I hate to say it, but—"

"Hey," one of the other guys said. "Awesome dog."

He bent and thumped Caramela on the side. Caramela just panted and wagged.

"Okay," Amethyst said. "I was going to say this is an invitation-only party, but be cool and you can stay."

They grinned down at her like, *See if you can make us leave.*

Amethyst smiled sweetly at them. If only they knew what she was. "Come on, Caramela."

She slid open the screen door and stepped into the house, but Caramela remained behind to socialize.

After all the activity outside, it seemed cool, dark and quiet. She crossed the living room, went down the hall to use the bathroom. Opening the door again, she stepped out and ran into Gary.

"Sorry," she said, disentangling herself.

He gave a lopsided grin and caught her by the shoulders as if to steady her. "No problem. No problem at all."

She eyed him. Something didn't seem right. A prickle ran down her back and along her arms. He wasn't as tall or as solid as Talys, but this close, he was bigger and taller than she'd realized.

Music thumped away outside. The sound of laughing voices drifted in from the backyard. She tried to step away, but his hands slid around behind her.

Damn, she thought. Gary had always been sort of annoying and embarrassingly persistent, but he'd never struck her as a creep.

"Come on, Gary. This isn't cool. Tom—"

"Forget him. Don't you know how I feel about you, 'Thys?"

He eased closer. How the hell much had he drunk? Amethyst's heart jackhammered.

She stiffened and put up her hands. "Look, if I have to be rude about it, I'm not interested. Now excuse me."

She made to push away, but he folded her in his arms and bent his head to kiss her.

Amethyst called power and sent a sizzling pulse of force between them. Gary yelped a curse and bounced back against the opposite wall.

"What the hell was that?" He pressed himself to the wall.

"That," she said, "was a warning. Don't ever do that again."

She turned and stalked away. She was shaking, with anger, with something that felt uncomfortably like fear. The smartest thing to do would be to go back outside, but she stopped in the kitchen and leaned over the sink, forcing herself to take deep breaths.

Footsteps approached through the living room. She pushed away from the sink and moved to flee to the backyard—and plenty of witnesses.

The screen door rolled open so hard it hit the stop and bounced back again. Melodie rushed in and would've brushed past her, but Amethyst caught her.

"Mel, what's wrong?"

Melodie tried to wrench free. Tears streamed down her face. "I'm going home!"

Amethyst hung on. "Why? What happened?"

Not much more than sobs came out. She put an arm around Melodie's shoulders. Gary slunk into the kitchen. Amethyst ignored him and he darted out the open screen door.

"Come on, Mel. It'll be fine." Whatever 'it' was. "Sit down. I'll get you some water."

"It's not fine!" Melodie said. "I can't believe he'd do this to me!" She dissolved into tears again.

Amethyst's stomach made a sick knot. "Who?" she asked, although she was pretty sure she already knew. "What's going on?"

"Marl!" Melodie gave a hard, angry laugh. "Look for yourself. Go on, take a look! Might as well. Everyone else is getting an eyeful."

Still holding on to her friend, Amethyst stepped to the side so she could see through the window outside. Lots of people were dancing, just as many guys as women now. One of the guys dancing was Marl. And he was dancing with...with...

"*Heather?* Oh, shit."

He wasn't just dancing. It was a slow, salacious slither, his hands firmly on her hips, hers twined around his neck. They pressed close enough they'd pop each other's buttons loose when they parted.

No way. Not Marl.

She looked around. Marl and Heather weren't the only ones acting...well, overly friendly. Couples were wrapped around each other all over the backyard.

Amethyst just stood with her mouth open. First Gary, now Marl—and everybody else. This went way beyond weird.

She stopped. And what had been going on the last time things went beyond weird? She cursed, long and foully. Magic, that was what.

Melodie, crying once more, tried to escape again.

Amethyst took a firm grip on her. "Melodie. This is not Marl's fault."

"Not his fault! Does it look like he's being raped? No, he walked up to that—that—*bimbo* and started coming on to her like he never did me!"

"Mel, listen, I can explain—"

A woman screamed. Melodie instantly gulped down tears. Amethyst surged for the door. By the time she got to the patio, she found Melodie right beside her.

Down at the far end of the yard, one of the three party crashers had Emily backed up to the wall, between the lilac bush and a Russian sage. Her fists flailed, but he laughed, caught her wrists. Amethyst started to run toward them, but Emily broke and bolted.

Like several others, Gary stood as if trying to decide what was going on and what he should do. Emily pelted toward him, grabbed his arm and swung behind him, squealing. The party crasher, the one with the goatee, made a grab for her and missed.

"Hey!" Gary said.

The guy took a swing at him. Gary jerked back to avoid it, then threw a punch of his own. His connected. Goatee Guy yelled and clapped his hands to his face, then his two buddies were on Gary like apes on a tree. Emily started screaming again.

Heather, shrieking obscenities, jostled past Amethyst, stepped in front of the guy who'd assaulted her cousin, reared back and kicked him. Goatee Guy went down, one hand clutching his bloody face, the other his groin. One buddy turned away from Gary and took a swing at Heather. She ducked, cursing, and the whole party converged on the fight.

Knots of men grappled. Women clawed and pulled hair. Liz, the woman who'd once been nervous around Caramela, threw efficient-looking martial arts kicks and punches. Two men writhed on the ground at her feet. Caramela barked, her voice echoing off the block walls. And Talys—where the hell was he?

Melodie's hand clamped on Amethyst's arm. "Holy crap," she breathed. "Call the cops!"

Amethyst called magic instead.

Clouds curdled out of a clear, blue sky, growing like some kind of time-lapse fungus into white towers with ominous black bottoms. Lightning flashed, thunder cracked, and rain roared down. It was a little more sudden and dramatic than the typical New Mexico summer cloudburst, but Amethyst was pretty sure no one was paying much attention to the weather at the moment.

In about thirty seconds, the backyard was half an inch deep in water and people were sliding like bumper cars. A couple of men rolled over and over in the swimming grass, pummeling blindly at one another.

"Amethyst!" Talys' voice bellowed behind her.

She whipped around. He came from the side yard—he must've been around in front. Anger knotted his face and she took an instinctive step back. She'd never seen him like this.

"Stop this!" he thundered. "Now!"

"I'm trying!" Amethyst said.

Talys snarled words in some unrecognizable tongue. Probably no one alive would recognize them, but they were obviously curses.

"Hey," Melodie said and stepped between them. "Don't you talk to her like that."

Amethyst caught her wrist and held it tightly. "I don't know what else to do," she told Talys.

He gave a furious snort, reached past Melodie and wrapped a hand around the back of Amethyst's neck. "Like this…"

He was her familiar. He could use her power to mold the magic. He'd done it before in moments of extremity. And this was, if nothing else, a moment of extremity.

The spell that unfurled was one of stillness. It sent out tendrils, infiltrating the seethe of people, the boil of air and electricity and clouds, the pounding rain.

The rain slowed and hung glittering, like some kind of CGI effect. The roaring hiss of the downpour ceased and the music stopped. The men brawling in the grass lay frozen in a fountain of water arrested mid-splash. Alex balanced on one foot, about half a second from landing on her butt, a look of shock on her face. A man hunched over Liz's karate punch. Emily stood behind Gary, her eyes wide and hands clenched over her mouth, while Gary's fist hung cocked for another punch.

Melodie's mouth hung open. Her eyes, round and shocked, darted. Apparently her physical contact with

Amethyst exempted her from the spell.

"There," Talys said. "That will give us time to get this sorted."

"What the hell is going on?" Melodie squeaked.

Amethyst looked a question at Talys.

He shrugged. "It was bound to happen eventually."

Amethyst took Melodie's other hand and made her face her. She took a long breath and said, "Mel, I'm a wizard."

Melodie stared at her. "What?"

"I'm a wizard."

She looked at Talys again. He gave a slight shake of the head. He didn't want her to say what he was. Okay.

Melodie gave a strangled laugh. "I'm dreaming. Or somebody slipped something into the punch."

"I know," Amethyst said. "You have no idea how hard it was for me at first, too."

Melodie turned to Talys. "She's not crazy, is she?"

"Thankfully, no," he said. "Reckless, foolish and inexperienced, but not crazy."

Amethyst scowled at him.

Melodie gave a laugh that came out a little too high. "Then I must be."

Talys rolled his eyes and heaved a sigh. "I seem to recall having heard that before."

"Remember when I asked you for that psychiatrist's number?" Amethyst said. "Save yourself some aggravation and just believe me, Mel. It'll make things a lot easier."

Melodie took a shaky breath and looked around. "I guess you couldn't do this with mirrors."

Amethyst had to stifle a wild laugh. "No. And like I was telling you before all hell broke loose, you can't get mad at Marl." She sneaked a nervous glance at Talys. "I think I know why that happened."

Melodie scowled. "Don't tell me. It was magic."

Talys folded his arms and raised his brows.

Amethyst wet her lips and cleared her throat. "It was a spell I worked. On Caramela."

"Ah," Talys said as if it were a matter of academic interest. "Would you kindly call her?"

Amethyst wasn't sure how that would work, but she felt him separate the dog from the spell that held everything still. Caramela shook hard, flapping her ears and spraying water everywhere, looked around at the funny statue people then came trotting over.

Talys bent and stroked her. Behind his sunglasses, he frowned. "What did you do?"

Oh, boy. "It was just a little glamour. Heather said I should lock her up somewhere so people wouldn't be afraid of her," Amethyst said in a rush. "I had to do something."

She turned to Melodie again. "I just wanted people to love her," she explained. "I didn't expect everybody to get all lovey with everybody else!"

Both of them stared at her, then Talys started laughing. Amethyst watched him, not sure whether to be alarmed, appalled or relieved. Judging from the look on Melodie's face, she felt pretty much the same. After a minute, he took off his sunglasses, wiped his eyes and put them back on.

"Amethyst, love, I think you may have used a bit too much magic for that poor spell."

"Seriously?" Melodie said. "Marl— It was all m-m-magic?"

She had trouble saying it. Amethyst knew exactly how she felt.

"I'm sorry, Mel," she said and took Melodie's hands again. "I swear I'd never do something like that on purpose." She turned to Talys. "So…" She swallowed and asked in a small voice, "What now?"

He folded his arms. "I believe the term is damage control." He eyed the frozen mayhem. "First order of the day is to remove that glamour."

"Are you a—a wizard too?" Melodie asked Talys.

He laughed. "Hardly. I simply possess a great deal of arcane and esoteric knowledge."

"And modesty to match," Amethyst muttered.

"And here I thought I'd uncovered your secret identity," Melodie said in an unsteady voice.

Amethyst swallowed a snort. Talys raised a brow at her.

She blew through her lips. "Okay. The spell."

With wizard's eyes, she looked at the magic. The glamour on Caramela fizzed and sparkled poppy red and sunshine yellow and spring green—and the damned spell had spread as if Amethyst had dusted Caramela with colored chalk. Everyone who'd come in contact with her had the same sparkle. Marl. Heather. Gary. The party crasher dudes. Poor Emily, of course, didn't wear a trace of it.

She sighed and searched her mind for a spell that dispersed glamours. The wizards who'd dumped the knowledge on her had known plenty of them. Apparently spin and packaging had been just as big in pre-industrial ages as they were now. And people were just as keen then to make decisions without all the marketing hype.

Amethyst called up the most straightforward, a spell that simply revealed the truth, and swept it over the whole backyard. The colorful glitter fizzled out.

"Rain." Talys pointed up. "Water." He pointed down at the wading pool the backyard had begun to resemble.

It wasn't easy to disperse the thundercloud overhead while keeping the spell of stillness in place. She struggled to separate the two, then finally worked on the cloud from the top down, sending it wisping away into the dry New Mexico air. The raindrops hanging in the air popped like tiny bath bubbles.

Messing with the weather made strange things happen.

Microbursts and dust devils, for example. A whirlwind started, and she scrambled to control it. Fortunately, it was just what she needed to get rid of the water.

With an ominous hiss, it swooped into the flooded yard. What had been an invisible disturbance of air turned into a grey funnel. Clothing and hair fluttered. A fine mist sprayed Amethyst, Melodie and Talys. Melodie yelped and scrambled backward, then set her jaw and feet. Amethyst gave her a smile, half apologetic, half encouraging.

Melodie swallowed visibly. "You really were telling the truth."

"Weather magic is rather impressive, isn't it?" Talys said.

The temperatures equalized, and the dust devil—well, waterspout, in this case—wandered off and dispersed.

"But what about them?" Melodie waved at the arrested melee. "How are you going to explain all this?"

Talys grinned. "People would far rather deny the evidence of their own senses than embrace the possibility of magic. Present company excepted," he said with a slight bow to Melodie. "However—"

"As far as they're concerned," Amethyst said, "when I remove the spell, no time will have passed. They were all fighting, and then the rain just stopped."

She nodded at Talys and released the spell.

Everything started up again. Alex landed on her butt on the grass. The man bent over Liz's fist gave a grunt and doubled over. Party Crasher Dude ducked Gary's punch.

"*STOP THIS AT ONCE!*" Talys roared and waded into the battle.

He jerked the two men rolling in the grass to their feet, spun Party Crasher Dude off balance before he could punch Gary, and lifted Alex, who was crying, to her feet.

Amazingly enough, everyone did stop.

When he wanted to, Talys had *presence*. All that black—

and the sunglasses—made him look like somebody you'd better not mess with. It also didn't hurt that he was a big guy.

Amethyst trailed in his wake, mopping up. Or trying to.

Most people were too embarrassed to do much more than apologize for their behavior, gather themselves together and beat a hasty retreat. Party Crasher Dudes were pitching Talys some attitude, though. She headed in that direction, Caramela trotting behind.

Gary, who'd put a protective arm around Emily's shoulders, stepped forward—though he stayed behind Talys.

"I think you guys had better do what he says and leave."

"Yeah?" One of the guys gave a significant glance at his bloody-faced friend. "Maybe we got something to do, first."

A rill of temper—and magic—burned through Amethyst. She stopped just out of reach behind them and folded her arms. "What's that, guys?"

Testosterone—or booze—still fueled Party Crasher Dudes. That was the only explanation Amethyst could come up with, since they were obviously sizing up their chances against Talys and Gary. Three to two, they probably thought. And Talys was the only one they really had to worry about. Certainly not his skinny girlfriend.

So when Loudmouth Dude took an aggressive step forward, *somehow* he went splat on his back in the wet grass. Emily squeaked. Gary goggled. Caramela barked. Talys gave Amethyst a small, approving nod.

"Oops," she said. "Too much beer."

That was all it took, and Party Crasher Dudes were on the stupid train again. Problem was, every time they tried to hit someone, they either missed, or ended up hitting one of their buddies instead.

It was like watching the Three Stooges. Amethyst snickered. Pretty soon she was doubled over, laughing. The Dudes weren't totally stupid. Eventually they caught on that something strange was going on and bolted.

Heather, Melodie and Marl had arrived on the scene at some point.

"Y'all don't come back now," Heather called after the Dudes.

"What in God's name was wrong with them?" Marl said.

Melodie took his arm, patted his hand and gave Amethyst a knowing tilt of the head.

"Who cares?" Heather said. "As long as they're gone." She turned to Gary and stuck out her hand. "I don't believe we've met yet. I'm Heather Purdy."

Gary had his arm around Emily's shoulders again. He had to release her to shake Heather's hand. Emily watched him with an admiring gaze. He snuck an uncertain glance at her, brightened and started to put his arm around her shoulders again.

Heather caught his hand first. "I just want to say how grateful I am that you stepped in to protect my cousin." She gave his hand a yank. He stumbled into her and she kissed his cheek. "No telling *what* those yahoos would've done if you hadn't been here."

Ah-ha, Amethyst thought. *Yes.* She glanced at Talys. He was pretending not to pay attention, but the little quirk at the corners of his mouth gave him away.

"Dammit, Heather!" Emily said and stomped up to her. "You're doing it again!"

Heather backed up, but didn't let go of Gary's hand. "What?"

"You know what," Emily said darkly. "The same thing you always do!"

Heather's eyes went wide. "I'm only thanking the man—for what he did for you!"

"I'm capable of thanking him myself," Emily said.

The look on Gary's face hovered somewhere between

disbelief and total bliss.

Two for one, Amethyst thought. *Even better.*

Talys put an arm around her and swept her away. Melodie followed, still smirking.

Marl, a couple of steps behind her, looked like he wished he could disappear. He caught Melodie by the hand, but had trouble meeting her eyes.

"Melodie," he said. "I don't know what to say to you. I can't begin to apologize." His lips thinned to a grim line. "I don't know what I was thinking—"

Melodie pulled him to her and kissed him. "I do, so don't beat yourself up about it."

"But—" he said.

"Believe me, Marl," Amethyst said. "It's not your fault."

He eyed her. "Okay. Something is clearly going on here today. I'd better know what it is."

Amethyst tried to ignore her squirming stomach. Her best friend finally knew the crazy truth about her. The problem was, telling anyone else wasn't going to be any easier. She shot Melodie a pleading glance.

"He's a lawyer, Wiz," Melodie said. "He's used to examining evidence. He shouldn't be that hard to convince."

Marl frowned. "Convince me of *what?* That someone spiked the punch?"

Melodie, stifling a giggle, snorted. Even Caramela gave Amethyst a laughing look.

Amethyst took Talys' hand for strength. His fingers, large and warm, curled around hers in a reassuring grip.

"Well, Marl." Amethyst hesitated, then plunged on. "Let me put it this way. Do you believe in magic?"

❖

Also by Kathlena L. Contreras:

SHADOWBOUND

The Land of Enchantment Series:

FAMILIAR MAGIC

CROOKED MAGIC

COULD IT BE MAGIC – a Land of Enchantment romance

FATED MAGIC – a Land of Enchantment novel

Kathlena L. Contreras writing as K. Lynn Bay:

BLACKTHORNE

CHANCESHAPER

SPRINGTIME IN HADES

About the Author

Kathlena Contreras has been writing since the age of eight, when while hanging out at her dad's office one summer, she typed out a story about a saber-toothed tiger that encounters a time machine. The story was three paragraphs long.

Many years and many paragraphs later and here she is, still writing about weird things. In between writing, Kathlena has been the owner of a successful small business, an assistant medical librarian, a database manager and a pusher of paper in countless offices. She's also been a copy editor for three nationally distributed rodeo magazines and the editor of a local literary magazine.

She currently lives with her husband, five dogs and assorted livestock on the edge of the woods above the valley east of Albuquerque, New Mexico, USA, the Land of Enchantment, a place where the view goes on forever.

Kathlena L. Contreras also writes as K. Lynn Bay.

Stop by and say hi at FlyingTigerPress.com

To hear about new releases, you can sign up on my website. I promise I won't spam you, and I'll never share your information with anyone.

> Email at kathys.wizards@gmail.com
> Flying Tiger Press on Pinterest
> Kathlena L. Contreras on Facebook

www.ingramcontent.com/pod-product-compliance
Lightning Source LLC
Chambersburg PA
CBHW070806180626
46818CB00001B/132